THE SIMON CRISP DIARIES

Simon Crisp would dearly love to be accepted among the smart, young set. He does try, and worry, and try again. But somehow . . .

A fine fat slice of contemporary life, rich as a syllabub and sometimes as messy, as carefully dissected as a GCSE Biology practical, artfully arranged as a *nouvelle cuisine* chef's special, sparkling as a 1989 Perrier water, fact packed as an executive's Filofax, imaginative as a Dockland developer's sales brochure, fast moving as a Golf GTi . . .

**Also by the same author,
and available from Coronet:**

FAMILY MATTERS
HOW TO SURVIVE MIDDLE AGE

About the author

Christopher Matthew was born in 1939. After
Oxford, he taught in a girls' finishing school in
Switzerland and had a short stint as an
advertising copywriter before becoming a full
time writer in 1970.

His books include two novels – THE LONG
HAIRED BOY and THE JUNKET MAN; an
annotated edition (with Benny Green) of Jerome
K Jerome's THREE MEN IN A BOAT; HOW TO
SURVIVE MIDDLE AGE; and FAMILY MATTERS
in which his famous hero Simon Crisp settles
down to married life. Here at last in one volume
are the earlier chronicles of Simon Crisp's life
and times as a young bachelor about town –
DIARY OF A SOMEBODY, LOOSELY ENGAGED
and THE CRISP REPORT.

Christopher Matthew is also a well-known
journalist and broadcaster, and he has serialised
and read most of the Crisp books on Radio 4.

The Simon Crisp Diaries

Christopher Matthew

CORONET BOOKS
Hodder and Stoughton

DIARY OF A SOMEBODY copyright ©
Christopher Matthew 1978 Illustrations
© Hutchinson Ltd
LOOSELY ENGAGED © copyright
Christopher Matthew 1980
THE CRISP REPORT © copyright
Christopher Matthew 1981

DIARY OF A SOMEBODY first
published in Great Britain in 1978 by
Hutchinson Ltd
Arrow edition 1980

LOOSELY ENGAGED first published in
1980 by Hutchinson Ltd
Arrow edition 1981

THE CRISP REPORT first published in
1981 by Hutchinson Ltd
Arrow edition 1982

Now published in one volume as THE
SIMON CRISP DIARIES in this Coronet
edition, 1988

British Library C.I.P.

Matthew, Christopher, 1939–
    The Simon Crisp diaries.
    I. Title   II. Matthew, Christopher,
    1939–   Diary of a somebody   III.
    Matthew, Christopher, 1939–
    Loosely engaged   IV. Matthew,
    Christopher, 1939– The Crisp report
    823'.914[F]

ISBN 0 340 43077 X

Printed and bound in Great Britain
for Hodder and Stoughton
Paperbacks, a division of Hodder and
Stoughton Ltd., Mill Road,
Dunton Green, Sevenoaks, Kent
TN13 2YA.
(Editorial Office: 47 Bedford Square,
London WC1B 3DP) by
Cox & Wyman Ltd., Reading.

Diary
of a
Somebody

For Robert Morley

September

Friday, September 2nd

I have decided it is high time I started to keep a diary. I simply cannot imagine why I have not done so before. When I think of the many interesting things that have happened to me over the years, I can only curse myself for not having had the sense to jot them all down.

I have travelled a fair amount – in Europe mainly – and come into contact with many interesting people, some of whom have been quite famous in their way. I cannot pretend that Simon Crisp is a household name, but that is not to say that the people I meet and the places I go to are any the less interesting for that. Indeed, in my opinion, fame can very often be a disadvantage in a diarist.

I do not suppose for a moment that anyone would wish to go so far as to publish my observations on life, and anyone who thinks that is why I have decided to start a diary could not be further off the mark. On the other hand, it might be interesting for my grandchildren and their children to browse through in years to come, and get some idea of how life in England was lived in the late 1970s. If ever I get married, that is.

Everyone in the flat is of the opinion that thirty-five is too old to be thinking of starting a diary. I cannot agree with them there and have made my opinions felt in no uncertain terms. I have never subscribed to this widely held theory that you have to have reached a certain stage in your career by a certain age in order to be considered a success. Look at Margaret Rutherford. She did not set foot on a stage until she was over thirty. And Milton waited till he was an old man before starting work on *Paradise Lost*.

Saturday, September 3rd

To Smith's to buy a diary. One of those substantial ones with a lock, I thought. Astonished to discover that the only diaries they had in stock were for next year. When I asked the woman at the desk for one for this year, she laughed and replied that they had sold out months ago. I said that, as far as I was concerned, we were still very much in this year, and that there must be many people who decide to start diaries in September. She said she had never heard of anyone doing it. I replied that it was extremely narrow-minded to assume that the year begins for everyone on January 1st and ends on December 31st.

'Narrow-minded it may be,' she retorted, 'but for everyone I know it does.'

'Even the Persians?' I asked.

She said that she was happy to say that she did not know any Persians, and what was more, I was holding up the queue. I pointed out that London had a large Persian population these days, and the sooner people like her came to terms with the fact, the better would be our chances of cheaper petrol.

'Well, all I can say is,' she snapped, 'they obviously don't keep diaries.'

'That makes two of you,' I said, and left.

No wonder big business in this country is in the doldrums if that is the way large firms carry on. And to think that only thirty-eight years ago to this day, we went to war with Germany. There is obviously nothing for it but to use a notebook, at least for the time being, but it is really far from satisfactory.

Arrived back in the flat just as Jane was leaving in true secretarial style to spend the weekend at her parents' in Oxted. If only she would do something about her hair. I am not surprised she has such difficulty finding a boyfriend. Her skin leaves much to be desired, too.

After tea, a couple of Victoria's weird friends came to take her off to one of their Workers' Workshops, whatever they may be. I fail to understand what an attractive, well-educated girl like her, with wealthy parents in Berkshire and a decent job in an art gallery, can possibly see in all this namby-pamby, lefty nonsense. I have tried to talk her out of it on several occasions, but I might just as well save my breath. If I didn't want to run the risk of looking like a fortune hunter, I might seriously consider setting my cap at her. She is very much my type.

Beddoes had his latest girlfriend Jackie round in the evening, and monopolized the television set again, to say nothing of the settee. If he must devote his spare time to a temporary waitress from Shepherd's Bush, at least he might get her to help out a bit at meal times. I do not mind cooking pork chops and vegetables for three people, but I do draw the line at being treated like a skivvy.

I restrained my feelings until the time came to bring the coffee in, when I banged Jackie's down on the table – rather too hard, as it turned out, since the cup tipped over, spilling coffee all down my trousers. I immediately sponged them with cold water and can only hope for the best.

Sunday, September 4th

Woken at nine by Beddoes knocking loudly on my door and calling out that he and Jackie were just off for the day to Brighton and there was no milk in the fridge. What he omitted to mention was that they had also finished off the rest of the loaf and covered most of the sink and draining board with a thin coating of burnt toast scrapings. How a man like that manages to hold down a responsible job in the City when he is incapable of calculating the number of slices in a loaf of bread is beyond me.

Victoria's political soirée had apparently turned into an all-night affair. Why I should feel so jealous of a bunch of second-rate Commies I simply cannot imagine, but I do.

I am definitely beginning to regret now that I asked her out to dinner on Monday night.

The coffee stain has still not come out of my trousers.

Monday, September 5th

A curious thing happened today in the office. Shortly after lunch, Armitage stuck his head round the door of the outer office just as I was dictating an important letter to Sarah, our new secretary, and said, 'Oh, by the way, if reception calls up to say Audrey Hepburn is here, ask them to send her straight up, will you?'

Not surprisingly, everyone was very excited at the news that the famous star was expected at any minute, and one or two began tidying their desks. Iversen even went so far as to slip out and have his hair cut.

I said to Sarah that I never realized Armitage knew Audrey Hepburn, to which she replied, 'Why shouldn't he? As the chairman's nephew I expect he gets to meet all sorts of interesting and important people down on his uncle's yacht on the Hamble.'

No matter how badly Armitage behaves, it is impossible to fault him in Sarah's eyes. She seems besotted by him, though heaven knows why.

More out of idle curiosity than from any genuine desire to meet the actress, I put off a couple of not very important meetings. I also rang Victoria to say that I might be a little late for our dinner date.

By five-thirty there was still no sign of Miss Hepburn, and at six, Armitage stuck his head round the door and said, 'Oh well, it doesn't look as though she'll be coming now, does it? Anyway, I'm off now. Good night, laddie.'

Arrived home to find a note from Victoria saying that she couldn't be fished to wait around any longer and had gone to the pictures with Beddoes. So much for left-wing manners.

Tuesday, September 6th

Have been thinking about this Audrey Hepburn business all day and can only assume it was meant to be one of Armitage's so-called jokes. If so, it certainly didn't cut much ice with me. On the other hand, I suppose there is no reason why he shouldn't have been telling the truth. The problem now is to find out if he was, without giving the impression that I give two hoots one way or another.

On the way in to work, I took the opportunity of button-holing George, the commissionaire, and asking him if by chance he had happened to see Audrey Hepburn going in or out of the building yesterday.

He thought for a while, then said, 'Audrey Hepburn, sir? Would she be with the frozen-food people?'

Either he knows something I don't, or else he has never been near a cinema in his life. Either way, it's decidedly rum. Asked Victoria out to dinner tomorrow night and she has accepted.

Looking forward to taking Victoria out to dinner so much that I was scarcely able to bend my mind to anything else all day. When Sarah came back from the coffee machine this morning, I found to my amazement that I had asked for hot chocolate, a drink I have not touched since childhood and heartily detest.

Decided to book up at a restaurant near Balham called The Soup Kitchen. Tim and Vanessa Pedalow recommended it and said that the last time they had been there, Prince Charles had been a fellow diner. They hadn't actually seen him themselves, but they had been told by one of the waiters that he was there somewhere. The theme of the restaurant, I gathered, was the American Depression – everything very plain and basic, especially the food. It definitely sounded the sort of thing that would suit Victoria with her proletarian views.

Unfortunately, we took rather longer to find it than I had anticipated, as a result of which they had given away our table, thinking we weren't coming, and we had to take a bowl each and stand in a queue outside in the street until a table became free. Luckily it wasn't too cold, although I was thankful I had brought a light overcoat. Victoria said it took the chill off her shoulders very nicely. After about ten minutes, she was all for leaving and finding somewhere else. However, I assured her that it was really well worth the wait, and at that moment a waiter in faded black trousers and a stained white shirt came out and told us he had a table for two ready. I was sorry we were not able to sit in the main part of the restaurant and spot the famous writers and TV actors who, according to Tim and Vanessa, use the place as their canteen. On the other hand, it was quite cosy and intimate behind the pillar, even if it was a little difficult to catch the waiter's eye.

When I did finally manage to hail one and ask him for a menu, he told me, rather rudely I thought, that it was chalked up on the wall on the far side of the room. I went to have a look, and when I came back, told Victoria that I would be going for the vegetable soup followed by the cheese omelette. She replied that, in that case, she would certainly choose the most expensive and exotic thing on the menu. I pointed out that that *was* the most exotic and expensive thing on the menu and that the whole point of the place was that everything was very much in keeping with the hard times we were living through.

She looked round at the rather stark grey walls and the plain wooden tables and said, 'What's this place called again?'

I told her The Soup Kitchen.

She said, 'The Soup Outside Loo would be a better name for it. Even the seats are round, hard and cold.'

I said that I thought *she* was being a bit hard, but she didn't seem to get the joke.

The soup, when it finally came, was quite tasty if a little tepid, and there were very nearly words when the waiter – accidentally, Victoria said; I still claim on purpose – shot an entire cheese omelette straight into my lap.

Victoria remarked, 'This sort of thing never happens at the Savoy Grill.'

I asked her when was the last time she had dined at the Savoy Grill, and she said that she and the others often popped in there for a bite after one of their Workers' Workshop meetings. I was astounded and said that that was hardly the behaviour one expected from socialists.

'We believe in spreading the money around instead of wasting our time salving our consciences by occasional bouts of pseudo-poverty,' she said.

I was dumbstruck, though not half so much as I was by the bill when it finally arrived. For that price we might just as well have gone to the Savoy Grill. At least we would not have gone home still feeling hungry, and I might now be on speaking terms with Victoria.

I only hope the egg stains come out better than the coffee.

Thursday, September 8th

Astonished to receive a telephone call from Mike Pritchard, of all people, asking if he could pop round and see me after supper on a matter of some delicacy. I doubt if I have exchanged a dozen words with him since we were at Oxford together nearly fifteen years ago. He had always seemed slightly older than the rest of us in the JCR, but nothing had prepared me for the balding, middle-aged figure to whom I opened the door this evening.

'Wizard,' he said as I showed him into the sitting room. Victoria and Jane were there with plates of scrambled eggs perched on their knees.

I introduced them to Mike who said, 'Wizard. I wouldn't mind seeing the news if that's all right by you.'

And before I could say a word, he marched forward and plumped himself down into the best armchair. I asked him if he would like some coffee, whereupon he produced two bottles of claret from inside his anorak and banged them down on the table saying, 'This'll do you more good than coffee any day.' Picking up a nearby glass he then proceeded to pour himself a large measure. 'Wizard,' he said, leaning back with his nose over the rim of the glass. 'Well, what have you been up to since we last met?' Before I could utter a word, he launched into a long account of his own recent life.

It appeared that his marriage had not been a success. He is now divorced from Babs and living in digs in Clapham. He has two children, Tom aged eight and Gerry (short for Geraldine) aged twelve, who stay with him at weekends. I'm not surprised he arrives at work on Monday mornings absolutely exhausted. He has already lost two good jobs in industry and looks set fair to lose a third. Even so, I was rather taken aback when he suggested I might be kind enough to look after the children for the day on Saturday, and the pretext of a slight acquaintance at university seemed decidedly thin. However, it is the least I can do. Besides, who knows, it might be rather an interesting experience to have to look after two children for a day. A sort of simulated parenthood.

Mike was obviously relieved when I agreed. 'Wizard,' he said, and drained the bottle. Then he got up to go.

Assuming he had left the second bottle as a sort of thank-you present, but not wishing to take it for granted, I said,

'Oh, you seem to have left something behind.' 'Oh, so I have,' he said, picked up the bottle and left the room.

In the hall he bumped into Victoria who was on the way to the bathroom in her nightie, and immediately invited her to have dinner with him in a 'cheap and cheerful little place' he had discovered in Kennington, specializing in different types of stew. To my astonishment, she agreed. I give up.

Friday, September 9th

Was on my way out to lunch when the lift stopped at the fourth floor, and in stepped Armitage, laughing rather too loudly, as usual, and a couple of his rugger-playing cronies – Prout from Accounts and Attenborough from Merchandising Development.

He nodded at me in a superior way and said, 'Basement for you, I presume?' at which the other two sniggered.

I decided it was high time he was taken down a peg or two, so I remarked casually, 'Funny about Audrey Hepburn not turning up the other evening, wasn't it?'

Prout said, 'What's all this then, Col?'

They both looked at him expectantly.

'Oh,' said Armitage, 'did I say Audrey Hepburn? How silly of me. I meant, of course, Katherine Hepburn.'

The others seemed rather baffled, as well they might be. It's hopeless trying to carry on a sensible conversation with Armitage when he's in that sort of mood, and so I maintained a dignified silence.

As we were leaving the building, there was some horseplay with the swing doors as a result of which I missed a perfectly good taxi and had to travel to my lunch date by underground.

Saturday, September 10th

Woke early with a shock to realize that I had accepted an invitation to Nick and Warthog's wedding in Newbury. Rang Mike at eight but there was no reply. Had barely replaced the receiver when there was a ring at the front door and there he was with the children, both dressed in jeans and T-shirts. Tom's had a finger on his, pointing towards his sister, with the words: THIS IDIOT'S WITH ME. Surprised to see she was much more grown up for her age than I had imagined.

I explained my problem re the wedding, but all Mike said was, 'Wizard, they enjoy weddings.'

And without another word he strode off down the corridor. Arrived at the church rather later than I had hoped. As we were being shown to our seats, I noticed a number of guests whispering and giggling. I looked down and realized that the finger on Tom's T-shirt was pointing at me. I gave them all a cold stare and took my place. As I was leaning forward to pray, I overbalanced slightly on the narrow seat, banging my forehead against the back of the woman's head in the pew in front and knocking her hat slightly askew.

In the middle of the service, just as the couple were making their marriage vows, I suddenly realized that, by an astonishing coincidence, the vicar had been at the same college as me at Oxford. Afterwards I went up to him and made myself known, but he did not remember me at all. However, now I come to think about it, although we were certainly contemporaries, I don't believe we ever actually spoke. At the reception I overheard a stout woman in a mauve hat confiding to a small, dried-up-looking man that Nick had only married Warthog – or Margaret, as she called her – for her money. This was the first I had heard of Warthog's family having the sort of money people marry for. Even if it were true, it does not seem to me to be a sound basis on which to build a happy and lasting union. But that is only my opinion.

The children behaved extremely well, helping to carry round trays of eats and refilling people's glasses. It was a pity Tom had to go and blot his copybook, not to say Warthog's mother's white shoes, by making himself sick on Coca-Cola, but people could not have been more understanding – especially Warthog's mother who assured me that her little woman in the village was a positive genius with stains.

As we were leaving, I caught my foot on the top of the front-door steps and stumbled forward, giving another departing guest a sharp blow on the back of his head with my elbow, and knocking his top hat to the ground. When he turned round, I saw that it was the husband of the woman whose hat I had dislodged in the church. I did not see that there was any call to be quite so offensive. It was only an accident.

Tom was sick again in the car going home. Thank heaven for Volkswagen's rubber floors.

Sunday, September 11th

A potentially good night's sleep disturbed by the most extraordinarily erotic dreams about Geraldine. I have been able to think of nothing else all day.

Beddoes, as usual, stayed in bed with Jackie all day,

'*As we were leaving I caught my foot on the top of the front doorsteps and stumbled forward . . .*'

emerging finally in time for a drink at six-thirty. Is it any wonder one has erotic dreams when this is the sort of atmosphere one has to live in? The sooner I discourage Pritchard from landing me with his children again, the better for all our sakes. Apart from anything else, I see no reason why I should be made a convenience of.

Monday, September 12th

Quite unable to sleep all night for thinking about Geraldine. As a result, arrived at the office exhausted.

'You look as though you had a skinful over the weekend,' Armitage called out as I passed his office, and laughed coarsely – as too did Sarah. She seems to be in there with him all the time nowadays. I am seriously thinking of saying something about it. While reading through the Barford projected sales figures before lunch, I fell fast asleep and would probably have slept until five-thirty had my elbow not slipped off the edge of the desk, bringing my chin down with a sharp crack on my blotter.

After lunch Uncle Ted rang to say he was in town for the day to see his accountant, and would I care to join him at the Athenaeum for tea?

Went straight in to see Roundtree, our group head, with some excuse about having a dentist appointment, and left at once for the Athenaeum.

An unpleasant scene with the porter at the side entrance who claimed to have no knowledge whatever of a Mr Rathbone. I made no secret of my irritation and pointed out sharply that he had been a member for forty years. 'Not of this club, sir,' said the porter impassively.

I finally had to tell him that I had expected something better of the Athenaeum. 'This is the Travellers,' he said. 'The Athenaeum is next door.' The situation was not made any easier by the fact that the chap was coloured.

After tea I set off home on my scooter, only to find the Mall solid with traffic, all heading towards Admiralty Arch. It was not until I reached Parliament Square that I discovered the reason the whole of central London had been brought to a virtual standstill was a demonstration by large numbers of ugly and ill-dressed men and women swarming all over the road carrying banners with such slogans as FIGHT THE

CUTS, SAVE JOBS and CUTS BASH GAYS. I have no idea what they were all on about, and I'd be the last person to condemn minority groups, but I wouldn't have minded bashing a few gays myself at that moment, and one or two others while I was about it.

Fortunately, thanks to some deft manoeuvring on my scooter, I was able to get in in time for the 'Six O'Clock News'. Even so, as I said to Jane in the kitchen that evening, the day decent, law-abiding citizens are no longer able to get home to their wives and loved ones after a hard day's work, it'll be the end of civilized life in this country as we know it.

As I might have expected, she took me far too literally and said, 'But you haven't got a wife or any loved ones,' which I thought was rather unkind. At that moment, Victoria walked in, and before long, heated words were being exchanged. 'I give up,' she said finally. 'It is quite obvious to me that you are, politically speaking, totally naive – and probably sexually impotent.' And she marched out, slamming the door behind her with such force that she cracked one of the frosted glass panels. I suppose I'll have to pay for that, as usual.

Later, to my surprise, she came to my room as I was lying in bed reading and said if I thought she had come to apologize, I'd another think coming, but that if I'd be interested in accompanying her to the following night's Workers' Workshop Session, I'd be very welcome. I said I'd think about it.

Tuesday, September 13th

Another restless night, thanks to a recurring dream that I was having tea with Lenin in the hallway of the Travellers Club. Awoke exhausted but enthusiastic about Victoria's invitation. I think perhaps I *am* a little out of touch with left-wing thought in this country and a glimpse, however brief, into how the other half thinks, could be only an advantage. On the way into work, bought a copy of the *Morning Star*, but left it behind on the tube before I'd had a chance to read a word of it.

For some reason had always imagined that Workers' Workshop meetings were held in a dingy basement room in the Gray's Inn Road. Was most surprised, therefore, to find myself in the sitting room of an expensively decorated flat in Covent Garden belonging to a smooth-faced man with carefully brushed grey hair and a double-breasted dove-grey suit by the name of Terry. I did not catch his other name, but he looked a bit of a nancy boy to me. At all events, he is certainly not my idea of a typical member of the English working classes.

In fact I doubt if any of them would have recognized a worker if he had walked in through the window. Nevertheless, they all talked at great length about the Englishman's right to work, and the dignity of human labour. I felt tempted to express the alternative view on several occasions, but since I was a guest, it seemed rude to interrupt. At eleven biscuits and hot chocolate were served, and a protest deploring the government's failure to reduce the level of unemployment was handed round for everyone to sign. I have never been very keen on the idea of putting my name to documents of any kind. However, not wishing to cause any ructions back in the flat, I decided not to make an issue of it. I had considered signing a false name, but in the end I wrote down my own, but very indistinctly.

As we were leaving, Terry took my hand and gave it a little squeeze. 'Britain needs people like you,' he said softly, 'and so do I.'

I'm pretty certain he's a pansy.

Was going to say something about it to Victoria on the way home, when suddenly she exclaimed, 'There's a horrible smell in this car. If you don't mind, I'll get out here and catch a taxi.'

I suppose I had better give the floor another going over. As if I didn't have enough on my hands.

Wednesday, September 14th

Woke in the middle of the night in a cold sweat about this thing I signed last night. What if it should ever fall into the hands of the Special Branch? Or worse still, supposing this country were ever to be taken over by a right-wing dictatorship, which is quite possible in my view? How am I ever going to explain to the Secret Police that I only signed it for domestic reasons? I know I signed my name illegibly, but was it illegible enough? Just to be on the safe side, every time the phone rang today in my office, I answered in a disguised voice. Once I gave such a good imitation of a

West Indian that I had Roundtree fooled for several minutes.

Later, Betty from Accounts rang, so I tried it out again on her, and launched into a long, satirical account of last night's events in Covent Garden. Suddenly I was interrupted by this woman's voice shrieking, 'You double-crossing, superior Fascist bastard. I'll get even with you for this.'

It's funny, but I had never realized before how similar Betty and Victoria sound on the phone.

I knew I should have left politics well alone.

Thursday, September 15th

I do not earn a particularly high salary, but I'd give ten pounds to know who sewed up the bottom of my pyjama trousers. I think I have a pretty fair idea, but no firm evidence. It's not the torn ends I mind so much as the sprained toe I received when I first drove my foot unwittingly into the leg.

Saturday, September 17th

To the National to see the Robert Bolt play about the Russian Revolution. Rather an apt choice in the circumstances. In the interval ran into the Pedalows who were at the Olivier seeing *The Plough and the Stars*. Vanessa said, 'Oh, we saw the Bolt when it first opened. I thought it rather a superficial view of what was, after all, the turning point of modern civilization.'

I didn't like to say so, but I thought it was very deep and at times quite difficult to follow – though not half as difficult as filling out the advance booking form, which is like sitting an entrance test for MENSA. I would have mentioned the matter to Peter Hall on the way out had he not been in conversation. 'We've had problems,' I heard him saying, 'like you wouldn't believe.' The fact that we have as the head of our National Theatre a man who cannot speak grammatical English I find far from reassuring.

Sunday, September 18th

An overcast day. In an effort to get rid of the nasty smell in the car, I tried a particularly strong type of cleaner, and after swabbing it all over the offending area, left it for a couple of hours to soak. When I came back, I found that it had dissolved the rubber and started eating into the metal floor underneath, leaving behind an even more unpleasant smell than before.

My toe is, if anything, worse.

Monday, September 19th

At lunchtime decided to try a new bistro that has just opened in the next street to the office. It is one of those places on several floors. Thought I'd try the basement. On the way down, who should I see sitting alone at a table for four but Hugh Bryant-Fenn.

When I asked him what he was up to, he said, 'Oh, I'm doing the restaurant column in *Bedroom*.'

It was all gobbledygook to me until he explained that *Bedroom* was a new magazine starting up, similar to *Penthouse* and *Mayfair*. 'The articles are frightful,' he said cheerfully, 'but the girls are fantastic.'

This was surprising news, since the last time I had met him at the Pedalows he had just set up as an interior design consultant with an office in Beauchamp Place. 'I see,' I said, 'so *that's* why you're here?'

'Why?' he said.

'To write this place up for your *Bedroom* column?'

'Good Lord, no,' he said. 'I wouldn't put this place in my column if they paid me. Which they do, as a matter of fact.'

He went on to explain in a confidential way that he was about to meet a chap to talk about the possibility of presenting Diana Ross and the Supremes for a season in the Rose Room at Bourne and Hollingsworth. I said that I had understood that Diana Ross had split up with the Supremes some years ago.

Bryant-Fenn tapped the side of his nose and leaned forward confidentially. 'Wait and see, chum,' he murmured, 'wait and see.'

Bryant-Fenn was still there as I was leaving – only now he was deep in conversation with two rather tarty-looking blonde girls wearing too much make-up. Whatever their professions, they didn't look to me the sort of people who'd know anything about presenting Diana Ross and the Supremes in the Rose Room of Bourne and Hollingsworth, or anywhere else. Not wishing to put Hugh on a spot, I tried to slip by without his noticing. However, he called me over and taking a card out of his pocket said, 'You look the sort of person who could make use of this. Take a few friends. If there's any trouble just mention my name.'

When I got outside I saw it was a printed invitation to a free meal at a restaurant called the Botticelli – somewhere in St John's Wood. I doubt if I shall ever be able to take advantage of it; but still, it was decent of him to think I might. In the bus going home this evening, some woman dropped an extremely heavy bag of shopping right on my bad toe. She looked Arabic, I thought.

Tuesday, September 20th

Was on the point of tackling a boiled egg at breakfast this morning when I happened to notice that the Picasso poster which hangs above the table had slipped down between the glass and the hardboard backing. I stood up, leaned forward across the table, and took hold of the glass frame which immediately split right down the middle. Not only does this mean I shall now have to have a new piece of glass cut, but since there was a very real possibility that glass splinters had fallen into my boiled egg, I had to throw it away along with the butter that was on my plate. Unfortunately, since I was by then rather late for work, there was no time to boil another egg. In addition, I discovered that we were out of butter. I only hope that broken picture glass does not carry the same curse as a broken mirror.

My toe is no better.

Wednesday, September 21st

I have been thinking: this free meal invitation of Bryant-Fenn's is obviously just a PR gimmick to drum up trade for the restaurant. It surely cannot matter to them *who* takes up the offer as long as *someone* does.

After lunch, rang the Pedalows who have had me to dinner several times lately to ask them to join me. 'How divine,' said Vanessa in her squeaky voice. 'You'd better check with monsieur first, though. I'll put you through to the study.'

'Sounds all right,' said Tim in his usual off-hand way.

'Just check the old almanac . . . No problem. I'm not going to Australia now till next week.'

Those two are a complete mystery to me. They have obviously made a lot of money but no one seems to know how. Hugh says he thinks it's something to do with land speculation. I thought he was meant to be a stockbroker. I have also invited Roundtree's secretary, Felicity. I wouldn't at all mind starting something up with her. She has a magnificent figure, and her accent is not really as bad as all that. Would have asked Victoria, but as she has refused point-blank to speak to me for a week, it's rather difficult.

Thursday, September 22nd

Our evening at the Botticelli started off very well. Tim and Vanessa seemed very much at home there, and spent a lot of time waving to people they knew. They seemed slightly surprised that the waiters kept calling me Mr Bryant-Fenn, but I explained that it was Hugh who had recommended the place to me and booked our table. Felicity obviously went down extremely well, at least with Tim who could hardly tear his eyes away from her bust. It was a pity that, as she has clearly never read a book or been to a play in her life, she was able to contribute very little to the conversation. However, she showed interest, which is the main thing.

The restaurant itself was decorated in a typically self-conscious style, I thought. Dark brown walls, potted plants everywhere, limited editions in silver frames and a great deal of indirect lighting. Remarked on this to Vanessa who said, 'Oh, we like it.' They would.

Wondered if they would have been as keen on the prices, which were steep, to say the least. Fortunately, however, cost was not on this occasion my concern, and we all did ourselves extremely proud: smoked salmon to start with, followed by veally things and salad. We had three bottles of Hospices de Beaune 1969 and brandy and liqueurs afterwards. I also decided, just for once, to join Tim in a large Romeo y Julietta. When the waiter brought the bill, I discreetly slipped him the invitation card and returned at once to the conversation. The waiter, however, instead of bustling about his business, tapped me on the shoulder and, holding up the card, asked in a loud voice what this was meant to be. I explained in a low voice that it was all perfectly in order. However, he insisted that he knew nothing about it, so I suggested he address any queries to the manager. I assumed that was the end of that, but a minute or two later he was back again, this time with the manager – a superior-looking fellow who was all olive skin and sideboards.

'Excuse me, sir,' he said, 'but was this given to you by TCP Public Relations?' I took a bow at a venture, and replied that it was. 'Oh, I'm very sorry, sir,' said the manager, 'but TCP stopped handling our account over three months ago. Under the circumstances, Mr Fern, I could possibly see my way to giving you a slight discount – say five per cent . . . ?'

I was on the point of suggesting we might discuss the matter elsewhere, when Tim said, 'That'll be all right, Gino. Just put it on my account.'

Gino said, 'Yes, of course, Mr Pedalow. Good evening, Mrs Pedalow. It's always a pleasure to welcome *old friends* to the Botticelli.'

I doubt if I have felt more humiliated in my life. I made it quite clear to Tim that I considered his offer to be merely a loan and told him I should be sending a cheque in the morning.

Felicity did not say much during all this, but I shall be astonished if the news is not all round the office by lunchtime tomorrow.

Friday, September 23rd

The instant I got in this morning, I was on the phone to Bryant-Fenn to say that he owed me an apology and £88·00. To my astonishment he feigned ignorance and innocence; and to add insult to injury, when I told him that his invitation was totally worthless, all he could find to say was, 'Oh. So you had to stump up then?'

I explained that Tim had very kindly come to my rescue, thus saving us all further embarrassment.

'It would seem to me,' Hugh said, 'that if I owe anyone eighty-eight pounds it's Tim.'

I said that was not the point.

'I don't understand,' he said, interrupting me rudely. 'You got a free meal out of it, didn't you? I don't see you have anything to complain about.'

I put the phone down on him. I have always said that public relations attracted the second-rate, and am only glad that I have nothing to do with it.

Returned from lunch to find a note pinned to my office door saying: 'How to Eat Out at the Best Restaurants Free in One Easy Lesson. Apply: S. Crisp. Ext. 7440 (Reversed charge calls not accepted).' The message was unsigned, but I detect the hand of Armitage in this. I shall certainly not give him the satisfaction of thinking I even noticed it.

Saturday, September 24th

Yet another reference in the paper to this chap who's leaving the Labour Party. If my experiences in Covent Garden last week are anything to go by, I can't say I'm entirely surprised. I wonder that intelligent men should ever join in the first place.

Jackie came round again this evening and made an enormous spaghetti for herself and Beddoes. I do not mind her not making enough for me, and am perfectly prepared to believe she thought I was out, but how she manages to get short lengths of uncooked spaghetti all over the kitchen floor is beyond me. I went in there after they had gone to bed to cook myself a boiled egg, skidded on the spaghetti which rolled under my feet and came down with a crash, catching the back of my head against the door frame.

Jane, who arrived on the scene at that moment, could not have been more helpful, dabbing Dettol on the bump and making me a cup of tea. We talked for quite a long time together afterwards in the sitting room. Although obviously very shy with men, she has a good sense of humour. All it needs is for someone to bring it out. The sad fact is, though, that she will never get anywhere until she does something about her complexion.

Noticed in the bath tonight that my toenail is beginning to turn quite black.

Monday, September 26th

At dinner at the Varney-Birches', I was introduced to a girl who said, 'Are you by any chance related to the Smith's Crisps?'

I presume she was trying to be funny, but you can never really tell with those sort of people.

Tuesday, September 27th

To Leeds on the train with Armitage and Roundtree to look round the Barford set-up. Their marketing chap, Neville Pratt, travelled with us. A more tedious and fruitless exercise it would be hard to imagine.

On the way back to the station to catch the evening train, we called in the bar of the Metropole for a quick drink. Who should be there but Bryant-Fenn who announced that he had been up in Leeds to give a talk to a local literary society on Dante Gabriel Rossetti.

When I expressed surprise, he said, 'Oh, I do quite a bit of lecturing, you know, up and down the country. Mainly to ladies' luncheon clubs. It's quite a good racket. Sixty quid in cash and a first-class return rail fare. My usual subject is "Me and My Stomach – Confessions of a Food Columnist". It always goes down very well.'

How a man who at dinner once at the Pedalows' could not tell the difference between Bœuf à la mode and Irish stew has the gall to set himself up as a gourmet is a mystery to me. Nor, as far as I am aware, do his literary tastes extend much beyond Hammond Innes and Lady Antonia Fraser.

'I never realized you were an expert on Rossetti,' I said pointedly.

'To tell you the truth,' he said, 'until this morning, I'd always thought he was a singer. However, the lecture agency sounded pretty desperate when they rang, and I thought: What the hell, it's only Leeds, and it's sixty quid and no questions asked. So I looked the fellow up in the encyclo-paedia, invented a lurid love life for him and hurried off to King's Cross Station. The chairman said it was one of the best talks they've had all year. In fact they've booked me for a return visit in the spring.'

He then announced that he had a matter of some delicacy he wished to discuss with me. Naturally, I assumed he was referring to the incident in the Botticelli Restaurant. But nothing could have been further from his mind.

'The thing is,' he said, 'I've been asked to lecture for a week on a Mediterranean cruise. "Roman Provincial Life in the First Century AD". It's five hundred quid all found, plus expenses. The only problem is what to do about Percy – you know, my budgerigar. You couldn't possibly have him, could you? I think you owe me a favour.'

I was astounded at his impertinence and said that in my book it was he who owed a favour to me; but it was like water off a duck's back. Anyway, I've said I'll think about it. It won't do him any harm at all to sweat it out for a bit.

Wednesday, September 28th

Morning spent wrestling with the problem of Hugh's budgerigar. I cannot imagine anything worse than having to share a room with a noisy cage bird. On the other hand, it's not as though I'm being asked to sit and talk with the creature, or take it out for drives in the country. A little added responsibility might be very good for me, and will, I feel sure, raise my stock in Victoria's eyes.

After lunch, put Hugh out of his misery by ringing him to say that if he really couldn't find anyone else to look after the budgie, I would be willing to take him on.

'Oh,' said Hugh, 'I never bothered to ask anyone else.'

Thursday, September 29th

Am quite looking forward to my little visitor. I have made a space for him on top of the chest of drawers. I only hope he is not going to be messy.

Friday, September 30th

Hugh dropped Percy off shortly after six. He seems a nice enough little chap, if not exactly bouncing with health.

'Ah,' said Hugh, when I mentioned it, 'that's because he hasn't been fed for a day or two. What with one thing and another, I haven't had a spare moment. I'm sure your local pet shop will oblige with a bag of seed. The large ones are more economical. Oh, and you might get him another cuttle-fish bone while you're about it. He becomes very bad-tempered if he doesn't get his cuttle-fish bone.'

It had never occurred to me they might have closed the pet shop in Holland Park Avenue. However, it really isn't all that long a walk up to Notting Hill Gate, and the chap there was very helpful, and most apologetic about being out of cuttle-fish bones. I sympathize with his comment that if he were a budgie he'd prefer a ladder and a mirror with a bell on it any day and can only hope that Percy sees it the same way. Arrived back at the flat to be confronted by Victoria demanding to know what the terrible noise was coming from my bedroom. I explained about Percy. 'If you ask me,' she said, 'keeping birds in cages is thoroughly inhumane, and I'm surprised at your agreeing to have anything to do with it.'

I see that he has already managed to break one of the rungs of his ladder. The super-strong model was certainly not worth the extra 25p, and I shall take it up with the pet-shop man next time I'm in.

October

Saturday, October 1st

Woken at the crack of dawn by Percy ringing his bell for all its worth. Under the circumstances, it is probably just as well that Jane, who sleeps in the next room to mine, is away for the weekend.

After breakfast, put my hand into the cage to remove the broken ladder only to receive a sharp peck from Percy that drew blood. I only hope that I have not caught one of those strange diseases that are occasionally transmitted from birds to human beings – like psittacosis. I certainly seem to be developing, for no very good reason that I can see, a very nasty sore throat, and I noticed tonight that my voice had become quite croaky.

Sunday, October 2nd

To Kent early with Percy for lunch with mother. The moment I arrived I made a solemn pact with her not to discuss politics. She is convinced I am a socialist – which compared with her I suppose I am – and she blames me personally for the mishandling of the economy by the Labour Government in general, and for the smallness of her pension in particular. No matter how hard I control myself, it invariably ends in a shouting match. To my astonishment, the entire morning passed without a single reference to Mr Callaghan, and for once I was able to read the Sunday papers in peace. Was in the middle of a very interesting piece in one of the colour supplements when she came up behind my chair and asked what I was reading. I explained that it was an article about the French Resistance during the last war.

'How interesting,' she said, peering at the page. 'What's that photograph?'

I said that it was of a group of Resistance fighters in Clermont-Ferrand.

'Oh really?' she said. 'They look like a lot of lefties to me.'

By the time lunch was on the table, she had driven me into such a state of fury that I had completely lost my appetite. Matters were not helped by her saying at regular intervals, 'I do wish you wouldn't peck at your food, dear.'

Under the circumstances she could hardly have picked on a more unfortunate choice of phraseology. However, my throat was by that stage so sore that I could not have replied, even if I had wanted to.

As I was leaving mother said, 'I hope Percy's a good traveller.'

When I asked her why, through the agony of streptococci, she said, 'There's an awful smell in the car, as though someone has been sick.'

Tuesday, October 4th

To dinner at Theresa Milne's. She is looking rather good for her age, I thought. She has just moved into a little house in Barnes and done it up very well. Philippe de Grande-Hauteville was there. I hardly knew him at Oxford, and yet I seem to bump into him everywhere. He has recently opened an antique shop in Notting Hill Gate, and I have promised to call in one day. He seems to me to be under the impression that I work for the BBC, I don't quite know why.

Sat next to a plain girl in beige who talked a great deal about people I had never heard of. I was giving her my views on the new Truffaut film when she suddenly interrupted me to ask if I wore false teeth, of all things.

I said that I did not, and she asked me if I was sure. I replied that I was positive, and asked her the reason for her question.

'Oh, nothing,' she said, 'it's just that you have a habit of doing something with your mouth that only people with false teeth do.'

I was quite taken aback and said that I hoped it wasn't something too off-putting.

'Not at all,' she said. 'In someone who doesn't have false teeth, it's really very charming.'

Why do I waste my time at such events?

Wednesday, October 5th

A bizarre footnote to the Horse of the Year Show now taking place at Wembley. Vanessa's father, who is a psychiatrist, has had two patients in this week, complaining that they are unable to make love to their wives unless they have a bit in their mouths, and their wives are dressed in jodhpurs and spurs. I dread to think what goes on during the Motor Show.

Thursday, October 6th

Percy seemed so depressed on his own in the bedroom this evening that I brought him through to the sitting room. Unfortunately he would insist on singing and chattering all through a TV programme we were trying to watch. Jackie said she thought having a pet around made the flat seem 'ever so cosy' and started feeding him pieces of apple. In the end, Beddoes became very cross indeed and said that one of these days he would strangle the bird with his bare hands. I wouldn't put it past him either.

Friday, October 7th

An extraordinarily tiresome day one way and another. My scooter is on the blink again which meant travelling to work on the underground for the third day running. Then, during the lunch hour, I remembered that I had left a pair of shoes to be repaired at a little place round the corner. Went to pick them up only to find that the shoe-repair shop was now a sandwich bar. Took my place in the queue and when it came to my turn said that I had come to collect my brown suede casuals. The man cutting the sandwiches said, 'That's a new one on me, squire. Brown suede casuals. Would that be some sort of hamburger?'

I said that I hadn't got time for games and that I wanted my shoes back. In the end the fellow became rather insulting, so I left. On the pavement outside I found a policeman. I explained my problem and asked if he would be so kind as to help me get my shoes back.

'Shoes?' he said. 'From a sandwich bar?'

I sometimes think I would be far better off living in the country, if not abroad. Meanwhile I am short of a pair of brown suede shoes.

Saturday, October 8th

A horrible shock. Lifted the cover off Percy to find him lying on the bottom of his cage, stone dead. He was in great form when I put him to bed last night. I suspect Beddoes had a hand in this – literally. My suspicions deepened yet further by the fact that when he finally got up just before lunch to mix himself a gin and tonic, he had a large plaster on his right finger. There was no point in beating about the bush, so I came right out with it and asked him how he had hurt his finger.

'If you must know,' he said, 'I cut it on that piece of broken glass from your Picasso poster which you left lying around in the kitchen.'

I still did not believe him and decided on a more direct approach still.

'You may be interested to know,' I said, 'that Percy is dead.'

'Oh, really?' he said. 'It must have been that smell in your car that did it. It's enough to finish anyone off.'

My real concern, though, was how to break the news to Bryant-Fenn when he calls to collect Percy tomorrow. In the end I decided that the kindest and simplest solution would be to replace him with an identical budgie. I therefore placed the dead bird in a large matchbox and carried him off to the pet shop where I was able to match him up with another bird so similar I would be prepared to give £100 to anyone who can prove that it isn't Percy sitting there in the cage.

Sunday, October 9th

Have been reading the biography of Lord Curzon, and am most interested to learn that he married for money. This puts quite a different complexion on things. If a man like Curzon is prepared to be mercenary over such matters, then who am I to waste time with scruples? I have had quite enough of this shilly-shallying with Victoria and at the earliest opportunity shall invite her to join me for a weekend in Hertfordshire at Nigel and Priscilla's. They are always asking me why I don't bring a nice girl down. I sometimes think my sister and brother-in-law are under the impression I have no social life or friends at all.

Bryant-Fenn arrived after supper with a peeling nose and bright red forehead to collect Percy. He obviously did not have the slightest suspicion as to the budgie's real identity, and actually remarked on how well Percy was looking. It was more than I could say for him.

Monday, October 10th

A beautiful, sunny day. Was just settling down over a cup of coffee with the new Barford development proposals when Bryant-Fenn rang to say that he was rather worried about Percy. When I asked him why, he said that he couldn't understand it: every morning for five years Percy had greeted him with the words 'Morning, cock, how's yourself?' but this morning he had peeled back the cover to absolute silence. He said, 'You haven't been messing about with him, have you? Frightening him or anything?'

Realizing that the truth was bound to emerge sooner or later, I said, 'Look, Hugh, I think I should tell you straight away that that is not Percy.'

'What do you mean, not Percy?' he said.

I said, 'I was going to ring you to explain. Percy died on Saturday. I didn't like to tell you last night and spoil your homecoming.'

'I see,' he said, 'so you decided to ruin this morning for me instead?'

'Well,' I said, 'you know what I mean.'

'Frankly,' he said, 'I don't. As I see it, this was a calculated attempt on your part to cover up Percy's death and deceive me into thinking that he was still alive and well. Well, if you want my opinion, it's the most underhand thing I have ever come across in all my life. Percy and I were extremely close – indeed he was in many ways my only real friend. If you'd just come right out with it and said, "Look here, Hugh, I'm afraid Percy has popped off," I would have quite understood. But to try and replace him with a second-rate double is beyond all belief. Well, as far as I'm concerned, you can have him back, and the cage, too, for all I care. There's no way I could ever warm to him now.'

And he put the phone down on me. I have always suspected that beneath that cool, worldly exterior was a deeply hysterical human being.

Arrived home to find that he had already returned the budgie – cage, cover, spare seed and all. That's the last time I offer to help out.

Spoke to Victoria after dinner, who said she would like to come for the weekend to Nigel and Priscilla's at Bishop's Stortford, but it did not mean that anything had changed.

Tuesday, October 11th

Left the office early on an urgent pretext and took the budgie back to the pet shop in the hope of getting my money back.

'What's wrong with him?' the owner asked.

I said that I was quite simply not satisfied with the bird. He asked me what sort of satisfaction I had been expecting. I said, 'Well for one thing, he doesn't say anything.'

He replied that if it was miracles I was looking for, I had come to the wrong place. I said that that much was obvious, adding that, in my opinion, pet shops in England are not what they were.

'Neither,' he said, 'are the customers.'

Rang the Joyces and spoke to Priscilla who said they would be delighted to have us for the coming weekend. I do hope Victoria is going to fit in to country life and will not be tempted to start any unpleasant arguments.

Wednesday, October 12th

Is the whole world going mad?

I was driving to work this morning on my scooter when the driver of a Ford Cortina wound his window down and spat a piece of apple core straight into my lap.

'Excuse me,' I called out as we drew level at the traffic lights, 'that went on me.' He looked at me for a moment, threw the rest of his half-eaten apple at me, and drove off up the Bayswater Road. I was so busy trying to remember his number that I drove into the back of the car in front that was trying to turn right. As if I didn't have enough to worry about.

Thursday, October 13

Life has become such a strain lately one way and another that I am seriously beginning to fear for my health. Just to be on the safe side, I have decided to go in for some of this Body Maintenance I keep reading about in the Sunday papers. I thought I might start off with something simple, like jogging in the park.

This evening a most extraordinary thing happened. At about six-thirty there was a ring on the front door. I opened it to find a black girl standing there, very tall, with the sort of hair that looks as though it has been ploughed. 'Hi, there,' she said. 'I'm Grace,' and marched straight past me into the flat. I said that I thought she must have come to the wrong address.

'Ralph does live here, doesn't he?' she said.

'Beddoes?' I said.

'Oh,' she said, 'is that his other name?'

Apparently Beddoes had picked her up on the underground on his way home from the office, invited her back to the flat and sent her on ahead while he went to get some cigarettes. She seemed a nice enough girl – a receptionist in a film company, she said. However, just to be on the safe side, I kept an eye on her till Beddoes returned.

'What do you think?' he said to me later in the kitchen, 'not bad for a choc ice, eh?'

One way and another I'm quite relieved to be going away for the weekend. Jane has very kindly agreed to look after the budgie.

Friday, October 14th

To the office in my brown tweed suit. I usually wear it on Friday mornings, largely to annoy Armitage who is convinced that I spend every weekend as a guest at some grand country-house party. It must be terrible to be so full of envy. 'Off for another of your smart house parties?' he asked as I walked in.

'Oh, not really,' I told him casually. 'Just some friends in Hertfordshire. A spot of shooting tomorrow morning: a little *mah-jong* and dancing to a wind-up gramophone in the evening – you know the sort of thing.'

Happy to see his knuckles went quite white.

Picked Victoria up at her office at five-thirty and drove straight on down. Unfortunately have still been unable to get rid of the sick smell completely, so sprayed the inside of the car with liberal doses of Flowers of the Forest air freshener. We were sitting in a traffic jam in the Euston Road, when she said, 'If there's one thing I can't stand it's strong after-shave,' and wound the window right down. As a result, the whole effect of the air freshener was lost and by the time we got to Holloway Road, the sick smell was back again.

'I'm so sorry about the smell,' I said.

She said that she hadn't noticed it, but now that I came to mention it, it was absolutely filthy and did I mind if we opened *all* the windows? I was glad I had had the foresight to throw my old anorak into the back of the car at the last minute. Victoria said it was remarkably warm considering its age. Any fears that I might have had about her not fitting in with my sister and brother-in-law's rural way of life were dispelled the moment we arrived. I have never been very keen on that take-us-as-you-find-us attitude that appears to prevail amongst country folk, but Victoria seemed to take to it very happily. As we were unpacking the car I happened to make a comment to her on how funny Nigel's clothes looked after London.

'I don't know what you mean,' she said. 'I think he looks very well in them,' and to my surprise began to discuss sugar beet with him. From what I could gather, she seemed quite knowledgeable.

I felt Priscilla might have come up with something a little more appetizing than sausages for supper. They seemed a little high to my way of thinking, and the cauliflower was definitely over-cooked, but Victoria appeared to notice nothing wrong and even asked for a second helping of both.

I hoped they had not taken too much for granted over the sleeping arrangements and wondered if I should give some hint of the situation. However, Priscilla solved the problem very simply by saying, 'I've put Victoria in the big room at the end, and you're in the box room. I'm afraid the heating doesn't work in there, but you could always use your anorak as an extra blanket, if you want.'

'That's fine by me,' Victoria said with an enthusiasm that was quite uncalled for.

The box room certainly is very cold.

Saturday, October 15th

Woke at nine with earache – presumably from driving all that way with the window down. Came down to find Victoria had gone out with Nigel in the Land-Rover to look round the farm. They seem to have hit it off surprisingly well.

A delicious breakfast completely ruined by James, aged six, who sat under the table, pulling at the hairs on my leg. I asked him to stop three times, but he took not the slightest notice and his mother said nothing to him, so eventually I leaned forward under the table and slapped him sharply on the wrist. He immediately screamed with rage and tried to bite me on the ankle.

I had expected Priscilla might have shown some sympathy. Instead she said, 'Would you kindly mind not hitting my child. It's very bad for children to be brought up in an atmosphere of violence.' I told her that was not *my* idea of bringing children up, at which she pointed out, rather unkindly I thought, that as I did not have any children I was hardly qualified to hold opinions on the subject.

At lunch (shepherd's pie and baked beans, which always give me terrible wind) Nigel suggested we might like to drive over to Braintree where some friends of theirs were having a clay-pigeon shoot. Victoria said she would love to, and I have always wanted to have a go at it myself. I went upstairs afterwards to change into something warm, but when I came down I found that Nigel and Victoria had already gone.

When I asked Priscilla why they hadn't waited for me, she said vaguely, 'Oh, I think they were under the impression you weren't very keen and had gone upstairs to read.'

In the evening, a small dinner party had been arranged in our honour.

'I think you'll like this other couple,' said Nigel. 'He's an architect, she writes. They're quite odd – well, that's to say, they're from London, too, so I expect you'll have a lot in common.'

In the event, it was a most successful evening, and we were

able to discuss a number of topics of interest to country folk –
the decline in village life, the rights and wrongs of foxhunting,
unemployment in agricultural communities, the preservation
of the countryside and so on. It was all great fun.

Afterwards, when they had gone, Nigel said, 'I couldn't
have kept all that up for much longer.'

'All what?' I asked him.

'All that chit-chat,' he said.

As I was getting into bed I caught my bad toenail on the
sheet, tearing it painfully.

Sunday, October 16th

Something very fishy was going on last night. Was so frozen
by about three a.m. that I simply had to get up to look for a
blanket. Not only was there a light showing under Victoria's
door, but the door to Nigel's bedroom was slightly ajar.
Yet I distinctly remember Priscilla telling me that they always
slept with their door shut. I thought at first that he might
have slipped downstairs for something, but there was no one
down there when I looked, and no one in the bathroom either.

This morning Victoria did not come down for breakfast,
and when she finally did appear, could not stop yawning.
Neither, I noticed, could my brother-in-law. When I asked
her if she had had a good night, she looked at Nigel, and said,
'A very good night indeed, thank you.'

I am not a suspicious man by nature, but I reckon there
was a bit of fun and games going on somewhere.

After breakfast we all went to church. I am not, I'm
ashamed to say, as regular a churchgoer as I might be, but I
never fail to enjoy it when I do go, especially when the
singing is good.

Evidently the Joyces' local church is not as well attended
as some, and this morning's congregation consisted of eight
elderly people who never opened their mouths from beginning to end. Under the circumstances one was hardly encouraged to 'Sing unto the Lord a new song'. Such singing
as there was came from the so-called choir which consisted of
a soft warbling from the district nurse, a growling basso
profundo from the tiny gamekeeper who insisted on his own
version of everything, and a piping tenor from Nigel who
was largely off-key. The organist groped about somewhere

in between. I heard Victoria make a half-hearted shot at the *Te Deum*, but she very quickly gave up the struggle. On the other hand, she gave a loud rendering of the General Confession, as well she might have.

Nigel read the first lesson – rather badly, I thought. He pronounced Micah as though it were Meecah. There was an embarrassing moment during the collection. Having anticipated a bag, it came as a bit of a shock to find that not only was it a brass plate, but that all the locals handed over their contributions in small brown envelopes. There was nothing for it but quickly to substitute the 10p piece I had ready for a pound note. I've enjoyed Mattins more, I must confess.

I was looking forward to a good, stiff walk after lunch, but Victoria said, 'Oh, I have to get back into town, I'm afraid.'

Having been brought up to believe that if you take a girl away for the weekend, it's your duty to bring her back again I had no alternative but to forgo my walk and drive back far earlier than I had expected.

Not surprisingly, we got caught in a bad traffic jam at Finsbury Park.

Whatever it was that Victoria had to get back for, it obviously was not very important, since she spent the entire evening in her bedroom.

All in all, though, I have a feeling I have made more progress with her than it may appear.

Monday, October 17th

A glorious autumn day. Wore my brown tweed suit again to the office to annoy Armitage. Called in at MacFisheries en route to buy a brace of pheasant to take in with me. Unfortunately, the best they could offer was a couple of pigeons. I hung them nonchantly on the hat-stand in my office. When Armitage came in, he looked at them and said, 'Well, you obviously didn't have a very good weekend's sport. I could do better than that in Trafalgar Square with a catapult.'

Tuesday, October 18th

Up at six, ready to start my jogging, but had hardly laced up my gym shoes when it started to rain, so returned to bed for another couple of hours of much-needed sleep.

Wednesday, October 19th

Up at seven to find the day overcast but dry. Set off eagerly on my first morning of jogging. Am thinking in terms of buying a track suit and a new pair of gym shoes, but have decided to wait and see how it goes before involving myself in a lot of expense. Anyway, the split in the sole hardly noticed after a while. Had never realized before how lucky I am to have Holland Park on my doorstep. I could as easily have been in the depths of the country – although I was surprised to pass quite so many other joggers on the way. Everything went extremely well for the first ten minutes, although I was somewhat alarmed to discover that I was barely able to cover a hundred yards at a time without running out of breath. I also began to experience sharp pains in my chest. One hears all too often of young men dropping dead from heart attacks as a result of too much sudden exercise, so I stopped and rested on a bench for a while. Nearby was a stretch of grass surrounded by a low iron railing, and beyond it a path where a rather pretty girl was walking with a small white terrier. I stood up, ran forward and vaulted lightly over the railing. Foolishly, I caught my foot on the top and came down heavily on the damp grass, giving my knee a nasty bruise. I was lying there, dazed and winded, when the terrier suddenly took it into its head to attack me. However, its owner, instead of calling the nasty little brute off, merely laughed and walked on. The interesting thing is that, apart from experiencing a certain difficulty in walking, I feel 100 per cent fitter already.

Thursday, October 20th

I would give a lot to know who it was who telephoned shortly after six o'clock this evening. I could hear the phone ringing as I was coming up the stairs. I hurried up the last two flights as best I could with my gammy leg and along the corridor. However, in my anxiety to extricate the front-door key from my inside pocket, I ricked my neck badly, and at the same time dropped the box of eggs I was carrying, breaking every one of them. I finally got the door open and had just reached the phone when it stopped ringing. I have rung up everyone I can think of, but none of them claims responsibility. Not only will my share of the telephone bill for this quarter be much larger than usual, but I am now incapable of moving my head without great pain. This will obviously put paid to my jogging for the time being.

Friday, October 21st

At Armitage's suggestion, have decided to pay a visit to a sauna-and-massage place he knows of, just off the Edgware Road. I got the distinct impression that there is more to it than meets the eye, and I made quite sure he understood that I was not in the market for any hanky-panky.

'I don't know what you mean,' he said, all innocence.

He must take me for a complete fool. At all events, whatever they may or may not get up to in this particular massage parlour, it's bound to be an interesting experience, and my neck couldn't be more uncomfortable than it is now.

I have booked a three o'clock appointment tomorrow afternoon.

Saturday, October 22nd

Hardly slept a wink last night for thinking of the massage parlour, and when I did, I kept having erotic dreams – one of which to my surprise involved Grace.

Arrived at the parlour in good time for my appointment. It all looked very respectable from the outside, with signs in the window for American Express and Access. I could not help reflecting what a strange world it is where you can even get pleasure on credit. Was surprised to find the receptionist was a man. He told me that I would be looked after by Michelle who was extremely capable. I said that it all sounded very satisfactory to me and that it would be a good opportunity for me to practise my French. At this he gave a little laugh, and called for Michelle through an intercom.

I was most interested to discover with what ease one slips into the demi-monde, and was beginning to feel quite at home when the door opened and in stepped a large, handsome young man with curly hair and a ring through one ear.

He was wearing white shorts, sandals and a T-shirt with the words I WANT TO GET MY HANDS ON YOU printed across the front.

The receptionist said, to my astonishment, 'Oh, there you are, Michel, this is Simon with a sore neck. It's the first time for him, so don't be too hard on him. I know how rough you can be.'

I remarked that I had expected the treatment to be performed by women.

'If you're looking for *that* sort of thing,' he said coyly, 'you've come to the wrong place.'

I decided the only thing to do under the circumstances was to play his game, so I said carelessly, 'Frankly, it doesn't matter to me one way or the other.'

He said that I was a devil, and hoped that whatever tensions I was suffering, Michel would be able to relieve them.

I followed Michel through some gaily coloured plastic strips into a sort of corridor with a number of doors leading into small booths. He showed me into the one at the far end and told me to take all my clothes off and lie face down on the couch. I heard him go into the next-door booth, where there was a lot of whispering, punctuated by laughter. I took everything off except my underpants and lay down as I had been told.

'I said *all* your clothes,' he said when he returned.

I remarked conversationally that he seemed to have a very good English accent. He said that, as he had been born and brought up in Cheltenham, that was hardly surprising.

When I was lying down again, he said, 'Is it just your neck that's giving you trouble, or do you require the full treatment?'

I had read enough of Beddoes's magazines to know what *that* meant, so I decided the best course would be to lay my cards on the table straight away. 'Now look here,' I said. 'I think I should tell you here and now that I am not that way inclined.'

'What a queer person you are,' he said, and started to massage my back.

I still can't make out whether he was having me on or not, but he certainly managed to put my neck right. I think the fact is, as soon as they realized they were dealing with a

40

serious customer, they decided to play it straight, rather than risk any trouble.

All evening I noticed Grace kept giving me knowing sort of looks, as though in some funny way she knew where I had been in the afternoon. It wouldn't surprise me one little bit to discover she does a bit of that sort of thing on the side.

Sunday, October 23rd

Was boiling myself an egg this morning in the kitchen when suddenly Grace rushed in wearing nothing but Beddoes's dressing gown, threw open the window and stuck her head out. For a moment I thought she was about to make some dramatic suicide bid, but she laughed and waved and even started cheering. I asked her what on earth was going on. 'It's Concorde,' she said. 'It always flies over at this time. I never miss it.'

I made some indifferent remark or other, at which she turned on me, her hands on her hips and her eyes flashing, and cried, 'But aren't you excited about it?'

I said that I was, quite.

'Well, I am,' she said, 'very. It's things like that that make me proud to be British.' And she marched off back to the bedroom.

It's extraordinary to think that someone like that should feel as responsible for the success of Concorde as I do.

While getting ready for bed this evening, I found that I have developed a nasty rash in a most awkward place.

No prizes for guessing where I picked that up from.

Monday, October 24th

This morning's post brings a letter from the Lord Chancellor's department, summoning me for jury service on December 5th. This is very exciting news.

Beddoes, who, as far as I can see, has no social conscience whatever, tells me that according to someone he knows who's up in these things, anyone can get out of jury service simply by slipping the Clerk of the Court a five-pound note and muttering the word 'incontinence'. I shall certainly do no such thing. As the enclosed, self-explanatory leaflet points out, 'Jury service is one of the most responsible duties that the individual citizen can be called on to undertake.' I quite agree.

Apart from anything else, it is sure to be an interesting experience, and one of those things everyone should do once in their lives. Who knows, I might even find myself involved in a sensational murder trial, like that of the Krays, and have to be put up in a West End hotel and given police protection and goodness knows what else.

Tuesday, October 25th

Am becoming increasingly concerned about this rash which shows no signs of clearing up.

Called round at the doctor's this evening after work, but he is obviously as baffled as I am. However, he prescribed some ointment, and said that it was probably just one of those things that go round from time to time.

I did not care for his implications one bit, but decided to let the matter drop rather than become involved in a long-winded explanation about my visit to the massage parlour and so on. It would almost certainly be misunderstood. I have long suspected that the majority of patients in his waiting room are there because they have been up to no good. In fact I have often seriously considered finding another doctor in a more respectable area.

Thursday, October 27th

Great excitement. The Harrods Christmas Catalogue has arrived. I have never actually bought Christmas presents from the catalogue, or from Harrods, for that matter, but mother always sends it on, and I enjoy speculating on what I might buy in a moment of desperation: the man's sheepskin coat with the coyote collar at £475, perhaps? The President's Cocktail Hamper at £350? The Black 'Top Hat' Ice Bucket with bottle of Moët & Chandon Première Cuvée Champagne, magician's rabbit glove puppet and pack of trick cards, for a mere £17·50? Or possibly the jumping dolphin in clear crystal on chrome stand from Daum of France, signed, at £180? I simply cannot imagine how I have lasted all these years without one.

Friday, October 28th

Rash showing no signs of improvement, despite the ointment. The doctor has finally admitted defeat and has made an appointment for me to see a specialist at the hospital on Tuesday week. I am beginning to wonder if I might not have contracted some rare skin condition that will set the entire medical world by its ears. Who knows, they might decide to name the complaint after me. Crisp's Disease. I can see the entry in the medical dictionary already.

Sunday, October 30th

Now my toenail has come off completely.

Monday, October 31st

A pink card arrived this morning from the hospital with an appointment to see a Dr Smithers. I only hope he is a little more *au fait* with his subject than my man.

A more immediate worry, though, is that it says on the bottom of the card: ON YOUR FIST VISIT [*sic*], PLEASE BRING A SPECIMEN OF URINE.

I have hunted high and low for a suitable container, but have been unable to come up with anything smaller than a 2 lb. Nescafé jar. What do other people do in similar circumstances? Frankly, I am rather stuck.

November

Tuesday, November 1st

The very mention of November for me conjures up images of leaves smouldering in London parks, roasting chestnuts over an open fire, and tea at the Ritz. Why this should be I cannot imagine, since I have never had tea at the Ritz in my life. Perhaps I should. It could be my next project.

The Pedalows have invited me to a firework party on Saturday. It seems rather short notice but have said I'll go.

Wednesday, November 2nd

Grace has been showing increasing interest in the budgerigar, so tonight I asked her if she would like to have it. Her delight was positively childlike. Anyway, she has taken the bird home with her – to eat, I shouldn't wonder.

Thursday, November 3rd

Armitage marched into my office this morning without so much as a by-your-leave and said, 'Oh, by the way, laddie. About the Barford project. They want suggestions on it in time for a meeting on Monday morning. I'd get my skates on if I were you.'

Who does he think he is?

Friday, November 4th

This business of the specimen has been on my mind for some days now. I wonder if hospitals have any idea of the problems and worries they create for people when they make requests of this sort? In the end, called round at Fortnum and Mason during the lunch-hour and asked for the smallest pot of jam they had.

'What sort of jam did you have in mind, sir?' asked the assistant.

I told him the actual jam was immaterial; it was the jar I was interested in. Finally, after a certain amount of misunderstanding all round, we settled for a small pot of damson, one of the few jams I have never much cared for.

Saturday, November 5th

To the Pedalows in Islington for the fireworks. It was all pretty much of a damp squib as far as I was concerned. Tim made a great fuss about a hot punch he had been working on all afternoon. He'd put far too much spice in it to my way of thinking and when no one was looking I tipped mine into a flower bed.

Philippe de Grande-Hauteville was there, and said, 'How's life at the BBC, then?'

I might as well talk to a brick wall as talk to him.

Also Theresa Milne, looking very old suddenly.

Hugh Bryant-Fenn much in evidence as usual, rushing about in a state of high excitement, letting off rockets in all directions and drawing everyone's attention to the ones he had bought. He made a particular fuss about a Catherine Wheel which he kept telling us cost him 85p. However, when it came to the point, the thing flew straight off the garden fence and into the compost heap where it fizzled pathetically for a second or two before going out. Thinking that was the end of it, I made my way towards the house, as did several others.

'Hang on,' we heard Tim shouting from the bottom of the garden. 'We haven't had the *pièce de résistance* yet. Everyone look at the flower bed.'

He then struck a match which he applied to a Roman Candle at one end of the bed. This duly went off, at the same time lighting a length of fuse which in turn lit another Roman Candle further along and so on. Everything seemed to be going according to plan, and everyone was congratulating Tim on his ingenuity when the fuse went out.

'Oh, hell,' Tim shouted, 'that's ruined the whole effect. It must be the damp. Will someone be an angel and light that next Roman Candle?'

Realizing that was the spot where I had ditched my drink, and not wishing him to discover the true cause of the failure, I volunteered and was just about to strike a match when the Candle went off in my face, scorching my forehead and completely burning off my eyebrows. Everyone was at once thrown into a frightful state. Vanessa became hysterical and had to be slapped round the face by the au pair girl. Tim kept trying to do a test he vaguely remembered from his Boy Scout days to check that I hadn't gone blind. Everybody agreed that I should see someone about it, so in the end Bryant-Fenn drove me down to the nearest hospital which by a curious coincidence was the very one I am due to go to about my rash. In fact I mentioned this to the nurse who took my particulars, but she didn't seem very interested. Casualty was full of people who had been injured by fireworks – many of whom had lost more than their eyebrows. I was all for going home after they had patched me up, but the doctor insisted on my staying in overnight, in case there was any damage to my eyes.

I was lent a pair of pyjamas and taken along to a men's surgical ward and put in a bed next to a chap who had just been operated on for impacted wisdom teeth. It was impossible to get a wink of sleep for the coughing, spitting and swearing that came from the next bed. It wasn't until four in the morning that I suddenly remembered that I was a subscriber to Private Patients Plan and could therefore afford a private room. I rang the night sister to explain this, but she was most unsympathetic and said that if I thought she was going to set to and move me at that hour of the night, I had another think coming, and that we'd all be getting up in another two hours anyway.

After she had left, the man opposite called out, 'I'd stay where you are if I were you, chief, and count yourself lucky. I knew a man in a private ward in a big London teaching hospital once who didn't get fed for two days.'

Spent the rest of the night composing a stiff letter to the PPP people cancelling my subscription.

Sunday, November 6th

Beddoes arrived at visiting time bringing a huge plastic
dahlia, a copy of *Spiritualist News* and an eyebrow pencil.
Discharged finally at four.

No one in the flat. Struggled with the Barford project. Ate
a boiled egg. Went to bed at nine.

I don't know which is more painful – my forehead or my
rash.

Monday, November 7th

If there's one thing I dislike more than men who carry hand-
bags, it's men who wear make-up. However, in the circumstances, it seems perfectly legitimate to imitate nature until
my eyebrows grow again.

Everyone at the office showed great concern for my misfortune, and Sarah even went so far as to buy me a coffee
from the machine at her own expense. Armitage, of course,
had to make light of the matter by calling out, 'Hello, it's
George Robey,' the moment I walked in.

I decided to sober him up straight away by discussing the
Barford project. I left him in no doubt as to the amount of
hard work I had devoted to the matter over the weekend in
the face of considerable difficulty, and suggested that the
sooner we got down to talking about the different ideas
before the meeting the better.

He gave me a superior look and said airily, 'Oh, you can
forget all about that. I talked it over with my uncle after
lunch on Sunday, and we will probably go ahead with a plan
based on my figures.'

Tuesday, November 8th

To the hospital, carrying my specimen wrapped in a piece of
Kleenex. Dr Smithers who examined me asked me a number
of rather personal questions about my private life which
under any other circumstances I should certainly have
declined to answer. I am beginning to think all doctors
these days have one-track minds.

Finally he said, 'In my opinion, you have got inter-
trigo.'

This was exciting news. 'Really?' I said. 'What is that exactly?'

'It comes from two Latin words, basically,' he explained, 'inter and trigo. In fact, it's a heat rash.'

I suppose I should be relieved that it is nothing more serious, but I must confess to feeling somewhat disappointed. As I was leaving he said, 'That's a nasty burn you've got on your forehead. I should have it looked at if I were you.'

I was halfway home when I remembered I had forgotten to ask the nurse for my jam jar back, which is a great pity since it had a rather unusual label.

Wednesday, November 9th

An unpleasant episode in the local grocer's. Called in on my way home from the office to buy a piece of their strong cheddar, and asked the girl if I could taste a small sliver first.

'Oh,' she replied sniffily, 'we don't allow that.' I said that in that case they were the only shop in London who didn't. But I might have been talking to half a pound of potatoes.

'Our cheddar is always very good,' she said. 'We always buy from the same people.'

I pointed out that it was not the quality of the cheese that was in question but the strength.

'Look,' she said, 'do you want a piece of this cheese or don't you?'

By now there was quite a queue building up behind me, so I replied calmly that I would take quarter of a pound. As she was weighing it out, I said, 'You see, if you had allowed me to taste it, I might have bought a much larger piece.'

'And if you hadn't liked it,' she said, 'you might have bought none at all.'

There is no arguing with people like that. It is a wonder to me they are still in business at all.

Thursday, November 10th

For reasons that I cannot explain, I have become more and more convinced lately that I have been chosen as a subject for 'This is Your Life'. Indeed, every time I am summoned to Roundtree's office, I feel sure that Eamonn Andrews is going to step out from behind the filing cabinet clutching the book, and pronounce the famous words. And why not?

They often have people on that I have never heard of and the programme has been just as interesting as those featuring the famous, if not more so. My only worry is that they might take it into their heads to fly Eric over from Canada, and I still haven't paid him back the £25 I borrowed the Christmas before last.

Friday, November 11th

Mike rang this morning to say that he was taking Victoria away for the weekend to stay with friends, and that he gathered I would be quite happy to have the children again. I asked him where he got that idea from.

'From Victoria, of course,' he said breezily.

Saturday, November 12th

Mike arrived with the children at noon, drank half a bottle of my gin, and left with Victoria at one. Gerry much less pretty than I remember, and *much* more childish.

Could not face cooking lunch, so decided to take them to my local Greek restaurant for a kebab. Jane was hanging about in the sitting room, looking glum, so invited her along too.

During lunch I asked Gerry who the friends were that her father and Victoria had gone to stay with.

'What friends?' she said. 'As far as I know, they've simply gone for a dirty weekend at the Spread Eagle at Midhurst.'

I was so upset I was quite unable to finish my souvlakia. Tom was also making slow progress with his moussaka. When I asked him why, he said, 'It's your face. It puts me right off my food.'

After lunch Jane suggested a trip down the river to Greenwich. Drove to Westminster Pier and arrived just in time for the 2.30 boat. I cannot imagine how I can have lived in London all these years and not been on the river. It is simply fascinating and I cannot wait to go again. It was rather embarrassing that I was able to answer so few of the children's questions. However, Jane turned out to be a great authority on the subject, and pointed out all the buildings of historic interest that we passed.

At Greenwich we looked over the *Cutty Sark*, visited the Painted Hall, and climbed the hill to the Royal Observatory, with the children hanging on to Jane's every word. The afternoon was such a success that I bought everyone an ice cream before leaving and another upon disembarkation. There was one unfortunate moment in the car going home when Tom started complaining about the nasty smell in the car, whereupon Gerry announced that it made her feel sick, and then suddenly Tom was. It was a pity he couldn't have done it on the same spot as before.

After dinner Jane and I sat together on the settee with a bottle of Riesling and watched a play about a honeymoon couple renting a cottage. Whether it was the play, or the wine, I do not know, but before long I found myself putting my arm round Jane's shoulders as though it were the most natural thing in the world. One thing led to another, and before I knew what, we were in my room and in my bed. I know there is a fashionable trend among diarists these days to commit the most intimate details of their private lives to paper willy-nilly, and I am as well aware that sex sells books as the next man. However, as I made quite clear when I started my diary, I did not embark upon it with a view to publication nor has anything happened in the meantime to lead me to change my mind. What took place in my bedroom on the night of November 12th is a private matter between me and Jane. Suffice to say it was both successful and enjoyable.

Sunday, November 13th

Woke up feeling even happier than I was yesterday, if such a thing were possible.

After breakfast, on a sudden wild impulse, I jumped up, threw open the window and shouted down into the street, 'A fiver for every man, woman and child who is happier than I am at this moment.'

A minute or two later there was a knock on the front door. It was Mrs Gurney from the flat downstairs.

'Aha,' I cried cheerfully, 'have you come to collect your prize?'

'I certainly have not,' she said. 'It may have escaped your notice, but today is Remembrance Sunday. If you must choose today for playing the fool, you might at least have had the decency not to do so in the middle of the two-minute silence.'

After lunch we all went for a long walk in Richmond Park. Any feelings I might have had for Geraldine have, I am delighted to say, disappeared completely, and my thoughts are now only for Jane.

I felt closer to her than ever this evening, and it came as a great disappointment when she said, 'I think I'll sleep in my own bed tonight, if you don't mind.'

When I asked her why, all she said was, 'I would rather.'

I lay awake for hours trying to work it out, and could only suppose I was suffering from a slight attack of bad breath. Eventually I got up and went to the bathroom and gave my teeth the scrubbing of their lives. When I got back into bed my gums were so sore I had to take a couple of aspirins to get to sleep.

Monday, November 14th

Was able to get very little done in the office this morning for thinking about last night. I have decided that the bad breath was a red herring and that, as usual, female psychology lies at the bottom of this. Having submitted to me on Saturday night, she is now suffering from guilt, and is, quite understandably, unable to face me.

Clearly the onus is now very much on me to put the situation to rights. Jane is a passionate girl, but at the same time obviously deeply inhibited. If I do not break down her inhibitions, no one will. It is unthinkable that she should finish up an old maid. My duty is clear, but not the way.

Against my better judgement, rang Beddoes at his office. I must say, for a successful City man, he always seems to have plenty of time to chat on the phone. I put the problem to him, as though it concerned someone in my office. He thought about it for a second or two and said, 'If I were you, I'd pay a visit to one of those sex shops. They've got all sorts of things for men with your problem.'

I said, 'There's nothing the matter with me,' but he just laughed and put the phone down. I shouldn't be at all surprised to learn that he has a problem himself. People who are forever trying to impute failure in others are frequently failures themselves.

Tuesday, November 15th

Was in the Edgware Road at lunchtime today when I happened to find myself passing a sex shop. Unfortunately, I was already late for a luncheon appointment, otherwise I might well have investigated further.

Wednesday, November 16th

Life is full of coincidence this week. Stepped off a bus in the Tottenham Court Road almost into the doorway of another of these sex shops. Purely out of curiosity, I decided to wander in and see what all the excitement is about. The middle of the shop was taken up by a book rack containing girlie magazines. I casually picked up one which had a picture on the cover of a girl with her hand down her knickers and went to riffle idly through it. However, this proved to be impossible owing to the plastic cover in which the magazine was firmly bound, and I was certainly not about to waste £1·50 on what would undoubtedly prove a great disappointment. There was also a rather unpleasant section containing more plastic-bound volumes with titles like *Pretty Boys* and *More of Bruce*. I doubt if that sort of thing would do much for Jane's confidence. On the other hand, what would?

The majority of the merchandise seemed to be aimed more towards the failed male than the unaroused female. I was particularly intrigued by a device called 'The Arab Strap' which claimed to combine 'visual pleasure with physical pleasure'. Since the effect of wearing the strap is to 'create a bigger bulge' the first part of the claim might conceivably be considered justifiable, but the second is surely so unlikely as to contravene the Trades Description Act? I took out my notebook with a view to jotting down the exact words when a voice behind me said, 'Can I help you?'

I turned to face a rather mousy girl with long straggly hair and no make-up, dressed in faded jeans and a cheesecloth shirt, through which a pair of large breasts could clearly be seen.

I told her I wasn't there to buy anything; it was part of some research I was working on.

'That's what they all say,' she said and returned to the cash register.

I was certainly not going to give her the satisfaction of thinking she was right, and so continued calmly to examine the goods, making the occasional note as I went. Was on the point of leaving when I happened to notice a book on auto therapy. One is always reading about women tuning themselves up sexually with practices of this sort, and despite the plastic wrapper it looked a more serious work than most. £5·95 seems little enough to pay for a happy and successful love life. Unfortunately the girl was still on duty at the cash desk, and I had no alternative but to leave it till another day.

Friday, November 18th

Returned to sex shop during lunch hour to find that a young man with a beard had now taken over. It is interesting how quickly one becomes accustomed to the most unfamiliar milieus, and it seemed the most natural thing in the world after paying for my book to stroll to the back of the shop where the sex films were being shown. It was rather like a public lavatory, with a narrow corridor and half a dozen doors leading off to either side. Men, many of them no older than me, were wandering from one to another as unselfconsciously as if it had been the Odeon, Leicester Square. There were three categories of film on offer: full length with talk, 2 × 50p; full length silent, 50p; and films in four sections, 10p per section. Not knowing quite what to expect, I decided to work myself in gently with 10p's worth. It was very dark in the booth, and I had a certain amount of difficulty in finding the slot for my coin, so that when the film started I was facing the wrong way, and by the time I had turned round, it had ended. I settled myself on the little wooden bench facing the white board on the back of the door before inserting any more money. The film appeared to be about two women on a bed, but the quality was so poor that I could not swear to this. When it ended, I could see that someone had written the word RUBBISH on the screen. Decided just for fun to try the booth next door which was showing *Hot Cheeks*. This concerned the activities of a man and two women on what looked very much like the same bed. Once again, the quality was so poor they appeared to be frolicking in a heavy rainstorm. However, just before the end there was a close-up of the man's face grimacing. I couldn't believe my eyes. It looked exactly like Beddoes. Before I had a chance to look more closely, the film ended. Discovering I had run out of 10p pieces, I hurried out into the shop to get some change, only to find that the bearded man had gone and his place had been taken by the girl again.

As I was leaving I heard her calling out, 'How's the research going then?' at which one or two of the customers turned and stared.

I ignored them all and hurried out into the street. It wouldn't surprise me to learn that Beddoes acts in blue movies; but how to find out for certain, that's the problem. One way or another I am going to find it very difficult to take him seriously from now on.

Saturday, November 19th

Having left the book on auto therapy on Jane's bedside table, I was quite surprised not to have had any reaction from her as yet. I couldn't believe she hadn't noticed it. Finally, this evening, I mentioned the matter.

'Oh,' she said, 'it was you, was it? Whatever made you think I would be interested in a subject like that?'

'Like what?' I said, pretending innocence.

'Car maintenance for relieving tension.'

Beddoes came in later with Grace, but I simply could not bring myself to look at him.

Sunday, November 20th

I see in the Sunday papers that someone has come up with yet more evidence about the fate of the Tsar of Russia and his family. Is Anna Anderson really the Grand Duchess Anastasia? The great debate continues. Oddly enough, I have always felt there was some doubt about my own origins. Every time I fill out a form for a new driving licence or a passport, I feel instinctively I should be putting something in the space marked *Title*. But what?

Until someone can come up with a satisfactory explanation as to why I am four inches taller than every other member of my family, I shall never feel entirely at ease in society.

'Oddly enough, I have always felt there was some doubt about my own origins.'

Monday, November 21st

To Ryman's at lunchtime to buy a proper diary. Finally chose something plain and simple, and why not? I am neither a gardener nor a sex maniac, nor an aficionado of any of the curious pursuits for which most diarists seem to cater nowadays. If there was such a thing as a Diarist's Diary, I suppose I might be tempted to buy it, but there isn't. *Tant mieux.*

Tuesday, November 22nd

My suspicions of Beddoes grow daily. The more I learn of him the more I am inclined to think that he is totally lacking in any moral sense whatsoever. Today he blithely admitted to me that he buys brand-new gramophone records, records them on his cassette machine, then takes them back to the shop claiming that they are scratched or in some way faulty, and gets his money back. A man who will do that will do anything.

Thursday, November 24th

Thanksgiving Day. Not that I have a lot to give thanks for. Not only has Armitage been appointed Assistant Group Head, which effectively puts him over my head, but I now hear that Mike Pritchard is to move into the flat to live with Victoria. Why is it that *I* seem to be the only one to raise objections? The next thing we know we'll have Terry from Covent Garden bringing his strange friends back here, not to say daily raids by the Special Branch. I cannot think what I ever saw in Victoria.

Beddoes appears to have booted Grace out and taken up with a surly looking French girl by the name of Marie-France. She looks the sort who might act in blue movies.

Friday, November 25th

Mike moved in this evening. I suppose it *is* more sensible for me to have Victoria's single bed in return for my double. As things stand with Jane, I do not seem to have much use for it at present. I hadn't realized Victoria's bed was quite so narrow, though. How they are going to fit the children in as well when they come tomorrow, I dread to think.

Fortunately, Jane has asked me down to her parents' at Oxted for the weekend which is a surprise, to say the least. There must be something behind it, but what?

Saturday, November 26th

On the way down in the car, I asked Jane the real reason for her not wanting to sleep with me on Sunday night.

'I told you,' she said. 'I didn't feel like it. Don't keep on.'

Is it any wonder that I do not know where I am from one minute to the next?

Her parents live in a modest, mock-Tudor house with a small garden on the outskirts of the town. They welcomed me in a most friendly way and showed me up to the spare room which seemed very comfortable and had a Russell Flint reproduction over the bed.

Jane's brother Roland arrived just before lunch. He is a lively fellow, if a little bumptious, with an amusing line in Irish jokes. I gather he is training to be an accountant.

We had steak and kidney pie for lunch and vegetables from the garden.

Mr Baker seems to be under the impression that I work in Public Relations. I tried to put him straight there, but he said, 'Public Relations, marketing, advertising, show business, they're one and the same thing as far as I am concerned.'

Roland kept up a steady flow of chaff and sexual innuendo which was rather embarrassing, but all Mrs Baker said was, 'Eat up your stewed apples, Roland. They're fresh from the garden.'

In the afternoon we went for a walk on Limpsfield Common. There was very nearly an unpleasant incident when we were mocked by a group of village boys. Things could have turned very ugly, but I quickly took the wind out of their sails by pretending to have a crippled leg, and they soon lost interest and drifted away.

In the evening we all played Scrabble. I was unlucky to draw quite so many poor letters, and came last in every game except one. Mr Baker said, 'I always thought you PR chaps fancied yourselves as masters of the written word,' and went off to watch 'Match of the Day'.

Read for a while in bed, thinking that Jane would pop in and say good night. Finally, after half an hour, got up and made my way along the corridor to her room. I knocked on the door and was on the point of opening it when Mrs Baker stepped out of the bathroom and said, 'Now, now, none of your London morals in this house if you don't mind.'

I doubt if I have ever been more embarrassed in my life.

Sunday, November 27th

A dull, overcast day. Spent the morning reading the *Sunday Express*. At noon we all drove up to the golf club for a drink. We went in my car. It was rather a squash, and the clutch started slipping slightly halfway up East Hill, but luckily it was only a short journey.

As we were climbing out, I heard Mrs Baker saying to her husband under her breath, 'I thought there was rather a peculiar smell in there, didn't you?'

Later, standing in the bar with our drinks, I remarked casually, 'Is it just me, or is there rather a funny smell in here?'

Mr Baker said, 'No, it's just you.' Everyone roared, but I think I'd made my point.

We had leg of lamb for lunch, with mint sauce made from fresh mint from the garden, and stewed plums and custard to follow.

At teatime Mrs Baker said, 'I expect we'll be seeing quite a lot of you from now on.'

This was news to me.

After tea Jane said that we ought to be getting back to town.

Roland said, 'Oh, I couldn't possibly bum a lift off you, could I?' I had rather hoped to have Jane to myself for once but was hardly in a position to refuse. I am not averse to giving anyone a lift, but even the best Irish jokes wear thin after a while, especially with a slipping clutch. I suppose he means well enough, but he's not what I'd call good brother-in-law material.

Monday, November 28th

This evening Jane suddenly announced, apropos of nothing, that it was ridiculous for a man of my age and position to be driving around in a clapped-out VW. I said I had never held with the middle-class idea that a man should be judged by the car he drives. In my book, if a chap doesn't like you for what you are, he's probably not worth knowing anyway.

Jane said that she was not suggesting that I should rush out that instant and buy myself a Maserati. However, she did think it was high time I got myself something with a bit more poke to it. I laughed and said that I had heard of cars being thought of as sex substitutes, but that was surely going a bit far. She replied sharply that I knew exactly what she meant, and while I was about it, I could buy myself some new shoes.

'If there's one thing that puts me right off,' she said, 'it's suede shoes. Especially ones that look like dead animals.'

I said that they were a perfectly good pair of suede shoes and had been hand-made.

'Who by?' she said. 'The Lincolnshire Poacher?'

She then added that unless I bought myself a decent car and a new pair of shoes she would not be coming out with me again. I was tempted to point out that she had not been *out* with me for over a week. However, I am still very fond of her, and do not wish to upset the apple cart at this early stage. I suppose I had better go through the motions.

Tuesday, November 29th

To the Haymarket Theatre to see the much-acclaimed revival of Ibsen's *Rosmersholm*. During the first act I turned to murmur something to Jane and was astonished to receive a sharp blow to the back of the head – delivered presumably by whoever was occupying the seat behind me. What does one do at such moments? I simply continued to watch the play as though nothing had happened. At the interval, turned round to find the entire row behind me occupied by very old ladies. I am mystified.

Wednesday, November 30th

Noted two possible cars in the *Evening Standard*, but both had gone by the time I called. It's a mystery to me that anyone has the time to get to Sidcup at such short notice. Anyway, it's probably a blessing in disguise. Vehicles that are offered for sale privately always sound in far better condition than they really are.

December

Thursday, December 1st

Spent most of the morning scouring *Exchange and Mart*.
However, my time has not been entirely wasted since I think
I may have found just the thing. A Jaguar XJ6 – 1971 – for
only £1300. Was surprised to find that what looked like a
private telephone number turned out to be that of a garage
in Tooting. However, Mr Woolcott to whom I spoke sounded
very nice and not at all like a second-hand-car salesman, so
I asked him honestly if he thought it was really worth my
while trekking all that way out for a look. He said that he
would be the last person to pull the wool over my eyes, but
that if I wanted his honest opinion, I'd do well to get down
there as soon as possible.

He has promised to hold it for me till six-thirty. He also
said he would be prepared to consider taking my VW in
part-exchange. One somehow does not expect to meet people
like him in the second-hand-car trade. I was putting the
phone down when I realised that Armitage was standing in
the doorway watching me. 'Hello, Crisp,' he said. 'Frittering
away the family profits on extra-mural activities again, I
see.'

I said that if he really wanted to know, *they* had called *me*.

'It's not the cost of the call I worry about,' he said, 'it's the
cost of your time. Do I gather you're thinking of buying a
new car?'

I said that I was, if it was any business of his.

He said, 'In that case, may I give you a word of advice?
Pay cash. They love cash, these car boys. Doesn't show in
the books, see?' He winked broadly. 'My mechanic, a mar-

vellous little Pole in Parson's Green, never takes anything but cash.'

'Mostly yours, it seems,' I said.

'Look, laddie,' he said, 'you can hardly expect to run a Natchford Special without spending a few bob on it from time to time.'

Really, for a so-called 'marketing man', Armitage is remarkably gullible.

'Now then,' he said, 'let's assume this heap of yours is worth a hundred at rock bottom. Thirteen hundred c.c. is it?'

'Twelve hundred, in fact,' I said.

'Yes,' he said, 'well there's nothing in it at that age. Sixty-two registration, you said. MOT?'

I told him eleven months.

'Eleven?' he exclaimed. 'Well, I mean, that's worth fifty quid in anyone's language. If I were you, I'd ask for £175 and settle for £140. Better still, how much is this thing you're thinking of buying?'

I said thirteen hundred pounds.

'Right then,' he said. 'If there's any trouble, offer him your car and a thou in cash, no questions asked. Tell him you'll bring it round in a suitcase. He'll probably waver for a bit and let you have it for ten-fifty. He'll be glad to have it off his hands.'

I was, I must admit, rather impressed at Armitage's know-how, and quite touched by his concern to get me the best possible deal, and thanked him very much indeed.

'That's all right, laddie,' he said. 'Any time. Oh, by the way, try not to use the phone on private business or we'll have to start docking your salary.'

Then, just as he was leaving, he looked down at the new shoes I had just bought and said, 'You might buy yourself a decent pair of shoes, too, while you're about it.'

He should talk!

Friday, December 2nd

After work, picked up Jane from her office and drove down to Tooting. Unfortunately, my new shoes have started pinching rather painfully, and what with that and the slipping clutch, we made rather slower progress than I had anticipated.

At one point we were overtaken by a cyclist. I was sorry Jane did not see the funny side of it.

Mr Woolcott was even more elegant than I had imagined. And so, too, was the Jaguar. The paint and chrome-work were in excellent condition, and despite its J registration it had done only 45 000 miles. Mr Woolcott took us for a short spin in it, and it seemed to handle very nicely. I asked if I could take the wheel, but he explained that would be impossible because of the insurance arrangements. I thought I could detect a slight knocking noise in second gear, which was accentuated when turning left, but he said it was nothing to worry about.

When we got back, I said that all now rested upon how much he was prepared to give me for my Beetle. I thought he might have devoted a little more attention to it than he did, but he obviously realized it had been well looked after, and when I mentioned the eleven months' MOT, he said, 'Oh, really?'

I was rather nervous he might wish to drive the car and thus discover the slipping clutch. At one point he made as if to open the front door. The handle has a tendency to stick sometimes and I hurried forward to open it for him. He stuck his head in, but all he said was, 'What a funny smell.'

I decided we had shilly-shallied for long enough, and asked him what he thought.

He said, 'I've seen worse. Fifteen quid.'

I was astounded, and pointed out that the tyres were worth more than that.

He said he was very sorry; he would have liked to make it twenty, but not in that condition.

'Look,' I said confidentially, 'supposing I were to come round tomorrow with a suitcaseful of notes. What would you say to a thousand nicker for the Jag, no questions asked, and you take my car?'

'Frankly,' he said, 'we're not really interested in cash these days. We far prefer customers to make use of finance. That way we get a kick-back from the hire-purchase company. Now, do you want the vehicle or don't you?'

I told him I'd think about it and walked firmly away.

It's hard enough for a chap to keep his end up with girls nowadays as it is without being insulted by second-hand-car salesmen.

Arrived back at the car to find my door handle had stuck. I tugged at it several times without success, and then, just as I thought I was getting somewhere, it came away in my hand.

Mike, Victoria, the children and Beddoes are all away for the weekend, which I suppose is some consolation.

Saturday, December 3rd

Was woken at eight this morning by Armitage, of all people, wanting to know how it had gone with the car. I told him it hadn't, and that I had obviously struck too hard a bargain. He sounded rather pleased at the news and said that his little Pole in Parson's Green knew a couple of chaps in Wimbledon who'd got a Cortina for sale.

'I've seen it myself,' he said, 'and I'd say it's a very nice motor indeed. It's got quite a bit of poke for its age.'

(I do wish people would stop using this expression. It quite sets my teeth on edge.)

There had to be a catch in it somewhere. 'How much are they asking for it?' I said.

'They're prepared to let this one go for three hundred,' he said.

When I asked him why, he said, 'Look, laddie. Don't ask too many questions. You're a friend of mine. Let's just leave it at that, shall we? The boys are on their way round to your place now. Good luck.' And with that he hung up.

Good luck?

It seemed a curious thing to say under the circumstances; and what did he mean by the boys? He made them sound like gangsters. At that moment there was a ring at the front door. I opened it to a small man in dark glasses and a pork-pie hat, smoking a small cigar.

'You the gent who wants to see the Cortina?' he said.

I decided that since he was there I might as well take a look, and, quickly throwing on a pair of trousers and a jacket over my pyjamas, I followed him downstairs.

The car was parked a few yards away down the street. It was bright green. As we approached, two big men in overcoats eased themselves out from the front seat. Just to show willing I looked the car over. I asked what year it was.

'Sixty-nine,' said Pork Pie.

I said I was surprised there wasn't more rust on it.

Pork Pie said, 'Fancy a little ride in it, do you, squire?'

I said that I didn't think that would be necessary, but that if they insisted, I wouldn't mind going just down to the end of the road and back. The two big men got into the front and Pork Pie and I sat in the back. We shot away from the kerb with such force that I was hurled back against the seat.

'Good acceleration,' I said with a laugh. We took the roundabout at the end of the road at about forty-five, but then to my surprise, instead of going right round and back again, we turned off and headed towards Hammersmith.

'I think you may have taken the wrong road,' I said.

'Harry knows what he's doing,' said Pork Pie, 'don't you, Harry?'

Harry nodded silently.

I suddenly felt convinced that I was being kidnapped. Any day now a ransom note made up of words cut out of a newspaper would arrive on mother's breakfast table in Kent demanding a vast sum for my safe return.

'I was hoping to borrow the money for the car from my mother,' I said casually, 'but she's even poorer than I am.'

'Oh,' said Pork Pie, 'we're not asking all that much.'

How much then? I wondered. Just a few hundred pounds perhaps. But was it worth it? And how humiliating if mother refused to pay. It was then that the thought occurred to me that all this was just an excuse to get me out of the way, and that meanwhile the rest of the gang were busy beating up Jane and doing the flat. I decided it was time for a showdown.

'Look here,' I said. 'I think I should tell you; I know what your game is.'

'Game?' said Pork Pie. 'What game would that be, then?'

'Well,' I said, playing it cool, 'you're trying to persuade me to buy this car, aren't you? Or am I very much mistaken?'

'Look,' said Pork Pie, 'we never try to persuade anyone to do anything against their will. If you don't want the vehicle, you only have to say so.'

I said that actually I had been thinking more in terms of a Jaguar.

Pork Pie said, 'A pity you didn't tell us that in the first place. Home, Harry.'

I decided to get out while the going was good, so I told Pork Pie that if it was all the same to him, I'd get out there, since I could do with a walk.

'Yes,' said Harry. 'Off a short pier preferably.'

I got out and they drove off at high speed towards the river.

The door to the flat showed no signs of having been forced, and Jane was still fast asleep. I spent a good half-hour going through all my things, but everything seemed to be in order.

Had planned to go down to Chelsea in the afternoon to look for a pair of trousers. However, under the circumstances, I thought it was wiser to stay indoors for the rest of the day, which was probably just as well, as it gave me an excellent opportunity to wash a few shirts.

Still no indication from Jane that she is interested in resuming our affair, which ended in such mysterious circumstances. I suppose it is up to me to make the next move, but not if it means further humiliation.

Sunday, December 4th

According to Beddoes there is to be a New Year's Eve party in the flat, starting at ten and going on till dawn. This is the first I have heard of it. I cannot imagine a less pleasant way to start 1978 than prancing around in a silly hat with Beddoes's drunken city friends, Mike Pritchard and Victoria and her lefty lot – and being kissed by a lot of people I don't know and don't wish to know. I am certainly not in the market for any of that sort of malarkey, and I made myself clear on that point straightaway. Needless to say, this did not go down at all well, but then nothing I say ever does.

Victoria got up and left the room in silence. Pritchard poured himself another large whisky and soda and grunted incomprehensibly. Beddoes said, 'Typical,' and lit one of his beastly small cigars. Only the French girl, Marie-France, had the grace to keep her counsel. Not that she ever speaks to me anyway. Or to anybody else, as far as I can see. Still, I have more important things to think about than surly Frenchwomen – namely, my duties as a juror which begin at nine tomorrow morning. I shall need my wits about me.

Early bed.

Monday, December 5th

My first day of jury service.

I drew up outside the court a good ten minutes earlier than requested only to discover they did not provide parking facilities as I had supposed. This meant driving around the neighbouring streets at the height of the rush hour looking for a free meter. As a result, I was five minutes late reporting for duty. To my astonishment, some two hundred people had also been called as jurors, and there was such a crush in the large courtroom in which we were assembled to be given our instructions that I had to stand in the doorway, thus missing much of what was said. Eventually, after much confusion and a good deal of sitting about in a smoke-filled waiting room, the jury to which I was assigned was summoned to its courtroom.

As soon as twelve of our number had been picked, the oath-taking began. The juror next to me, a coloured chap, was about to take the oath when he was asked by the judge what his religion was. 'Methodist,' he replied firmly. I was glad I was not asked to make a similar affirmation in open court since, although officially I have been a member of the Church of England all my life, I have recently begun to harbour certain doubts and have found myself leaning more and more towards Reincarnation. Only the other day I was in the British Museum buying some postcards when I found myself irresistibly drawn towards the Egyptian Room, a part of the building I have hitherto never felt the slightest desire to visit.

Once the formalities were over, counsel for the prosecution gave his opening address. The case concerned the handling of stolen property, and from what I could gather, things were looking far from rosy for the wretched-looking fellow in the dock. At all events, it was most interesting, and I was looking forward keenly to the parry and thrust of cross-examination when the judge announced that an important crown witness had failed to turn up and consequently we were dismissed until the following morning.

Jane came home early, very excited, wanting to hear all about it. I pointed out that her curiosity was entirely understandable, but that unfortunately it would be quite out of the question for me to divulge information that might prove prejudicial to the cause of justice.

'Oh, come off it,' she said laughing, 'that doesn't apply to me.'

I said that I was afraid it was impossible to make any exceptions, to which she replied that I was a pompous twit and marched out, taking my evening newspaper with her.

I wonder if Lord Widgery has to put up with this sort of behaviour every day from his friends? Incidentally, I am surprised that no mention has been made so far about appointing a foreman of the jury. However, I daresay a natural leader will emerge in time.

Tuesday, December 6th

No sooner had we gathered in the jury room this morning than one of the women members announced, 'Well, as far as I'm concerned, I'm ready to cast my vote here and now.'

When I asked her what on earth she meant by this astonishing remark, she replied, as cool as a cucumber, 'It's obvious. Any fool can see he's as guilty as all get out.'

I reminded her in no uncertain terms that in this country a man is innocent until proven guilty, and that since all we had been given thus far were the barest outlines of the prosecution's case, we were hardly in a position to draw any conclusions.

'That's quite sufficient for me,' she replied crisply, and began to unwrap a packet of sandwiches.

I was reflecting that, were I by any chance to be appointed foreman of the jury, she would certainly be feeling the rough side of my tongue, when we were called into court and informed that, since yet another key witness had failed to materialize, the case would have to be held over and that consequently we were discharged.

A great disappointment, I must say, but the way things were going in the jury room, probably just as well.

Wednesday, December 7th

Was woken shortly after seven this morning by an insulting telephone call.

'Hello,' said the man's voice. 'You're a fruit.'

I may not be up in all the modern jargon, but I have been around long enough to know that the word 'fruit' is a euphemism for a pansy. Naturally, I was pretty angry, and made my feelings known.

'I don't know who you are or what you are on about,' the man said, 'but I am trying to ring a company called Euro-fruit.'

'In that case,' I told him, 'you have the wrong number,' and slammed the receiver back on to the cradle with such force that I damaged the mechanism and it has been out of order ever since.

I have asked for an engineer to call round and repair it, but whether anything will come of it is anybody's guess. It is incidents of this sort that make one doubt the wisdom of our ever joining the Common Market.

Thursday, December 8th

Finding myself alone in the sitting room this evening with Marie-France, I attempted to converse with her in French. I would not go so far as to claim that my command of the language is total. However, I have spent several holidays there – in Paris mainly – and can certainly make myself understood when I want.

'*Bonsoir*,' I said conversationally. '*Comment ça va?*'

She looked up from the French newspaper she was reading, shrugged and went on reading. I decided to try a more rewarding line of approach.

'*J'aime beaucoup le France*,' I said, giving a particularly authentic roll of the 'r'.

She looked up again, frowned and said, 'Huh?'

I said: '*Je disais que j'aime le France.*'

She continued to stare at me in blank incomprehension, and then suddenly her face lit up. 'Ah!' she exclaimed. '*Vous aimez* la *France*!'

I am not surprised Beddoes never speaks to her if this is what he has to go through every time he opens his mouth. It is certainly the last time I shall try. My doubts about the Common Market increase daily.

Saturday, December 10th

Am completely stuck for a Christmas present for mother this year. She did mention something about a Burmese kitten, of all things. Out of curiosity called in at the pet shop in Notting Hill Gate and enquired if they happened to have such a thing as a Burmese kitten in stock. The man, who obviously did not recognize me, said he knew where he could lay his hands on one, and that they were £50 each. I may have to think again.

Sunday, December 11th

Pritchard and Victoria set off early for a Vintage Car Rally in Basingstoke, leaving me with the children yet again. Jane and I decided to give Tom a treat by inviting the Pedalow children over for lunch.

We had my favourite: roast lamb with roast potatoes and Brussels sprouts, followed by caramel-flavoured Instant Whip.

The Pedalows arrived at twelve-thirty with Justin and Emma, and a friend of Emma's called Natalie who, the moment Tim and Vanessa had gone, began to behave in an atrocious manner, shouting, running in and out of the bedrooms, and bossing the other children about in a most unattractive way. She also had a streaming cold.

Lunch went off rather badly, thanks to Natalie. The lamb was very slightly underdone, just the way I like it, but Natalie announced that she was not in the habit of eating raw meat and threw hers on the floor. She then sulked.

I wouldn't have minded that, had it not been for her constantly running nose which made me feel quite sick. Unfortunately, Jane had made only enough Instant Whip for the six of us, so I had to forgo mine in favour of Natalie who took two mouthfuls and announced she didn't like it.

I would have finished it off myself but did not want to risk catching a heavy cold.

What a terrible thing it must be to have a child who is both plain and bad mannered. It makes me more determined than ever to think twice before bringing children into the world.

Mike and Victoria's outing was evidently not a great

success since they are now on non-speaking terms. A pity the same cannot be said about the children.

Monday, December 12th

To Hyde Park for a stroll during lunch hour. Paused to watch a group of small boys enjoying an improvised game of soccer. One wild shot came in my direction, so I thought I would make myself useful by kicking the ball back to them. Obviously there is some special way of kicking a football that has to be learned. All I know is that I stubbed my toe so badly that I have been in considerable pain ever since.

It would have to be my bad toe, of course.

Curious how often I find myself thinking about that Instant Whip. I suppose it has to do with my horror of waste, so in that sense it is perfectly understandable. Pritchard moved out this evening, thank goodness. Now perhaps I can get my own bed back and enjoy a decent night's sleep for the first time in weeks.

Tuesday, December 13th

In the middle of a meeting with the Barford client, I began to feel that unmistakable dryness at the back of the throat that presages a cold. I might just as well have eaten the Instant Whip after all. Home early and straight to bed with a glass of hot lemon and honey and the *Radio Times* for company.

Mother rang later to say that since she had heard nothing to the contrary, she presumed I would be going to her for Christmas as usual. But I was feeling far too ill to bend my mind to such trivial domestic concerns and told her I would confirm my plans as soon as I felt up to making decisions. In fact, I shall almost certainly be doing as she said. Christmas for me has always meant a time of peace and love and understanding, all three of which are sadly lacking in the flat this evening. For one thing, I still have not got my bed back.

Wednesday, December 14th

Woke exhausted after a perfectly dreadful night. Throat like a raging furnace. Jane has been the only one of my so-called flat mates to show the slightest concern for me, bringing me hot tea and aspirins, and generally cossetting me like a baby. What a wonderful wife she will make someone. Possibly me.

Spent most of the afternoon changing the beds round, slightly ricking my back in the process. But at least I can now be ill in comfort. Not that I would have expected Victoria to understand. That's socialism for you.

Thursday, December 15th

Cold taking its usual course. The sore throat has faded away to be replaced by a streaming nose and thumping head, both of which I infinitely prefer. Leafing through a pile of women's magazines which Jane very kindly left by my bed, I came across a most interesting article on Prince Charles and his girlfriends. He is quoted as saying how difficult it is for him, since every time he takes a girl out for the evening, he finds himself wondering if she would make the right sort of wife. I know just how he feels, and am only sorry we are not able to get together and talk this over as one bachelor to another.

What an extraordinary accident birth is. I could so easily have been born to the Queen in Buckingham Palace, and Prince Charles to my mother in Ashford General Hospital – had I not been conceived six and a half years earlier, that is. All in all, though, I am glad it turned out the way it did.

Friday, December 16th

Rather than run the risk of passing my cold on to everyone else at the office, I have decided to delay my return until Monday morning. Despite my natural anxiety about how they are coping with the workload in my absence, I managed to enjoy a quiet, ruminative morning and afternoon. One so rarely has the opportunity these days to sit and think about things – particularly with Beddoes walking round the flat with a handkerchief tied round his nose and mouth, humming the theme tune from 'Dr Kildare'. It was quite funny the first time, but even the best of jokes wear thin after a while.

The only person for whom it does not, apparently, is Marie-France, who bursts out shrieking every time he appears. But then, of course, the French are renowned for their cruel sense of humour. I have a feeling he only keeps it up for her benefit; although I must say, a man who has to resort to facetiousness to keep his girlfriend sweet must be pretty desperate.

Saturday, December 17th

Feeling 100 per cent better and dressed for the first time in nearly four days. Finally finished reading *Vanity Fair*. I have always suspected that Thackeray is a thoroughly overrated writer, and now I am even more convinced of it than ever.

Sunday, December 18th

To bed with Jane tonight for only the second time since that marvellous weekend with the children, though why she should have picked on tonight to revive our affair I cannot imagine. I have always thought of Sunday evening as a time for reading, washing one's hair and going to bed early in order to be fresh for Monday morning, and had rather assumed she did too. Whether it was this, or the debilitating effects of my cold, I do not know, but the fact is it was not a success.

However, like the understanding girl she is, she said she didn't mind, and that it was probably just as well as she still had not read *The Sunday Times* colour magazine.

Monday, December 19th

Was in the bath shortly before seven this evening when there was a ring at the front door. Since I was alone in the flat I jumped out, threw a towel round my waist and hurried along the passage. I opened the door to be confronted by three small boys who broke into a feeble ragged version of 'We Wish You a Merry Christmas' before seizing their noses and collapsing into helpless giggles. I told them I could see nothing funny in making a mockery of Christmas, and that if they wanted to get a penny out of me, they'd be well advised first, to get to know a few real carols, and second, to learn to sing. Needless to say, they ignored my advice completely and ran off down the corridor shouting 'Silly old git' and making rude gestures.

So incensed was I at their insolent behaviour that I set off down the corridor after them, meaning to give them a good box round the ears. Unfortunately, silly Miss Weedon from the flat next door had to choose that moment to emerge with Poppy, her loathsome snuffling pug, all done up in a woolly jacket. Instead of encouraging me in my efforts, she shouted, 'People like you ought to be locked up.'

I stopped and turned towards her in an attempt to explain the situation, whereupon she shrieked, 'Don't you try any of your tricks on me. Get back to the jungle where you belong.' And, snatching up the ghastly Poppy, she slammed the door on me.

I returned along the corridor only to discover that meanwhile my own door had closed and I had locked myself out, which meant trudging all the way downstairs and across the yard at the back to borrow a spare key from Gidney. At this rate I shouldn't be surprised if I have double pneumonia by Christmas Day. Not a very auspicious start to the festive season. Not only may I now have to start thinking in terms of moving, but in the neighbourhood I live in, I wouldn't put it past boys like that to make life extremely uncomfortable for me.

Indeed, as I was getting into my car later, they emerged from the block of flats next door, saw me, and began whispering and giggling together. I don't suppose they would go so far as to let my tyres down or bend my aerial. However, just to be on the safe side, when I returned, I took care to park several streets away. I have also taped up the inside of the letter box.

Tuesday, December 20th

At lunchtime I popped round to the nearest charity card shop to buy my usual packet of six cards to send off to people who send cards to me. The worrying thing is that, with less than a week to go to Christmas, I have so far received only one card – from my local wine merchant. I only hope that friends who are planning to send me cards will not leave it much longer, otherwise it will be too late for me to send my cards back in time. Meanwhile I have sent off a card to the wine merchant.

Wednesday, December 21st

My postman has become unusually civil of late despite
delivering no mail to us. However, if he supposes that his
ingratiating behaviour is going to earn him a Christmas box,
he is sadly mistaken. This time last year, I slipped him a
pound note with the compliments of the season and came
home a few days later to find a large flat packet lying bent
double on the hall floor. On it were printed the words:
GRAMOPHONE RECORDS DO NOT BEND, underneath which
was scribbled, 'Oh yes they do'.

Thursday, December 22nd

Still no cards and, more astonishingly, not a single invitation
to a Christmas party of any sort. I can perfectly understand
firms cutting back on this sort of thing, but surely one's
friends are not so hard-up that they cannot afford to offer one
a glass of wine over the festive season? I would ask a few
people in myself if only I could trust my flat mates to behave.
I was lamenting this dismal state of affairs to Iversen in the
office when Jane rang to say we had been asked to a dinner
party this evening by some rather grand friends of hers who
live behind Harrods.

My first reaction was to refuse. We were obviously asked
only because some other couple had dropped out at the last
minute, and in my book it never pays to be too readily
available.

However, Jane insisted. Apparently she and the wife
were at school together. Theresa Milne was there, looking
rather pretty for once. Apart from her, the party turned out
to be even worse than I had feared. The conversation was
either about the City or skiing, in neither of which subjects
do I have the slightest interest.

I attempted to introduce a little cultural relief into the
proceedings at one stage by mentioning that I had just been
reading the new John Fowles novel, and saying how astutely
he had pin-pointed the Englishman's oppressive sense of
guilt. But they all looked at me as though I were mad. I
thought for a moment that the husband of Jane's friend was
going to take me up on it. He lowered half a glass of brandy,
looked at the others and said, 'Sounds pretty *foul* to me!'

Everyone roared like lunatics and helped themselves to more drinks. Unfortunately, neither Jane nor I had come out with our watches, and the evening dragged interminably. Finally, I could stand it no longer, and giving a great yawn, announced it was way past our bedtime and apologized for outstaying our welcome. Our hostess uttered the usual polite protests, and Jane said she did not want to break up the party; but I was adamant.

Naturally, I imagined that our fellow guests would take the hint and follow our example, but they made no attempt to move, and one or two of them even began to refill their glasses yet again. One of the men called out, 'Hello, a couple of love birds, eh?' and laughed coarsely.

It was an unfortunate remark under the circumstances, and one which in my view deserved a cutting reply. However, I think my cold stare was probably just as effective.

When we got home, we found it was only ten o'clock. I could not help bursting out laughing, and I was only sorry Jane did not see the funny side of it too. Not only are we now not on speaking terms, but I have since discovered that at some point during the evening someone had bent my car aerial nearly double. So much for the season of good-will.

Friday, December 23rd

To Selfridges at lunchtime to buy Jane a pair of slippers. Rather expensive, I thought, for what they were. Tried at the same time to find something for mother, but had an altercation with woman at glove counter and left in a rage before I had had a proper chance to look round. The cat is definitely out of the question. Other considerations apart, I do not much relish the prospect of driving down to Kent on Christmas Eve on roads solid with drunken drivers with a strange cat jumping about in the back. I may very well have to fall back on a Marks and Spencer voucher, like last year.

To the pub for a lunchtime Christmas drink with the people from the office. Everyone ordered much more expensive drinks than usual – double whiskies, crème de menthe on the rocks, and so on – on the assumption that Roundtree, as head of the department, would stand the round. However, just as it came to the moment to settle up, he announced that he had an important phone call to make and disappeared into the crowd. By then everyone else was busy talking, and it was left to me to pay. No one appeared to notice, however, and when it came to the next round, Roundtree announced that we should all pay for ourselves. I could not help noticing that everyone immediately reverted to half-pints of bitter and small sherries. Even so, a great deal more drink was consumed than usual, and one or two people behaved rather badly. Felicity, Roundtree's secretary, passed out into a plate of shepherd's pie, and at one point I saw Armitage kissing Sarah Smith with a lighted cigar stuck in his mouth. She didn't seem to mind at all.

Arrived home at four, rather the worse for wear, to find a note from the postman pinned to the front door saying that he had tried on several occasions to deliver some letters, but had been unable to do so, due to a malfunction of the letter box.

Now I have to trudge off to some post office miles away to collect them. If I were not so concerned that some of them might be Christmas cards, I really do not think I would bother. It only shows how little interest the others take in the day-to-day running of the flat that none of them had even noticed my anti-hooligan precautions – let alone done anything about them.

I had seriously been looking forward to a festive drink with Jane in congenial surroundings, possibly over a meal, so I made no other arrangements for the evening. However, it was nearly eleven when she finally appeared, and when I asked her where she had been, she replied that she had been making up for time lost last night. I do not know quite what she meant by this nor was she prepared to elaborate further. At all events, her behaviour was certainly not what one expects from a friend, and I not only did not give her her slippers, but I also made no attempt to kiss her under the piece of mistletoe which I have hung above the front door.

Before going to bed, I removed the greetings label from the slippers and wrote out another one, substituting mother's name for Jane's.

Saturday, December 24th

To the post office to collect the letters. To my surprise, found I had received cards from many more people than I had expected, including Nick and Warthog, the Pedalows, Buffy and Moo, Mr and Mrs Baker, and Nigel and Priscilla.

Fortunately I had my five remaining Oxfam cards with me, so I was able to send them off straight away. I am only sorry there was no time to reply to the rest.

Returned to the flat to find an envelope propped up on my bedside table. It was a Christmas card from Jane saying that she was sorry to have missed me and that she thought it was just as well Christmas had come along, as we both needed time to think things over. She may; I certainly don't.

Beddoes and Marie-France were still in bed, but Victoria was up and about looking rather pretty for once in a long brown dress. She was also a great deal more friendly than usual, and even insisted on dragging me under the mistletoe and giving me really quite a passionate kiss. I have no idea what it was all about, but I must admit that I set off for Kent feeling more optimistic about life than I have for many days.

Arrived shortly before lunch to find mother busy preparing her traditional table centre. The motif has been the same for as long as I can remember: a mirror surrounded by cotton wool, representing a lake in winter. On the lake there are a number of white swans and a red Indian in a canoe, and on the snow, polar bears, penguins, and several tiny Christmas trees flecked with white.

The sight of it never fails to bring a lump to my throat. I was surprised to see that as yet there was no sign in the sitting room of the Christmas tree, which I always enjoy decorating. When I mentioned this to mother, she said, 'Oh, that's all right. Nigel and Priscilla said they would bring one with them.'

This was the first time I had heard that they were spending Christmas with us. They have not done so in the past, and I made a pointed remark to this effect.

The really annoying thing was that I had left all their presents in London, thinking to hand them over when I next saw them. After lunch I had to drive over to Ashford to see what I could find.

Shops solid with pushing, sweating, last-minute shoppers. Why *will* people leave all their Christmas shopping to the last minute? After an anxious and exhausting hour and a half, I came away with a woolly hat for Priscilla, a Farmer's

Diary for Nigel, and a modelling kit of the *Golden Hind* for James.

Arrived back at the car to find a traffic warden standing there writing out a ticket. I explained that I had not parked but merely stopped there for a second to pick up some last-minute shopping for an elderly lady. But I might have saved my breath.

'That's what we call parking,' said the warden, putting the ticket in a plastic envelope and sticking it on to my windscreen.

I suggested that as it was Christmas, he might be a little bit Christian about it.

'I don't see why,' he said. 'I'm a Jew.'

I may pursue the matter further or I may not.

Was watching the circus on television after tea when I heard Priscilla and Nigel arriving. There seemed to be rather more commotion in the kitchen then usual, so I went out to discover a tiny Burmese kitten rushing around the floor after a piece of wrapping paper. I have never seen mother so happy and excited. I asked Priscilla how she had managed to bring it down in the car. She said: 'In a cat basket, of course.'

Fortunately, they had also remembered to bring a small Christmas tree.

Just before dinner, James crept up behind my chair and rammed a piece of holly into the back of my head. Everyone seemed to think it was a great joke. It's a pity they don't pay a bit more attention to him than they do to the kitten.

Had very much been looking forward to Midnight Mass. However, somebody had to stay behind and babysit, and my neck was still very sore.

Dozed off in front of the fire and woke up to find the kitten had made a mess in the corner of the room. Cleared up as best I could and went to bed feeling slightly sick.

Sunday, December 25th

Woken at six-thirty by James jumping on top of me dressed in commando outfit and firing a noisy plastic machine gun. Tried to get back to sleep after booting him out but failed.

Exhausted by breakfast time.

Afterwards we opened the presents.

Mother seemed quite pleased with her slippers, but she is so besotted by the kitten that very little else seems to register with her. Thank goodness they fitted – which is more than could be said for the pyjamas which she had bought for me. Still, they are a very nice colour, and they're always very good about changing things at Marks and Spencer.

When I gave the Joyces their presents, Priscilla said, 'Oh, I'm afraid we haven't got anything for you. We thought we'd be seeing you at a later date.'

I said that was all right and that anyway my presents were really rather dull. James said, 'Yes, they are, aren't they?'

To church on my own. Congregation as thin as the singing. I attempted to fill out 'Oh, Come All Ye Faithful', by singing the harmonies, which I happen to know; but as no one else joined in, it simply sounded as though I was out of tune.

Lunch, when it finally appeared on the table, was an unexpectedly jolly and touching occasion. After I had carved the turkey, Nigel stood up and made a rather moving little speech about the importance of family life. He then proposed a toast to mother who was so overcome she burst into tears all over the Brussels sprouts. It was a pity the turkey was quite so tough. I suppose one should be jolly thankful one has anything to eat at all when one thinks of all the starving millions the world over. On the other hand, no amount of thinking will make a tough turkey tender.

After we had eaten we pulled some crackers. Mine wouldn't pull properly, so I reached inside to pull the crack out and it went off unexpectedly, giving my finger a nasty little burn.

James became over-tired after tea and mother suggested that an early night might not go amiss. Personally I think that a hand firmly applied to the seat of his pants would be more effective and told Priscilla so. But all she said was, 'When you have your own children, you may do as you wish.'

I certainly shall. I know Christmas is supposed to be a time for children, but surely not *all day*?

In the evening I proposed a game of canasta, which Priscilla and I used to play a great deal when we were young.

Unfortunately, I drew some very bad cards, and was thus unable to support mother as much as I should have liked. It was really rather humiliating. But then I am used to being humiliated these days.

Monday, December 26th

Came down this morning to find that the kitten had got hold of my new pyjamas which I had left, I thought safely, on top of the piano, and not only ripped the cellophane cover, but also torn a small hole in the material itself.

Nigel suggested that I should pretend to the people at Marks and Spencer that they were like that when I took them out of the bag. I shall certainly do no such thing.

All mother could say was, 'You didn't know any better at his age.'

I certainly do not remember going around making holes in people's brand-new pyjamas – or making messes wherever and whenever the mood took me.

I seriously wonder if this creature has not turned her mind. If so, there is no doubt in *my* mind who is responsible.

As they were leaving after tea, Nigel enquired idly after Victoria. I told him that it was all off. He seemed rather pleased, I thought. I am more certain than ever that the two of them got up to something that weekend.

Tuesday, December 27th

Another day's holiday to make up for the one we missed on Sunday.

Mother is convinced that some old hunting prints which she has found in the attic are worth a lot of money. They are by someone called J. Herring Senior and to my way of thinking are completely without artistic merit. However, I have promised to take them in to Sotheby's when I get back to town. It will set her mind at rest.

Wednesday, December 28th

Beddoes has now taken up with a Chinese girl, if you please. What's more, they appear to have spent Christmas together in the flat. In bed I shouldn't wonder. The whole place positively reeks of stale Chinese cooking, and the sink is piled high with dirty crocks. I simply do not know where to begin.

If this is what happens when two of them get busy, I

81

dread to think what the place will look like after Saturday night's party. I shall certainly make sure my bedroom door is locked. Jane is staying at Oxted till Saturday. As for Victoria's unexpected show of affection last week, I fear this must be put down to seasonal enthusiasm. She could not be more off-hand if she tried. Who cares? I have far better fish to fry.

Thursday, December 29th

To dinner with Mollie Marsh-Gibbon. I have not seen her for months.

She is easily the cleverest woman I know; rude, witty and critical of everything and everyone. She claims to be sixty-five but does not look a day over fifty. When I last saw her, she said she was going to redecorate the whole house; but the only difference I can see is that she has stuck back the peeling wallpaper with stamp paper. Food as bizarre as ever: Heinz tomato soup from the tin, fish fingers and a whole Stilton. We drank some red Australian wine which she had found in a closing down sale in Kidderminster. She insisted that most people would not be able to distinguish it from claret. Most coal miners possibly. When I mentioned the J. Herring Senior prints she said, 'My word, you're in luck if they're the real thing. He was the foremost print maker of Victorian times and is very much sought after nowadays.' Had another look at them when I got home. On second thoughts, they are really rather charming.

Friday, December 30th

Armitage finally condescended to ask me if I had a good Christmas. I replied that it had been very pleasant and quiet.

'Everyone always says that,' he said. 'Well, I'm glad to say that I had a very noisy Christmas. We all ate and drank so much we made ourselves quite ill.' I do not see that is anything to boast about.

Rang Sotheby's about the pictures. The man I spoke to in the prints department was polite, though less enthusiastic than I had expected. But then I was playing my cards pretty close to my chest, too. I said, 'I have some Victorian hunting prints I think you might be interested in.'

'Oh, yes?' he said.

'They're by J. Herring Senior,' I added.

There was no doubt that his attitude towards me altered dramatically at that moment. 'Of course,' he said, 'we should have to see them before making any promises.'

I said that I quite understood and asked him when would be a convenient time to bring them in.

'Oh, any time during the week,' he said. 'There's always someone here.' I pointed out that under the circumstances, I would naturally prefer the opinion of someone of experience.

'We are all experts here,' he said. I asked him if I needed an appointment. He said that would not be necessary and that if I'd just like to bring them along, any time. I checked my diary and suggested Monday morning at about eleven. He said that would be fine, and that any time would do. It all sounds most encouraging.

Saturday, December 31st

The last day of the Old Year, and one on which far too many people in my view indulge in retrospect. I understand the temptation, but prefer to take the positive line myself and look forward to the year to come. But then, of course, I do have plenty to look forward to, not least of which is the possibility of making some real money at last with these pictures. Indeed the only black spot on the horizon when I rose this morning was this so-called New Year's Eve Party. Clearly I could not possibly remain in the flat, but where else was I to go?

By an extraordinary coincidence, Hugh Bryant-Fenn rang just before lunch to say that if I happened to be at a loose end he had asked a couple of girls round for the evening, and perhaps I'd care to help him out? I could think of several people I'd rather see the New Year in with than Hugh, but needs must, and I agreed to go.

Spent the morning with the New Year's Honours List. Delighted to see the England cricket captain has been recognized, and not before time. By an odd coincidence, he was up at Cambridge at the same time I was at Oxford. I'm surprised we've never met. On the whole, though, an uninspiring list of dull businessmen, flashy show-biz personalities, and civil servants whose names mean nothing to me. As for the new Companion of Honour, it's extraordinary to think that a Trades Union official should now have the right to put the same letters after his name as Kenneth Clark. From now on, I shall certainly not be making any special effort to have my name included.

Arrived at Bryant-Fenn's shortly after nine, as arranged, to find him sitting in an armchair staring disconsolately at a blank TV screen, and not a girl in sight. He explained that they had just rung to say that they had remembered they were expected at a fancy-dress party in Fulham, but might look in later. This was disappointing news, but I put a brave face on it and pointed out that there was a rather good film on the TV.

Hugh said: 'Actually, the TV's on the blink. I've rung the people, but they won't be able to send anyone to look at it till next Wednesday at the earliest.' I won't pretend this was not something of a body blow. However, knowing Hugh's expertise in the kitchen, I consoled myself with the prospect of an excellent dinner with some first-class wines, and said cheerfully, 'Never mind. After all, what's an old film compared with a good meal?'

Hugh said that he was very sorry but he had arranged with the girls that they would bring the food and there wasn't a thing in the house.

'We could go out to a restaurant,' he suggested, 'if you really wanted. But frankly it's a bit of a busman's holiday for me. On the other hand, there's an excellent Indo-Pak take-away round the corner. I could write it up for my column. You don't happen to have any money on you by any chance, do you?' I am perfectly prepared to admit that my taste in curries may not be shared by all, but I still do not see that was any reason for him to insist quite so firmly on the Prawn Biryani and the Tandoori Fish, especially as I thought I had made it quite clear that I'm not that keen on fish.

After dinner we played Monopoly, a game I have never much cared for and for which I must admit I have very little natural talent. I thought he behaved very selfishly in not selling me Liverpool Street Station when I already had the other three, and I was very unlucky to miss the chance of buying Park Lane and Mayfair.

At ten to twelve there was a ring at the front door. Hugh, thinking it was the girls, rushed to open it and I followed.

To our surprise it was two other girls, both extremely attractive, dressed in leather motor-cycling gear. We could not believe out good fortune.

'Can I help you?' Bryant-Fenn asked them in a rather obviously suggestive tone of voice.

'We was looking for Tony, actually,' one of them said.

'There must be some mistake,' Bryant-Fenn said. 'I'm Hugh.'

'So I see,' said the girl, and the two of them walked off down the stairs.

Hugh put the kettle on for coffee after that, and said he would tune in to the BBC on his transistor for Big Ben. I do not know if it was the curry or what, but I suddenly had to rush to the loo.

When I came out, Hugh said, 'You've been an age. The New Year's ten minutes old already.' This is the first time in over twenty years that I have missed seeing it in. Unable to face going back to the flat, so stayed the night on Bryant-Fenn's sofa, which is far from ideal for a full night's sleep. Not exactly a propitious start for the year ahead.

January

Sunday, January 1st

Awoke stiff and cold after an extremely uncomfortable night. Rice Krispies and instant coffee for breakfast. I am more convinced than ever that someone should expose Bryant-Fenn for the gastronomic fraud he is. Lunched alone off pork pie and Guinness at the Cricketers. Returned to the flat at four. Victoria and Jane still busy clearing up. Beddoes in bed, as usual. Rehearsing for another blue film, no doubt. Astounded to find my bedroom door open. Went in to discover my bed had been slept in and obscene anatomical additions made to my bullfighting poster. Although I immediately changed the sheets and took down the poster, I could not rid my mind of the feeling that I had been personally violated. Needless to say, neither of the girls claimed any knowledge of the incident, and when I mentioned the matter to Beddoes, all he said was, 'The trouble with you is that you're jealous.'

He seems to see everything in terms of sex. The thing that really concerns me is how anyone managed to get into my room in the first place. Someone obviously must have a spare key, and until I know who, I shall not feel at ease in this flat again. The only good thing to be said for the New Year so far is that I can at last start making my entries in a proper diary. Extraordinary how much more significant everything now appears.

Monday, January 2nd

To the office by taxi. A great extravagance, but one has to be prepared to spend money if one wishes to make any, and I could not run the risk of the prints being ruined by a damaging scratch from a careless umbrella on the Underground. To Sotheby's for my eleven o'clock appointment. I was interested to note as I entered that there is to be a sale of prints later in the week, which no doubt explains their interest in mine. There were many more people waiting in the print department than I had expected. However, I went straight up to the desk and addressed myself to a young girl employee. 'I've come about the J. Herring Seniors,' I told her in a low voice. 'Someone is expecting me.'

She looked down at my brown paper parcel. 'May I see them?' she asked.

'I did ring yesterday,' I reminded her.

'If you'd just undo the parcel,' she said.

As I struggled with the Sellotape and tissue paper, I said that I supposed they had to ask customers to undo their own parcels just in case there was any question of damage. She did not reply but picked up one of the prints and ran her fingers lightly over the surface. Her colleague, a young man, looked across at her and gave her a knowing nod.

'I'm sorry,' she said, 'but I'm afraid it's a reproduction. Next, please.'

I was perfectly astounded and reminded her of the trouble and expense to which I had gone, entirely at the suggestion of her colleague. But all she said was, 'I'm sorry. Next, please.'

As I was wrapping up my rejected wares, I remarked casually that she might be interested to know that I had already been offered a not inconsiderable sum for them elsewhere. 'I doubt it,' she said, 'but if it's true, take it. They're quite worthless. Next, please.'

I suppose it is easy enough to make mistakes when you spend so much of your day looking at real rubbish. As I was leaving, for example, an old lady shuffled forward and produced from a worn shopping bag a small oil painting.

'A pound,' the girl told her.

'A pound?' squawked the old lady. 'A pound? But the frame alone is worth more than a pound.'

'Actually,' said the girl, 'if you must know, the frame is really rather nasty.'

It was all a bit pathetic.

Tuesday, January 3rd

Jane seems very friendly all of a sudden, and tonight gave me some sprouts to go with my pork chop. Does this mean she wants to start up the affair again, and, if so, should I encourage her? I am not entirely convinced that she is the girl for me, and I do not want to lead her up the garden path.

How difficult these affairs of the heart are.

Wednesday, January 4th

Beddoes said something extraordinary this evening. 'I find it helps if you refuse to answer a single thing a woman says to you for at least an hour after you come in in the evening.'

What can he mean? Since most of the women he takes up with do not speak a word of the language anyway, I cannot see that it makes the slightest difference whether he talks to them or not.

Thursday, January 5th

Christie's are as unenthusiastic about the J. Herring Seniors as Sotheby's. I shall certainly seek a third opinion.

Friday, January 6th

Twelfth Night. Sorry to say Bonham's even less interested in the prints than the other two. I am reluctant to admit defeat, but I do have better things to do with my lunch hour than travel round London being snubbed by art dealers.

After supper took down the Christmas decorations watched by Beddoes. He contributes less and less to flat life. I also have a sneaking suspicion he might be carrying on a secret liaison with Victoria, but have as yet no proof.

Saturday, January 7th

Jane asked me down to Oxted with her for the weekend, but I declined the invitation. It won't do any harm to keep her guessing for a while longer.

An unfortunate incident in the greengrocer's. Was standing in a queue waiting for a cauliflower when Victoria appeared behind me. She said she wanted some carrots and onions for 'our' stew. As far as I know she has not seen Pritchard for some time, so she could only have been referring to herself and Beddoes. A black man was in front of me, buying a great number of oranges. He went out looking so depressed that I remarked to George on the fact.

'Yer,' said George. 'What you might called browned off.'

Naturally I roared, but Victoria was absolutely furious and accused George of racism, threatening to report him to the Race Relations Board and goodness knows what else. Not only did she slam the sitting-room door in my face this evening, but I obviously shan't be able to go into that shop again for a very long time.

Sunday, January 8th

To Kent for the day to return the prints. When I broke the news to mother, she said, 'Oh, I knew they were reproductions. I thought it was worth a try, though.'

During tea she told me that the other night as she was leaving after drinks at the Scott-Percivals, Denys Ramsden, who must be eighty if he's a day, put his head through the car window and gave her a French kiss. I do not believe this story. Apart from anything else, I am certain mother would not recognize a French kiss if it was handed to her on a plate.

Something is definitely going to have to be done about that kitten. I was sitting reading the Sunday papers in the wing chair when the wretched creature suddenly launched itself off the top of the drinks cabinet straight on to the top of my head. When I tried to pull it off, it sank its claws and teeth into my hand and drew blood.

Mother seemed to think the whole incident a cause for great hilarity. I wonder more and more about her sanity.

Monday, January 9th

It may be a little late in the day to start making New Year resolutions, but mine are none the less serious for that. I shall write them down to remind myself:

1. To make some money.
2. To think seriously about getting married – possibly to Jane, but ideally to someone with money.

3. To find somewhere else to live. I am getting too old for this type of flat life.

4. To move more freely in society. I am always reading in the diaries of the famous how they dined here and lunched there; sat next to this person at table and met that one at the theatre. I see no reason why I should not do the same. My problem is that my life is too often taken up with domestic trivialities, and I allow my time to be wasted by people of little worth and influence. I shall take steps to break out of this little world in which I have become trapped in recent months, and give far freer rein to my personality and talents.

Wednesday, January 11th

Invited Jane to dine with me. Normally, I would have chosen a modest trattoria like San Frediano, or an amusing dive like Joe Allen. But now I feel I have reached a stage in my life when I should be aiming for quality in all things. A pair of hand-made shoes from Lobb's may cost three times more than a pair bought at Freeman, Hardy and Willis, but they last three times as long, if not longer. I realize this argument does not apply in quite the same way to food, but the principle is the same. One should not be afraid to spend money; the more one spends, the harder one is obliged to work to replace it. This is how successful people get on in life, and it is probably one of the main reasons why I have not. Expansion is the key word from now. I therefore ordered a table for two at what Hugh Bryant-Fenn tells me is the best restaurant in town, Le Gavroche in Lower Sloane Street.

Jane was clearly surprised at my choice, and rightly made more of an effort than usual with her appearance. The food was simply delicious, and the wine excellent. I am not sure it was quite worth £55, and it is not something I am planning on doing again for a while. But there is no doubt Jane's attitude towards me has changed dramatically, and although I have not gone so far as to resume our affair in the technical sense, I certainly left her in no doubt of my feelings, which I am happy to say are stronger than ever. It is extraordinary what a sense of confidence money gives one. I only wish I had more.

Thursday, January 12th

I did not speak to Jane for at least an hour after coming in this evening, yet it does not seem to affect her feelings towards me one little bit. I have not felt more cheerful for years.

Friday, January 13th

My attention has been drawn to a curious phenomenon of modern life. Nine out of every ten young people I pass in the street appear to be acquiring small bruises on the sides of their necks. When I mentioned this to Jane, she laughed and said, 'Well, what's so extraordinary about that? They're love bites. We always gave them to each other when we were young – didn't you?'

I replied that, as far as I knew, I had never bitten anyone on the neck, nor had anyone ever attempted to bite me. Jane said that it all added to the fun of love-making, and the trouble with me was that I was far too inhibited.

I do not understand what she can mean.

Saturday, January 14th

To the theatre on my own to see this new sex show. Normally, I would not dream of going to such a thing, but I was interested to find out what all the fuss is about. After all, how on earth can one be expected to give one's opinion on important issues of the day unless one has had first-hand experience? Never having been to a sex show before, I was absolutely astounded by the whole thing. I had no idea that such things were said and done on the public stage in this country.

Indeed, on more than one occasion I was compelled to close my eyes, put my fingers in my ears and hum loudly in order to drown what was being said. And yet, in the interval, perfectly normal and respectable-looking people were walking about and chatting and smoking as though nothing whatsoever had happened. I can only suppose that there are many more devotees of this lewd form of entertainment than I had realized. I understand now how poor mother must have felt when she was staying with friends recently and unwittingly started reading a copy of *Penthouse* which she found on her bedside table.

As far as I am concerned, the only good thing about the evening was that I did not, as I had feared I would, come away with an inferiority complex about my private parts.

Sunday, January 15th

Nor, I am glad to say, does it appear to have inhibited my sex drive, if last night's performance was anything to go by. I am more and more convinced that the basis for a happy marriage is a happy sex life.

On the other hand, I thought Jane's comments about my figure were rather uncalled for. She is far from perfect herself, but I do not draw attention to the fact. Besides, I have always understood that women like men to carry a little weight. Perhaps I am very old-fashioned.

Monday, January 16th

Sarah in the office tells me she is on a diet that is so successful that she has lost five pounds in as many days. The essence of the regime, I gather, is fresh unsugared grapefruit with every meal.

Breakfast consists of half a grapefruit, followed by fried eggs and bacon and one cup of coffee without milk or sugar. Lunch is half a grapefruit followed by meat and green vegetables; dinner ditto. One cup of tea is allowed per day plus an optional glass of skimmed milk before going to bed. It sounds remarkably painless, and according to Sarah, really works. I shall start it tomorrow.

Tuesday, January 17th

First day of my diet. Breakfast actually more substantial than usual.

Lunched at Italian bistro round the corner from the office. Half a grapefruit, a plain veal escalope, undressed green salad and coffee. Simply delicious.

Dinner very similar except for a small steak in place of the veal.

I feel better for it already.

Wednesday, January 18th

Diet still going well. Surprised not to have lost any weight yet. However, bathroom scales notoriously inaccurate. Sarah says the headache is all the poison coming out, which strikes me as rather far-fetched.

Suggested to Beddoes that he might well consider trying the diet, too, since he has put on quite a bit of weight lately. But all he said was, 'People who think thin, think small.'

Is it my imagination, or is he losing his hair?

Thursday, January 19th

Delighted to discover I am able to tighten my belt by one notch. Interested to note on the way to work just how many overweight people there are in London. They none of them look very happy to me.

Lunched with Barford client in smart new restaurant in Covent Garden.

Astounded to find they did not have grapefruit on the menu. It would not matter quite so much if my diet were not the sort that must be followed to the letter. Pointed out the omission to the waiter who said that he might be able to find me some grapefruit juice. I asked him if that would be sweetened or unsweetened, and he said he would enquire. He returned with the news that it was very slightly sweetened. I said that I was very sorry but that would be quite out of the question, and would he mind terribly if I slipped out and bought myself a grapefruit? He said that that was up to me, but that of course he would have to charge me skinnage.

The client chuckled at this, and I joined in with a rueful smile, but I really do not care for waiters who make jokes at the customer's expense.

Fortunately, there was a fruiterer's nearby and despite a short queue, I was back in no time at all.

Surprised to find on my return that the client had disappeared. The waiter handed me a note saying: 'Your guest left this for you.' Apparently he had remembered he had some urgent shopping to do, and although he was sorry not to have had a chance to hear my marketing strategy proposals, he felt sure they could wait until I was able to give the matter my wholehearted attention. He also wished me luck with my diet.

What a pleasure it is to work with such sympathetic people. If nothing else, our meeting has certainly been a great help in cementing client relations.

In the afternoon found I had developed a nasty tummy-ache. Sarah said, 'Perhaps you've got your belt done up too tight.' I said that it was far more likely to be the effect of my stomach contracting – an observation that was shown to be founded on fact when I stood on the bathroom scales this evening and discovered that I had lost no less than six pounds.

Beddoes pointed out that the scales had not been right ever since they had been used in a game at the New Year's Eve party. He may be telling the truth or he may not, but on balance I think I prefer to believe my own eyes than anything he tells me. (No joke intended.)

Friday, January 20th

To my local barber's after work for my usual monthly trim only to discover the place completely empty, the windows covered in white paint, and a sign announcing: OPENING HERE SOON. KEBAB HOUSE. If his kitchen is half as dirty as his washbasins, we can expect a few gippy tummies around Holland Park from now on.

Saturday, January 21st

Oddly enough, my own stomach is still none too settled. Am wondering if it is something I ate.

Sunday, January 22nd

Find I really look forward to my egg-and-bacon breakfasts, despite attacks of indigestion that often follow. Tummy also slightly upset still.

Remarked on this to mother when I drove down for lunch. She said: 'I'm not surprised with all that grapefruit you eat. You're obviously suffering from too much acidity.' I'd rather suffer from an excess of acidity any day than an excess of Burmese cat, but said nothing.

Decided to make a spot check on the weight on mother's

bathroom scales. Incredible as it may seem, I found I was five pounds heavier than when I got up this morning. As I was leaving I remarked to mother *en passant* that her scales needed adjusting. She said, 'That's most unlikely considering I had them tested only two days ago.'

Who by, I wonder? Cyril Smith?

Monday, January 23rd

To the office still feeling far from well.

Bumped into Armitage in the lift who said, 'You look terrible. You know your trouble, don't you? You're putting on weight. You ought to do some exercise.' Had a long talk with Jane this evening. I cannot remember a time when I was more pleased to see her. By no stretch of the imagination could she be described as an ornament to society, but I really believe I enjoy her company more than anyone I know. At least she does not spend all her time criticizing every move I make, like some people I know.

Tuesday, January 24th

Have decided to give my diet a rest for a few days. A week is quite long enough, and despite the fact that the weighing machine at my local chemist's appears to concur with the one in mother's bathroom, I definitely *feel* thinner which is the main thing. It's a pity I don't feel better.

Wednesday, January 25th

This morning at breakfast Jane said, 'Has anyone told you that you have blackheads on your nose?'

At first I thought I must have misheard her, but she repeated this extraordinary observation, adding that in her experience a good rub with a nail brush would not go amiss – and after all no one should know better than she about facial blemishes.

I did as she suggested, but unfortunately went rather too far and made the tip of my nose bleed so profusely that I had to go round all day with a small piece of cotton wool attached to it – a fact that did not go unremarked by Armitage, needless to say.

Thursday, January 26th

This morning's post brings a sensational offer: the chance to buy a magnificent new book entitled *Wildlife in Britain* at £1·75 less than the normal price. I cannot imagine why I have been picked out of so many millions of householders to be the recipient of this remarkable offer, but clearly it is an opportunity not to be missed. 'Just think,' it says in the glossy leaflet, 'with the help of this magnificent volume you can now learn to identify pied wagtails in the Mall or lone buzzards in the Scottish Highlands!' The possibilities are endlessly fascinating. 'Why not plan exciting day-trips to explore your own ecological area? Experience the thrill of seeing a badger; catch a glimpse of the rare pine marten; watch a lone otter gambolling in a Hebridean stream; wonder at the strange barking of the muntjak.' And all of this for less than ten pounds.

I have always been very keen on wildlife, and although I do not manage to get out into the field as often as I would like, I always make a point of looking in at the nature programmes on TV. I shall certainly send off for the ten days' Free Examination straight away. I shall also say YES to my name being entered for the Great £50000 Holiday Wildlife Game. The first prize is a round-the-world trip for me and my family, or £7000 in cash. I know which I shall choose.

Friday, January 27th

To the opera with Mollie Marsh-Gibbon. It is an art form for which I have never really acquired a taste, and second-rate productions of *Carmen* in English are hardly guaranteed to change my opinion.

To her flat for supper afterwards. Noticed the wallpaper has started to come away again. We ate cold chicken and tongue and potato salad with a bottle of English hock-style white wine which Mollie declared was barely distinguishable from the real thing. I am bound to say that there was something in what she said – although I wished I'd had the expertise to refute it. It is high time I started educating my palate.

Knowing Mollie's interest in the countryside, I mentioned

the wildlife book. She said, 'Sounds to me like yet another of those cockeyed schemes that are forever being dreamed up by seedy entrepreneurs to make money out of the idiot public by exploiting their desire for instant, potted knowledge. Anyone with a genuine interest in nature discovers what he wants by first-hand observation, not by flipping through the pages of books that are designed primarily to adorn the coffee tables of middle-class suburbia.'

It is always a mistake to reveal one's ignorance to Mollie, and if I do decide to find out more about wine, I shall certainly take care not to mention the fact in her presence.

Saturday, January 28th

Last night I had the most extraordinary dream in the course of which Fiona Richmond lay naked in a huge plate of fried eggs and bacon. When I told Jane about this, she said that in her opinion there was nothing more boring than other people's dreams, and that anyway I should have been dreaming about her.

The point about it, which she clearly failed to grasp, is that it just goes to show the effect these sex shows can have on perfectly normal, well-balanced people without their realizing it.

Monday, January 30th

I really feel I cannot allow this business of my nightmare to pass without making my feelings known to the proper authority. Devoted much of the morning to penning a pithy letter to the managing director of the company responsible for putting on the sex show, with copies to the producer and the cast. I pointed out that if a perfectly sane, well-balanced member of the audience could have his subconscious distorted in such a dramatic way, I dreaded to think how such an entertainment might affect those already mentally and sexually unhinged. I added that from a purely artistic point of view, the show had been well beneath the standard one expects from a West End show, and that I thought the least the management could do by way of recompense was to return my money. I sent it by recorded delivery. I shall be most interested to hear what they have to say.

No sign of my wildlife book as yet.

Was in the middle of washing up this evening when Jane suddenly announced that she felt our relationship was not getting anywhere.

I asked her where she thought it ought to be getting. She replied, 'I have no idea, but wherever it is, it quite obviously isn't getting there, is it?'

I said that, as I understood it, relationships were not supposed to *get* anywhere; they were meant to *be*. At this stage she accused me of trying to evade the issue, as usual, and before I knew what, I found myself involved in a quite unnecessary row. In an attempt to assure her of my affection, I stepped forward to embrace her. Unfortunately, our two pairs of spectacles became locked, with the result that when I pulled away from her, I dragged hers off her nose and into the sink, smashing both lenses and bending one of the side pieces.

I do see, it *is* rather annoying to have to go round for the next week or so in a pair of round black National Health frames, but I still do not think that is any reason to take quite such a strong line against me. We must all learn to take the rough with the smooth, and the fact that she is not prepared to be forgiving over a comparatively unimportant misfortune like this, does not bode well for our future married life together.

February

Wednesday, February 1st

Penelope's birthday. It will be eight years this summer since we decided we were not really meant for each other, yet I often think about her still. On an impulse, I decided to ring her, but found that the last number I had for her was the Queensgate flat. After much telephoning, I finally traced her whereabouts through Harry Jeavons, of all people, who told me that she had finally married an out-of-work sociologist and become self-sufficient in a converted ploughman's cottage near Barnstaple. Got through after lunch. Surprised to discover my heart gave a little jump at the sound of her voice, just as it always used to. She seemed genuinely pleased to hear from me again after all this time, and suggested I might like to drive down for lunch on Saturday.

I said that I thought it was rather a long way to come for lunch, but she said, 'In that case, why not stay the night? We've got plenty of room, as long as you don't expect the Savoy. I know Ben would really love to meet you.'

Oddly enough, I have been thinking more and more recently about the possibility of escaping the rat-race for a simpler, more wholesome existence in the country, and I shall be most interested to see how they have got on.

Thursday, February 2nd

Still no sign of my wildlife book, but so looking forward to seeing Penelope again that scarcely anything else seems to matter. Refused coffee from the machine for the first time in four years. From now on I shall avoid touching food or drink that has not been made from natural products.

At lunchtime popped out to buy the Seymours' book on self-sufficiency. It makes fascinating reading. Am particularly interested in the section on the cow. They write: 'The cow should be absolutely central to the economy of a small-holding.' I could not agree more. Section on the pig less interesting.

Planted some mustard and cress in an old ice-cream container.

Friday, February 3rd

Called in at my local grocer's on the way home to buy half a dozen eggs. When the girl produced them, I asked her if they were fresh.

'Fresh in yesterday,' she replied in an off-hand manner.

'I am not interested in the date you received them. It's the date they were laid that I need to know,' I said.

'How should I know when they were laid?' she replied. 'I'm a shop assistant, not a chicken farmer.'

I told her that there was no necessity to take that tone with me, and although it may not be a shop assistant's job to watch eggs being laid, it *was* her job to be civil to customers. I then asked her if they were farm eggs. 'Says so on the box,' she said with a shrug. 'Dairyfield Farm.'

I said that sounded like a made-up name if ever I had heard one, and reminded her that it is an offence against the Trade Descriptions Act to describe eggs as farm eggs if such is not the case.

'Here,' she said, 'are you some sort of policeman, or what?'

I said, 'Merely an ordinary member of the public who wants to know precisely what he is paying for.'

'If you ask me,' she said, 'you're making a lot of fuss over nothing. You asked me for six large eggs, and I gave you six large eggs. For all I know they may be ostrich eggs that have been interfered with by the head-shrinkers of Papua, but that's no concern of mine. Now, do you want them or don't you?'

I said not unless she could guarantee to me that they were real fresh farm eggs, adding for good measure that there were no ostriches in Papua. She simply put the eggs back on the shelf and walked away without so much as a word.

I could have pursued the matter with the manager, given the time and patience, but a quiet word with the Trades Description people will certainly prove very much more effective. I shouldn't be surprised if there isn't quite a stink about this.

No sign yet of my mustard and cress – or of my wildlife book.

Saturday, February 4th

Made an early start for Barnstaple, but traffic terrible anyway. Is it any wonder people like Penelope and Ben opt out of modern society?

Finally drove in through the open gate and immediately ran over a chicken or, to be more precise, a cockerel. Apparently he was the very first creature they bought when they arrived. By way of consolation I remarked that they must have become used by now to sudden set-backs. Ben said: 'Yes, but not quite as sudden as that.'

Had for some reason pictured Penelope in a long, flowing patterned dress, looking very romantic and beautiful like Dorelia John, and was most disappointed when she appeared in the doorway in jeans and T-shirt looking rather fat and unwashed – just like every other girl one sees in London. Ben looked more the part, in his collarless shirt with sleeves rolled up to his biceps, his old army trousers tied up with string and his heavy brown boots. He might have stepped straight out of the pages of a novel by D. H. Lawrence. He also hadn't shaved, I noticed.

After a while they offered me a glass of their home-made wine which tasted exactly like mouldy vinegar.

Then the children came in to be introduced – Seth aged seven, Job five, and Amos three. Penelope said, 'It's about time you started a family.' I felt like saying, 'Not if they turn out to look anything like these.'

They all appeared to have the most extraordinary number of holes in their pullovers, and when I remarked on this fact, Ben said, 'They're meant to be like that. It's called open weave. We finished them only the other day on the hand loom.'

Penelope said, 'We thought they were rather successful.'

Ben added, 'And they cost only a fraction of the sort of thing you find in the shops.'

And look it, I thought.

Lunch took an extraordinarily long time to prepare so that it was difficult for me to refuse a second glass of their vinegary wine. It was unfortunate that they had chosen to make every single stick of furniture with their bare hands since there was not a single chair or bench that was remotely comfortable.

Needless to say, there was no gas or electricity; such heating as there was came from open wood fires, and lighting was all by oil lamps. I noticed there were only two bedrooms, but did not like to ask where I would be sleeping – in the stable no doubt with the three sheep, two goats, cow, donkey, pregnant white New Zealand doe rabbit, eight Khaki Campbells and as many Buff Orpingtons as had escaped the wheels of visitors' cars. Lunch appeared finally at 2.15 in a large, steaming casserole.

'How delicious,' I said. 'Chicken.'

'Yes,' said Penelope. 'To be precise, the one you ran over this morning. Nothing goes to waste here.'

Ben then produced a small jug of their home-made ale which tasted to me exactly the same as their wine. I hoped they might close the window while we ate, since there was a cold wind out and it was blowing straight down my neck. But when I drew Ben's attention to this, he said: 'You city people don't know what fresh air is. You'll soon get used to it.' I daresay I might have done had it not been for the appalling stench of manure that came in with it. It was so strong that at one point I really wondered if I was going to be able to finish what was on my plate.

When I mentioned Tim and Vanessa, whom Penelope had known, she said, 'We're different now, and there's no point in pretending we're not.'

After lunch Ben slaughtered one of the goats and Penelope sprayed the fruit trees with tar wash, some of which splashed on to my suede shoes, leaving a nasty mark. Later we had a cup of dried pea tea which seemed to me to taste no different from the wine and the beer. They seemed genuinely disappointed when I announced that I had suddenly remembered I had a lot of work to do in the morning and would therefore be unable to stay the night after all. However, I promised to return again in the summer and try some of the goat's-hoof jelly. As I drove out through the gate, I felt a strange bump under my rear wheel but decided not to stop.

Sunday, February 5th

Got up late. Still tired after long drive yesterday. Weather cold and wet. Thank goodness I decided not to stay. Went into the kitchen and found someone had moved my mustard and cress. Hunted high and low all morning, but without success. Mentioned the matter to Beddoes when he finally appeared at tea time. He said, 'Oh, Birgit and I decided to have a tidy up yesterday and we threw it out with the rest of the rubbish. We wondered what it was.' When I asked him who Birgit was that she should take it upon herself to interfere with other people's property, he told me airily that she was 'a piece of Scandinavian tail' that he'd picked up on Aldgate East Underground station on Friday afternoon. I did not conceal my distaste at the crudeness of his language, and commented coldly that, as I understood it, he was going out with Victoria.

He said, 'Well, I'm not now, so there.'

While I am relieved to hear that Victoria has seen sense at last, the fact that some foreign girl whom I have never met, and never want to meet, should decide to throw away my mustard and cress is something which I can neither forgive nor forget. Thought about penning a note to the Trade Descriptions people re the eggs, but really I have better things to do with my time. Suddenly the winter seems very long indeed.

Monday, February 6th

Despite a particularly unpleasant journey to work and the continuing non-appearance of wildlife book, I am happy to be back in civilization once more. Dr Johnson was right of course. 'A man who is tired of London *is* tired of life.' Self-sufficiency is for the bored and the boring, and I do not think anyone could accuse me of being either of those. Celebrated my return with two cups of coffee from the machine and felt rather sick for the rest of the morning.

Tuesday, February 7th

With Jane to dinner at the Pedalows'. I quite agree, their little mews house is charming, but not as charming as all that. Tim was very full of his new BMW 528, and after coffee he took Jane for a quick spin in it. On the way home, Jane said, 'I do not understand why you cannot have a nice car like Tim's.'

I said, 'Because I do not happen to be a partner in a family stockbroking firm where a large expensive car goes with the job.' She replied that I always had an answer for everything, and I am afraid we had words about it. Frankly, the sooner I make some money the better for both our sakes, but I am certainly not going to tell her that.

Wednesday, February 8th

This evening I asked Beddoes if he could ask around his influential City friends and see if he couldn't come up with a tip that would make me a shilling or two on the stock market. He said he was very sorry, he didn't have anything to do with that side of the business. What *does* he do? I'd like to know.

Thursday, February 9th

Have decided to hand over my portfolio to Tim instead. He is very enthusiastic and says he has had a sniff of something that might turn out to be very interesting indeed, and will let me know in a couple of days.

Friday, February 10th

Bought the *Financial Times* on the way into work. Looked up the share prices, but was quite unable to make head or tail of them. However, I daresay I will get the drift in time, and anyway the arts pages are excellent.

Saturday, February 11th

My wildlife book has arrived at last and is every bit as fascinating as the leaflet suggested. I had no idea there were tawny owls in Regent's Park. I must remember to look out for them the next time I am up that way. Disappointed not to have heard any news of the Holiday Wildlife Game, but perhaps one should not expect more than one excitement in a day.

Monday, February 13th

No news as yet about my investment. Rang Tim as soon as I got into the office. I gave my name to the secretary and she asked me to hang on for a moment. There was a brief silence and when she returned she said she was very sorry but Mr Pedalow had just gone out to a meeting and would not be back until late afternoon. I cannot explain why, but I had a funny feeling that she was not telling me the truth and that Tim was trying to avoid me. I had expected better treatment from a friend, and hope that he is not going to start acting the goat with me, otherwise I shall seriously have to think about removing my portfolio and entrusting it to someone who is prepared to take it more seriously.

Tuesday, February 14th

Received a Valentine card of appalling sentimentality depicting a young couple walking hand in hand through a bluebell wood. The printed message inside read: GIVE ME YOUR HAND AND I WILL LEAD YOU TO PARADISE. Assuming this to be one of Beddoes's feeble jokes, I confronted him with it at breakfast saying that I might be desperate, but I wasn't as desperate as all that! Beddoes then made a coarse joke and we both roared and slapped our thighs. Then Victoria made an excellent joke to the effect that I should be very grateful that it had been *handed* to me on a plate, and we roared all the harder. Suddenly, to our surprise, Jane threw down her toast and marmalade, burst into floods of tears and rushed from the room slamming the door behind her. Naturally, I went after her and asked her what was the matter. 'If you must know,' she blubbed, 'I sent you that card, and what's more, I meant every word of it.' Oh dear, oh dear.

Wednesday, February 15th

Tim rang to say he was planning to put me into Benganese Conglomerates, whatever they may be, and how much did I have in mind to invest? Obviously it is one of those very rare occurrences, a copper-bottomed certainty, so I decided to throw caution to the wind and plunge my entire savings

'Then Victoria made an excellent joke . . .'

of £500. As Onassis said in his biography, which I have recently been reading, if you want to make a lot, you've got to risk a lot – a philosophy that certainly paid off for him. On the other hand, of course, Onassis did not have to waste his time hoovering the sitting-room carpet and generally cleaning up other people's messes. I do not quite understand why I have been landed with this job, but I have.

Thursday, February 16th

At the risk of tempting providence, I have decided to treat myself to a new suit: a blue double-breasted worsted, I thought, with a heavy pin stripe, in keeping with my new image as a man of affairs. However, despite visiting over half a dozen reputable men's outfitters in the West End, I am quite unable to find anything remotely approaching this. Where *do* people go nowadays if they want traditional off-the-peg tailoring?

Friday, February 17th

Again bought the *Financial Times* to see how my shares are doing. But try as I might, I am quite unable to find anything that sounds like Benganese Conglomerates. Have I been taken for a ride? I have always had my doubts about Tim Pedalow.

Saturday, February 18th

Spent all morning going round the shops but still unable to find the suit I want. In the end settled for a similar thing in plain dark grey worsted. I think it looks rather good on me. I only hope I shall be in a position to pay for it.

Sunday, February 19th

To Regent's Park to try to catch a glimpse of these tawny owls I have been reading about in my wildlife book. But not an owl to be seen or heard. A most unproductive day in all respects. I do not know which disappoints me more: my wildlife book or Regent's Park. However, I am looking forward to wearing my new suit tomorrow.

Monday, February 20th

Armitage most insulting about my suit. Said I looked as though I had stepped straight out of the Munich crisis and that the pre-war look might go down very well amongst my country friends, but it was not the sort of image the firm wished its young executives to project. I said that in my opinion – and I was not alone in this – there is a correct way for business people to dress and an incorrect way. He might think it perfectly acceptable to go round in a pale green Terylene three-piece with six-inch wide lapels and a tie with a knot the size of a cottage loaf, looking like an out-of-work hairdresser, but I happened to believe in such old-fashioned traditions as good English cloth and decent English tailoring. Armitage laughed in a superior way and said that if success had anything to do with it, he'd rather be mistaken for an out-of-work hairdresser than the poor man's Anthony Eden any day. I replied that it was very easy to sneer at Anthony Eden, but that in my book, if we had a foreign secretary today who dressed half as well as he did, we might carry a little more weight at the international conference table. Armitage said, 'Churchill went round dressed in an old boiler suit, but he was still prime minister.' I simply could not be bothered to argue with him, and turned my attentions instead to the *Financial Times* Ordinary Share Index. I only wish someone could explain what it all means. I also wish I could find a single reference to Benganese Conglomerates.

Tuesday, February 21st

Foolishly happened to mention to Beddoes that I had invested a monkey on a snip. He looked completely baffled and said he hadn't the faintest idea what I was talking about. I said, 'I thought as a City man you were familiar with the jargon. I was saying that I had invested five hundred pounds on a sure-fire winner.' He said that he had been in the City for twelve years but he had never heard any of those expressions used by anyone. 'If you really *do* work in the City,' I said quietly.

He said, 'What is this so-called snip that you have invested your monkey in, then?'

I said, 'Benganese Conglomerates.'

'Benganese Conglomerates?' he exclaimed.

I smiled and nodded.

Beddoes said, 'I wouldn't touch those with a barge pole. They're a real flash in the pan. Australian Mining all over again.' I was completely taken aback and reminded him that he had told me he was not on that side of the business.

'I'm not,' he said, 'but anyone with the slightest knowledge will tell you that Benganese Conglomerates are a bummer.'

I said, 'I think I will allow my stockbroker to be the best judge of that.' And left the room closing the door firmly behind me.

Wednesday, February 22nd

Rang Tim first thing and said that a little dicky bird had just whispered in my ear that Benganese Conglomerates were a dead loss. He said, 'I don't know what sort of dicky birds you mix with, but this one is pulling your worm.' And he gave a not very convincing laugh.

I do not pretend to have a lot in common with Onassis, but I fancy I have a pretty good nose when it comes to sharp practice. I said, 'That may be so or it may not. At all events, I should like you to sell my shares immediately.'

'Don't be a bloody fool,' he said. 'If you sell now, you'll lose a penny per share; but if you are patient, you could make yourself a small fortune.' The only good decisions in business are the ones that are made quickly, and I wasted no time over this one.

'Sell,' I told him, and hung up. I do not know whether Sarah was listening in or not, but I have the feeling her attitude towards me has suddenly become unusually respectful.

Thursday, February 23rd

No copies of the *FT* at the station this morning. I can't say I was entirely sorry. The *Daily Mirror* made an excellent substitute. Turned to page three to find a photograph of a girl with magnificent breasts who looked exactly like Beddoes's ex-girlfriend Jackie. According to the caption her name is Annabelle de Woolf, but that does not mean anything these days. It wouldn't surprise me a bit if she hadn't acted in a blue movie or two before now. Read a long and fascinating article about soccer hooliganism. Curiously enough, I have never once attended a first-class soccer match. Perhaps I should. It might be very useful to see some of this violence at close quarters.

Friday, February 24th

Tackled Armitage re this question of a football match. He suggests tomorrow's game at Chelsea, and says there is sure to be some rough stuff. This is excellent news. Tim rang after lunch in a great state to ask if I'd seen the evening papers. Apparently Benganese Conglomerates have taken off even more dramatically than he had forecast. He has made a small personal fortune, and is already talking about changing his BMW for a Ferrari. I said I hoped he had not taken my instructions too literally the other afternoon.

'Of course I did,' he said. 'I'm a stockbroker, not a mind reader, more's the pity. Still, you only lost twenty pounds. On the other hand you could have made yourself four hundred; but that's the stock market for you.'

Beddoes was looking a damned sight too cheerful for my liking when he came in this evening. I was in no mood for pussyfooting, and told him straight out that he owed me £420. Of course he feigned total innocence, and when I explained why, he said, 'It's no good your taking my word on these things. I've told you already, I don't work on that side of the business.'

I said the only satisfaction to be derived from the whole sorry affair was that he had not gone into Benganese Conglomerates himself.

'Oh,' he said, 'I did. Made myself a tidy packet, as a matter of fact.' I told him that I was now quite convinced that he was a man who was totally incapable of telling the difference between right and wrong.

'The difference is crystal clear to me,' he said. 'I got it right, and you got it wrong.'

Saturday, February 25th

Set off for the match in my oldest clothes and thickest shoes, having first made sure I had some 10p pieces in my pocket which in case of trouble I could quickly slip between my fingers and make into a knuckleduster. Arrived rather later than I had hoped, as a result of having to make a few small adjustments to the headlights on my scooter. Decided to park a good, safe distance from the ground, and joined the fans in their blue-and-white scarves. They certainly looked a pretty rough crowd to me, and I was glad of my coins. After much jostling and horseplay at one of the side entrances, I was confronted by a hefty-looking man with an official badge on his arm who told me, 'Sorry, no entrance without a ticket.' It had not occurred to me before that one had to book in advance, and I was on the point of making an official complaint when I felt a hand on my shoulder. Spun round to find myself face to face with Hugh Bryant-Fenn, of all people, who said he had a spare ticket if it would interest me. In spite of our lateness, we managed to find a couple of seats with an excellent view of the whole pitch, and settled down to enjoy the game. I pulled my coat collar up high around my neck so that, in the event of receiving a bottle on the back of the head, I could be sure of some protection. However, the first half passed off without incident, and not one of the fans around us showed the slightest sign of wishing to pick a fight with me or anyone else.

'Not much hooliganism today then,' I murmured to Hugh out of the corner of my mouth. He looked surprised.

'I wouldn't know about that,' he said. 'That sort of thing happens down on the terraces, not here in the numbered seats.'

Chelsea won 3–1, not that it mattered a hoot to me one way or the other. An unfortunate incident occurred after the game when I became involved in a misunderstanding with a passing motorist outside the ground. Heated words were being exchanged when a policeman appeared from nowhere and told me to turn out my pockets.

Naturally, I protested in the strongest possible terms, explaining that if it was anyone's fault it was the driver's for not looking where he was going. I might have been addressing a lump of wood for all the sympathy I received, and it was with extreme reluctance that I acceded to his request. I had quite forgotten that I was still carrying the spanner, and the policeman pounced upon it with a cry of satisfaction. 'Hullo,' he said. 'Looking for a bit of aggro, were you?' I told him that I had never been so insulted.

'If you think that's an insult,' he said, 'wait till you get down to the station.' And before I knew what, I was frog-marched away, bundled into a police van along with half a dozen vicious-looking youths and driven off at high speed to Chelsea police station. One of them, who had a safety pin through his nose and a length of lavatory chain hanging from his ear lobe, said: 'What you been up to then, dad? Misbehaving with small boys?'

Fortunately, there was a policeman present, and I pretended not to have heard. Upon arrival at the police station, I informed the desk sergeant that I wished to speak to my solicitor but was told to wait my turn with the rest.

It was not until my name was called out and I was asked for my solicitor's name that I realized that I did not actually have one. Luckily, I was able to remember the name of father's solicitor in Kent. His wife answered the phone and said she was very sorry but her husband had died on Tuesday and she was just leaving for the funeral.

I remember seeing a film on TV about a man who is wrongly arrested and accused of murder, but is unable to persuade anyone of his innocence, and that is precisely how I felt as the sergeant took down my statement. It soon became obvious, of course, that it was all a misunderstanding and after a cup of tea I was told I could go home.

I am seriously considering bringing a complaint against the police for false arrest. But first I must find myself a solicitor.

Tuesday, February 28th

I have just about had enough of Beddoes's constant reference to prisons and criminals. This evening he introduced me to this new girlfriend of his, Birgit, as 'the well-known jailbird'. I was strongly tempted to point out that, if throwing away a tub of mustard and cress that does not belong to you is not a criminal act, I'd like to know what is, but could not be bothered to waste my breath. How a man who contributes to the sale of pornographic material can seriously sit there puffing away at one of his ill-gotten cigars and accuse anyone else of disreputable behaviour is beyond me. Talk about mote and beam.

March

Thursday, March 2nd

I am reminded of Hugh Bryant-Fenn's joke that if the actress Tuesday Weld had married Frederick March II, she would have become Tuesday March II. It always makes me chuckle. But of course it doesn't really apply this year.

Friday, March 3rd

Suddenly realized that I have now had my wildlife book for over ten days, so shall not be able to send it back as I had hoped. This is probably just as well, since the postage on a book of that size is almost as much as the book itself. Besides, it's always useful to have in the car. One never knows when one might need to find one's way to Whipsnade Zoo, or identify a bird one has just run over. I am also sure that the people who keep the book stand a better chance of winning the Wildlife Game than the ones who send them back.

Saturday, March 4th

Jane has gone to Oxted for the weekend, thank goodness. Our affair is not going at all well, and I have grave doubts about our future together. Matters are not improved by her insistence on wearing her National Health frames despite the fact that her other pair have been ready for collection for several days now. I am sure she does it purely to reproach me. Her increasing plainness might be less obvious if it were not for Birgit's great beauty. I simply do not understand what she sees in Beddoes. I suppose it's all to do with sex, as usual.

Sunday, March 5th

Had a most erotic dream about Birgit last night. She was dressed in a policeman's uniform and wearing a pair of National Health glasses which made her look more desirable than ever.

I hope I am not falling in love with Birgit. It could complicate matters no end.

Monday, March 6th

Armitage marched into my office this morning and said in an off-hand way, 'If you're not doing anything better on Saturday, we're having a few friends round for a bit of a do. We'd love to see you. Alone preferably.'

I suppose by 'we' he must mean himself and Sarah. At all events, it is not *my* way of inviting someone to a party. However, am quite looking forward to it already. Knowing Armitage he is sure to have laid on a few pretty girls with loose morals, and after all, it's not as though I were married to Jane.

Tuesday, March 7th

Flirted outrageously with a most attractive dark-haired girl on the Tube this morning. Am only sorry I did not have time to follow it up. She was obviously pretty easy meat, and I noticed that the moment I got out she went straight across and sat next to a chap who had been standing next to me all the way from Notting Hill Gate. What *is* coming over me these days?

Thursday, March 9th

This evening, I kissed Birgit on the cheek while Beddoes was in the lavatory. Heaven knows what made me do it. All I know is that it seemed the most natural thing in the world. Instead of being shocked or angry, as I had expected, she merely smiled and went on watching TV. There is definitely electricity there between us, and as long as things like this can happen, it would be quite wrong of me to consider tying myself down to one woman.

Friday, March 10th

Nothing of interest to report. To bed early, which was probably just as well the way I'm going.

Saturday, March 11th

To Armitage's party.

I have long suspected that he moves with a fast crowd for whom drug-taking and other forms of loose behaviour are very much second nature, and it seems I was not mistaken. A strange aroma hung over the proceedings, and although I have never partaken myself, only a fool would have failed to recognize it for what it was.

Got into conversation with a girl with an appallingly scarred face who offered me a cigarette from what looked like an innocent packet of Players No. 6, but I was not taking any chances, and left her to puff away contentedly. It is always difficult to know what to say to someone who has obviously suffered a serious misfortune. Some people try and ignore it, but I have always believed you should bring it out into the open quite naturally. I said, 'I'm so sorry about your face. How did it happen?'

She replied calmly, 'In the normal way. I just mixed up the henna, took out a small brush and painted it on.' I managed to laugh off my *faux pas* but could not help reflecting that, as make-up goes, hers was in a particularly bad taste.

Later a huge risotto was brought in. Sarah came up and told me she had found the recipe in her Alice B. Toklas cook book, the implication obviously being that one or two ingredients had been added of a somewhat spicier nature than usual. I know pot is supposed to be non-addictive and less harmful than a whisky and soda, but there are exceptions to every rule, and although I do not see myself trying to fly off the mantelpiece, I was not about to make a fool of myself in front of anyone – let alone people from the office. Apart from allowing myself one small mouthful from the henna-ed girl's plate, I stuck firmly to wine. Even so, I began to feel quite light-headed and had the strangest feeling that everything in the room was advancing and receding from me in an oddly surrealistic way. By the end of the evening I was in such a peculiar state that Roundtree had to drive me home and put me to bed. All very embarrassing, but a lesson well worth learning.

Sunday, March 12th

One often hears it said that one of the great things about pot is that it does not give you a hangover. I do not know what it was they put in the risotto last night, but I would rather have gone the whole hog and tried to fly out of the window than have had to suffer what I have suffered today. I am too ill to write any more.

Monday, March 13th

To work rather later than usual, still feeling decidedly shaky. Surprised to find Sarah as bright and perky as ever, apparently having experienced no ill-effects at all. Same thing with Armitage, who bounced into my office at eleven-thirty, noisy and extremely full of himself.

'My word,' he said, 'you were certainly knocking back the wine the other night. You really should have had some of that risotto. It's always a great mistake to drink heavily on an empty stomach.' I suppose that in his circle you have to keep up pretences for the sake of the outside world.

Tuesday, March 14th

Feeling marginally better this morning. Was in the middle of a not very important Barford meeting in Roundtree's office when Sarah rang through to say she had some television people on the line asking for me urgently. My first thought was that it was 'This is Your Life' people at last, but to my surprise I found myself speaking to Nicola Benson. I have not seen her since we used to appear in undergraduate revues at Oxford. It seems that she is now something very high up in television. She is busy planning a major new series for BBC 2 and thinks that I might be just the person to anchor it. I do not quite understand what this would entail, but it all sounds most exciting, and I am to lunch with her and her executive producer on Friday to talk about it further. One often hears of people suddenly being plucked out of obscurity to become TV stars, but somehow one never thinks of it happening to oneself. Why not, though?

Thursday, March 16th

Am so excited at the prospect of tomorrow's lunch that nothing else seems worth mentioning.

Friday, March 17th

Lunched with Nicola at the Terrazza, always a great favourite of mine, but scarcely noticed what we ate or drank. All I did notice was how very much more attractive she was than I had remembered. At Oxford I could hardly be bothered to give her the time of day, yet now I feel she is a girl I could go for in a very big way indeed. What a strange thing life is. Her executive producer, a cocky young man called John, explained the idea of the programme which is to take a typical young man about town and transport him to a remote part of northern Scotland with a minimum supply of modern aids, and see how well he succeeds in looking after himself – building a hut, hunting for food, etc.

It is a far cry from sitting in a studio chatting to interesting people which was how I had envisaged the programme, and I must confess that at first I was disappointed. On the other hand, as I pointed out, it was an extraordinary coincidence that they should have picked on self-sufficiency, a subject which I had only recently researched at close quarters. They agreed that it was rather extraordinary, and that they had obviously been quite right to think of me. However, they warned that before any firm decision could be arrived at, I should have to undergo some sort of test to find out how I reacted to a camera and so on. I pointed out that I was a very busy man and might not necessarily be free at the drop of a hat. John said he thought it would probably be some time next week, but that he would be in touch nearer the time.

As we were leaving the restaurant, Nicola said, 'I know that a self-sufficiency programme on BBC 2 may not seem at first glance very glamorous, but if this thing catches on – and we think it will – it could turn you into a very big television star.'

Spent the afternoon practising my autograph and went home early. The temptation to break the news to the others in the flat was almost unbearable, but am determined to say nothing until I know for certain. I have no wish to make a fool of myself.

Saturday, March 18th

For the first time in weeks, found myself alone in the flat this evening with Jane.

I have definitely come to the conclusion that I could do a great deal better for myself – and if all goes well, probably shall. Even so, I am pretty fed up with her bossy attitude towards everything I say or do. This evening, for example, she said, 'Do you know, you're becoming a real telly bug. You have watched everything from "Dr Who" onwards.'

I explained that I had to do it for professional reasons, and that it was not exactly something I enjoyed. Any normal girl would have asked me what I meant. However, there's no doubt she is intrigued.

Monday, March 20th

Nothing from the television people, but I suppose it is early days yet. Snubbed Armitage in a Marketing Strategy meeting.

Tuesday, March 21st

Took Jane to dinner at the Bordelino and broke the news to her over coffee. Although she appeared indifferent, I'm pretty sure that deep down she is beginning to regret not taking her chances when she had them. To underline the point, I said, 'It's extraordinary to think that tonight I am able to walk into this restaurant, just like that, and no one gives me a second look; nobody knows who I am and nobody cares. And yet in a few weeks from now I'll walk into this same restaurant and people will stop talking, and point, and whisper, and the waiters will scurry about and make a lot of fuss of me and ask me to sign the menu, and I'll be obliged to leave a larger tip than usual with the woman who looks after the coats. And yet basically I'll be exactly the same person.'

She thought for a moment and said, 'I simply could not bear to go out with someone famous. It would be too embarrassing for words.' That's what she *says*.

Wednesday, March 22nd

Thinking back to last night, I am beginning to understand now how Plantagenet Palliser must have felt when faced with the decision of giving up the chancellorship of the exchequer or his marriage. How can a man, who is unable to order his own affairs, dare to attempt to direct those of the nation? Or for that matter of BBC television? I am seriously beginning to wonder if I should not consider giving the whole idea up.

Thursday, March 23rd

Mystified not to have heard anything still from the television people. As a result have been quite unable to get down to any serious work.

Finally, after lunch, rang Nicola's office. The phone was answered by a secretary. I told her that I was Mr Crisp's assistant and that I was ringing to say that he had had to go away for a few days on urgent business but that if they had any news, I would be glad to pass it on. The girl said she knew nothing about it. She also asked who Mr Crisp was, which is ominous, to say the least.

Friday, March 24th

Nicola rang at last to say that there had been a slight setback to their plans, but there was nothing to worry about and they would be calling me next week to fix a date for the test. It's just as well, since a small spot has suddenly come up on the side of my nose.

Victoria has suddenly become more friendly of late. Women are all the same: the tiniest sniff of fame and they all come running. I suppose it is something I shall have to come to terms with.

Saturday, March 25th

To Kent for the Easter weekend – alone.

Finally succeeded in distracting mother's attention away from the cat sufficiently to give her my news. All she said was, 'That's nice, dear. Perhaps now you'll be asked on to "Any Questions" and meet Edward du Cann.'

Spent the whole of the afternoon trying to build a hut at the bottom of the garden with my bare hands. It is a good deal more difficult than it sounds, and the fact that mother's garden consists of quarter of an acre of lawn and two small flower beds tested my powers of survival to their limits. Mother could not have been less helpful if she had tried.

I tried to tell her that the programme was an experiment in living; but she replied that, as far as she was concerned, it was an experiment in being very silly indeed and that anyway tea was on the table and if I didn't come at once it would be stewed.

After tea, I constructed a makeshift tent out of a broom, a garden fork and the cat's blanket. Mother had to point out the obvious fact that the chances of my coming across a cat's blanket in the wilds of northern Scotland were remote in the extreme. I explained that, in the nature of things, it could only be a simulated model and that the object of this particular experiment was simply to see if I could survive a night out in the open in the middle of winter. She asked me what I was planning to do for food – make a surprise raid on Mrs Agar's bantams down the road, or slum it on worms and leatherjackets? And added that if I really thought she had nothing better to do than make up my bed and get in half a rolled shoulder of lamb specially, then I had another think coming.

I said that when the time came I would probably snare a rabbit or shoot a ptarmigan with a rough bow and arrow, and repeated that my concern for the present was sleeping and keeping warm.

Set off into the garden shortly after eleven, with a pile of straw and wood shavings from a box in the garage which had been used to deliver a special offer spin drier.

All was going to plan, and I was just settling down with the help of my old skiing anorak and an extra pair of thick

'She had also taken the opportunity of bringing two cellular
blankets, a cushion, a hot-water bottle and a cup of Bovril.'

socks, when mother arrived to say that the cat wouldn't settle and would I mind changing the blanket for an old one she had found in a trunk in the spare room. She had also taken the opportunity of bringing two cellular blankets, a cushion, a hot-water bottle and a cup of Bovril.

Finally dozed off at about two-thirty.

Surprisingly warm.

Sunday, March 26th

Easter Day.

Mother woke me with a cup of tea at seven. I do not believe I have slept so well or felt so fit for years. Suddenly, Easter has taken on a whole new meaning for me. Was so excited that, despite a badly thought-out sermon, I put two pounds in the collection plate at Mattins.

Monday, March 27th

Returned to London to find a letter from the managing director of the company that put on the sex show. I had forgotten all about it. He says that he is amazed by my comments; the show is a great success and this is the first complaint he has received. And not the last, I shouldn't wonder, if many more people start having the sort of dreams I had. I notice he says nothing about returning my money. I am in two minds whether to refer the matter to a higher authority.

Tuesday, March 28th

Rang Nicola about my night of survival, but she was in a meeting, so left a message to call me back. I do think it's important to be seen to be taking an *active* interest. None of us is so good at our job that we cannot do with a few helpful suggestions now and then.

Wednesday, March 29th

Have suddenly gone quite mad and ordered a pair of contact lenses – the ordinary hard variety. I know some people think I look rather well in my glasses, and they certainly have not done any noticeable harm to Ludovic Kennedy's career.

Still, I cannot help feeling that, in matters of communication, glasses do tend to act as a sort of psychological barrier, and actually I happen to think I look marginally better without them.

The man who tried them on for me in the shop had such bad breath that I felt quite sick. Most relieved when he suggested I should walk around the streets for twenty minutes or so and see how I got on. In fact unable to see anything or to get on much either due to the tears that poured continually from my eyes. It is just like a severe attack of hay fever. I have never actually suffered from hay fever but imagine that is what it is like. Was so blinded at one point that I went hard into a lamp post, bruising my forehead painfully and dislodging one of the lenses. Decided to return at once to the shop, but by now rendered virtually sightless and had to be shown the way by Irish traffic warden. It took over five minutes to remove the lenses, during which time the optician breathed malodorously into my face.

I have agreed to go ahead with a pair, and only hope that I shall not suffer a Pavlovian reaction and feel violently ill every time I take them out or put them in.

Thursday, March 30th

A message from Nicola's office to say that they should have a definite answer for me next week. If they mean a definite *date*, why don't they say so? For people whose job is communication they seem to have a curiously slap-happy way of using the language.

Friday, March 31st

Rang the local telephone manager's office and asked for my number to be made ex-directory. One of the many drawbacks of being a public figure is that one lays oneself wide open to unsolicited phone calls.

Last year Mollie Marsh-Gibbon was rung up every day regularly for a week by a man who said, 'Next time we meet it's roll-ons and panties down and smacked bottoms for you.'

Not that Mollie is a public figure – and as a matter of fact I think she secretly enjoyed it – but as the man in the telephone manager's office agreed, you can never be too sure these days. It was perfectly normal for TV people to go ex-directory and by an odd coincidence the new A–D books were due to go to press any day now, and he would look into it straight away. I doubt if I would have received such prompt service if I had been just any old member of the public.

April

Saturday, April 1st

Woke this morning to find a note pushed under the door. It was from Beddoes to say that someone had rung while I was out last night to know if I would be interested in taking over from Michael Parkinson, and, if so, would I ring the controller of BBC 1 as soon as possible.

Had just dialled the number when I heard shrieks of laughter from the next room and Beddoes and Jane came in shouting, 'Who's an April fool, then?'

They all roared till the tears ran.

I'm afraid I was unable to see the funny side of it. A stupid joke like that could destroy a man's career in seconds.

Sunday, April 2nd

An uneventful, unproductive day, filled with doubts and misgivings.

Monday, April 3rd

Am in a quandary to know what to wear for the television test. The pin-stripe is probably rather too formal. I do not wish to appear stuffy. Nor do I think that the brown tweed suit strikes quite the thrusting note that I am sure they are looking for. Finally decide on an excellent compromise. A velvet suit. Dark brown, perhaps, or bottle green. Elegant and slightly daring with a touch of cosiness.

Set off at lunchtime for the shops. Walking along Oxford Street I had the distinct feeling that people were looking at me in a quite different way from usual. But, of course, it is quite well known that fame – or even imminent fame – can imbue hitherto quite ordinary people with a peculiar aura which sets them apart from the crowd. I remember I once saw Stewart Granger outside Safeways wearing a safari outfit. Somehow one simply could not help looking at him. It is most interesting to notice how quickly and effortlessly I am beginning to acquire some of that star quality myself. Very pleased with the suit. It is dark blue. Victoria said that she has never been able to resist men in velvet. She seems to have very little difficulty with me.

Wednesday, April 5th

Horrified to realize, while shaving this morning, just how pale I am looking. This evening borrowed Victoria's sun lamp and had a session while listening to an indifferent radio programme. A light tan can do me nothing but good, although, of course, people with black and white sets will hardly reap the benefit. The effect so far is rather on the red side, but I daresay if I keep it up for a few days, it will gradually turn brown. The white rings round the eyes are a bit of a worry, too.

Thursday, April 6th

Was on my way out to an early lunch when the phone rang. It was John, the executive producer, to say that there had been a muddle over budgets and that they had had to re-think the programme in terms of a studio discussion. This could not have suited me better, and I told him so. He said, 'Well, actually that rather puts you out of court, I'm afraid. Frankly, you just haven't got the weight to carry that sort of thing.'

I am not up in this media jargon and asked him what sort of person he had in mind.

'We're thinking in terms of Michael Parkinson,' he said.

I do not understand any of it, and neither, I suspect, do they. All I do know is that I am landed with a blue velvet suit and a pair of contact lenses which I now no longer need nor want.

Friday, April 7th

Took the suit back at lunchtime. They were not at all pleased. Neither was I when they gave me a credit note for £39·50. When I told the manager I would prefer the cash, he said, 'I daresay you would, sir.'

I tried on a three-piece in a Prince of Wales check, but found I looked exactly like Armitage. Couldn't get out of it fast enough. Nothing else caught my eye. I might just as well have kept the blue velvet after all.

Suddenly life seems extraordinarily flat.

Saturday, April 8th

Unless I am much mistaken, something very fishy is going on between Beddoes and Jane. When I walked into the sitting room this evening, I had the distinct feeling that they had been kissing each other. Beddoes said, 'Oh, hello, matey. I've just been trying to get a fly out of Jane's eye.' But no amount of levity could conceal the obvious guilt on both their faces.

If she thinks that by throwing herself at another man's head she is going to make me come running, I am afraid she is much mistaken.

Sunday, April 9th

Unable to sleep a wink last night for thinking about Beddoes and Jane. It is not jealousy that consumes me, but indignation at Beddoes's attitude that anyone is fair game. The one chance in the week to get a really good night's sleep completely ruined.

Was reading the papers after lunch when Beddoes breezed in and announced that he and Jane were just off to the cinema and would I like to join them. I replied pointedly that I was not in the habit of playing gooseberry, and besides I did not hold with cinema-going on Sundays.

He said, 'Please yourself,' and left – for some cheap hotel in Paddington, I shouldn't wonder. Happily I am beyond caring.

Victoria continues to be friendly, if reserved. She says that she has seen Mike again, but that he is very mixed up and depressed about his failed marriage, and does not think there is any future for them. I know it's wrong, but I must admit I am immensely cheered by the news. It would just serve Jane right if I did catch Victoria on the rebound. I have decided, for the time being at any rate, to say nothing about the failure of the TV programme.

Monday, April 10th

Armitage said, 'You *might* catch her on the rebound, but if I were you, I'd stand well back.'

That is absolutely the last time I ever confide in him. Dave Garwood rang to say he had been trying to get hold of me all weekend over a matter of some freelance work, but had been unable to find my number. He had lost his A–D directory and when he rang Directory Enquiries, they had told him that they were not at liberty to give him my number since it was now listed as ex-directory.

I had completely forgotten about this and rang the telephone manager to ask if my name could be reinstated in the book after all, but he said I was too late since they had already gone to press. This effectively puts paid to anyone I do not know ringing me up with offers of work.

One small crumb of consolation: I have a feeling I may be able to get the contact lenses off tax.

Tuesday, April 11th

I have never been so bored at work. Armitage tried to score off me in a meeting this morning, but I simply could not have cared less.

Wednesday, April 12th

Watched an old Cary Grant film this evening. I have always rather identified with him. Interested to notice that he is actually much broader across the beam than I had realized. I do not know why I should find this so cheering, but I do.

Thursday, April 13th

The most terrible thing happened today. I was in a meeting in Prout's office discussing the Merchandising Development

Programme for the new Barford project when I gave such an enormous yawn that my jaws became locked wide open. I struggled for half an hour to close them but in the end had to take a taxi to the Middlesex Hospital where they gave me a local anaesthetic and did the job for me. It would not have been so bad if I had not had to wait for over an hour in a crowded out-patients' department.

A small boy who was sitting opposite could not take his eyes off me. Finally his mother said to him, 'You shouldn't stare like that. He can't help being wrong in the head.'

Naturally I attempted to register my complaint but all that came out was an unpleasant gargling sound. At this the woman seized the child by the arm and bundled him away to the other end of the room.

Without question the most humiliating day of my life.

Friday, April 14th

I daresay there are people who would accuse me of turning Victoria's unhappiness to my own advantage. I do not see it that way at all. I obviously represent for her a safe harbour after storm-tossed seas. After all, what are friends for if they cannot proffer comfort in times of need? If she doesn't need it, she is perfectly at liberty to say so.

Saturday, April 15th

A sensational turn of events. Mike Pritchard rang to say that he had woken this morning to discover that during the night all his hair had fallen out. He had found it lying beside him on the pillow like a small sleeping cat. He sounded pretty shaken. Victoria announced that, of course, she would have to go to him at once. I don't really see why. He has lost so much hair already, I wouldn't have thought that losing the lot would make very much difference one way or the other. Still, who am I to dissuade her?

All I can do now is wait and see how she feels when she returns. Waited up till one, but still no sign of her, so went to bed, a deeply disillusioned man.

Sunday, April 16th

Woke early after a troubled night to find a strange smell in
the flat. Discovered that amid all the excitement last night,
I had forgotten to take the bœuf bourguignon out of the
oven, as a result of which it had become welded onto the
casserole. Threw the whole thing into the dustbin. No sign
of Victoria all morning.

Beddoes appeared bleary-eyed at lunchtime, followed
shortly by a large angry Italian lady whom he introduced as
Stephania. She completely took over the kitchen, regardless
of the fact that I was trying to cook myself lunch, and
proceeded to make herself and Beddoes an enormous cheese
omelette. She was not only extremely messy but also very
noisy, and kept shouting out to Beddoes at the top of her
voice through the kitchen door. I felt compelled to point out
that we had recently suffered a tragedy in the household and
I would be obliged if she would respect other people's
feelings. Naturally she got hold of the wrong end of the stick
and started jabbering away at me in Italian and rolling her
eyes, and would, I have no doubt, have assaulted me physically
had Beddoes not appeared in the doorway and let out an
enormous bellow. He certainly knows how to keep his
women under control, I'll give him that.

Where Jane is, I have no idea. Or Victoria, come to that.
It's like living in a madhouse.

Monday, April 17th

Jane walked into the flat this evening after work, glared at
me, and without a word, stormed into her bedroom and
slammed the door behind her. I mentioned this extraordinary behaviour to Beddoes when he came in. He said,
'I'm not surprised, the way you've treated her in the last few
days.'

I was perfectly astounded and said that if anyone had
treated her poorly it was him – making great play for her one
minute, then throwing her over in favour of some mad
Italian woman the next. Beddoes said, 'Why should I make
any play for her, great or small? She's *your* friend. Besides,
she's not nearly pretty enough for my liking.'

He must take me for a complete fool.

I wondered if I should talk the whole thing over with Jane, but decided to let sleeping dogs lie. Now that I have finally made the break and things are going well with Victoria, there's no point in raking over old coals. As Beddoes once remarked, you've got to be cruel to be kind in these matters – except, of course, that in his case, he's cruel to be cruel.

Still no sign of Victoria. I am beginning to fear the worst.

Tuesday, April 18th

Victoria rang at last to say that Mike needed her and she had decided to return to him after all, and would I be very kind and run a few of her things over in the car – including her blue woolly hat. I suppose I should have kicked up a fuss. But really what is the point?

Thursday, April 20th

Victoria came round to collect a few remaining bits and pieces and to say goodbye. I do not mind admitting that tears came to my eyes as she kissed me on the cheek. I only hope she knows what she's doing.

Lying in bed this evening, I decided that it really does not pay to saddle oneself with lame ducks, and I do not intend to do so again. In fact, I have no intention of saddling myself with anyone. Beddoes has got the right idea. Play fast and loose; it's the only way.

The London Season is about to burst upon us at any moment and, taking that as a basis, I shall throw myself wholeheartedly into society and live purely for pleasure from now on. Marriage can wait – probably for ever. It brings nothing but unhappiness.

Friday, April 21st

To the opticians to collect my contact lenses. Enormously cheered to find a different fitter in attendance. His breath could not have been fresher. Unfortunately, just as he leaned forward to place the first lens in my eye, I noticed he had something nasty protruding from his left nostril. I do not know which made me feel iller: that or the thought of the quite unnecessary expense.

Saturday, April 22nd

Read a most fascinating article in the paper this morning about Venice. According to its author, unless drastic steps are taken to stop the industrial pollution that is eating away the façades and the very foundations of this beautiful city – and taken very soon – Venice, as we know it, will cease to exist. Ashamed to realize that I do not actually know it at all, and so have decided to get out there as soon as possible to find out for myself what all the fuss is about.

Sunday, April 23rd

St George's Day and the birthday of our greatest poet and dramatist. To be perfectly honest, I have always found Shakespeare's plays rather difficult to follow and wonder if too much isn't made of him altogether.

Monday, April 24th

Rang Hugh Bryant-Fenn re Venice. He is always going over there in his capacity as chairman of the British Carpaccio Society, and has written one or two good articles about the place.

By an odd coincidence he is planning to go himself next week and suggests that I should join him. He says he should be able to get any number of 'freebies', as he calls them, at all the best hotels.

I asked him which of us should get the tickets. 'Oh,' he said, 'I think you had better make your own travel arrangements. I shall probably go as the guest of some airline or other.'

I asked him, half-jokingly, if he couldn't take me along free as his assistant. He told me that would be quite out of the question, but that he'd see I was all right once we got there. I presume this means he will be organizing a 'freebie' for me in one of the hotels he was talking about, but didn't like to ask outright.

Tuesday, April 25th

To my local travel agent to buy my ticket for Venice. The Getaway Weekend comprising return flight, bed and breakfast for three nights in a first-class hotel and free transfers to and from the airport certainly sounds excellent value, but not, of course, if one is being given one's accommodation free anyway, and I settled for just the return air fare.

This evening Jane said if I wasn't doing anything at the weekend, perhaps I might like to go down to Oxted with her. I explained about Venice. She was not quite as impressed as I had hoped.

Wednesday, April 26th

To Hatchards to look for a good guide book on Venice. The *Companion Guide* seems as good value as any. Bumped into Mollie Marsh-Gibbon who announced that Venice was the most overrated tourist trap in Europe.

There appear to be as many opinions about this subject as there are people who give them. Thank goodness I shall soon be in a position to speak upon the matter with some authority.

Friday, April 28th

Woken at the crack of dawn by Bryant-Fenn to say he would not now be able to get away until tomorrow morning, but that if I went to the Hotel Browning and asked for Signor Domenico and mentioned his name, I would be well looked after. We have arranged to meet tomorrow morning at eleven on the Rialto Bridge.

On the plane sat next to a man whose face seemed very familiar, but for the life of me I could not put a name to it. I am normally very good at remembering names. Eventually we got talking, but although I asked him all manner of questions, he left me none the wiser. Finally, I steered the conversation round to the subject of passports and how unrecognizable people were in their photographs. I said, 'I mean, just look at this dreadful picture of me,' and handed my passport to him. Naturally I assumed he would recipro- cate with his, but all he did was look at mine, roar with laughter and hand it back again. Soon after that he went to sleep. The flight seemed never-ending; nor was it made any the shorter by the couple sitting behind me. There was apparently nothing he did not know about Italy, Italian art and Venice. If only she had known *something*, she might have been able to staunch the flow of information that poured from him ceaselessly. At one stage he struck up a conversation in loud, obviously schoolboy Italian, with an Italian family sitting opposite. As we were disembarking, I turned to him and remarked in a loud voice that he was obviously quite an expert on Italy.

'I should be,' he replied, 'I am an Italian and I am bringing my new English bride home to visit my family here in Venice.' He went on to explain that he was a lecturer in Italian art at some college in London, and added that if there was anything he could do for me during my stay, he would be only too delighted. He knew one of the leading hoteliers intimately and would be very happy to show me some of the work that's being carried out on the famous bronze horses on the front of St Mark's. I thanked him and said that I was already being well looked after.

Finally arrived at the Hotel Browning. It had a warm, welcoming look to it, although it was far from de luxe. Asked for Signor Domenico only to be informed that the hotel had recently changed hands and he had gone to Pisa. Mentioned Hugh's name but it meant nothing to the receptionist. However, have decided to stay anyway. It is a little further from the centre than I should have liked, but it is not all that expensive and anyway tomorrow I shall be moving into something a good deal more comfortable with Hugh. It hardly seemed worth unpacking, but I did remove a few valuable items from my case, such as travellers' cheques, passport, wallet, guide book etc., and concealed them beneath the spare blanket in the wardrobe.

Interested to note that the decay is already beginning to work its way indoors. It is particularly noticeable just behind my bed.

Saturday, April 29th

Woken early by sun streaming through tear in curtains. Threw open windows and breathed in morning air. Apart from nasty smell from small canal below, a perfect morning. After breakfast, checked out of hotel, and made my way plus suitcase to Grand Canal where I caught a *vaporetto* to St Mark's Square. No sooner entered St Mark's than I remembered I had left my guide book, cheques, passport, etc.,

'He finally rolled up at ten to one, if you please, dressed in blue sleeveless shirt, shorts and sandals.'

under spare blanket in hotel wardrobe. No time to go all the way back, so rang the manager to ask them to look after it until later. As a result had to cut down visit to Cathedral and Doge's Palace to twenty minutes.

Even so, arrived at Rialto Bridge twenty minutes late. No sign of Hugh. He finally rolled up at ten to one, if you please, dressed in blue sleeveless shirt, shorts and sandals. I don't know why, but sandals always set my teeth on edge, especially when worn with socks. I might have expected Hugh to dress like that abroad, but that did not make them any the more bearable. He offered no explanation or apology for his lateness, but merely announced that it was time for lunch. I asked him where he was planning to take me. He replied that he disliked making plans when travelling and preferred to walk about until he found somewhere that took his fancy. I said that surely, as an old Venice hand, he must know of many good trattorias.

'Not in this part of town,' he snapped.

I suggested that in that case we might just as well go straight to his hotel where I could leave my suitcase and have lunch at the same time.

'Oh,' he said, 'are you turning out of the Browning then?'

I replied that I certainly was and explained why. He appeared quite unconcerned at being so utterly discredited and asked where I was planning to go. I said that, if I had understood him correctly, I would be moving in with him on a complementary basis. He replied that he had had enough trouble fixing himself up without worrying about me as well. I reminded him of all the 'freebies' we had heard so much about. He said, 'If there's one thing I can't stand, it's people who are not prepared to pay for their pleasures.'

Finally ate lunch in a funny little restaurant in a garden. Food excellent, if rather dear. When the bill arrived, Hugh said he couldn't bear fiddling about trying to divide bills into two, so why didn't I deal with this one and he'd pay for dinner.

'I know of a marvellous little place called the Madonna,' he said. 'All the Venetians eat there. The tourists haven't discovered it yet.'

On the way out, bumped into the art historian from the plane and his wife. I told him I'd very much like to take up his offer re the horses. He said he would call me at the hotel as soon as he knew what his plans were.

Afterwards Hugh told me his name was Carlo Mendotti and that he was one of the leading experts on Venetian art. Obviously we are very lucky to be asked, but Hugh said, 'I thought he sounded pretty keen to get out of it, if you ask me.' There is nothing I dislike more than professional jealousy.

Suggested popping in to the Accademia for a quick look at the Tintorettos and Canalettos. Hugh said that the only thing worth seeing there were the Carpaccios, and that anyway the best Carpaccios were in the church of San Giorgio del Schiavoni. 'You can see the Accademia any time,' he added.

I reminded him we had still made no arrangements re my accommodation. He replied, 'If I were you, I'd try and get your room back at the Browning tonight. I should have fixed up a freebie by tomorrow morning.'

Returned to Browning. My room already let, but luckily they were able to give me another, slightly cheaper, and actually I have always rather enjoyed sleeping in attics.

Left suitcase and set off for San Giorgio, but arrived just as they were closing for the night. Returned to Browning via Accademia which was also closed.

Was in the bath when Hugh rang to say he had been asked to dine with some marquesa and we should have to scrap our plans for dinner. In fact rather relieved. In my experience one always finds out so much more about a city on one's own.

Decided to try Madonna anyway. Arrived to find place jammed to the doors with groups of tourists and not a table to be had. In the end, ate a plate of risotto in a modest trattoria, felt rather ill and went to bed early.

My new room may be a little less spacious than last night's but the bed is certainly softer. Unfortunately, kept awake for rather a long time by couple in the next room making love – or possibly playing Italian Scrabble.

Sunday, April 30th

Woken early by gondoliers shouting beneath my window. Another glorious sunny day.

Took the boat out to the island of Torcello for lunch at the famous Locanda Cipriani. Hugh assured me he would be able to change a travellers' cheque there, and that lunch was on him.

Arrived at restaurant in good time. A large room with tables spilling out into the garden. Ours was not exactly in the best position, but certainly not in the worst, and we had a good, if slightly restricted, view of the bottom half of the cathedral campanile.

Had just started on plate of green tagliatelle when Hugh said, 'Hullo,' and Carlo Mendotti and wife walked in and sat at a table near the garden. Finally caught their eye and nodded my head in the continental manner, but obviously they had not seen me after all. But then who sees anyone when one is in love?

Afterwards went across and spoke to them. Hugh said he knew when he was not wanted and disappeared mumbling something about the bill. Carlo full of fascinating information. He said he could remember a time when Torcello was a place for getting away from the tourists, but that these days it was worse than St Mark's Square. I said I quite agreed and that I expected I'd be seeing them again soon. Carlo said, 'Venice is very small. It is difficult to avoid people.'

Disappointed that he made no reference to our visit to the horses. Also that the restaurant refused to change Bryant-Fenn's travellers' cheques. I do not mind coughing up for everything on a temporary basis, but the fact is I am rapidly running out of cash myself. After a hurried visit to the cathedral to look at the mosaics, caught the boat back to Venice, with a view to seeing the Carpaccios in San Giorgio. Disembarked and went straight to nearest café for coffee and ice cream. Suddenly Carlo and his wife appeared from nowhere and sat down at a nearby table. Hugh muttered, 'This is getting downright embarrassing,' and leaping to his feet he marched off down the street.

There was nothing to do but pay the bill and set off after him. Luckily, I don't think the Mendottis saw me. Had words with Hugh, as a result of which we both completely lost our sense of direction and arrived at San Giorgio five minutes after closing time.

Agreed to meet Hugh for dinner at the Colomba at eight-thirty and returned to Browning. Arrived half an hour later to find message from Hugh saying that the manager of his hotel would be delighted to offer me a room for the night at a special reduced rate. Immediately made an excuse about a sick relative, checked out of Browning and set off for Hugh's hotel.

The reception staff made me most welcome and showed me up to a magnificent room with private bathroom on the first floor overlooking the Grand Canal. There was even a large bowl of flowers with the compliments of the management.

Shaved, dressed, picked one of the flowers for my buttonhole and rang Hugh's room. No reply. Surprised to find myself at the restaurant before him. Ordered a nice table for two, a Campari and soda, and waited. An hour later he still had not arrived, so I ordered. By 10.15 I had finished my meal and there was still no sign of him, so I paid my bill and returned to the hotel. Had been sitting in the lounge for half an hour when he walked in looking, I thought, rather tight.

'Where the hell did you get to?' he called out at the top of his voice.

I replied calmly that I had been at the Colomba, as arranged, and more to the point where the hell had *he* got to?

'The Colomba?' he exclaimed. 'I said quite clearly Al Colombo. Too bad. Carlo and his wife were there and invited me to join them. He was absolutely fascinating about Tintoretto and Canaletto. Right up your street.'

I asked him if he had said anything about the horses.

'No,' he said.

May

Monday, May 1st

May Day. An annual reminder of how lucky I was to have
been born in England, and not in Russia.

Woken early by waiter banging on my door by mistake
with someone else's breakfast.

By nine-thirty still no news from Carlo about the horses,
so decided to go sightseeing alone. Arrived at Accademia to
find it was closed all day Monday. Returned to the hotel
around noon meaning to give Bryant-Fenn a piece of my
mind, but he had gone out.

Presented with my bill. Even with the 75 per cent reduction, it came to far more than the Browning. As it was, I
finished up with only 200 lire in my pocket, which meant
that until Hugh paid me back, I would not be able to buy
presents for Jane, etc.

Hugh finally appeared carrying a lot of parcels. 'Oh, there
you are,' he said. 'I've just been to San Giorgio. The
Carpaccios were looking better than ever. You really missed
something.'

I said that, thanks to him, there was scarcely a thing in
Venice that I had *not* missed.

'Oh, I wouldn't say that, old man,' he replied cheerfully.
'If it hadn't been for me, you'd never have had such a cheap
night in this hotel, and you certainly never would have got
to Torcello.' I pointed out that that might well be so, but at
least I'd have had some money left over to do some shopping.

Hugh said, 'If you'd called up this morning before rushing
out, I could have paid you back. I changed a couple of
travellers' cheques last night. As it was, I assumed you were

all right, so I blew the lot on a set of Murano wine glasses. Never mind, I'll write you a cheque in London. Wouldn't want you to be out of pocket.'

I am not a man who bears a grudge, but I simply could not bring myself to speak to him or even look him in the face all the way out to the airport.

In the lounge he offered to buy me a farewell drink. 'Never let it be said that I cannot stand my turn,' he said. Even so, he was short and I had to give him my last 200 lire to make up the difference. Our flight was being called when I felt a tap on my shoulder. Turned to find Carlo and his wife. 'Sorry you couldn't make the horses,' he said. 'They were fascinating.'

I was astounded and said I thought it was all off.

Carlo said, 'But didn't you get my message at the hotel? Hugh assured me last night you would receive it first thing this morning.'

I turned to Hugh for an explanation, but all he said was, 'I've been meaning to remove my custom from that hotel for years. The rooms and the food are marvellous, but the service is terrible.' How fortunate I am not to have to depend on freeloading for my livelihood. It leads only to dissatisfaction and meanness. I shall certainly not travel under similar conditions again.

Tuesday, May 2nd

An astonishing piece of news. Beddoes is to join the European Commission at a salary of £20000 a year, tax free, if you please. He takes up his new post in Brussels in the middle of June. He announced this when he got in from the office this evening. Naturally I said that I was very pleased for him and offered him my warmest congratulations – although frankly I should have thought that the sum total of his knowledge of the Common Market, not to say foreign languages, could be jotted down on the back of a postage stamp.

A more pressing worry, however, is what will happen to the flat? Jane and I certainly could not afford to keep it up on our own, and I do not relish the prospect of sharing it with people we do not know. The first week of May should bring with it a prospect of blue skies and warm days; instead all I can see ahead are the black clouds and cold winds of uncertainty.

Is it my imagination, or did I read somewhere that there is a thriving market for blue movies in Belgium?

Wednesday, May 3rd

Is it any wonder people are so depressed these days? Set off at lunchtime to buy a birthday present for my nephew who is seven on Saturday. With James Joyce for a name, what else could one give him but books?

In the bookshop near the office I was confronted by an eager young assistant with a moustache. I told him that I was looking for Arthur Ransome.

'Does he work here?' the young man enquired.

I told him no, Arthur Ransome, the author.

'What sort of things does he write, sir?' he asked.

At first I assumed he was trying to be funny. However, it soon became clear that, despite my mentioning some of the better-known titles and a brief résumé of the plot of *Pigeon Post*, he had never heard of either the author or the books. Finally, between us, we succeeded in locating a shelf full of Ransomes, and I chose *Winter Holiday* and *The Picts and the Martyrs*. As he was wrapping them, he confessed that today was his first day in the shop and that anyway he was there only on a temporary basis.

I asked him what he did normally and he told me he was studying at the Open University.

'What subject?' I asked him.

'English literature,' he replied.

I was sorely tempted to ask him if he had ever heard of William Wordsworth, but felt I had probably made my point sufficiently strongly already.

Thursday, May 4th

To drinks at the Pedalows'. In view of Tim's gross mishandling of my portfolio, I had made up my mind not to go – a decision I knew I should have stuck to the moment I set foot through the front door. What Vanessa had described gaily as 'a few close friends' turned out to be half the stock exchange.

Tim thrust a glass of champagne in my hand with the instruction to 'go on up', and disappeared into the arms of a tall, rather common-looking blonde towing an even taller man in Gucci shoes and hair that curled under his ears.

Made my way up the stairs to the sitting room on the first floor, to be faced by a large room jammed to the door with shouting, smoking party-goers. The couple near the door stared at me coldly. I took one look, turned, and walked quickly downstairs to the dining room, which by now was as full as the sitting room. An arm in a white sleeve reached out with a champagne bottle and attempted to refill my glass. I waved it away impatiently and a voice said, 'You're getting very grand in your old age, aren't you?'

Turned to find the waiter grinning at me in a knowing sort of way. I was in no mood for badinage with the staff and frowned at him coldly.

'You don't recognize me, do you?' the waiter said.

I confessed that I did not.

'School House?' he said. 'Togger's Room? 1955?'

It still meant nothing to me, and I shook my head.

'You must remember,' he said. 'Maddocks, C. M.'

I said, 'Not Wanker Maddocks?'

His face positively lit up at this and he said, 'I knew it would all come back eventually.'

It didn't, as a matter of fact, since as far as I could recall he had been in a quite different set from me at school and I had barely exchanged two words with him the whole time we were there. Even so, it did not particularly surprise me that he should be a waiter at a party where I was a guest. I decided to cut the conversation short by telling him that if he stuck at it he'd probably do very well one day.

'Oh, I'm doing quite well already,' he replied. 'I very rarely take home less than three hundred a week.'

I was so taken aback I could hardly speak.

'Do you ever go back to the school?' he enquired.

I said that, as far as I was concerned, a man who kept returning to the scenes of his childhood was unlikely ever to get on in the world. Maddocks said, 'I wouldn't know about that. I cater for all the Old Boys' Dinners now, and I clear enough from them to pay for a month's holiday in Barbados every year.'

He then handed me a business card saying, 'You might be very glad of this one of these days,' and made off into the crowd brandishing his champagne bottle. Now I come to think about it, he was reputed in Togger's to have been half Jewish, if not wholly so.

Friday, May 5th

My birthday. I can hardly believe I am thirty-six. I do not feel a day over twenty.

Cards from mother, Nigel and Priscilla, Mollie Marsh-Gibbon, and Mrs Veal.

Jane, looking quite attractive for once, gave me a scarf which she had knitted herself. I was quite touched and asked her to have dinner with me. She accepted immediately.

Beddoes strolled in smoking a cigar and threw a small parcel into my lap saying, 'Many happy returns, matey.'

It was a pack of playing cards with a couple on the reverse side involved in a series of sexual acts. If you arrange the cards in a certain order and then flick them, the couple perform as though in a film.

The man involved was unrecognizable, but just for fun I asked Beddoes if this was by way of being a personal show reel. However, he did not rise to the bait so I let the matter drop.

As he was leaving he said, 'Oh, by the way, this is also for you. It came while you were away.' And he tossed another small parcel on to the table.

I opened it up to find inside a pair of plastic bloomers plus a leaflet which explained that if you inflate them and then do a number of prescribed exercises in them, 'You will see the inches literally melting away from your waist and hips.'

I detect the hand of Armitage in this.

Had planned to confront him with them, but then he and the others in the office invited me out for a celebratory lunchtime drink at the Stoat and Anvil, so had to postpone it. As it turned out, he spoiled the whole occasion by getting tight and trying to persuade all the other customers to join in singing 'Happy Birthday to You'. But then, of course, if you're the chairman's nephew you can get away with any-thing.

To dinner with Jane at the San Sebastiano off Beauchamp Place. Aside from bumping into Armitage, a most promising start to my thirty-seventh year, and to the renaissance of our romance.

Saturday, May 6th

After breakfast, locked my bedroom door and tried on the plastic pants. Blew them up with special hand pump and had just embarked on first exercise when Jane called out that Tim was on the phone. I threw my dressing gown on and hurried into the sitting room. Jane there drinking coffee and reading the *Express*.

Tim unusually agitated. It appears that on a recent business trip to Germany, he started up a passionate affair with a blonde typist from Hamburg. He is keen to continue the relationship by letter and has suggested to her that she write to him c/o my flat. I was so astonished that I fell back into the nearest armchair.

Stupidly, I had clean forgotten the inflated plastic pants which exploded with a loud report, causing Jane to tip coffee all over herself and Beddoes to come rushing in, stark naked, thinking someone had been shot. I could hear Tim's voice calling out, 'What's happening, what's happening?'

I shouted back, 'I've finally exploded,' and put down the phone.

I am still very much in two minds what to say to Tim. One thing I do know: there is no danger of my ever becoming a sexual deviant – at least in plastic.

Sunday, May 7th

On a whim, decided to drive down to my old school. Terrible traffic in south London, and arrived only just in time for Maters. Was parking in Pegram's Piece when I realized with a shock that this was the first time I had been back in seventeen years. It felt most peculiar walking into chapel in a double-breasted suit without having to worry about how many buttons I had done up. Service most disappointing. Singing very thin and ragged compared with my day. Tried to set an example by shouting out the descants in 'Guide Me, O Thou Great Redeemer', as we always used to do, only to discover that I was absolutely on my own. The whole school turned round and stared at me. I have never felt such a fool in my life. Sermon by Head Magister similarly second-rate.

Afterwards bumped into Dickie Dunmow, of all people, in Apthorpe's Bottom. Went straight up and introduced myself. At first he had difficulty placing me, but then he remembered me absolutely and said that I might be interested to know that my record for the lowest mark ever achieved in A-level Latin verse still stood. He asked me what I was up to now and when I told him, he said gloomily, 'No more than I would have predicted, and no less.'

I should have known it's always a great mistake to go back, and I decided the time had come to return to London For old times' sake, exercised my privilege of strolling across the grass in Upper Bummers with my hands in my pockets, as I had done countless times on my way to Sunday Refec. Was halfway across, reflecting dreamily on the old days, when I heard a voice calling out, 'Excuse me, but visitors are not allowed on the grass.'

Turned to see a Top Swine striding towards me, his blue gown flapping behind him. I pointed out that as an OF who had in his time been a Top Swine, a Swotbag *and* in the Upper Sixth, the term 'visitor' was hardly applicable. The boy said, in an insolent tone of voice, 'Well, you're not any of those things now, are you?'

For two pins I'd have boxed his ears, but I kept my temper and pointed out that he obviously knew nothing of Common Law under which a privilege, once granted, can never be removed. The boy replied that, as a matter of fact, he had been taking Law as an optional second subject instead of Estate Agency for the last two years, and he had never come across anything like that in his textbooks. He then suggested that I might perhaps like to discuss the matter further with the Head Magister.

I had better things to do than waste my time on such infantile argy-bargy, and, giving him a cold stare, I walked away towards my car in dignified silence. Nevertheless, I have no intention of letting the school get away with it scot free, and this evening I wrote a stiff letter to the Secretary of the OF Society cancelling my membership, my free copy of the School mag, and my standing order for the New Bilge Lab Fund. I also tore up Wanker Maddocks's visiting card into small pieces and threw them into the waste-paper basket.

Monday, May 8th

Thirty-three years ago the German High Command surrendered to Field Marshal Montgomery at Lüneberg Heath. It seems scarcely credible. I never actually met Monty personally, although I did once see him at Windsor at the Garter ceremony for which Auntie Bettie had managed to get us tickets. Although not physically large, he gave the impression of being a big man in every sense of the word. He was often accused of being a cold, rather remote figure. I must say, that was not my experience at all; rather the contrary. I remember that when I called out, 'Good old Monty,' he broke off a conversation he was having with Winston and looked straight at me. And although I would not go so far as to say that he actually smiled, there was no doubt whatever about the keen personal interest he took in people from quite different walks of life from his own. I miss him.

Tuesday, May 9th

Whether it was the memories of the great Allied victory that preoccupied my thoughts yesterday or what, I do not know, but the fact is that I have had the strangest feeling all today that something important and momentous is about to happen to me. And yet it has turned out to be one of the dullest and most uneventful days I can remember for a very long time.

Wednesday, May 10th

The morning post brings a letter addressed to Tim Pedalow and bearing a German stamp. I have been giving this matter a certain amount of serious thought in the last few days, and while I am far from happy at the idea of acting as a private *poste restante* for the furtherance of Tim's extra-marital sexual liaisons, I have known him for very much longer than I have known Vanessa, and therefore I suppose that my loyalties should be more towards him than towards her. Besides, I daresay it's all fairly harmless.

Rang Tim who rushed in on his way home from the office, tore open the letter and sat on the edge of my bed wearing as silly an expression as I have seen on a grown man in a long time. He read it through no less than three times, then said he thought it would be better if I were to keep all the letters here for the time being. I told him he was a swine, to which he replied, 'I know. Don't you wish you were one, too?'

I replied that I wished for nothing less and that, in my view, if one really loved a woman, one did not gad about with bits on the side. Tim said, 'That's the trouble with all bachelors. They're hopeless idealists. Show me a man who has stayed faithful to his wife through the years, and I will show you a man who is sexually impotent.'

I was speechless.

As he was leaving, he said, 'Don't worry. I'll make it worth your while.'

I was sorely tempted to remind him that the last time he said that, he lost me £420, but really what is the point in trying to reason with those sort of people? Even so, his remarks have set me thinking again about the advisability of tying myself up permanently with Jane. But as things stand, what is the alternative?

Thursday, May 11th

When I take stock in years to come, today will, without any question, stand out as the happiest and most momentous of my life. I still cannot quite believe my good fortune. Arrived at the Varney-Birches' dinner party rather late to find everyone already at table and halfway through the artichoke soup. Took my seat, rather hot and flustered, turned to the girl on my left to apologize, and found myself face to face with the love of my life.

Her name is Amanda Trubshawe, and she is not only very beautiful, but she happens to be the daughter, no less, of my chairman, and Armitage's uncle, Derek Trubshawe. The coincidence is too extraordinary for words. Even more extraordinary is the very idea that this exquisite creature of eighteen with her round, childlike face, enormous green eyes, and her long slim legs should be even remotely related to Armitage – let alone his first cousin.

I could not take my eyes off her all evening, nor she off me, and as far as I can remember, neither of us exchanged a single word with anyone else.

As I was waiting in the hall afterwards for Amanda to collect her coat prior to driving her home, Nan Varney-Birch came up and said, 'Normally I charge ten per cent for this kind of service, but you two looked so sweet, I'll only charge you five.'

I laughed, but secretly thought her rather common.

Obviously it was quite out of the question to take Amanda back to the flat for coffee. However, she seemed perfectly content to be driven straight home. I said that I imagined she had to be up early in the morning for work. She replied, 'Oh, I don't work. I'm doing the Season.'

I said, 'How extraordinary, so am I. Let's do it together.'

And she laughed and said, 'Yes, let's.'

The Trubshawes live in an enormous house in The Boltons. Amanda said she would have asked me in for a drink, only her father always sets the burglar alarms at eleven. I laughed and said I didn't mind at all, and we kissed.

As she was getting out of the car, she said, 'I hope you don't mind my mentioning it, but either your suit needs cleaning, or else there's a very peculiar smell in this car.'

I apologized and assured her I would be changing the car any day now – for a company car, a more ambitious man might have thought to himself as he drove away. But then very few men are lucky enough to be as much in love as I am.

Friday, May 12th

Lay awake most of last night thinking alternately about Amanda, and poor old Jane. There's no doubt she has been making quite a play for me recently, and I could not bear to hurt her feelings. Slept fitfully and woke exhausted just before seven. Determined to tell Jane at the earliest opportunity. However, when she appeared at breakfast, she had so obviously made a special effort with her clothes and make-up, that I hadn't the heart to say anything. Another letter arrived for Tim from Germany. What a sordid business it all seems suddenly.

If only he had had the good fortune to marry a girl like Amanda, he would never have been forced to resort to this kind of cheap subterfuge. I feel sorry for him. Almost said something to Armitage about having met his cousin last night, but checked myself at the last moment.

Knowing him, he would almost certainly have found a way of using the information as a rod to beat my back. Stayed in all evening half hoping Amanda might ring, but no such luck. I would have rung her myself, but do not wish to appear too keen. To bed early with the *Evening Standard* and an apple.

Saturday May 13th

Blew my nose so hard this morning I made it bleed. Rinsed the handkerchief immediately in cold water, but the stain had still not entirely disappeared, so popped it into a saucepan with some bleach to soak. Phone rang soon afterwards. It was Amanda inviting me to dine there this evening with her parents. My heart was beating so hard with the excitement that I felt sure she must have heard it on the other end of the line. Needless to say, accepted at once, and hurried out to buy Mrs Trubshawe some flowers.

Skipped along the street like a mad thing, singing and waving at everyone who passed. So anxious to share my happiness with others that, as I was overtaking one man, I gave him a cheery slap on the back. What I did not realize until too late was that he was carrying an enormous parcel of shopping, which he promptly dropped, spilling groceries and vegetables all over the pavement. I was sorry he chose to take it quite so badly.

Arrived back in the flat rather later than expected with a huge bunch of mixed roses. Went to deal with my handkerchief only to discover that it had dissolved into a mass of holes, at the same time making a funny mark on the bottom of the saucepan. Cleaned it out as best I could and made a mental note not to use that one for cooking. Noticed later that Beddoes used it for scrambled eggs, but said nothing. Car decided to pick this evening, of all evenings, to let me down, so forced to resort to a taxi.

Arrived at The Boltons to discover I had come out without any money. Nasty scene with the taxi driver who got very hot under the collar and called me all the names under the sun.

'You're all the same, you lot,' he shouted, gesturing

towards the Trubshawes' front door. 'Honesty's just a word to you.'

I pretended to be a total stranger to the neighbourhood and eventually he drove off grumbling and swearing. Try as I might, I simply cannot find it in my heart to like the working classes. Amanda met me at the door looking enchanting in blue, and took me through to the sitting room where she introduced me to her parents.

The chairman, a large, craggy man, said, 'We haven't met,' which was true. Indeed he seemed scarcely aware of my existence within the organization. When I reminded him I was in Armitage's group he said, 'I'm sorry to hear that.'

I said that I had understood that his nephew was doing very well.

'If you believe that,' he grunted, 'you'll believe anything.'

So astonished was I that I almost forgot to say good evening to Mrs Trubshawe who was seated in a large, squashy armchair by the fireplace. She was much younger than I had expected and in many ways just as attractive as her daughter.

I happened to notice she was wearing a rather unusual pair of lace-up boots and said I had never seen anything quite like them before.

Amanda said, 'They're a form of surgical boot. Mummy has to wear them for support. She broke her leg very badly last Christmas running for a taxi outside Peter Jones.'

I apologized for my tactlessness and said I was quite sure she had recovered by now.

'I haven't, as a matter of fact,' she said. 'Hence these hideous boots.'

Dinner was a simple affair: smoked salmon, tournedos Rossini, raspberries and cream, with Krug '66 and Château Mouton Rothschild, served by two oriental women in black frocks and white aprons. The Trubshawes asked me a number of personal questions, relating to my family and education.

On hearing that I was up at Oxford in the mid-sixties, they enquired if I had known someone called Arthur Croucher. I replied that I had not, but that with a splendidly Dickensian sounding name like that, he should go far. Enid Trubshawe said that was hardly likely since he was the only son of their dearest friends and had been killed in a car accident in Spain ten years ago.

Fortunately, things began to look up slightly when I mentioned my interest in the theatre. The chairman said, 'My wife likes to go. I normally get enough theatre during the day to last me for weeks.'

Enid asked me what playwrights I particularly admired. I thought for a while and finally said, 'Alan Bennett.'

The chairman grunted and said, 'Bennett, eh?'

It was difficult to tell from his tone of voice whether my answer had been very good or very bad.

Afterwards Amanda and her mother disappeared to make the coffee and the chairman took me into his study where he asked me a number of searching questions about the work of my group and the Barford project in particular. He then offered me a glass of his best brandy.

As I was leaving, Amanda said, 'They really like you.'

I said, 'Are you sure?'

She said, 'Yes, but not half as much as I do.'

I danced all the way home, swinging on the lamp-posts.

Sunday, May 14th

Hugh Bryant-Fenn called round this morning to say he had a couple of free press passes to the Chelsea Flower Show tomorrow, if I was interested. I certainly am.

Every year I see those tents going up in Royal Hospital Gardens, and every year I promise myself I will go, but somehow I never seem to get round to it.

As Hugh himself pointed out, not only are the flowers at their freshest on the Monday, but it is traditionally the day on which the Queen pays a visit – presumably to plan her famous herbaceous border at the Palace.

Not that I would expect to meet her personally, but you can never tell with the Royal Family. They are becoming more relaxed and informal by the day. At all events, it is not everyone who is afforded the opportunity to launch into the London Season in such an auspicious manner.

Told Beddoes who said, 'What do you want to waste your time there for? You don't even have a window box.'

I tapped the side of my nose and said, 'I may have considerably more than a window box before long.'

Naturally he wanted to know what I meant by that, but I said, 'Never you mind,' and left him to stew in his own juice.

I cannot help feeling that he is unlikely to get far in Brussels if he does not take drastic steps to curb his tongue. I understand that tact and decorum are very much the key words in the social life of the Commission.

Rang Amanda to invite her to Chelsea with me tomorrow, but unfortunately she had promised to go with her parents on Tuesday which is the Society Day, whatever that may mean.

Wrote a long and, I think, rather witty thank-you letter to the Trubshawes. Must remember to post it tomorrow.

Monday, May 15th

To Chelsea by taxi at four. I do not think I have been inside a tent of such proportions since I last went to Bertram Mills's Circus as a small boy.

The arrangement around the memorial column in the centre was particularly impressive. None of the exhibitors' names meant anything to me. Not that it mattered. I simply wandered about as the mood took me, smelling a rose here, admiring a rockery there, as I would in somebody's private garden.

Surprised to find workmen still busy constructing some of the stands. Also many fewer people than I had expected for the opening day. Commented on this to one of the rose growers who told me that it was only press day, and that it is tomorrow that all the nobs come.

I said that if Her Majesty wasn't a nob, I'd like to know who was, and enquired casually if she'd been yet. 'She always comes at five-thirty sharp,' he told me. 'That's why everyone's rushing to get their stands finished.' Could not help congratulating myself on having timed my own visit to coincide with the Royal Party's, and set off to look at some greenhouses.

Bumped into Philippe de Grande-Hauteville who said, 'I suppose you must be covering this for the Beeb.' Bloody fool.

Was on my way back into the tent when an official stepped forward and asked me to leave. I pointed out that I was not just any old passer-by off the street but an official member of the press, and I showed him my invitation. 'I don't care if you're Lord Beaverbrook,' he said. 'The rule is that everyone has to be out of here before the Queen arrives, and that means everyone, sunshine.'

I said that I could perfectly well understand Her Majesty wishing her visit to be of a private nature, but that I could not help thinking how distressed she would be to hear that members of the public, not to say the press, were treated with such discourtesy on her behalf. 'If that's all she has to worry about this week,' the official said, 'she can count herself lucky.'

I somehow managed to control my temper, but unfortunately in doing so gave myself another nasty nosebleed.

Walked up to Peter Jones to buy some handkerchiefs and browse round Smith's for half an hour before catching the 19 bus down the King's Road.

Immediately became stuck in the most appalling traffic jam. When I complained to the conductor, he said, 'What can you expect when the Queen goes to Chelsea in the middle of the rush hour?'

I'm not blaming Her Majesty, but it is incidents like this that cause one to wonder if the monarchy is not more trouble than it is worth.

The moment I got home, I jotted down a verbatim account of both incidents and penned a stiff letter on the subject to *The Times*. I have a feeling it could stir up quite a controversy.

Nose still bleeding slightly.

Tuesday, May 16th

Mollie Marsh-Gibbon rang to say she had a spare guest ticket for Chelsea, if I was interested. I described my previous day's experience and said I was not surprised the London Season had declined if that was the sort of treatment one could expect.

'My dear fellow,' she shrieked, 'for one thing Chelsea has never been considered part of the Season; the Academy Exhibition is traditionally the opening event. And secondly, what can you expect if you will go on Press Day? Half the stands are still being built, the place is swarming with half-naked workmen and seedy photographers, and the flowers are only half out. The point is, the whole thing is geared to today when all the members of the RHS go, not to the Queen.'

I daresay Mollie is right. She usually is, which is maddening. Even so, I sometimes wonder if she has a good word to say for anyone.

Have not blown nose all day, and nose-bleed quite cleared up.

Wednesday, May 17th

Quite without thinking, gave nose hard blow on waking up, with disastrous results. Two more letters have arrived from Germany – a bitter reminder that I still have not broken the news to Jane about Amanda. Oddly enough, she has never looked more cheerful, and when I said how sorry I was not to have seen much of her lately, she seemed remarkably unconcerned. No sign of my letter yet in *The Times*.

Thursday, May 18th

Unable to find a clean handkerchief anywhere, so had to set off to work without one – a thing I have not done for many years. I felt as uncomfortable as if I had gone to the office without any underpants. Not that I have ever gone to the office without my underpants, or anywhere else for that matter – although I understand there are people who do.

Friday, May 19th

By a curious coincidence, my rash has suddenly taken it into its head to return. Whether this is due, in some psychological way, to my thinking about not wearing underpants yesterday, or simply because of the unusually warm weather, I do not know. At all events, it is extremely irritating, in every sense of the word.

So, too, is the non-appearance of my letter in *The Times*.

Saturday, May 20th

Have been feeling rather faint and dizzy all day – probably as a result of losing so much blood. It has hardly been the most propitious start to the Season. However, I would rather be physically below par than mentally – which is what Tim obviously is. He arrived this morning to collect the latest outpourings from his Teutonic paramour, and announced that he had decided to take all the letters home with him. I asked him if this was really wise to which he replied, 'If we all confined ourselves only to what is wise, nothing would ever get done in this world.'

I said that considering I had risked, and very nearly lost, £500 at his hands, that remark was singularly ill-advised. He replied, 'Pah. What's five hundred these days?'

I told him a great deal to some people, and that he need not expect me to risk my good name, or my savings, on his behalf again in a hurry. He left without another word.

After tea, while soaking handkerchiefs, wrote a stiff note to the editor of *The Times*, reminding him of the public's enormous interest in all matters relating to the Royal Family, and drawing his attention to my letter of the 15th.

Sunday, May 21st

Vanessa rang after breakfast to say that she had just found Tim's letters in a box under the bed, and that not only was she leaving Tim, but she never wanted to speak to me again as long as she lived.

I attempted to defend myself but found I was speaking into a dead telephone.

Was so angry and upset I simply could not bring myself to have a heart to heart with Jane this evening, as I had planned. As it happened, she went out anyway. She always seems to be going out these days.

On the subject of letters, I am reminded that I never actually heard that I had *not* won the Wildlife Game. What a joy to have some clean handkerchiefs at last.

Monday, May 22nd

To the Royal Academy with Amanda for the opening day of the Summer Exhibition. The Season is well and truly under way at last, and despite everything that has happened in the last few days, I could not be more cheerful.

It's extraordinary to think that in all the years I have lived

'. . . to my astonishment found myself face to face with a
portrait of Dickie Dunmow, of all people.'

in London, I have never actually set foot inside the Academy. Every year I plan to go to the Summer Exhibition, and every year they take it off before I have had the chance to get round to it. I daresay it's a problem many busy people experience. Still, better not to go at all than rush off willy-nilly to absolutely everything that comes on, like some people I know.

Entrance hall swarming with people. Surprised and disappointed not to recognize any famous society faces in the crowd. Also surprised that the so-called security men did not give us a second glance as we entered the building. Just because neither of us was carrying a brief case or a carrier bag did not mean that we could not have been concealing a bread knife or a razor blade somewhere about our persons. After what happened to Rembrandt's 'Night Watch' in the Rijks-museum in Amsterdam, you'd have thought they'd have learned their lesson.

Paused briefly at the top of the stairs where they were selling catalogues, but did not bother to buy one myself. If a painting is not immediately self-explanatory, it is probably not worth bothering about anyway.

Amanda, I am glad to say, is of the same opinion. Entered the first room and to my astonishment found myself face to face with a portrait of Dickie Dunmow, of all people. The artist's name meant nothing to me, but I must congratulate him on achieving an excellent likeness, especially from a distance.

I was only sorry to see that it was not for sale, otherwise I might have been tempted to purchase it myself. Realizing that the man standing beside me was also admiring the portrait, I said to him, 'It may interest you to know that that man was my Latin beak at school.'

He stared at me for a moment, said something in a foreign language, and walked away. I simply do not understand why foreigners bother to come to traditional English events like the Summer Exhibition if they have not the slightest interest in learning about the English way of life.

At one point listened to two middle-aged women in hats discussing a picture and distinctly heard one of them say, 'In a way it's rather like going to see *Electra*. If you're not up in Sophocles, you probably won't understand the half of it.' The painting under debate was a self-portrait of a naked man standing in front of a bedroom mirror. Two women could be seen out of the window, gardening. The only thing I could not understand was why, on a nice sunny day, the painter was not out there in the fresh air with them instead of fiddling about indoors.

Very disappointed by the depressingly low standard of dress of most of the people present. Few of the men were wearing ties and many of the women actually had on T-shirts and jeans. I felt positively over-dressed in my pin-stripe suit.

We can only hope for better things at Ascot.

Tuesday, May 23rd

Was describing my experiences at the Academy to Sarah over coffee this morning when Armitage marched in and said that if it was big hats and social chit-chat I was after, I should have gone to the Private View Day, which was last Thursday. Since I have been quite unable to take anything Armitage says seriously after the recent conversation with his uncle, I merely ignored him and left the room.

Enid Trubshawe rang in the afternoon to thank me for the unexpected letter describing my experiences at the Chelsea Flower Show, and to ask me to the theatre tomorrow night. I was so dumb-struck on both counts that I completely forgot to ask what the play was. Wondered about dropping a line to the editor of *The Times* explaining that there had been a mix-up in the letters, but finally decided we both have enough on our plates as it is.

Wednesday, May 24th

Arrived at The Boltons in good time for a drink, as instructed. No sign of Amanda or the chairman. When I remarked on this, Enid said coolly, 'It's just the two of us. I hope you're not one of these people who has old-fashioned scruples about going out alone with married women.'

I replied that I had for some reason expected a small party. She laughed lightly and said, 'How sweet. I do believe you're blushing.'

Frankly I was beginning to feel rather uncomfortable at the somewhat suggestive tone of the conversation, and pointed out that if we wanted to be at the Lyric in time for the curtain, we had better go.

I remember very little of the play or of our supper afterwards at the Ivy, except that I had the impression Enid touched me on the arm rather more often than was necessary, and on one or two occasions deliberately pressed her leg against mine under the table. We arrived back at The Boltons at midnight to find the chairman still not back from his business dinner and Amanda still out at her girls' bridge party. Naturally, I did not wish to be caught in a compromising situation; on the other hand, it is never advisable to give a frustrated middle-aged woman the cold shoulder. In the end settled for a neat compromise by announcing that I had to be up early for a meeting and kissing her on the hand.

She said, 'I think that, under the circumstances, a chaste kiss on the cheek might be more in order.'

I had no alternative but to oblige.

On my way home in the taxi, I found myself thinking more and more about the phrase 'under the circumstances'. What precisely did she mean by this? Was she referring to my friendship with Amanda and looking forward to the time when she would be my mother-in-law? Was she perhaps in the habit of being taken to the theatre by young men and being kissed afterwards on the sofa? Or was she simply implying that some sort of relationship between us had been set in motion? And, if so, where does that leave me *vis-à-vis* Amanda? Am I expected to carry on with the two of them at the same time, or are the Trubshawes one of these sexy families one reads about for whom anything goes?

My head is in a complete whirl, and matters are not helped by the realization that in fact I am as attracted to Enid as I am to her daughter, if not more so.

How difficult these affairs of the heart can be. One sometimes wonders if they are not more trouble than they're worth.

Thursday, May 25th

Hugh Bryant-Fenn rang almost as soon as I got in this morning and said in a facetious tone of voice, 'Who was that lady I saw you with last night?'

I replied that I hadn't the faintest idea what he was talking about. 'Don't be silly,' he said. 'That gorgeous older number you were being so intimate with in the dress circle of the Lyric.'

His suggestive manner, combined with the fact that he had still made no effort to repay me the money I lent him in Venice, made my hackles rise, and I told him sharply that if it was any business of his she was my aunt up from Leighton Buzzard for the day.

Hugh laughed and said, 'Aunt, my big toe. Aunts don't look at nephews like that.'

I replied that I was not in the habit of discussing my private affairs with people who owed me money, and put the phone down on him.

Armitage looked in a couple of times, but I pretended I was too busy to speak to him. He seemed to me to have a peculiarly crafty look on his face that I have not noticed before. Does he know something?

Not a word all day from Amanda. Does she know something? The only person who certainly knows nothing is the unfortunate Jane.

This evening Beddoes made a coarse joke about a Negro and a ship's captain which I did not get. He tells me he is to start taking evening classes in French on Monday, which I suppose is something to be thankful for.

Friday, May 26th

Now the cat is really out of the bag. Was working on the revised Barford figures this morning when Armitage walked in, threw a newspaper down on my desk with the words, 'You're for the high jump now,' and marched out again.

The paper was open at the gossip column. Ran my eyes quickly over the various items but could find nothing that concerned me. Finally, my eye was caught by a brief paragraph at the bottom of the page, which read:

Is the rather continental fashion of young men squiring older women around town beginning to make a comeback after all these years? Eligible marketing executive, Simon Cusp, 36, who was seen in intimate conversation with Mrs Enid Trubshawe last night at the Ivy, once London's most fashionable after-theatre supper place, had a strangely pre-war look about him. Mrs Trubshawe, 46, wife of Harley Preston chairman, and sometime Conservative candidate, Derek Trubshawe, was formerly musical comedy actress Enid Trehearne, which perhaps accounts for her old-fashioned theatrical tastes.

I had often wondered what it feels like to achieve sudden overnight fame, but had never dreamed of it happening in quite this way. Needless to say, I was shocked and horrified at the appalling implications.

Obviously my career is in ruins.

My romance with Amanda is at an end, as are any chances I might have from now on of making a good marriage. My friends will never let me hear the end of it, and it may be many months before I can go down to Kent again.

On the other hand, I must admit that I am rather excited at being mentioned in such a famous gossip column and am only sorry that they spelt my name wrong.

Decided to adopt the tactics traditionally employed by those involved in scandals, and disappeared – firstly into a pub unfrequented by people from the office and thence into the dark anonymity of the Academy Cinema. Unfortunately realized too late that they were showing *Les Enfants du Paradis* which I have seen three times and have never much cared for anyway.

Stayed in all evening, but although the phone rang several times, not once was it for me. I daresay the Trubshawe family is suffering enough agony as it is without my adding to it. Quite unable to concentrate on any TV programme, so tidied my room instead. Found myself looking at my possessions as if for the last time.

Saturday, May 27th

Have always believed that the best form of defence is attack, so after breakfast took my courage in both hands and rang the Trubshawes. Enid answered. She sounded strained and tired – quite unlike her usual bubbling self. I said, 'I have been thinking things over and have decided to go abroad for a while.'

There was a long pause from the other end and then the voice said, 'I see. Well, they're all away for the weekend, too.

On the Hamble. I'll tell them when they get back tomorrow, shall I?'

I told whoever it was that it didn't matter and rang off. Spent the rest of the day in an agony of doubt and self-reproach. Jane seemed at a loose end, too, for once and under the circumstances decided I had nothing to lose by asking her out to dinner and did so.

I was surprised that, having made such an effort with her appearance over the last week or so, she seemed to have made almost none this evening. But then it was not as though we were going to the Savoy – or the Ivy.

Sunday, May 28th

Woke this morning with a terrible pain in my chest. Thought at first I might have suffered a mild heart attack but decided it was probably only indigestion.

I have finally come to the conclusion that I do not like Indian food.

Read the papers in a desultory way and walked in Holland Park with Jane. Saw a dog that reminded me very much of the Trubshawes' West Highland. Bent down to stroke its head and it bit me on the hand quite sharply.

As if mental pain were not enough.

Monday, May 29th

The call came at last at half-past ten. As I was going up to the fourteenth floor in the lift, I reflected how ironical it was that the only time I should set foot in the chairman's office was in order to be asked to leave.

And to think that less than a week ago he was well on his way to becoming my father-in-law.

Under the circumstances he seemed remarkably cheerful. Before I could utter a word, he said, 'I've been thinking things over at the weekend and have come to the conclusion that the best answer would be to shovel Colin off into Merchandising Development and move you up to Assistant Group Head. That way, no one's going to get shirty.'

I was struck literally dumb for a moment or two and

stared at him in amazement. He asked me if I had any objections. Obviously he knew nothing of my relationship with his wife or of the newspaper item. I decided that there was no point in trying to pull the wool over his eyes any further. I said, 'I think I should tell you, sir, that your wife and I have struck up a relationship.'

'I should hope so, too. My wife is a very warm and open woman.'

I said, 'I am sure she is, sir, but I do not think you quite understand. On Wednesday night she and I went to the theatre alone and dined afterwards at the Ivy.'

'Excellent,' he exclaimed. 'I hope you had a good time. As I told you, I do not care for the theatre myself, and I am delighted that you enjoy it as much as she does. If you do become a member of the family one of these days, as seems likely, I'm sure there will be many opportunities for all three of you to go together.'

I could hardly believe my ears. Promotion and a virtual offer of marriage in one day. It was almost too much to take in at one go.

Even so, I felt it my duty to explain about the newspaper item, but all he said was, 'My wife still enjoys a little publicity from time to time. It wouldn't surprise me to learn that she'd rung up the paper herself.'

As I stood up to leave, my feet seemed scarcely to be touching the carpet, so intoxicating was my sense of relief and happiness. And as if that were not enough, he then asked me to join them all in their villa near Antibes on Saturday for a couple of weeks. Arrived back in the office to find Armitage emptying his desk. He seemed quite defeated and for once I actually felt quite sorry for him.

Tuesday, May 30th

Unable to keep the news to myself any longer and told Beddoes quietly this evening of my good fortune. All he said was, 'Good. Perhaps now you can get on and find yourself a few decent mistresses.' I simply cannot imagine how I can have lived with him for all these years, and can only thank heaven that I shall not be doing so any longer.

Found myself alone in the flat with Jane for the first time in days and so was able finally to break the news to her. She said, 'I'm so glad. I hope you'll be as happy with her as I am with Colin Armitage.'

For the first time in my life, I was completely stuck for words.

June

Thursday, June 1st

Unable to get any serious work done all morning for reflecting on my future and the strange way life has of taking one completely unawares. One moment everything looks as black as it could be, and the next thing you know, the clouds have dispersed and all is sweetness and light. Less than a week ago, I seemed to be a man without any prospects, and now suddenly I am poised to make my mark on the world in no uncertain terms.

The way ahead is clear at last.

Friday, June 2nd

The twenty-fifth anniversary of the Queen's Coronation, and a red letter day for me, too, since today I officially take up my position as Assistant Group Head with special responsibility for the Barford project. I have also decided to discontinue my diary. Obviously, from now on I shall have neither the time nor the need for introspection, and my mind will doubtless be occupied with more important matters than the trivial activities of my friends and acquaintances.

Amanda rang after lunch from Antibes to say that she and her father had decided at her mother's suggestion to fly on ahead, and did I mind terribly driving down slowly with Enid in the Rolls. I suppose this is wise?

Sorry to discover in the bath tonight that my rash still hasn't quite gone.

Loosely
Engaged

To Nicholas, with love

June

Sunday, June 11th

Villa Les Roches Blanches, Cap d'Antibes.
What an extraordinary thing life can be at times. One minute,
all is sweetness and light. The sky above is blue and the way
ahead seems straight and untrammelled. The next, dark
storm clouds have gathered overhead and suddenly the road
is strewn with sharp stones and pot-holes at every turn.

It is a mere week since I closed my diary for the last time,
confident that, with my new-found love for Amanda Trubshawe and my promotion to Assistant Group Head, I should
have neither the time nor the need for introspection. Yet
already I feel the urge to take up my pen once more and
commit my innermost thoughts to paper. I am only sorry I
did not bring my faithful old diary down with me. However,
the cheap exercise book I bought in Antibes will have
to serve for another week. Is there really still a week to go?
Frankly, there have been days when I have felt like buying
my own ticket and taking the next plane to London. However, when one is the guest of one's chairman and his wife –
not to say the boyfriend of their daughter – it is not only bad
manners to walk out, but very bad public relations. It is also
extremely expensive. I see no alternative but to stay and see
the holiday out. Unfortunately, no amount of hot sunshine,
beautiful surroundings, excellent food and wines, and
twice-daily water-skiing can disguise the fact that relations
between Amanda and me have turned decidedly frosty.
I am sorry that I do not share her enthusiasm for the Pot à
Gogo discotheque or for lounging around in cafés, with dark-

skinned layabouts, smoking Gitanes and talking twaddle, but there it is.

As I said to her, I somehow can't imagine the Scott Fitzgeralds and the Gerald Murphys frittering their time away on the Riviera on such mindless pastimes, but the names mean nothing to her. I suppose this is one of the penalties one has to pay for falling in love with a girl half one's age.

Matters not made any easier by my feelings toward Enid Trubshawe which are equivocal, to say the least. I continue to find her tremendously attractive and I'm pretty sure she feels the same way about me.

On reflection, it was perhaps unwise of me to have agreed to travel down alone with her in the Rolls. Even though nothing actually happened at the hotel in Orange, it could have, which amounts to the same thing.

How very confusing it all is.

The sun doesn't seem to be doing my rash much good either.

Monday, June 12th

The chairman has had to fly back to London on unexpected business. Strongly tempted to ask if I could join him. However, Enid suggested that after dropping him at Nice Airport we should drive up to Saint Paul-de-Vence for lunch at the Colombe d'Or. The opportunity to experience one of the great restaurants of the world is not one that should be lightly dismissed. Luckily we had a table outside on the terrace. Amanda silently intent on her sun-tan, as usual, until Enid mentioned that the last time she had been there she had seen Dirk Bogarde having a drink in the bar. At this A. perked up no end, leaving the table at frequent intervals and disappearing indoors.

When I asked her if he was there, she said. 'Who?'

I said, 'Dirk Bogarde, of course.'

She said, 'I've no idea. I was looking for Jean-Jacques. He said he might be here.'

I asked her who Jean-Jacques was. 'Oh', she said, 'just someone I met at the discothèque.'

Her mother said nothing and neither did I. But honestly. . . .

Think I may have spotted Graham Greene in the street this evening. It's reassuring to know that the literary tradition of the Riviera is alive and well. Am rather hoping I might have the chance to meet him sometime. Although of different generations, we have remarkably similar minds.

Tuesday, June 13th

Swam, sun-bathed and wind-surfed the whole day. I really believe I'm getting the hang of this curious sport at last. Managed to stand for several minutes on end without toppling into the water. Haven't quite mastered turning yet, or indeed moving forward, but it's only a matter of time. I daresay I do look a little ungainly compared with the skinny local boys whom Amanda seems to attract in such numbers; but then, of course, it's easy enough to acquire a flashy superficial skill in these fringe sports if you have nothing else to do all day, and I feel Amanda's unstinted admiration for their self-conscious cavortings is disproportionately enthusiastic.

When I made a pointed comment to this effect, Amanda said, 'I'm not making any comparisons. We all of us have our different talents.'

We certainly do. I'd like to see some of those sun-tanned merchants trying to compile a Barford New Product Development proposal document.

In the evening played Scrabble and won every game! It's a relief to know I'm good at something.

Drank three cognacs and went to bed feeling decidedly more cheerful than for several days.

Pity I had to catch the sun again quite so badly across my shoulders. I thought I'd surmounted that hurdle last week.

Wednesday, June 14th

After breakfast Enid drove to Nice to collect Derrick from London.

Sun-bathed with Amanda in the garden.

Object of the exercise almost totally nullified in my case owing to having to wear an aertex shirt and a towel across the top of my legs to protect nasty sunburn. Amanda even darker brown than usual in the briefest bikini I have ever seen. I seem to remember reading somewhere that some

9

people have more oil in their skin than others. I'm not surprised; she certainly puts enough of the stuff on. After a while she took off her bikini top. I said, 'Are you sure that's wise?'

'Very,' she said. 'Why?'

I said, 'We wouldn't want your parents to arrive back suddenly and get the wrong idea.'

She said, 'What sort of wrong ideas could they possibly get? We're going together, aren't we? Supposed to be, anyway.'

I said that the fact that one was going out with a girl did not automatically entitle one to play the goat in broad daylight at eleven o'clock in the morning.

She replied that I didn't seem to be interested in playing the goat at any time of the day or night.

Oh dear. I was afraid that this touchy subject would raise its ugly head sooner or later. The truth is, I shall be quite ready to play my full part in this regard as and when the time is right. Our love is still in its blossoming stage and I feel that, if we wish it to ripen and produce an abundance of fruit, to pluck the flowers at this early stage would be rash and foolish.

Also, the problem of hanky-panky in other people's houses is always a tricky one – viz: the humiliating incident at Jane's parents' in Oxted. Funnily enough, I have dreamt about Jane once or twice recently. I cannot imagine why.

By way of a welcome-home for the chairman, Enid cooked an absolutely delicious *pintade à la Rousillonne* which Derrick complemented, as usual, with some first-class burgundy. What a joy it is to be marrying into a family of real gourmets. It's all a very far cry from the middle-class fare dished up by Jane's parents.

Sorry to discover later as I was undressing that, despite my careful precautions this afternoon, my skin is even redder and more painful than before. I can scarcely lie down without experiencing severe discomfort. This will definitely put any 'goat-playing' out of court for several days.

Thursday, June 15th

To the Grand Hotel du Cap for lunch at the Eden Roc pavilion. One has the feeling that at any second one will look up and glimpse Scott and Zelda, the Murphys, Ernest and

Pablo strolling through the pines in their bathing wraps, sipping dry martinis and swapping amusing repartee. Amanda certainly in sparkling form.

Lunched extremely well off cold *loup de mer* and Pouilly Fumé at one of the umbrella-ed tables on the terrace overlooking the pool. While waiting for coffee, thought I'd take a few snaps of the lunchtime scene purely for reference purposes, so moved amongst the tables with my Instamatic, snapping away at random rather as I imagine Tony Snowdon does when he's working on an assignment. My discreet and casual manner obviously paid off, since most people took no notice of me at all. Was quite surprised, therefore, when one stout, rather red-faced couple waved their arms at me as I passed their table and said, in English, 'Not for us, thanks.' I stopped and asked them what they meant. 'Oh,' said the man in an unmistakably North Country accent, 'aren't you one of them beach photographers then?'

I replied that I was certainly no such thing.

His wife said, 'You look just like one in your dungarees.'

I said nothing and returned to my table. How people who cannot tell the difference between 'dungarees' and a pair of extremely well-cut jeans manage to get past the doorman of a place like the Eden Roc, let alone afford the prices, I simply cannot comprehend. They must feel so terribly out of place. And yet, only moments afterwards, I saw the head waiter dancing attendance on them. As I remarked this evening to Enid, 'Scott and Zelda must be turning in their graves.'

She said, 'He might, she wouldn't. She was burned to death in a fire.'

What a pleasure it is to be in the company of such a witty, well-read woman.

Friday, June 16th

Life with the Trubshawes is a non-stop round of pleasure. This evening we drove to Monte Carlo for dinner at the Hotel de Paris. An excellent and, as it has turned out, unique opportunity to wear Tim Pedalow's white dinner jacket.

A pity my nose had to choose today of all days to start peeling. Even so, everyone commented on the jacket, and in the car Amanda squeezed my arm, gave me a kiss and said, 'Ooh, I quite fancy you this evening.' I whispered back, 'Me too,' at which Enid called out from the front seat, 'Come along now, you two love-birds.' I felt rather foolish.

Dinner in the huge, ornate dining room excellent. On a platform at the far end, a small orchestra played suitably old-fashioned melodies. At one point the violinist strolled round the tables asking for requests. I asked for 'The Man Who Broke the Bank at Monte Carlo'. He gave me a blank look, announced that he had never heard of it and moved on to the next table. Some sort of joke, I imagine.

Amanda spent much of the meal singing the praises of Bjorn Borg, the tennis player who, I gather, lives in Monte Carlo, though goodness knows why.

After dinner, Derrick announced that he fancied trying his hand at the tables. This was excellent news. I have always wanted to see the famous casino, and a visit to Monte without chancing a bob or two on the green baize would be as unthinkable as driving through Avignon without stopping to look at the *pont*.

Suggested they go on ahead while I took a short walk to settle a slight attack of indigestion. After a while, felt slightly better and made my way into the sumptuously decorated interior of the most famous gaming rooms in the world. Surprised to fine most of the players dressed in a most casual way. Some were even wearing jeans. No sign of the Trubshawes. Made enquiries of one of the employees. He looked me up and down and said, 'I think your friends must be at the new Sporting Club down on the beach.'

Took a taxi, which cost me all the money I would otherwise have splurged on the tables. Just as well, probably, since all the Trubshawes lost theirs. But then, of course, they can afford to. I have better things to do with my money than chuck it away in such joyless and fruitless pastimes. The philosophy of something for nothing is thoroughly alien to me, and for all his great writing, it certainly brought little happiness to Dostoievsky.

Was strolling around, hand in hand with Amanda, when an American couple came up and asked her if she was Princess Caroline. I don't know if they thought I was Philippe Junot. I hope not.

Saturday, June 17th

Our last day at Les Roches Blanches. Am really quite sorry to be going, even though, from a romantic point of view, the holiday has been very much of a curate's egg.

But then, in my experience, everyone's judgement tends to go to pieces when they're abroad, and I am confident that we shall quickly find ourselves on the same wave-length once we are back in London.

For all her childish ways and unformed tastes, Amanda still sets my heart skipping every time I see her, and I am certain that beneath that frivolous exterior her feelings for me are as genuine and serious as ever. Really, my head is in as much of a whirl as it was before the holiday began. We leave tomorrow after lunch. Enid and Amanda and I take the plane; the chairman drives home in the Rolls. No mention of my accompanying *him*, I'm glad to say.

Sunday, June 18th

While buying croissants for breakfast in Antibes, bumped into the head waiter from the Eden Roc. I hardly recognized him in mufti. He certainly didn't recognize me, but then in that sort of job one must meet so many people.

Had a most interesting conversation about the hotel. Happened to mention the elderly North Country couple who had seemed so obviously out of place the other day.

'Ah, yes, *monsieur*,' he said, 'Sir Eric and Lady Maxwell. A charming couple. They have been coming to the Grand Hotel ever since they had their honeymoon here in 1928. They were great friends of the Scott Fitzgeralds, you know.'

Waiters are such snobs, one never knows if they are telling the truth.

On our way out to the plane at Nice, felt a hand on my shoulder and turned round to find myself face to face with Bryant-Fenn of all people. I gathered he had been on the Riviera for the best part of a week, writing an article for some in-flight magazine about the Monegasque royal family. He nodded towards Enid and murmured, 'Isn't that the woman I saw you with at the theatre a week or two back?' I told him I really couldn't remember. 'Yes, you do,' he persisted. 'I asked you who she was the next day and you told me she was your aunt up for the day from Haywards Heath or somewhere.'

Attempted to brush him aside but he went on, 'You're a sly one. I congratulate you.' Decided to put an end to this charade once and for all by introducing him to the wife of the chairman of Harley Preston.

'What fun,' he said cheerfully. 'Let's all sit together.' I pointed out that we had specially reserved seats at the back.

'Oh,' he said, 'in that case we can't. I'm travelling first class.'

For nothing presumably, as usual.

As we were taking off, Enid said, 'Who was that? A friend?'

I laughed and said, 'Hardly.'

Ten minutes later a stewardess arrived with a bottle of champagne and three glasses, compliments of Monsieur Bryant-Fenn.

Of course I said that we could not possibly accept such a gift from a comparative stranger.

Enid said, 'I don't see why,' and asked the stewardess to pour it out for us.

She took a couple of sips and said, 'It's a pity you don't know a few more people like Mr Bryant-Fenn.'

Arrived back at the flat at ten thirty to find that Jane has moved out, lock, stock and barrel, and gone to live with Armitage in his 'house' in Clapham. It is disappointing enough to think that one's ex-girlfriend should have seen fit to ally herself with the man one has recently ousted as Assistant Group Head, but that she should give up a good address in Holland Park in favour of a shabby workman's cottage in a poor street in South London is beyond my understanding.

No sooner stepped through front door than I was confronted by a small, dark, Arabic-looking girl, dressed in shocking green, skin-tight trousers and one of *my* best shirts, tied in a knot at the hip, who said in a rude voice, 'I think you have made a mistake. This is Ralph Beddoes's flat.'

I said, 'On the contrary, it is *you* who have made the mistake. This is *my* flat.'

At that moment, Beddoes emerged from the bedroom wearing just a towelling dressing gown (no prizes for guessing what *they'd* been up to) and introduced the girl as his fiancée. He must take me for a fool. Her name is Shusha and she comes, like all bad news these days, from Iran.

'Her family is one of the best in Teheran,' he told me, 'but they have fallen on hard times.'

'So hard apparently that they can't even afford their own shirts,' I said. 'I understood you were leaving for Brussels last week, Beddoes.'

'Well,' he said, 'you obviously understood wrong.'

How he has managed to make such a success in the City with manners like that I can't imagine. As for this new job, I dread to think how he is going to cope at the polite dinner tables of EEC high society. Roy Jenkins will make mincemeat of him, and rightly.

Compelled to eat scrambled eggs to the accompaniment of evil-smelling eastern cooking and toneless, oriental, so-called music on the gramophone.

Also had to sleep without sheets or pillowcases owing to Beddoes' failure to collect clean laundry.

What a wretched homecoming and how I long for a quiet life. Possibly a married one.

Monday, June 19th

My first day as Assistant Group Head and one on which I should have set out fresh and eager to face up to my new responsibilities; yet I do not believe I have ever known a more depressing start to any week. Things got off on the wrong foot at breakfast when Beddoes said, 'I suppose you will be resigning your job at the earliest opportunity.'

I told him I had no intention of doing any such thing.

'Oh well,' he said. 'If you have no scruples about nepotism.'

I laughed and said that it was Armitage who was the chairman's nephew, not me.

He said airily, 'Nephew, son-in-law, it all boils down to the same thing in the end.'

I replied that what was good enough for our ex-ambassador in Washington was certainly good enough for me.

'And look at the trouble that caused,' he said, and marched off into the bathroom.

He may have a point or he may not. Time alone will tell. A real friend, of course, would not have raised the subject in the first place.

Arrived at the office to find that not only had no one made the slightest effort to move my things out of my old office, but that my new room (Armitage's old one) was now occupied by a tall, blonde American girl who announced herself as Ruth Macmichael.

She has recently arrived in London after eight years in a large New York advertising agency and is, I gather, to be my junior assistant.

'I believe that if one is in the business of selling, one should get to have as wide a perspective on the market place as possible,' she announced.

I said I quite agreed, and that as soon as we had the office situation sorted out we must sit down and exchange a few ideas.

She replied that, according to the latest psychological research carried out in America, status symbols at work are a hindrance to positive thinking.

'I mean,' she said, 'who cares a damn whether I have a bigger office than you? How's that going to help shift our clients' products off the supermarket shelves?' If she couldn't see how, I certainly was not about to tell her.

I do hope we're not heading for an ugly confrontation. The omens are far from favourable.

Tuesday, June 20th

Still no progress re my new office. Mentioned the matter to Roundtree, as group head. He *says* he'll look into it. There seems to be an awful lot of talk and very little do in this place nowadays. May very well say something to the chairman next time I see him.

Shortly before lunch, went to see Ruth about the Barford sales figures, only to learn from Sarah that she is away all day on private business.

It is not easy being an Assistant Group Head without a group to be Assistant Head of. Talk about too many chiefs and not enough indians. In the flat, of course, it's quite the reverse – if you can call Persians indians.

Wednesday, June 21st

This evening I said to Amanda, 'I suppose you'll be throwing yourself wholeheartedly into the Season from now on.'

She laughed and said, 'Don't be silly. No one does the Season any more.'

I reminded her that when we first met she'd told me she was doing precisely that.

'Oh yes,' she said, 'but it's only a manner of speech. All that Berkeley Dress Show, Ascot, Goodwood stuff is as out-of-date as the Rolling Stones. Occasionally someone throws a thrash, but most of the time we just bomb round to Wedgies or Tramps and have a bit of a giggle.'

In my opinion, there is no more pathetic sight than that of an older man trying to ingratiate himself with a younger girl by pretending to be *au fait* with her world. On the other hand, one does not wish to appear an old fuddy-duddy, so I remarked casually that I had been quite a dancer myself in my time and had once won a Twist competition during a skiing holiday in the Austrian Tyrol.

Amanda said, 'Oh yes, I've heard of the Twist. I think my parents used to do it.'

Thursday, June 22nd

An astounding thing happened. Strolled into Ruth's office to ask if she would mind collating the Barford projections for tomorrow's meeting.

'Why?' she said, 'Can't you?'

I replied in a light-hearted way that I was her superior and, as such, expected a bit more respect.

'I don't see why,' she said. 'Frankly, as far as I'm concerned, you're a bit of an ass-hole.'

I made it quite clear that I was not about to put up with that sort of talk from anyone by turning and leaving the room without a word.

These Americans are getting above themselves. They are guests in our country, and Harvard Business School or no Harvard Business School, a modicum of politeness and modesty is surely not too much to expect.

Any more of this behaviour and she'll be feeling the rough side of my tongue.

Friday, June 23rd

I thought I had made it perfectly clear, following the unfortunate incident during my visit to the school in May, that I wished to resign from the OF Society and to have no further communication with them. And yet today through the post comes a booklet containing minutes of the annual general meeting of the Society, details of the Society's accounts, reports of the progress of OF Cricket, Rugger, Golf, Fencing, Cross-Country Running, Hockey and Darts, and news of the trivial activities of fifty or more OFs, none of whom I have ever heard of – even though some claim to have been contemporaries.

Of what possible interest can it be to anyone that L. G. Rasper (Brough's, 1949–54) has given up his job as Deputy Agricultural Supervisor in southern Botswana to become Banqueting Manager of the Ibn Bin Saud Palace Motel in Qatar? Or that Andrew Smellie (Newby's, 1970–75) has passed his chartered accountancy exams and has been making a name for himself in the Plymouth area with his mobile discotheque and lighting-à-gogo roadshow? As for the information that Wilfred Ng (Boshier's, 1955–59) 'who will be remembered by all of us for his epic battle against Kenneth Singh (Parkinson's, 1954–58) in the finals of the Pemberton Squash Cup in 1958' (not by me, for one) married the sister of G. G. Cartwright (Lomas's, 1951–56) and now has a son and daughter, it seems to me sheer conceit on the part of Ng to suppose that his private life is of concern to any but his family and most intimate circle of friends. I notice someone has enclosed a roneo-ed sheet of paper with the words, 'I should like the following news of myself published in the OF News section of the school magazine. Name . . . House . . . Dates . . . Address and phone number. . . .'

Strongly tempted to commit it to the waste-paper basket, but have decided on second thoughts to put it away in a safe place until I feel I have something really worthwhile to publish. I only wish more OFs would follow my example.

Saturday, June 24th

Standards are dropping daily. Called in at my local off-licence this evening on way home from the office to buy a bottle of Robinson's Barley Water.

'Sorry, dear,' said the woman behind the counter, 'we've had a bit of a run on cordials.'

I said that I thought she must have misunderstood me; it was not some fizzy peppermint or blackcurrant drink that I was after, but a bottle of Robinson's Barley Water.

'Look,' she said, 'are you in the drinks business or am I? I know perfectly well what a cordial is, and Robinson's Barley Water is a cordial.'

I told her that, as far as I knew, Robinson's was, and had been for generations, a fruit squash. If she insisted on referring to it as a cordial, that was fine by me, but I doubted if she was in the majority.

'I do insist,' she said, 'and we're out of it anyway. What's more, I shall be very surprised if you'll find a bottle of it anywhere in this weather.'

I told her that was the silliest thing I had ever heard, since there were obviously plenty of bottles of the stuff somewhere in London.

'You're welcome to go and look,' she said.

What is the point in arguing with the lower orders when they are in that sort of mood? Tried every other shop and off-licence in the area, only to discover there wasn't a bottle of it to be had anywhere.

I can only assume that, if all off-licences are as ill-informed as mine, people have simply stopped asking for it.

Sunday, June 25th

To Kent to introduce Amanda to Mother.

Arrived shortly before lunch to find that she had asked Denys Ramsden over for a drink to meet us. I have never really been able to look him in the eye ever since Mother claimed earlier this year that he had given her a French kiss. I know he's nearly eighty, but I wouldn't put it past him. It's the way he twiddles his moustache I don't trust. Things were going extremely well, with the compliments flying in all directions, and Denys twiddling, and much lively discussion about the weather and the traffic on the journey down, when Mother suddenly launched off into a long discourse on Nabokov's *Lolita*, a novel which, as far as I was aware, she had neither read nor heard of. Unless, of course, Denys has been trying to force his tastes on to her in addition to his tongue. At all events, she proceeded to outline the plot of this older man's passion for this very young girl in startling detail, and had I not had the presence of mind to suggest a stroll round the garden before lunch, I really believe things could have taken a very uncomfortable turn indeed. As it was, she spent most of lunch making pointed references to the difference in our ages. When she asked Amanda what she was hoping to do when she left school, I really felt she had gone too far, and after coffee I proposed an early return to town.

At least the cat didn't get a chance to sink its claws into Amanda's leg, a trick in which it appears to be encouraged by Mother who is even more besotted by the creature than she was when Nigel and Priscilla gave it to her last Christmas.

As we were getting into the car, Mother said, 'Do get Simon to bring you down again soon. It's been such fun.' Amanda replied, 'I certainly will.' as if she really meant it.

Glanced in my rear view mirror as we set off down the road and saw that Denys Ramsden had his arm round Mother's waist. I only hope that's as far as she allows him to go.

Apologized to Amanda for Mother's tactless behaviour. She said, 'I thought she was sweet. She reminds me of my grandmother.'

Just so long as we are not about to acquire a grandfather.

Only a week to go now before Beddoes leaves for Brussels. I have designed a small chart listing the seven remaining days which I shall tick off as BB Day (Beddoes to Brussels Day) approaches. Anything to make the time go quicker.

Monday, June 26th

Woke feeling unusually excited. For a moment or two I could not think why; then realized, of course, that today is the start of Wimbledon fortnight – an event in the sporting and social calendar that I always look forward to with keen anticipation. Every year I promise myself that I am going to get up a small party and spend a day there roaming the courts, eating strawberries and cream and watching the great stars in action, but somehow time always seems to fly by and before I know what, Harry Carpenter is previewing the fortnight on TV and discussing the seedings with Dan Maskell before I have had a chance to send off to the ticket office – wherever that may be.

Still, the BBC coverage is always so good and Dan's comments are invariably so sensible that I wonder anyone bothers to go at all. Not that anyone I know ever does.

Said as much to Amanda this evening. She replied, 'Oh, we always go every year. It's such a good opportunity to meet one's friends.'

I gather they make two trips – once during the first week and then again on mens' quarter-finals day. No mention I notice of my joining them. However, I have a feeling the chairman also takes people along for business reasons, so perhaps she assumes I will be in on one of those.

Only six days to BB Day.

Tuesday, June 27th

Five days to BB Day. The time cannot go fast enough for my liking.

Wednesday, June 28th

A dreadful night's sleep, thanks to the non-stop antics of Beddoes and his Islamic paramour. I do not often sleep with women but when I do, I certainly do not find it necessary to broadcast the fact to the entire neighbourhood.

Still wide awake at 1.30, so turned on my radio and listened for a while to an excellent Schubert concert from Holland. On the point of dozing off during slow movement of C Major Quintet when jerked back to life by loud hammering on the door and Beddoes's voice calling out, 'Would you mind turning off that terrible row? Some of us are trying to get to sleep.'

Finally got off shortly before three.

Overslept badly, leapt out of bed in panic and ricked my neck.

Felt so wretched all day, was quite unable to tackle Ruth re Barford figures or Roundtree re my new office.

To dinner with the Trubshawes. Amanda in excellent form and full of plans for party going, etc. Sadly incapable of joining in with any degree of enthusiasm. Enid most sympathetic about my neck and has arranged for me to see her man in Harley Street.

I have wasted far too much of my life hanging around bleak corridors in National Health hospital clinics, waiting for hours to see some apparently non-existent consultant before finally being fobbed off with an assistant. Time is money for a man in my position, and to deny oneself private medicine is short-sighted and uneconomic.

All other considerations apart, I cannot risk another journey on my scooter like this morning's when I was unable to look either to right or left and ended up being knocked over by a pedestrian in South Audley Street.

Four days to BB Day.

Thursday, June 29th

To Harley Street at noon. Place stiff with Arabs, largely of the brown-robed, scruffy-bearded variety. After waiting for ten minutes in a small, quite well-furnished room with a Peter Scott reproduction over the fireplace and a large pile of out-of-date copies of *Vogue* on the table, the receptionist arrived to say she was very sorry but Sheik Somebody-or-other had just flown in from the gulf with a slipped disc, and would I mind terribly hanging on for another quarter of an hour or so.

I may not be earning a thousand pounds a minute, but my time is not so worthless that I can afford to have it wasted at the whim of some rough Bedouin. Receptionist finally condescended to show me into large panelled consulting room.

Dr Andrews seemed a little too off-hand for a Harley Street man to my way of thinking, and when I introduced Enid's name into the proceedings, he seemed scarcely to remember her at all.

Am wondering if there might not be a hint of the Levant in Dr Andrews, if not the actual tarbrush.

He sat me in an upright chair, twisted my arms behind my back and started to manipulate me.

I remarked that it was a wonder people didn't finish up with broken necks.

'Oh, they do,' he said, and at that moment gave it an immense wrench.

'Well,' he said, 'that seems to have done the trick.'

I didn't like to say so but the pain was, if anything, even more severe.

He has made arrangements with my local hospital for me to be fitted with a surgical collar which I must wear constantly for a week and every night thereafter.

I have often seen people wearing these in the street and wondered what it must feel like to walk about like an African tribesman.

I shall soon find out.

Friday, June 30th

To the hospital first thing to be fitted with my surgical collar.

Oddly enough, it is a great deal more comfortable than I had imagined, and can easily be disguised with a silk scarf.

Few people gave me a second glance, but one or two did stare rather rudely, so I stared back and they soon stopped.

One middle-aged man on the bus went on staring for so long that in the end I stuck my tongue out at him. At this he came across and said, 'For two pins I'd break your ruddy neck, if it wasn't broken already.'

I pretended not to have heard him.

Beddoes, who can never let anything pass, walked into the flat and said, 'Good God, it's Eric von Stroheim.'

I reminded him that it was thanks to him that I was compelled to wear the wretched thing in the first place, adding that if he really wanted to know, I happened to have a weak cervical vertebra, and that if I don't wear a collar, it's liable to come out.

He said, 'You mean like that debutante bird of yours?'

As feeble a joke as I have heard in a long while. He'll have to do a great deal better than that in Brussels. Is it any wonder I cannot entertain my girlfriend in my own home?

Still, only two more days to go and I can once more call my life my own.

I feel like Laocoon wrestling with the serpent.

July

Saturday, July 1st

To lunch at the Trubshawes in my collar. Steak and kidney pie with peas and new potatoes and rather too many uncalled-for jokes at my expense. Was just about to tuck in when Derrick called down the table, 'You're supposed to be educated – Oxford and all that. What does this mean?' And he pushed a large grey pot of *Moutarde de Meaux* in my direction.

The label contained an account in mock medieval script of how in 1760 the Pommery family acquired the secret of the *Moutarde de Chanoines* from the monks of Meaux. I read it carefully, then said, by way of a little joke, 'I believe this is what is known in the mustard business as a potted history,' deliberately stressing the word 'potted'.

However, my little *jeu de mots* (or should I say *jeu de meaux*?) obviously escaped Derrick altogether. 'I did not get where I am today by not being able to read mustard pot labels,' he said irritably. 'It's the Latin I'm referring to.'

And he pointed at the words 'HUIC CONDIMENTO EST IMPERARE OMNIBUS CIBIS.'

Try as I might, I was quite unable to make any sense of it whatever, and said that in my opinion it was probably some meaningless tag dreamed up by a clever marketing man in order to invest an ordinary everyday product with some specious aura of tradition and antiquity. Derrick seemed genuinely impressed, as did the girls. Even so, it doesn't say a lot for Dickie Dunmow's teaching methods that, despite my having spent three years in the Classical Sixth, I am now quite incapable of understanding a single word of Latin. It's one more nail in the coffin of the OF Society as far as I'm concerned.

Sunday, July 2nd

I can hardly believe that today is the last day I shall ever have to share my home or my life with Beddoes.

One would have thought he'd have enough to occupy himself with – packing suitcases, writing out cheques for his share of the household bills and generally making himself pleasant and useful around the place for once. But no. He has to devote the large part of his last day in this country lounging around in bed with Miss Teheran. Had been gearing myself up to a final outburst of noise, celebration and general bad behaviour on his part to such an extent that, even though he did not emerge from his room until half past three in the afternoon, I had exhausted myself with anticipation, and the tension had made my neck ache so badly that I had to take two Codein and lie down. I can't think of many people capable of upsetting others by doing nothing.

Finally got down to the Sunday papers just before supper.

By all accounts, I have missed absolutely nothing by not going to the first week of Wimbledon. Since I am still barely able to move my neck, let alone swivel it from side to side, I'm really quite glad the Trubshawes didn't ask me after all. I'd only have had to refuse.

Monday, July 3rd

Hurrah, hurrah. The day I have been looking forward to for so long and thought would never come.

Ralph Beddoes, my so-called flatmate for the past two and a half years, left these shores (or at any rate these rooms) at nine-thirty this morning, taking the ghastly Shusha, his beastly smelling cigars, his towelling dressing gown, his collection of pornographic magazines, and his irritating air of lecherous superiority with him.

The moment I saw him stepping into the taxi in the street below I rushed round the flat throwing open all the windows.

The one in his room had been closed for so long that I had quite a struggle shifting it, and when I did, it shot up to the top, breaking two panes, and would not come down again.

Even when he is not here, Beddoes costs me money. Still, a little broken glass is a small price to pay for the pleasure of feeling his presence blowing out through the window along with the months of accumulated dust. I shall send him the bill in Brussels. If he shows signs of dragging his heels over it, I shall have no hesitation in putting pressure on him through the appropriate government body here at Westminster. Which reminds me, I still haven't the faintest idea what he will be doing in Brussels. Neither, I suspect, does he.

Tuesday, July 4th

In the words of the song, I feel as corny as Kansas in August *and* as high as a flag on the Fourth of July. However, while I have nothing against Americans, ex-patriate or otherwise, celebrating their independence, I do draw a line at junior executives from Des Moines, Iowa, trying to teach me how to draw up a Barford New Product Development plan.

Miss Ruth Macmichael has tried to force-feed me with her slick Madison Avenue marketing methods just once too often. I am not by nature a vindictive man, but I must confess I took great pleasure this morning in slapping her down in no un-certain terms. I was disappointed that Roundtree should have seen fit to take her side in the matter, though not half as much as I was at Enid and Amanda setting off for the men's quarter-finals without so much as a mention of my joining them.

Wednesday, July 5th

Amanda came round after work to watch Wimbledon on the TV. Considering it was her first visit to my home since we met in May, and thus something of an historic occasion, I felt she might have shown a little more interest in the place. I had made quite an effort – hoovering right through, polishing the furniture, putting out a new roll of loo paper, etc.; yet when I asked her what she thought, all she said was, 'It's all right. Where's the TV set?'

A strangely incurious attitude towards her possible future home.

I also thought she made rather a meal about my not having

a colour set. In my view, one loses nothing in black and white, and as far as sport is concerned, the definition is, if anything, slightly sharper.

Despite the high standard of the men's doubles matches we were watching, she talked of nothing but Bjorn Borg. She seems positively obsessed by the fellow, and is evidently quite blind to his scruffy, rather bad-tempered appearance.

Eventually could not resist remarking that I was beginning to wish he had never been bjorn.

She stared at me blankly, so I repeated my little joke. She still didn't get it and I gave up. Later we watched a recording of a ladies' semi-final. I said that in my opinion Yvonne Goolagong was the most elegant player to have emerged since Maria Bueno.

'Who's Maria Bueno?' she asked.

The generation gap raises its ugly head at the most unexpected moments. One longs to bridge it, but how? I hardly know where to begin.

Vaguely at the back of my mind was the thought that we might celebrate the occasion by breaking the sexual ice. However, quickly realized the time was not right and scrapped the idea.

It never did anyone any harm to wait.

Thursday, July 6th

Men's semi-finals day at Wimbledon, but still not a word from the Trubshawes about my going with them. Returned to my desk after my usual ten o'clock visit to the coffee machine to find an envelope addressed to me in the unmistakable hand of Miss Ruth Macmichael. Scrawled across one corner was the word URGENT.

Decided I had had quite enough of these curt transatlantic business methods and tore the whole thing up without so much as a second glance.

Enjoyed a rare coup at lunchtime. Called into the delicatessen near the office and, after some deliberation, bought myself a piece of cold game pie. Astounded to be informed by sniffy, over-made-up girl at the cash desk that the modest slice I had chosen came to £1.30. In my confusion, handed over a single pound note, at which the girl gave me 70p in change. I suppose I should have said something, but I have never much cared for her manner, and it will do her no harm to take the rap.

Ate pie in square and afterwards fell asleep in the warm sun. Woke just before three and hurried back to the office, much refreshed. Spent a comparatively pleasant afternoon with the Barford figures and left promptly at five-thirty. Bumped into the chairman in the front hall who said, 'Hello, you're leaving it a bit late, aren't you?' I had no idea what he was talking about and said so. He frowned and said, 'You did get the ticket, didn't you? Miss Macmichael promised me faithfully she'd leave it on your desk in good time. Centre Court tickets are hard enough to come by at the best of times, but on men's semi-final day they're like gold dust.'

Rushed upstairs to my office to find that the cleaners had, for once, decided to empty the waste-paper baskets early.

Every bus crammed to bursting point, so did not arrive home until six-thirty by which time recording of afternoon's big games was over.

Consoled myself with thought that I could still watch it on Match of the Day. However, suddenly struck down by violent stomach upset and forced to retire to bed.

So much for game pie. I've a good mind to say something to that girl at the delicatessen.

Friday, July 7th

Woke feeling extremely queasy and decided to treat myself to a morning in bed for the first time in months. At least no-one can accuse me of hypochondria. Tried reading *Tess of the d'Urbervilles* for the umpteenth time and, as usual, failed to get beyond page two. Is it just me, or is Hardy a wildly over-rated novelist?

I doubt the so-called intellectuals would rate Ed McBain alongside the great masters of the written word, but at least one can get through his books at a sitting.

Saturday, July 8th

To the Trubshawes for lunch followed by the men's tennis finals. Try as I might I simply cannot warm to Bjorn Borg. I'm sure that, if one were to get to know him, one would discover that he is a quiet, simple lad, as capable of enjoying a pint and cracking a joke as the next fellow. Even so, I do not believe one can ever quite trust a man whose eyes are set so close together.

Sunday, July 9th

The day following some great sporting occasion inevitably brings with it a sense of deep anticlimax and today was no exception.

In an effort to liven up proceedings, invited Amanda to new Woody Allen film. How a girl with an expensive education like hers can have reached the age of eighteen without having seen one of Woody's films beats me. The prospect of trying to fill her in on the required background between The Boltons, Kensington and The Screen on the Hill, Belsize Park, was daunting to say the least.

Was perched in the drawing room at The Boltons, idly riffling through the new *Queen*, when the chairman stuck his head round the door and said he would like a short chat with me in his study. Naturally I assumed it had something to do with my new responsibilities at the office, so that when he asked me, 'What exactly are your intentions towards my daughter?' the wind was slightly taken out of my sails.

'I intend' I told him, 'to make her happy.'

He frowned impatiently and said, 'Yes yes, but how exactly?'

I was rather non-plussed by his line of questioning and said, 'I don't think I'm quite with you, Derrick.'

'It's quite simple,' he said. 'Are you or are you not planning to marry Amanda?'

I said that I was very much thinking along those lines.

'When?' he said. '2001?' – and left the room, tongue firmly in cheek I trust.

Amanda took so long getting ready that we were too late for the film and had to content ourselves with a sentimental piece of soap about tennis, called *Players*.

At least Bjorn Borg wasn't in it.

Monday, July 10th

Scooter on the blink again, so compelled to travel to work on the tube.

Arrived at the office in a rage and went straight to coffee

machine. What I had failed to notice in my nervous condition was that the stupid thing was out of plastic cups, so stuck my hand casually into pouring area only to have it scalded by a shower of boiling hot liquid. Managed to alleviate pain to some extent by plunging it immediately under nearby cold tap.

Was on my way back to the office when Armitage stalked past and made for the machine, a coin ready in his hand. Said nothing. Had just sat down at my desk when Ruth marched in without so much as a by-your-leave and asked if I had any comments on her suggestions for revising the Barford projected sales figures. She pointed at a green file on the top of my in-tray. I said I was afraid I had not had time to look at anything, and explained about my scalded hand.

'We all have our crosses to bear,' she said, 'and one of mine is that I have you as my Assistant Group Head. Frankly, if I were you, I'd get my ass out of the sling pretty damn quick.'

I was astounded by her insolence and would have replied that if anyone needed to get anyone's ass out of any sling it was hers, but I simply could not bring myself to utter the words. No sooner had she left than Armitage stuck his head round the door and said leeringly, 'Some people get all the luck.'

When I asked him what he meant, he replied, 'Who needs a group when you've got a piece of tail like that at your beck and call every day?'

And he winked suggestively and sipped noisily at a plastic beaker.

'Where did you get that?' I asked him.

'Out of the machine, of course,' he said, and with another loud laugh he walked off.

I do not give a fig for his opinions of Miss Macmichael, yet I have to admit, she is, for all her abrasive New York ways, strangely attractive. But then the way things are with Amanda at the moment, even Brenda from Accounts could set my loins ablaze.

Tuesday, July 11th

With Amanda and a group of her friends to see the new James Bond film. The most preposterous hotch-potch of gadgetry, sexual innuendo and over-acting I have ever wasted good money on in my life. Timmy and Joanna screamed with laughter throughout like a couple of excited school-children. Sorry to note that Amanda showed no less discrimination and joined in even more loudly. Dave, who has a stall in Camden Lock market, appeared to be the only one with the nous to see through it all.

As we were leaving he commented, 'Bloody immoral, that's what it is.'

I said that I quite agreed, and was reminiscing briefly about the great days of Sean Connery, Ursula Andress, Honor Blackman et al., when Dave interrupted me to say that it was not the morality he was complaining about but the cost. I said that, speaking as a practitioner in the communication business, I knew only too well the lengths to which one has to go these days to attract the public.

'No, no,' he said, interrupting me again. 'I meant the cost of the ticket.'

Business may not be booming at Camden Lock, but I noticed that did not prevent him from joining us for an expensive jumboburger at one of those ubiquitous, quasi-American fast-food joints that are so popular these days amongst the young, the ex-patriates and the indiscriminating.

Place full, hot and loud with pop music so that I could scarcely hear a word anyone said. Not that anyone had anything very interesting to say anyway – at least, not to me. Had barely placed our orders with a surly waitress with pink hair when Joanna said in a loud voice, 'Pooh, what an awful smell,' and Timmy said, 'I reckon someone's just let off.'

Noticed that there was a fat corgi asleep under the table of the couple next door.

Finally the smell became so bad that I leaned across and said to the owner, 'Excuse me, but I think your dog is suffering from flatulence.'

He put down his knife and fork, turned to me and said, 'If you must know, *I'm* suffering from flatulence.' To which his wife added, 'And I think it's jolly mean of you to draw attention to other people's medical conditions. How would you like it if I suddenly started shouting round the restaurant that you have bad breath?'

I said coolly, 'I do not happen to have bad breath, and if I did, I would certainly take care not to inflict it on innocent strangers in public places.'

'As a matter of interest,' said the man, 'you do have bad breath and it's putting me off my food.'

And with that they got up and left, taking their smelly Welsh dog with them. After they had gone, I said with a laugh, 'Talk about mote and beam.'

Amanda said, 'Actually, he was quite right; your breath is peculiarly pungent this evening.'

'Yes,' said Joanna. 'In fact, I thought the smell came from you.'

Needless to say, they did not get much change out of me for the rest of the evening.

Wednesday, July 12th

The morning post brings Dr Andrews's bill for dealing with my neck. Forty guineas, if you please.

As soon as I got to the office I rang Harley Street and pointed out to the secretary that whoever it was who made out the bills was obviously labouring under the misapprehension that I had been there twice.

'If you must know,' she said tartly, 'I made out your bill and, unlike you, I am not suffering from anything. One consultation with Dr Andrews – forty guineas. We have made a slight reduction in consideration of your relationship with the Trubshawe family. However, we'd be quite happy to waive this, if you would prefer it.'

I replied that I was simply checking and put the phone down. Thank heavens for my private patients' scheme, that's all I can say.

Thursday, July 13th

Rang the private patients people in Eastbourne to ask them to send me a claim form.

Spoke to a Miss Hart who asked me when I had seen my own doctor. I told her that I had gone straight to the specialist.

'Oh,' she said, 'I'm afraid we cannot contemplate a claim unless we have a statement from your own doctor saying that he recommended the treatment in question.'

I pointed out that when one is suffering from a stiff neck, one does not need a doctor to tell one what is wrong or what to do about it.

She said, 'That may be your opinion, but I'm afraid we're quite firm on this point.'

I decided the time had come to read the riot act to Miss Hart and did so.

When I had finished she said, 'What is your name again?' I told her. There was a brief pause, then she came on the line again.

'I'm sorry, Mr Crisp,' she said, 'but according to our records you cancelled your subscription last November.'

And just as well, if this is the standard of service one can expect from private medicine nowadays.

Friday, July 14th

Le quartorze juillet as our neighbours on the other side of the Channel have it. I do not hold much of a brief for the French, especially in the light of their high-handed behaviour towards us in the EEC. On the other hand, for all their rudeness and over-eating and smelly cigarettes, they are very much of a piece as a nation. Their policemen do not drive round on German motorbikes, nor does one hear the phrase '*société multiraciale*' being bandied round smart Parisian dinner tables. It's a pity *we* do not set aside a special day every year when we can express our pride in our nation with eating and drinking and dancing in the streets. That way we might feel more confident about putting our so-called *confrères* in their proper place at the conference tables of Brussels and Strasbourg. It might also do something towards improving the standard of food in motorway cafés.

Saturday, July 15th

At somewhat of a loose end, as Amanda has agreed to go down to the Hamble for the weekend with Enid and help choose fabrics for the saloon of the yacht which they are having redecorated at huge expense.

We seem to see less and less of each other these days. Still, that may not be such a bad thing. Familiarity *does* breed contempt, and it never pays for two young people to be constantly on top of each other. Not that we ever are, of course, but there's plenty of time for all that sort of thing in due course.

Am seriously thinking of asking Ruth out to lunch next

week with a view to clearing the air and re-establishing the lines of communication. Meanwhile, decided to improve the shining hour by walking up to Kensington High Street and buying myself a new pair of underpants from one of the large stores. Found the perfect pair in dark blue with red piping. Asked the girl for a pair in medium, but was told they only had them in small and large. I suggested she might care to look in the stock drawer before coming out with such a definitive statement.

She said, 'I don't have to look in the stock drawer to know that we only have those in small and large.'

I pointed out that, if that was true, it was extremely bad marketing on the part of the store, since the majority of male customers took medium.

'I know,' she said, 'That's why we've only got small and large left in stock.'

I replied that frankly I did not believe her and suggested she called for the floor walker. After a long wait, a young man came hurrying up, all teeth and smiles and rimless glasses, to explain that they were expecting a new supply of mediums in on Monday.

I said, 'Do you absolutely promise me they will be here? I have to come from quite a long way specially.'

He said, 'You have my word.' For what that's worth.

Sunday, July 16th

I'm sorry now that I didn't take a pair of the plain light blue since I discover this morning that I am completely out of clean underpants altogether. However, my bathing trunks will act as a perfectly satisfactory substitute until tomorrow.

Devoted most of the morning to washing out a few shirts and socks and the afternoon to cleaning the car. There's no more healthy therapy than manual labour, even if it does give you chapped skin.

Monday, July 17th

Lunch hour given over entirely to collecting underpants. Incredibly, they were still out of mediums. Demanded to see the floor walker.

'Can you remember his name?' the assistant asked me.

I told her that we had not been introduced. After a certain amount of to-ing and fro-ing, a quite different young man appeared from the nether regions to say that they had been expecting the mediums in at eleven o'clock that morning, but that there had been a hold-up with the van. I reminded him that I was promised they would be there, which was why I had given up my valuable free time to come all that way. 'Not by me, you weren't,' said the young man.

I suppose I could have kicked up a real stink if I'd wanted, but in the end said I'd settle for a pair of the plain pale blue.

'We sold the last one of those on Saturday morning,' he said. I suppose the white ones are really just as good and, as the young man pointed out, as long as they do their job what difference does it make what colour they are?

Tried them on this evening after supper only to discover a small hole in a most awkward place. Why is it that one has to go shopping twice for everything these days?

Bang goes my lunch date with Ruth tomorrow.

Tuesday, July 18th

Ruth surprisingly nice about my cancelling our tête-à-tête. Although she said it was all the same by her, there was no disguising the disappointment in her voice. Have suggested dinner tomorrow night instead and she has accepted. It won't do her any harm to be on tenterhooks for another 36 hours.

A pity someone doesn't think up a way of keeping shop assistants a bit more on their toes. First of all the girl pretended she couldn't see where the hole was, and when she did finally admit its existence, she peered at it for a moment, then said, 'Are you sure you're not to blame?'

I did not care for her implications one little bit and I'm afraid we had sharp words about it.

However, in the end she agreed, rather grudgingly, to let me take another pair. I also bought some socks while I was about it. Dark blue, rather nice.

Wednesday, July 19th

Amanda rang this morning to say she had been asked to a charity dress show and did I want to go? I explained about my previous engagement with Ruth in as tactful a way as possible but got no reaction. I'd have expected her to show some sign of jealousy. Called Ruth just before lunch to ask where she'd like to dine. She said, 'Oh, is it tonight? I'd quite forgotten. Actually I've just agreed to go to Covent Garden. Can we make it another time?'

I was astounded at her casual attitude and made my feelings felt. But all she said was; 'I didn't realize it was such a big deal. I thought it was just an informal business reappraisal.'

I said stiffly, 'It all depends on how much of a big deal you think your career is,' and quietly put the phone down.

The maddening thing is, I was actually rather looking forward to it all. But I'm certainly not going to let her know that.

Rang Amanda to say I would be free for the dress show after all.

'Oh, that's a pity,' she said coolly, 'I've arranged to go with Colin.' Suppose she must mean Armitage, but didn't labour the point. The prospect of him and me becoming relations is too awful to contemplate.

Thursday, July 20th

Mother rang this evening to ask me if I'd remembered Priscilla's birthday on Saturday. I hadn't, as it happened, any more than my sister remembers mine, and to be reminded of the fact makes me even less willing to do anything about it.

Really, the sooner Mother stops treating me like a small child, the better for both our sakes. As I was leaving with Amanda the other day, I'll swear I heard her asking me if I had a clean handkerchief.

Friday, July 21st

Arrived in the office to find a note from Ruth saying that she hoped I wasn't planning anything elaborate for this evening, since she was lunching with the Barford New Product people. This is the first I've heard of it. If anyone should be lunching with anyone round here it should be me. Rang Roundtree and kicked up a stink, only to be informed that it was his idea, that Alec Giles was very partial to a pretty face, and that any company in this day and age that did not put itself out to make its client feel loved and wanted needed its head examined.

I didn't like to say so, but there are one or two people I can think of who need *their* heads examined. Including me. Am I a Group Head or aren't I? I understand now how poor old Wavell must have felt in the desert in 1941. Added the word INSUBORDINATION to my list of matters to be discussed this evening.

Went to put on new socks this evening and big toe went straight through the end. Not surprisingly, arrived at Bordelino in a fury. Also rather later than I had said. No sign of Ruth. Mentally added UNRELIABILITY to the list.

I must have eaten at that restaurant a score of times over the last couple of years, yet the head waiter appeared not to recognize me at all. However, when I mentioned my name he said, 'Ah yes, of course,' and began to scan the book.

'Your table was for eight-thirty,' he said.

'I know,' I said. 'I booked it myself. The corner one.'

'It is quarter to nine,' he said.

I said, laughingly, 'In my book, eight-thirty means anything between eight-thirty and nine o'clock.'

'Really,' he said, 'in mine it means anything between eight-thirty and eight-thirty!'

The upshot of this absurd exchange was that he had assumed we were not coming and had given the table away. However, if I cared to wait . . . ?

I replied stiffly that I did not care to do anything, least of all eat in his restaurant, and was on the point of leaving when Ruth arrived, looking, I must admit, very glamorous in a red velvet trouser suit.

To my astonishment, she and the waiter rushed at each other and embraced warmly, showering each other with compliments of a most intimate kind.

Frankly I felt a bit of a fool standing there, though not half as much as I did when 'Franco' rushed us to the best table in the house, muttering inanities like 'If I'd known it was you, *cara mia* . . .' and similar twaddle.

If there's one thing I dislike more than an obsequious head waiter it is an obsequious Italian head waiter. They're so *obvious*. As it turned out, though, dinner could not have been a greater success. I do not believe I have enjoyed myself so much for years. We hardly mentioned the office at all, and my list remained firmly in my pocket throughout.

Bill rather larger than I had anticipated; however, I shall almost certainly be able to claim it back on expenses.

As we stepped into the street Ruth said, 'Your place or mine then?'

Was momentarily thrown off balance by the bluntness of her approach, but quickly recovered my composure and said innocently, 'Oh, I think I've had enough coffee for one evening.'

'Who said anything about coffee, dum-dum?' she replied.

I said, 'I'm afraid I don't quite follow you.'

'What's there to follow?' she said. 'Do you want to fool around or don't you?'

One reads about this sort of thing happening in certain types of American literature, and I'd be the first to admit that there have been moments when I have day-dreamed about receiving such a proposition myself.

All I can say is that the fictional characters who take women up on those sort of offers (a) are obviously never feeling under the weather, (b) do not have to get up and go to work in the mornings, and (c) don't go out on dinner dates on their scooters.

On the other hand, I must confess I was not indifferent to her suggestion, and certainly did not want to close the door on it completely.

'I've heard about romance in the office,' I said with a laugh, 'but this is ridiculous.'

I suppose I should have realized that, like all Americans, Ruth has very little sense of humour.

'Thanks for nothing,' she said, and began to walk off down the street.

Decided to play things casually and called after her, 'I'll call you a cab.'

'Call me what you like,' she shouted over her shoulder, 'I only live a couple of blocks away.' And with a wave she disappeared from sight.

Though not perhaps a successful conquest in the accepted sense, I have a feeling I may have done myself more good than it may appear.

Saturday, July 22nd

How glad I am to have given up jogging when I did. Holland Park seems to have been turned into one vast cross-country running course. At every turn one is confronted by yet another sweating, red-faced fanatic, heaving his unhealthy bulk along on pink and white flabby legs, coughing, spitting, panting and generally spoiling the beauty and tranquillity of this historic preserve. Do people have no sense of place? If they want to do that sort of thing there are plenty of running tracks set aside for the purpose. I am seriously thinking of starting up an anti-jogging campaign. I can see it already: public meetings in Kensington Town Hall, articles in the paper, interviews on the 'Today' programme with Brian Redhead (or better still, Libby Purves), questions in Parliament, compulsory wording on every pair of gym shoes sold – JOGGING CAN BE HARMFUL TO YOUR HEALTH'. There's no end to it. Moreover, it's a well known fact that there is no better way of making one's name these days than by taking up some popular cause. Look at Peter Hain. His name is a household word. And Mahatma Gandhi. Who had ever heard of him before he took up non-violence?

Half expected Ruth to ring all evening.

She probably hasn't got my number.

Sunday, July 23rd

Still nothing from Ruth. Or from anyone else, come to that. Was walking in Holland Park again this afternoon following a morning of heavy rain. Stepped out of the way to avoid an on-coming jogger only to discover I had put my foot straight into a dog dirt. In those wet conditions it was indistinguishable from the surrounding mud.

Spent several minutes trying to wipe it off and was heading towards the car park when a large labrador jumped out of a Volvo and bounded towards me. I stood to one side, assuming it was setting out for a walk, but instead of rushing by, it leapt straight up at me with its dirty paws and slobbering jaws and then rushed back to the car, leaving my fawn trousers completely covered in black mud. I picked them up from the cleaners only yesterday.

Am thinking of changing my cause from anti-jogging to

anti-dogs. To judge by the state of the London pavements, I think it would do me every bit as much good.

Supper on a tray in front of the TV, again. How lonely it is in the flat these days. I never thought the day would come when I would actually miss Beddoes' presence.

Life is strange.

Monday, July 24th

I give up. Not only am I still no nearer to getting a new office, but I arrived this morning to find that over the week-end someone has seen fit to substitute my homely, if somewhat cigarette-scarred, wooden desk for a metal monstrosity half the size.

Not only that, but Miss Macmichael even more difficult and insulting about my Barford projections than ever.

I said that the mood of *détente* achieved on Friday night appeared to have been constructed very much on shifting sand.

'Friday night was pleasure,' she replied sharply, 'or rather it might have been. Today it's back to business as usual.'

So I see.

It's interesting that the most attractive women are also frequently the most ruthless. It would make an excellent subject for a thesis. Or even a book. The *Sunday Times* would snap it up like a shot. If they weren't on strike that is.

Took sub-standard socks back to shop and had further words with buyer. I may very well refer the matter to a higher authority.

Tuesday, July 25th

By one of those coincidences that are almost too astonishing to be true, I opened the paper in the tube this morning to find an advertisement for something called the Creative Writing Academy, with an address in South London.

'ARE YOU THE NEW SOMERSET MAUGHAM?' demanded the headline. 'How do you know unless you try?' continued the sub-heading.

If the copy is to be believed, by the simple device of giving up the equivalent of one evening's TV viewing time a week,

I can learn how to write and sell TV and film scripts, newspaper articles, short stories, even novels.

Have written off for the free booklet *Writing for Money*, enclosing a brief letter explaining that I have already completed half a novel while at Oxford, and that although one or two of my friends at the time commented that it was far too obviously based on Evelyn Waugh, I could not see it myself and still cannot. I agree that *Brideshead Revisited* is a very good book in its way, but that does not necessarily put all novels about undergraduate life completely out of bounds. I do not know how this will go down with the Director of Studies, but I wanted to make it clear to whoever runs the course that I am not a complete beginner.

Wednesday, July 26th

On my way in to work on the tube this morning, found myself reading *Daily Telegraph* with an altogether fresher and more critical eye. At one point, got out Pentel and found myself instinctively correcting an article about Norman St John Stevas. Also jotted down a few notes for a short story. I have long suspected that beneath this hard commercial exterior lies a deeply creative nature.

Over coffee read an interesting, though not very well written, article bemoaning the fact that TV is spoiling cricket, and that to get the real feel and atmosphere of the game one must be there in person.

I quite agree.

As one who was privileged to see the great Cyril Washbrook come out of retirement to score 98 against the Australians at Leeds in 1956 but who these days prefers the easy option of the armchair in front of the TV set to the real thing, I am only too aware of the short-comings of the medium and long for the noise and smell and excitement that are the very warp and woof of this great British institution.

By a happy coincidence, the Second Test starts at Lord's tomorrow and I think I owe it to myself, both as a sportsman and a writer, to slip up there for the day.

Informed Roundtree that I should not be in, due to dentist appointment.

He said, 'That's all right. Ruth is quite capable of making those changes for the sales conference charts we discussed.'

I said nothing. What is the point? It is impossible to fault her in his eyes. I'm beginning to wonder if he might not be having a bit of a thing with her.

Thursday, July 27th

To Lord's for the Test Match.

Paid my entrance fee at one of the side gates and made my way to the Warner Stand, to which John Arlott and others are constantly referring, only to discover that a further charge of nearly three pounds was being asked. I told the official that, as far as I was concerned, I had already paid my entrance.

'Not to the Warner Stand, you haven't,' he replied.

'There are plenty of free seats at the Nursery End, you know.'

I said that this was the first I had heard of it and that in my view it was a pity this fact was not more widely and clearly advertised.

Made my way to the Nursery End, but had no sooner taken my seat than the umpire drew stumps for lunch.

En route for a beer and a sandwich, bumped into Armitage who said, 'I'd rather you didn't mention in the office that you've seen me here. I'm supposed to be at home, working on the Morton-Johnson figures.'

I've suspected for some time now that his position in the firm is shaky, to say the least, and now I'm sure of it.

After lunch, found a seat at the very front in the sun, and settled down to the afternoon's play.

It's really most interesting to see the great stars of modern cricket in the flesh after watching them for so many years on TV. Somehow they assume much more human proportions.

Also interested to note how much smaller Lord's is in real life. One really does miss these details on TV.

Not perhaps the most exciting afternoon's cricket; indeed at one point, nodded off for quite fifteen minutes.

All in all, though, I wouldn't have missed it for anything.

Friday, July 28th

Bumped into Roundtree on my way back from the coffee machine this morning. He said, 'I didn't realize they'd taken up dentistry at cricket matches.'

Assumed that Armitage had ratted on me, and feigned innocence.

'Come off it,' said Roundtree. 'I know you were at Lord's yesterday afternoon.'

'Lord's?' I exclaimed.

'People lie, but cameras don't,' he said. 'We were having a client meeting with the Morton-Johnson people in the chairman's office yesterday afternoon when David Johnson asked if he could see the Test score. We switched on the TV and there you were, large as life and twice as natural, in the front row of the public stands. And you were asleep.'

I replied that the standard of TV outside broadcast camera work is not so perfect that it is not capable of distorting the odd face from time to time, and walked away with dignity.

My problem now is whether to mention the matter to the chairman or say nothing. Silence certainly did Jeremy Thorpe's case no harm, and it can do me none to follow his example.

Have made a few more notes on my short story. It's shaping up well.

Saturday, July 29th

Slept collarless for the first time in weeks and feel all the better for it.

Lunched *chez* Trubshawe. As coffee was being poured Derrick announced he was off to his study to watch the Test Match on TV. He turned to me and said, 'Care to join me? I understand you're quite a keen cricket fan.' To have denied it or refused might have led to a confrontation, so I said, 'Yes, I am quite,' and followed him from the room.

He did not refer again directly to my enthusiasm for the game, but I am sure he is *au courant* with my escapade in St John's Wood. All very embarrassing and awkward. According to Mollie Marsh-Gibbon, TV companies are legally bound to pay a fee of five pounds to anyone who appears, however fleetingly, in any of their programmes. I may very well take the matter up with the BBC. In the meantime, I have more pressing and delicate matters to attend to, not least of which is knocking my story into shape. It is called 'Dog', which the other way round spells God.

Sunday, July 30th

I have been thinking. I have no alternative but to tender my resignation to Roundtree tomorrow morning. It is the only honourable course open to me.

Story going less well today. I think I may be suffering from writer's block.

Mentioned it to Amanda who said, 'Housemaid's knee more likely.' Has she really got what it takes to be a writer's wife, I ask myself?

Monday, July 31st

Spent most of the day wrestling with my letter of resignation. I know now what Anthony Eden must have gone through in 1938.

Armitage stuck his head round the door later and said, in a suggestive tone of voice, 'If you have any problems with my cousin, just let me know.'

I told him that would not be necessary.

What *has* Amanda been saying to him? I have never really trusted cousins ever since reading *Rebecca*.

August

Tuesday, August 1st

A truly extraordinary coincidence. Was on my way out of
the office to deliver my letter to Roundtree when the phone
rang. It was the Barford marketing chap, Neville Pratt,
wanting to know if I was at all interested in changing jobs,
because, if so, he had a proposition he wanted to put to me. I
could hardly believe my ears. However, I have always held
that it never pays in business to express unqualified enthusiasm over anything, so have merely said I'd be interested to
hear more, and we have arranged to lunch at the Ritz. I have
always said Barfords is a company that's not afraid to spend
money when necessary. Was tempted in my excitement to
tear my letter of resignation into tiny pieces and scatter them
over Ruth Macmichael, but sanity prevailed and I put it
quietly away in a drawer. One never knows.

Wednesday, August 2nd

As we were leaving the Bordelino this evening after a difficult
dinner, Amanda suddenly put her arms round my neck, gave
me a smacking kiss and said, 'You're a funny old thing, but
I do rather love you.'

Am not sure whether to be pleased or not.

Thursday, August 3rd

A day of decisions for which I dress accordingly in dark grey.

Great hotels like the Ritz have a way of bringing out the best in one, and as I entered the restaurant, I noticed that more than one person looked across in my direction. The fact that the head waiter had never even heard of Mr Pratt, or of Barfords, slightly spoilt the effect. However, all was explained a few moments later when Pratt arrived, full of apologies, with a colleague named Keith Hardacre. We went straight to the bar where Pratt had a large vodka and tonic, Keith had a large whisky and water, and I had a small Campari and soda, a drink that is lively without being too alcoholic.

'Not a serious drinking man, then?' Keith asked with a laugh. I said that I could be on occasions, but that I preferred to keep a clear head at lunchtime.

'Sensible man,' said Keith, swallowing his whisky. 'Another one for you, Nev?'

Neville said, 'Hold your horses, Keith,' swallowed his vodka and banged his empty glass down on the table.

Keith looked at me and said, 'Simon?'

I shook my head politely.

'Sensible fellow,' said Keith, and nodded at Pratt who nodded back, and they both nodded at a passing waiter and ordered another round of the same.

After that they had another round and then we went in to lunch, and a first-class lunch it was too. Barfords certainly know how to push the boat out.

I drank one glass of white wine and one of red. Keith and Neville got through the best part of a bottle each, and yet, apart from the moment when Keith tipped a spoonful of *petits pois* into his lap, it seemed to have no effect on them.

When the coffee came, Keith said, 'Liqueur, Simon? Cognac? Tia Maria?'

I said I wouldn't have anything.

'Sensible chappie,' said Keith. 'Nev?'

They both ordered large Green Chartreuses on the rocks. We then got down to business.

Keith, who is a director of Barfords and Neville's boss, did the talking. The idea apparently is that I should join them in a PR sort of capacity, as a kind of roving ambassador, travelling here and there and generally handling the corporate image of Barfords. It all sounds most exciting and very much my sort of style, and when they mentioned the salary (£12,000 a year) I nearly fell off my seat. That's half as much again as I am getting at Harley Preston.

Talk about offers one can't refuse.

It is high time I got out and about a bit in the world before married life pins me down once and for all. Like T. S. Eliot, I could easily fit my writing in in the evenings and at weekends.

Was quite tempted to say 'yes' and be done with it. On the other hand, it will be interesting to see the lengths to which Harley Preston are prepared to go to keep me on, and I said I would let them know in a few days. 'Sensible fellow,' said Keith, and we all had a celebratory Green Chartreuse which made me feel rather sick.

As we were shaking hands on the steps, Keith said in an earnest sort of way, 'Do join us,' and gave my hand an odd little squeeze.

I had the distinct feeling he was trying to tell me something. Walked back to the office in the warm sunshine in a strangely puzzled mood.

Friday, August 4th

Once one has made up one's mind to a thing, there is no point in prolonging the agony and I pinned Roundtree down to a confrontation at 3.15. I cut the chit-chat and came straight to the point. 'I think I should tell you,' I told him, 'that I have been offered a post at Barfords at £12,000 a year. I'd be interested to hear what you have to say.'

'Congratulations,' Roundtree said.

I said, 'So you're not interested in matching the offer?'

'No,' he said.

'I see,' I said. 'Still, I daresay you'd like me to work out my notice. As you know, I have quite a bit on at present.'

He said, 'I don't think that will be necessary. Ruth pretty well knows the form by now.'

I was, and still am, dumbfounded. For two pins I'd leave tomorrow.

Unfortunately I have not yet received an official letter from Barfords offering me the job. Am hoping Roundtree will not mention the matter to Derrick for a day or two, just in case.

Rang Neville's office to be told he was in Leeds. Keith Hardacre also away. Had a row with Ruth and went home early.

Have decided to scrap short story in favour of a novel about a man who suddenly at the age of 36 decides to change his job. It's coming along rather well.

Saturday, August 5th

Surprised and disappointed to have heard nothing yet from the Creative Writing people. However, novel going so well I'm beginning to wonder if I'm really going to need the course after all.

Amanda rang to ask me to Joanna and Timmy's party, but I pleaded pressure of work.

She said, 'You never want to do anything any more. I don't know why we bother to go on.'

I pointed out that relationships with writers have always been notoriously difficult and quoted as examples Byron and Hardy.

She said, 'I don't know about Hardy, but at least Byron was sexy.'

I said that if a cripple who was mad, bad and dangerous to know was her idea of sexy, then I gave up.

'Yes,' she said. 'It is.'

I reminded her that sex appeal and literary talent were totally unconnected; the whole point was that one could not afford to be distracted by trivial social activities, adding that it was well known that, when Nancy Mitford was writing a book, she never saw anyone for weeks on end.

She said. 'Don't say you're changing sex. That would explain everything.'

And she rang off.

All very distressing, but as a writer one will have to learn to live with this kind of thing.

Sunday, August 6th

Damn and blast it. I've missed Glyndebourne again. Every year I promise myself I will join the dinner-jacketed revellers on the famous afternoon train, hamper in one hand, a pretty girl in the other. I have never cared a lot for opera. On the other hand, the idea of wandering around the lawns of a country house, sipping champagne in the cool of a summer's evening in the company of Bernard Levin, Arianna Stassinopoulos and others has always appealed to me, and to have never experienced it is surely to have missed one of the essential pleasures of English life as we know it. Or don't, in my case.

I wonder if I shouldn't try and work it into my novel in some way?

I'm thinking of calling it *The Long Look Back*, but may change it later.

Monday, August 7th

Lunched with Mollie Marsh-Gibbon in what she described as the best fish restaurant in London and turned out to be nothing more than a glorified fish and chip shop. Wandsworth is a long way to go for the doubtful pleasure of deep-fried hake. I'm not surprised that very few people know about it. Still, one can't tell Mollie anything, and I didn't try.

True to form, she was most scornful of my lunch at the Ritz, saying that only jumped-up media people and second-rate estate agents ever eat there nowadays. When I mentioned the curious handshake Keith had given me, she shrieked, 'My dear fellow, don't you know anything? The chap's obviously a Mason. I'd steer clear of that firm if I were you.'

I had neither the time nor the inclination to take her up on the matter, but her comments have certainly set me thinking. Perhaps Keith *was* inviting me to become a fellow Mason, and is waiting for me to take him up on this before he will commit himself to offering me the job officially. But how to find out for certain? This is one of those tricky little situations one meets from time to time in one's professional life and which, if handled badly, can lead to disaster.

First things first: I must do a bit of research into this whole subject of Freemasonry.

Curiously enough, I have always been very interested to know what it's all about, and this is an excellent opportunity to find out at last.

Tuesday, August 8th

I have never really had a lot of truck with astrology, and when I skim through the horoscope in my newspaper every morning, I treat it very much as I treat theatre and cinema reviews – as good entertainment but not to be taken too literally.

However, this morning the forecast for the weekend reflects my life with an accuracy that is surely more than coincidental.

'This could turn out to be one of the most outstanding weekends of your life, and one of the happiest. Forge ahead confidently with everything you are doing at present, and take care to accept every invitation you are offered. Refusal at this stage could cause you much unhappiness in the long run.'

It's almost as if the writer is thoroughly *au fait* with the most intimate details of my life. I wonder if it's anyone I know?

Wednesday, August 9th

To the Westminster Public Library to consult the standard history of Freemasonry by Brother Ellis. Most interested to discover that there is scarcely a great man in history who was *not* a Mason: Christopher Wren, George Washington, Robert Burns, Mozart, Edward VII. Were I to join, I should obviously be in good company, and I have no doubt I am as well fitted to become a member of a lodge as the next man. I am over 21, a free man of good report and integrity, and would certainly come of my own free will. On the other hand, do I really want to become a Lodge Master, or an Inner Guard, or even a Junior Deacon? A writer's life is full enough as it is.

Indeed, if Brother Ellis's report is anything to go by, it is going to take all my time just to grasp the fundamental principles of Freemasonry. I have no first-hand experience of the building industry, and lines like 'We cannot properly consider the square without associating it with Euclid's 47th Proposition' set my mind reeling.

I am also suspicious of this connection with Solomon's Temple. I'm wondering if the Jews have a hand in it somewhere.

Frankly, after an hour's concentrated reading, I am as baffled as ever. So, I daresay, are the large majority of Masons, if they would but admit it. What an intelligent fellow like Mozart saw in it all is beyond me.

On the other hand, I think I would be unwise to dismiss the whole idea willy-nilly. I am not a superstitious man, but my horoscope was quite specific on the subject of invitations, and for the moment I intend to reserve judgement.

Thursday, August 10th

Still nothing from Barfords. Morning spent in an agony of doubt and indecision. Other considerations apart, if I don't receive confirmation of my new job soon, I shall seriously have to consider taking lodgers. I really cannot afford to keep this flat going at this rate.

After lunch, could stand suspense no longer and rang Keith's secretary, Miss Hippo. Said who I was and explained that I had been away for a few days and that I was just ringing to find out if by chance he had been trying to get in touch with me. She said, 'No. Why, should he have been?' I said, 'Not really.' She said, 'Mr Hardacre is a very busy man. Why should he ring for no reason?'

I said, 'It was just that he'd promised to let me have some information about a club he belongs to.'

'Club?' said Miss Hippo. 'What sort of a club?'

I told her it was not exactly a club, more a society. She said she was not aware of his belonging to any societies. I said in a confidential tone of voice, 'It has loose connections with architecture, or more precisely the building industry, if you know what I mean.'

Miss Hippo said, 'I can only suggest that I pass the message on to Mr Hardacre and let him come back to you in person.' And before I could stop her, she had put the phone down on me.

I hope the secretaries at Barfords are not as hopeless at passing on messages as Sarah is in our office.

Friday, August 11th

Was on my way to the coffee machine this morning when Keith rang and said, 'I understand from my secretary that you are interested in joining the National Trust. This is excellent news. We need as many members as we can get. I've asked them to send you all the requisite bumph. You should be getting it any day now. Must dash.' And he rang off.

Curiously enough I have often considered the possibility of joining the National Trust.

Saturday, August 12

The 'Glorious Twelfth' indeed, since the morning post brings a fat manilla envelope from the Creative Writing people. As well as the booklet *Writing for Money*, there are various vouchers and a free copy of *The Moon and Sixpence*. Are they somehow in league with the Maugham family, one asks oneself?

Also included is a personal letter addressed 'Dear Writer' from the Director of Studies, Mr Brian Silver. I seem to have heard that name somewhere before. What he has to say is certainly to the point: the secret of successful writing is simply knowing *what* to write, and *how* to write.

Skimmed through *Writing for Money* which, among other things, contains letters from satisfied and successful students. One read: 'I have had two articles accepted by a gourmet magazine. . . . My life has been completely transformed. . . . I owe it all to the Creative Writing Course.' Signed H.B-F. London.

If that isn't Hugh Bryant-Fenn I'll eat my hat. If he's an example of one of their successes, I'd hate to think where their failures wind up.

At all events, have decided to accept their free trial offer to read and criticize any piece of descriptive writing of no more than 500 words that I care to send within the next twenty-one days. Oddly enough, I have had the feeling for several days now that I am about to give birth to an outburst of creativity.

After much agonizing, settled for a walk in Richmond Park beneath the shade of the beeches – alone, of course. Set off after lunch. A perfect summer's afternoon: warm and sunny with just the faintest hint of a breeze kissing the panting grass. Above, an azure sky was decorated with tiny puffs of white cloud, like blobs of cotton wool on a child's painting.

Butterflies lolloped from wild flower to wild flower, pausing briefly to sip at the warm honey before skipping on their way, while deep in the woods, turtle doves cooed seductively to the dozing deer. An English summer at its very best. . . .

Cut across towards Thatched Lodge, home of the Ogilvys. Slithered down the steep bank below the house and crossed the road. Was strolling happily through the thick bracken when I heard a strange sound away to my left, as though an animal were in pain.

Tip-toed towards the sound and hid behind a tree. Peered round the trunk to discover, as I thought, a young man in the process of murdering a young girl. Moved forward to protest when I suddenly realized that they were half naked and making love. Understandably I was frozen to the spot for a moment or two with embarrassment. Unfortunately, before I had a chance to move away, the girl spotted me and cried out, 'Bugger off, you dirty old man.' Was thinking I'd seen her before somewhere, when the man looked up.

I could scarcely believe my eyes. It was Colin Armitage. The girl, I suddenly realized, was Roundtree's secretary, Felicity. I do not believe I have been more shocked and embarrassed in my life. At the same time I was oddly excited, and all I could think about as I walked back to the car was how much I wanted to see Amanda. For two pins I'd have gone round to The Boltons there and then were I not so anxious to get the story down on paper while the events were still fresh in my mind. As a writer, one cannot afford to let such moments of inspiration pass and be dissipated in the pursuit of bodily gratification.

Finally settled down at the Olympia portable at six and worked on till Starsky and Hutch. Am experiencing some problems with the opening, but then even Maugham was prepared to sit all morning staring at a blank sheet of paper. The hardest thing of all is the title. I may call it *Summer Madness*.

Sunday, August 13th

Woke exhausted and disturbed after a restless night. At one point had a strangely erotic dream of a vaguely pornographic nature, concerning a member of the royal family. As a result, quite unable to settle to any serious work all day. Have definitely decided to change the title, though to what I am not as yet sure.

After supper watched 'Face the Music'. Lord Norwich, Mother's favourite, not on. Have come to the conclusion that there is only one item I dislike more than the Funny Opera and that's the Dummy Keyboard. Tonight they had both.

Monday, August 14th

The morning's post brings the long-awaited letter from Keith, officially offering me the job and laying down the conditions of employment. I am to be known as Deputy Marketing Manager, with direct responsibility to Neville Pratt, at a salary of £12,000 per annum, payable monthly as usual, and I am to begin as soon as my present commitments will allow. No further mention, I notice, of Freemasonry. Immediately drafted a letter of acceptance. The key to success in business is recognizing opportunities when they arise and seizing them with both hands. As Sir Freddie Laker said in a recent TV interview, re his executives: one can tolerate almost any fault except indecision. Spoke to Roundtree about date of leaving and have told him I am prepared to stay on for a further week. There are still one or two odds and ends to be tidied up and besides, there are many who would feel most aggrieved and hurt if I were to leave before they'd had a chance for a whip-round.

Sarah will almost certainly wish to organize some sort of farewell do in the pub.

Worked on my piece in the evening. I'm calling it *Summer Sonata*.

Tuesday, August 15th

Woke early and put finishing touches to the piece. It is faintly reminiscent of H. E. Bates. Decided to treat myself to small celebratory lunch at my favourite Greek restaurant near the office and posted Barford letter en route.

Was on way out when I felt a hand on my arm. Turned to find Bryant-Fenn reaching out from a table by the door, and inviting me to join him for a drink. He told me he was there in his capacity as restaurant critic for this much-heralded news magazine which is supposed to change our lives for the better. He ordered a glass of retsina for me and a brandy for himself.

When I told him about my new job he said, 'Good. It's about time you started living high on the hog at someone else's expense.'

I replied stiffly that if he thought I'd risk my career for the sake of a few perks, he had thoroughly underestimated me.

Hugh threw back the remains of his brandy and shook his head. 'What a very naive chap you are,' he said. 'All the best people live at someone else's expense, and always have done. No one in his right mind would rush to become Deputy Marketing Manager of anything unless it involved free travel, a company car, jolly good expenses and probably school fees, clothes, interest-free mortgage and free hairdressing for the wife thrown in for good measure. Not, of course, that you have a wife. Never mind. You can always invent one.'

I told him that obviously all those minor details were being well taken care of. I said, 'You don't honestly think I'd walk into a set-up like this with my eyes shut, do you?' 'Knowing you,' he replied, 'yes.'

Was so rattled by his remarks that I quite forgot to tackle him about the Creative Writing Academy. Left restaurant and ran to post box on off-chance of intercepting collection, but arrived just as van was driving away up the street. Grabbed taxi and told driver to follow van, but lost him in Euston Road. Returned to office by tube, but even so was the best part of thirty bob out of pocket.

Yet another terse note from Ruth about the Barford projections set a miserable seal on what should have been a very happy and satisfying day.

Wednesday, August 16th

Posted *Summer Sonata* to Creative Writing people. I could scarcely bring myself to put the envelope in the box, and as the brown manilla slipped through my fingers, I felt as though part of my soul had gone with it.

Rang Mother this evening for no particular reason. She took an age to answer. When she finally did, I said, 'I hope you're not going deaf; I've been ringing for ages.'

'Not at all,' she replied briskly. 'If you must know, that

dreadful Tony Benn was on TV again and I've been watching with my fingers in my ears.'

Thursday, August 17th

Was clearing my desk before lunch when Hugh rang to ask if I would be interested in his proposing me for American Express Card membership.

Funnily enough, I have been thinking of applying for some time now, largely as a result of those TV commercials I keep seeing. I have never been a great advocate of the 'live now, pay later' way of life, but to be in a position to book theatre seats over the phone, rent a car without leaving a deposit, and earn the respect of head waiters in the best restaurants is no bad thing for a rising executive. Indeed, to be thought uncreditworthy by potential clients would be to undermine the whole purpose of one's existence.

I realize that not everyone is eligible for membership by any means, and I told Hugh that I was most flattered to be asked.

He said, 'There's no need to be. I only mentioned it because they're offering six bottles of rather good wine to anyone who introduces a new member. I'll fill out the form straight away. You're the fourth scalp I've bagged this morning.' And he rang off.

Arrived home this evening to find an application form for membership of the National Trust. £7 a year seems little enough to pay for the privilege of walking into any of the Trust's properties free of charge, and can do me nothing but good in the eyes of my new employers. Have sent off cheque straight away.

Friday, August 18th

Read a fascinating report in the paper about a drugs raid in Chelsea. It seems that the police had been watching the flat for some weeks, but when they finally decided to pounce, they got stuck in the lift between two floors and by the time they'd extricated themselves, the suspects had poured most of their merchandise into the water cistern.

I am rather worried about this, since there is nothing to prevent the stuff getting into the London water system and thence via the taps into our homes. Why they couldn't have shoved it down the loo like every other drug smuggler, I can't think.

One would have thought the authorities would be as concerned as I am, and yet, so far, no warnings have been issued in the papers or on the radio. Really, the public is held in less and less regard these days.

This morning my coffee tasted most peculiar, and I have been feeling decidedly light-headed all day. Mentioned the fact casually to Sarah, our secretary, who said she felt fine and that for as long as she had known me I have been rather airy-fairy.

There's no talking to her since Armitage ditched her for Jane. It's as if the fact that he's gone off with my ex-girl-friend was in some way my responsibility.

Am seriously considering penning a stiff note to the Metropolitan Water Board.

Saturday, August 19th

It never rains but it pours. Have deliberately been maintaining a lowish profile with Amanda during these tricky times, largely to avoid another possibly embarrassing scene with Trubshawe *père*.

Matters taken rudely out of my hands by sudden appearance shortly after breakfast on the doorstep of the young lady in question, carrying a small suitcase, a selection of magazines, and a moth-eaten toy panda.

Any doubts that I might have been harbouring concerning my feelings for her dissolved in an instant, and I opened my arms to her. 'Thank God you're in,' she said, and marched firmly past me into the flat.

'Is anyone else here?' she asked.

I told her that we were quite alone. 'Good,' she said. 'I need your help.'

I said, 'It's right that I should be the first person you turn to at times like this.'

'Actually,' she said, 'you're the third. All the other people I tried were away for the weekend.'

People tend to say things they don't really mean when they're upset. The long and the short of it is that she has had the most almighty row with her parents, given them back her

Mini and left home. I said I hoped I was not the cause of it.

She said, 'Why ever should you think that?'

She then announced that she was planning to move in with me. While I am obviously excited at the prospect of our living together if only temporarily and while I welcome having someone else in the flat to help out with housekeeping, cooking, bills, etc, I certainly do not wish to fall out with Enid and Derrick.

Until this business of expenses, etc. is settled with Barfords, there is always the possibility I may still be working for Derrick for some time to come.

At all events, have decided to play it by ear, at least until after the weekend.

After supper we watched an absurd American detective film on TV, curled up together on the sofa, sipping wine and canoodling.

As I write these words, Amanda is in bed next door with a magazine. The moment of truth is nigh. . . .

Sunday, August 20th

Last night rather a flop – in every sense of the word. Undressed in bathroom, washed carefully all over standing up, and gave teeth a strenuous seeing to – rather too strenuous, as it turned out, since I carelessly knocked the hard part of the brush against my upper gums, drawing blood and slightly loosening a molar. Rinsed as best I could in Listerine and finished toilet with modest dash of after-shave in various strategic places. Arrived in bedroom to find Amanda lying on her back with her eyes closed and magazine face down on her chest.

Thinking to surprise her, I tip-toed across the room. In doing so, small Abyssinian prayer rug beside bed slipped on lino floor, bringing me to the floor with a crash and badly ricking my neck. Amanda did not even stir.

Tip-toed from room again to bathroom where I took two Disprin in water and put on my surgical collar. Realizing I was still naked, I reached behind door for my pyjamas only to remember they were hanging on line over bath, still damp from yesterday morning's wash.

Put on underpants, returned to room and slipped into bed

beside naked, sleeping figure. Despite pain, finally nodded off.

Woken soon afterwards by telephone. Staggered to sitting room to answer. It was Derrick, at his iciest, wanting to know if Amanda was with me. Did the only thing possible in the circumstances by adopting West Indian accent and saying he must have dialled the wrong number. Hurried back to room to find Amanda sitting up anxiously in bed. As I entered, she shrieked with laughter, pointing at me, stuffing the sheet in her mouth and rolling around helplessly. I suppose a surgical collar does look rather funny if you're not used to such things, but not as funny as all that. Against my better judgement, removed offending article and hopped back into bed but sadly unable to respond to her enthusiastic advances. I doubt that even Beddoes would have fared better in the circumstances. Amanda said it really didn't matter and went back to sleep, leaving me to long hours of sleepless agony. Finally dozed off just before seven and managed to get in an hour or two before Amanda appeared with newspapers and breakfast on a tray.

I am not normally one for lying around in bed at weekends, but there are exceptions to every rule. Suffice it to say that one thing led to another and before I knew what, it was lunchtime. I've said it before and I'll say it again, a happy sex life is fundamental to any relationship. Apart from anything else it has also done wonders for my neck.

Monday, August 21st

Rang Hardacre the moment I got in this morning and as tactfully as possible tackled him over this matter of expenses. He said, 'Of course you get an expense account. How could you possibly do the job otherwise?'

Said that I was just checking on a few details, adding that I presumed that included a company car.

He said, 'Oh, I'm afraid that's quite out of the question. We're cutting back on perks like that.'

Obviously I shall now have to get rid of the VW once and for all and buy myself something more in keeping with my new position. A Rover 3500 perhaps or a Citroën CX. Or even a BMW, though why we should support the German car industry in this country after all the trouble they've given us over the years I cannot imagine. If only Amanda hadn't been so hasty in giving her Mini back to her parents. Much as I am getting used to her presence in the flat, I may seriously have to consider turning her in.

Arrived home this evening to learn that she had spent all day cleaning the flat. To my eye, it seemed slightly dirtier than when I left this morning. Spaghetti for dinner. Her idea of cooking this simple dish is to take a handful of the stuff and force it into the saucepan breaking off all the outside bits which, if they do not fall into the flames of the gas and become welded on to the enamel, scatter in all directions so that the floor becomes like an ice rink.

She also forgot to put salt in the tomato sauce.

I could not be more fond of her if I tried, but really if the last few days are par for the course kitchenwise, I'd do better to revert to the Indian takeaway. On the other hand, no amount of spicy food can make up for a healthy helping of spicy sex!

Tuesday, August 22nd

Had just got in after a longish lunch with Iversen and Attenborough when the chairman's secretary rang to say he would like to see me at 4.15.

I do not think I have experienced a more nerve-racking half hour in my life.

Arrived in Derrick's office to be greeted with the words, 'I hear you're leaving us.'

I replied that in my considered view it was best for all concerned.

'Quite right' he said. 'None of us can afford to turn down good offers nowadays, not with wives and families to support.' Decided to play the innocent and asked him if he happened to know where Amanda was. He said, 'At home, having tea with her mother when I last heard of her. I gather she found all that cooking and housework too much of a strain. Still, plenty of time for all that, eh?'

I said, 'So you know everything?'

He said, 'You mean about her staying with you? Of course.'

I said, 'When? How?'

'Oh,' he said, 'the moment I rang up the other night. That

was quite the worst bit of acting I've come across in a long time.'

Rang Amanda later who said she thought it would be better for both our sakes if we didn't meet for a few days. Had no choice but to agree. Feel I should be putting my foot down over all this, but how? I never thought the day would come when I would value Beddoes' advice. If he hadn't rushed off leaving so many unpaid bills, including his share of the telephone, I might have rung him in Brussels, but not at those prices. Finally decided to do so, reversing the charges.

After a certain amount of to-ing and fro-ing, the operator informed me that Mr Beddoes had refused to accept the call. I can only assume there was some sort of breakdown in communications. What uncertain times we do live in.

Wednesday, August 23rd

Mother's birthday. Hope the flea collar for the cat went down well. Not perhaps the most personal of gifts but, for one who thinks more of her animal than herself, highly suitable, I think. Can she really be 68?

On way to coffee machine this afternoon, spotted Sarah in Iversen's office, obviously collecting money. I wonder what they're thinking of buying me? I could really do with a new wallet. The problem is how to drop a big enough hint without letting on that I've twigged.

Still nothing from Amanda. I miss her dreadfully, but am determined to leave the running to her for once.

Thursday, August 24th

On way into work, stopped off at my local BL dealer to see if they had anything to catch my eye. I feel it is my duty to support the British car industry at this low point in its fortunes. Mr Aylott, a tall, well-spoken young man in a dark suit, sat me down with a cup of coffee and delivered a fascinating lecture on the history and manufacture of the Austin and Morris. He then took me out for a test run in his Rover 3500 and allowed me to experience what he called 'the magic of BL motoring'.

Was particularly impressed by the brakes which are most efficient, if a little sharp – to wit the sharp crack Mr Aylott gave his knee against the dashboard when I stopped suddenly at a pedestrian crossing.

Still, he couldn't have been nicer about it and said he was sure the limp was only temporary and that provided *I* was convinced, it was worth the odd unexpected knock.

We then looked at a selection of second-hand models any of which I'd have been happy to own. Was particularly taken by a white 1976 Austin Maxi. According to Aylott, they are spending £300 on doing it up, including a new clutch, and four hours of paintwork. He says it will look very nice indeed when they've finished with it. I have said I'll think about it. He told me to take my time, pressed some sales leaflets into my hand and limped off towards his office.

Made a point of getting out my wallet in front of Sarah this afternoon and saying it was high time I got a new one.

She said, 'Yes, it certainly is.'

I think the message has got through.

Friday, August 25th

My last day at Harley Preston. In a symbolic gesture, threw my old wallet out of the office window and watched it flutter, like an autumn leaf, into the dustbins below. Then went to wash my hands in gents. Just before five-thirty, strolled into Sarah's cubby hole to find her putting the cover on her typewriter.

'Hallo,' she said, 'you still here then?'

I said, 'If it wasn't for the party, I'd have gone hours ago.'

'Oh,' she said, 'are you having a party? You might have asked me.'

'There seems to be some sort of misunderstanding,' I said.

'Obviously,' she said. 'Well, I must be off.' And she began to gather up her things.

I said, 'About the you-know-what, I couldn't help noticing you were making a collection the other day.'

'Oh, that,' she said. 'It's for Roundtree's secretary, Felicity. She's getting married, you know. As you were leaving, I didn't think you'd be interested.' And with a curt goodbye, she walked off down the corridor.

Was hunting in the dustbins for my old wallet when Armitage walked by.

'What's all this then, Crisp? A last minute spot of industrial espionage?'

I couldn't be bothered to reply.

Saturday, August 26th

My article came back today from the Creative Writing people. Hardly a sentence has escaped the furious attentions of the red pencil, and the margins are filled with lengthy and, to my mind, totally unjustified criticism. *Summer Sonata* was considered 'a sloppy title'. My description of the sights and sounds of Richmond Park in high summer were 'overblown and hackneyed'. As for my unexpected encounter with the young couple making love, this was thought to be 'not credible and rather crude', and my expressions of regret and the loss of innocence 'mawkish and naive'. The comments are signed H.B.-F. It may, or may not, be Hugh – who cares? The point is, a set-up that employs a tutor who is so incapable of recognizing talent when it leaps off the page and hits him in the face is hardly likely to get my vote, and I have written to say so.

Amanda rang this morning to ask me to lunch tomorrow at The Boltons. Have said I'll go, but may easily pull out at the last moment. Later, called round to car showroom to find a stout, middle-aged man with handlebar moustache sitting in Aylott's office. Asked where Aylott was.

He said, 'He's away for a fortnight in hospital, having an operation on his knee. There's a rumour he may never play squash again.' Had been planning to ask for a test drive in one of their Range Rovers, but in the circumstances it seemed only polite to buy the Maxi that caught my eye the other day.

Mr Balditch told me that there were still one or two little things that needed looking at in the workshop.

'We're putting over £350 of work into this car,' he said. 'The paintwork alone will take twelve hours.'

I doubt if one would have met with that quality of service from a foreign car dealer.

Spent rest of day composing two advertisements: one for my Beetle and another for some new flatmates. I obviously cannot rely on Amanda to help out on either score.

I may definitely slide out of this lunch date tomorrow. One

good thing about her departure: at least I can now wear my surgical collar in bed *sans peur et sans reproche*.

Sunday, August 27th

If the Sunday Supplements are not trying to sell off cheap continental quilts and curtain materials, they are trying to foist clock radios and digital watches on to the unsuspecting public. Why anyone should feel the need to be woken up by the inane chatter of Irish disc jockeys first thing in the morning I cannot think. I have woken regularly at 7.30 for the last five years without the need of any artificial alarm, and see no reason to change my habits in the future.

Rang Amanda at noon to say that I had been unexpectedly struck down by a violent attack of food poisoning and would therefore be unable to make lunch.

She said, 'I think it would be to our advantage if you came.'

Arrived in time for drinks. Derrick said cheerfully, 'Something soft for you, I suppose?' And before I could utter a word, he had poured me a glass of Perrier water. Lunch was my favourite: roast leg of lamb, garden peas and new potatoes. Derrick had brought up one of his best clarets.

'Plenty of everything for you?' said Enid and piled up my plate. Amanda came into the room and exclaimed, 'You shouldn't be eating that with your food poisoning,' and took my plate away.

'Just a glass of wine then,' I said.

'Certainly not,' said Derrick.

After a while they relented slightly and allowed me to nibble on a dry biscuit and sip some water. While we, or rather they, were waiting for the pudding, Amanda announced that Derrick had agreed to throw a party for her on September 16th, in return for which she is to undertake a two month's course in shorthand and typing. I'm the last to know – as usual.

We then went through to the sitting room for coffee – or not in my case.

Derrick poured himself a brandy and announced that he had had enough of our shilly-shallying and the sooner we got on with it and made the whole thing official the happier he would be.

In the meantime he has bought Amanda a small house in Parsons Green, if you please. Whether this is intended as a juicy carrot to lure me to the starting gate I do not know. At all events, I was certainly not about to let him think I can be bought that easily.

I said, 'What a very good idea,' and immediately changed the subject to the forthcoming Barford client meeting. By three-thirty was feeling so hungry I made an excuse and hurried home where I ate baked beans on toast followed by cheese and biscuits, two cups of coffee and a Mars bar.

An hour later had one of the worst tummy upsets I have ever known. Still, at least it gave me a much-needed opportunity to lie down and review my situation.

I suppose I am very old-fashioned, but I had always assumed that in the event of my marrying, the role of bread-winner would fall fairly and squarely upon my shoulders. On the other hand, I don't recall the Duke of Marlborough adopting a high moral tone when he married the Vanderbilt girl, and Dickie Mountbatten very quickly adjusted to the idea of marrying an heiress. The alliance of beauty, brains and breeding with money and property is as traditional a part of the English way of life as the Eton Wall Game and Swan Upping. In this life some of us fall on our feet, and some don't, and I must learn to accept my fortune with good grace and press ahead with cheerfulness and humour. I suppose I must now think seriously about putting our relationship on a proper footing and buy Amanda an engagement ring. Now that the problem of accommodation has been settled, I shall be able to spend a little more on it than I had expected.

Monday, August 28th

A ghastly thing happened. I still cannot believe it is true. Woke refreshed and full of optimism after an excellent night's sleep. Looked at my watch to discover it was 9.15! As a result arrived to take up my new appointment three-quarters of an hour late, in a muck sweat and minus my usual bolstering breakfast.

Asked the commissionaire at the front desk for Mr Pratt's office and when lift wouldn't come, ran to the eighth floor, still wearing my motorcycling gear. Flew in through door marked N. G. PRATT, MARKETING MANAGER (NEW

PRODUCT DEVELOPMENT) and came face to face with extremely attractive red-headed girl who said, 'Messengers are on the fifth floor.' I laughed and explained who I was, but she seemed never to have heard of me. At all events, Pratt and Hardacre are both away in Stockholm until next Monday. Hardacre's secretary, Miss Hippo, also away.

The girl told me her name was Pippa Robinson and that she was Pratt's secretary. Suggested she made a few enquiries on my behalf, but she could find no-one who even knew of my presence in the company. I had a mind to kick up a bit of a stink, but did not wish to embarrass Pippa who did her very best to make me feel at home, and made me a cup of coffee on a real Cona machine.

While eating one of her digestive biscuits, I bit hard on the tooth I had loosened with my toothbrush and broke it clean in two. Pippa was most concerned and immediately rang her own dentist and made an appointment for me tomorrow at two-thirty.

I do not think I have ever got on so well with anyone so quickly as I did with her. We seem to laugh at exactly the same things, and there is definitely electricity between us.

At noon, the door opened and a large, shambling man of about forty-five with straggly fair hair round a bald head and strikingly bad teeth stuck his head round the door and said, 'Hallo, who are you?'

I explained who I was, at which he said, 'Good, good. Settling in well, I hope?' and left.

I said to Pippa he looked like a man who had just escaped from a loony bin. She said, 'Actually, that was Harold Hill. He's the chairman.'

Lunched alone at a sandwich bar near the office. One sardine, one cheese and sweet pickle.

At three o'clock a surly looking black woman arrived with the tea trolley. Asked for milk and no sugar and got lemon and three lumps. Later Pippa gave me a Rolo which got stuck in my broken tooth and hurt so much I had to go home. Was almost at the front door when I remembered I was supposed to pick up the Maxi.

Rushed back to the showroom and arrived just before they closed at five-thirty, only to learn that they have had a couple of blokes off sick. Balditch said, 'We do want to bring the vehicle up to standard. After all, we are putting nearly

£400 into it. We should have it ready this time Thursday. No sweat.'

Maybe it wasn't for him, but then he hadn't run half the length of Kensington High Street.

To bed early with the *Evening Standard* and a couple of Veganin. Jane always used to pronounce it as though it were a Russian astronaut. Strange how much I still miss her. She would have been very much my type if it hadn't been for the bad skin. And the hair. The *Standard* has made my sheets quite black.

Tuesday, August 29th

Arrived in Pratt's office, on time, to be told Miss Hippo would like to see me. Confronted by a petite blonde woman in glasses.

She said, 'I'm most terribly sorry about this, but we were expecting you next week. Anyway, I think I've found an office for you. If you wouldn't mind sharing Miss Robinson with Mr Pratt for the time being.' She then led me along the corridor to the back of the building. Couldn't help noticing that she had a pronounced limp, so said conversationally, 'That leg of yours looks nasty.'

'I've got used to it myself,' she said, 'ever since I had polio as a child.'

My office slightly smaller than I had imagined, but it could be worse. It's a pity that in an office block that overlooks such a pretty square I should have a comparatively uninspiring view of the back of the Carshalton Building Society building. Still, I shall probably hardly ever be there.

Hung my calendar from Drake's garage depicting British wildfowl on the wall above my head. Thought of placing photograph of Amanda in black leatherette frame on the desk, but finally decided against it.

I wouldn't want to give the impression unnecessarily that I am spoken for.

After a while, heard the sounds of a trolley being wheeled along the corridor, and cups being chinked. Waited for several minutes but no-one came. Rang Pippa to suggest lunch but no reply. Decided to risk sandwich bar again. Tongue on white with mustard excellent but chicken on brown very nasty indeed.

Bought *Evening Standard* to check on my ad. It certainly stands out very well. I'm glad now I allowed myself to be talked in to the semi-display.

To the dentist at two-thirty. He says I'll need a root filling, followed by a crown.

Although claiming to be National Health, this will set me back £150.

Have said I'll think about it. At that price, it's worth getting some quotes from other dentists. I never thought the day would come when I would have to shop around for a new tooth.

Wednesday, August 30th

Picked six dentists at random from Yellow Pages and they all quote a similar figures, except one in Cricklewood who quoted only £80. Have never been one to spoil the ship for a ha'p'orth of tar, but for £70, it has to be worth the detour and the man sounds really very nice indeed. Have made an appointment for Friday.

After lunch a woman rang to enquire about the car. She seemed very keen indeed and we arranged to meet outside the flat at five-fifteen. Left the office early in order to give the vehicle a quick wash and brush-up prior to inspection. It was a pity a large piece of paint should have chosen today of all days to come away completely, but then it is for good, sound engineering that so many millions have been buying VWs over the past fifty years, not fancy bodywork.

She arrived punctually by taxi, a small, grey woman, not unlike Mother in looks. Name of Miss Timms. The entire transaction took slightly less than fifteen minutes. I was naturally disappointed not to get the £150 I was asking, but I must agree with Miss Timms that 98,000 miles *is* steep, even for a Beetle, and the bodywork *has* seen better days, and the smell inside *is* rather pungent, and although £65 is hardly what I'd call a near offer, I'm frankly quite glad to have the thing off my hands. Whether she really would have reported me to the Trades Description people I don't know, but one cannot afford to take those sort of risks nowadays. Not in my position anyway.

Called at showroom to collect my new Maxi, but it seems they came across something in the gearbox this afternoon they don't like the look of.

What I'd like to know is, if the car was supposed to be ready by this evening, what were they doing inside the gearbox *this afternoon*?

Did not feel inclined to kick up too much of a stink, however, since they have offered to lend me a two-year-old Mini until Monday evening.

Browsed round a few jewellers' at lunchtime. I had no idea engagement rings were so expensive. Anyway, in my view, if a couple need to resort to flashy jewellery to prove their love for each other it's a pretty poor look-out.

September

Friday, September 1st

To Cricklewood by Mini to see the dentist. I don't know why it had not occurred to me he might be a coloured chap, but it hadn't. However, he appeared to go through very much the same routine as white dentists, so I daresay my misgivings are without foundations.

He seems confident that he can do a good job on my crown for £90, so I have told him the contract is his. We meet again in a week's time.

The only drawback with black dentists is that after staring up into gleaming white mouths for a few minutes one comes away with such an inferiority complex about one's own stained, grey, metal-filled monstrosities. It's a pity *our* ancestors didn't chew a few more roots.

Saturday, September 2nd

It is exactly a year ago to the day that I decided to start my diary. And what a fascinating year it has been. Looking back, I see that in my first entry I remarked that if anyone thought I had undertaken a diary with an eye to publication, they had another think coming. And yet I venture to suggest that my view of the late seventies is every bit as fascinating and revealing and publishable as Harold Nicolson's was of the thirties and forties, if not more so.

I am well aware that the exploits of the rich and famous make for popular publishing, yet Francis Kilvert and Parson

Woodforde scarcely met or wrote about a figure of note in their lives and today their diaries are considered classics.

Sunday, September 3rd

Woke to discover that I have developed some sort of infection in my broken tooth. Rang dentist, but no reply. Like plumbers, they are never there when you want them. Patched up tooth as best I could with oil of cloves and took a healthy dose of Codein, which I have repeated at three-hourly intervals. As a result, left later than expected to collect Amanda for Tim and Vanessa Pedalows' cocktail party.

Had not in fact realized they were back together again, and can only hope Vanessa has forgiven me for my seemingly treacherous behaviour re Ti.n and the German air hostess. Hared along Earls Court Road and was waiting innocently at traffic lights by tube station when a young man in a Morris Minor drew up next to me, wound down his window and called out, 'Afternoon, Fittipaldi. You were hammering it a bit back there, weren't you?' If there's one thing I can't abide it's self-righteous busybodies, and I decided to cut him down to size straight away.

'I think that's a matter for a policeman to decide, don't you?' I replied.

He got out of his car, came across and waving an identity card under my nose, said, 'I am a policeman. May I see your driving license, insurance and MOT certificate?' I tried to explain that it was not my car, but this only made matters worse. Whether he thought I'd stolen it, I don't know, but before I knew what, we were both standing at the side of the road while he took down particulars. He explained that he would have to report the incident and that I might be hearing more about the matter or I might not. He also insisted on a complete examination of all my tyres, including the spare. As a result arrived at The Boltons three-quarters of an hour late, with filthy hands, only to receive an even greater shock, if such a thing were possible. Amanda has gone punk. Vivid green- and orange-striped hair sticking up like a gollywog, funny signs painted all over her face, skin-tight pink satin trousers, tee-shirt knotted at the hip, the lot. She took one look at my filthy hands and said, 'Great. Wipe them all over me.'

There's only one way to deal with people who set out deliberately to shock one's sensibilities and that is to pretend one has not even noticed.

Everyone at the Pedalows' so taken by her appearance that no apology or explanation was needed. Philippe de Grande-Hauteville, who is still convinced I work for the BBC, put on a typically Gallic performance, kissing his fingers into the air in an exaggerated fashion. I had no idea that he and Theresa Milne had married. Obviously they've wasted no time in producing a family: Theresa was looking like the side of a house.

'When's the baby due?' I asked her.

'I had it two months ago,' she said, and walked away. Oh dear, oh dear.

Bryant-Fenn came bouncing up, gave me a friendly slap on the face and said, 'You're a dark horse and no mistake.' He would have to choose the side of my bad tooth. Announced he had just been appointed Wig and Hairpiece Editor of *Barbershop Quarterly*, and thought he might do a feature on punk wigs, and could he use Amanda as the model?

Tempted to bring up subject of Creative Writing Course and show him up for the shallow poseur he really is, but honestly he is so obviously second-rate, one can't help feeling sorry for the fellow.

'My dear chap,' I cried. 'Feel free.'

He gave me a sickly grin and rolled off into the crowd. Had been studiously avoiding Vanessa but need not have bothered.

'How's my favourite traitor?' she shrieked, rushing up to me and patting me enthusiastically on my bad cheek.

Mentioned my unfortunate brush with the law to Tim who said, 'Oh, that's nothing to worry about. Take my advice and write a nice cringing letter to the Chief Traffic Officer saying what a naughty boy you've been and you'll never hear another word about it. I do it all the time. Never fails.'

He and Vanessa have asked us to Covent Garden on Tuesday for a gala evening of ballet. Had in fact been planning on watching the first episode of the much-heralded TV series about the Prince Regent that night. However, when Tim explained that not only would we be guests in their box, but that we were invited to the glittering party afterwards, I decided Prinnie could do without me for one week. After all, what is TV glamour compared with the real thing? There's no knowing who one might not meet at that sort of do. Amanda, to my surprise, has said she'd love to come too. Not looking like that, she won't.

On the way out from the party, felt a tap on the shoulder and whirled round only to receive a sharp blow on the side of the face from a man who said cheerfully, 'Sorry, old boy. Thought you were someone else.' No need to say which side of the face.

Spent the rest of the day swilling down Codein and hot tea. I don't know which is more painful: my toothache, or the prospect of walking into the Crush Bar at Covent Garden with a green-haired zombie on my arm.

Monday, September 4th

Rang Amanda first thing to re-state my views concerning tomorrow night, only to be told by Enid that she had already left for the secretarial college. I had completely forgotten she was starting there today. I said, 'If she gets bored she can always staple her ear lobes.' Enid claimed not to know what I was talking about, but I think she got the point.

She has suggested an outing to the theatre on Saturday evening – just the two of us. I am not sure how to interpret this. Asked what play she had in mind.

'You're the expert,' she said, 'I leave it entirely to you.' If she's not hatching something I'll eat my hat.

Had my first meeting with Neville Pratt and Keith Hardacre. It could not have gone better. My first task is to prepare a proposal document for a major presentation of Brand X, as the new product is now known, in a fortnight's time in New York! Am so excited at the prospect of my first visit to the New World, I can think of nothing else. Not only that, but I am also to work in close co-operation with Roundtree and Ruth Macmichael at Harley Preston. I cannot wait to see their faces when I confront them for the first time as the client. There'll be a few old scores settled now and no mistake.

Arrived back from lunch to find a man painting my name on the office door. Pointed out that it was Simon, not Stephen. He has said he has another job on today but will do something about it as soon as possible.

Tooth still extremely painful, despite Codein. I am up to ten a day now.

Collected car after work. It seems to go very well, apart from the slight stammering in top gear. Rang Balditch when I got home. He says it is probably just the new clutch settling in. I wasn't even aware it had a new clutch.

Tuesday, September 5th

So nervous at thought of how Amanda will go down with this evening's balletomanes that I was scarcely able to concentrate on anything else all day.

Left office early, bathed, dressed and drove to Boltons to collect her. Stomach full of butterflies. Could hardly believe my eyes when she walked down the front stairs in a most elegant black evening dress, blonde hair done up in elaborate creation with ribbons and wild flowers. I suppose it must be a wig. I have never seen her looking lovelier, and said so.

Set off in excellent time for the Garden. No sign of Pedalows, so stood by bar with Amanda viewing audience. Shocked to see how few men had followed my example by dressing. One or two were actually wearing jeans and open-necked shirts. I'm surprised they were allowed in.

Just as the first bell was sounding, in swanned Tim and Vanessa, cool as cucumbers, asking if I'd collected the tickets. Had been looking forward to a leisurely pre-performance whisky and soda, but instead had to battle in long queue at box office. Was making my way across to the others when who should I bump into but Armitage and Jane? He in one of his cheap, off-the-peg three-piece monstrosities, she in a particularly frumpy peasanty number. Most unsuitable.

'Evening, Crisp,' said Armitage loudly. 'Fancy seeing you here. We're in the stalls; where are you?'

I told him Box 69.

'Bad luck,' he said, and the pair of them walked away. I put it down to envy.

Naturally had imagined that at £11 a head we would be prominently placed in first tier and the fact we had to climb several sets of stairs did not bode well. Arrived finally at box. I have never been higher up in a theatre. Since there was room for only three chairs at the front, I had to stand at the back from where I could barely see half the stage. Not surprisingly, much of the first item lost on me – literally.

During first interval, spotted a chap I once met at a dinner party, named Cyril Bunting. I smiled at him but he did not smile back. Such a crowd, I was quite unable to get near enough to bar to order drinks before bell went.

Had assumed that after the interval Tim would suggest taking turns with the standing, but he said nothing and resumed his seat. Item two starred the famous Russian dancer Baryshnikov. From the few glimpses I caught of him as he flashed on and off the small portion of the stage that was visible to me, he certainly seemed a very lively young fellow.

In second interval, I was all for going straight to bar, but Tim announced we should change seats.

We eventually found some in the stalls which we took just as the lights were dimming. I was sorry the man in front of me had quite such a large head; however, by crouching slightly and bending to my right, I had an almost uninterrupted view.

To the Lyceum Ballroom, of all the unlikely venues, for the exclusive gala party. Rather too exclusive as it turned out, since Amanda's and my name not included on invitation. As a result had to battle in undignified fashion with three sets of bouncers before being admitted.

Sat near the door in order to spot the famous as they arrived. Tim and Vanessa pointed out several including, I think, Princess Margaret. It was a pity they didn't actually know any of them to speak to.

Later, several elderly people took to the dance floor in an abandoned sort of way. Amanda was all for joining in, but I put my foot down. Or rather, I didn't!

Ordered coffee which did not come and left at 11.45. So much for the all-night revelry I had been anticipating. Still, an instructive evening, though I was sorry to have missed Prince Regent. With TV you really feel you get to know the famous.

Wednesday, September 6th

It's an extraordinary thing, but the more Codein I take, the worse my toothache seems to get. Am now up to two every two hours. Rang the dentist but he cannot see me till Friday.

Amanda rang after lunch to say that Timmy and Joanna

had suggested we all go on Thursday to the opening of a new discotheque called the Top Hole. A typically suggestive name, I thought, but she couldn't see it. When I asked her why she wasn't at college she said she was so tired after last night she had decided to take the day off. I said, 'You'll be even tireder after tomorrow night.'

'Oh do stop fussing,' she said. 'Anyway, dancing's like rugger. The spectators are always more tired after a match than the players.'

I should have thought the sum total of her knowledge of rugger could be jotted down on the back of a postage stamp. However, have agreed to make an exception to my night-club rule for no other reason than that it might take my mind off my toothache.

Have also bought two tickets for *Once in a Lifetime* at the Aldwych. I have heard excellent reports of it. At £5.30 a ticket, it ought to be good.

Thursday, September 7th

Our soirée at the Top Hole as dismal and depressing an affair as I had feared and expected.

Place so full of freaks and grotesques that Amanda looked positively square in her punk gear. Oddly enough, my dark suit and OF tie came in for much favourable comment. Spotted several faces that were vaguely familiar from the newspaper. Also had quite an interesting chat at the bar about the weather with a girl who might or might not have been Britt Ekland. Timmy and Joanna shared several cigarettes during the course of the evening.

'Pot?' I enquired casually.

'No,' said Joanna. 'Poverty.'

I laughed. It was a good try but I'm too old a hand to have the wool pulled over my eyes.

Tooth started playing up later, so took a couple more Codein.

'Uppers or downers?' Joanna asked me.

'Neither,' I replied coldly. 'Codein. For toothache.'

Timmy said, 'You don't want to take too many of those; before you know what, you'll be hooked.' A marvellous joke suddenly occurred to me. 'Talk about the *pot* calling the kettle black,' I said, but of course the joke went way above their heads. I am beginning to wonder if the younger generation have any sense of humour at all.

Dancing on the whole abysmal compared with the days when I pulled off Twist competition in Obergurgl.

I don't know what got into me but on a whim I grabbed Amanda's arm and before I knew what, I was in the middle of the floor, shaking my hips and waving my arms like a mad thing. Was in the middle of one of my famous shoulder shaking routines when I distinctly heard a girl's voice behind me say, 'It's pathetic to see these middle-aged people making fools of themselves.' At this everyone within earshot, including Amanda, burst into gales of laughter. I left the dance floor at once – probably forever.

In the car going home Amanda announced that the theme of her party on Saturday week is to be punk; anyone who comes dressed in any style other than punk will not be admitted. Oh dear. Trouble.

Friday, September 8th

To the dentist at long last. Mr Nwachukw most concerned about the pain in my tooth, and when I told him how many Codein I was taking he tutted in a most worried way. Having never been in a position to stretch a dentist's skill beyond a straightforward filling, I was rather pleased at being able to present him with a problem he could really get his teeth into. (No joke intended there.)

After a long, muttered conversation with his female assistant, also black but rather attractive in an African sort of way, he turned to me and announced he would have to give me a general anaesthetic and 'have a bit of a look-see'. Luckily, it was some hours since I had last eaten, and I agreed to his suggestion without any hesitation.

While under the gas I had the most extraordinary erotic dream concerning Mr Nwachukw's assistant. Came round to find the pair of them roaring with laughter. I said, 'May I be allowed in on the joke?' at which they roared all the harder until the tears ran down their cheeks. I grinned foolishly, until Nwachukw announced that he had just removed the whole tooth.

I was astounded and reminded him that he had referred to inspection rather than extraction.

He said he was very sorry, but that under the circumstances he had no alternative, and once again the two of them shrieked with laughter. I pointed out stiffly that the pain was, if anything, worse.

Nwachukw told me, that was because I'd become too reliant on pain-killers. The more one takes, the worse the pain.

I laughed and said, 'You make me sound like a junkie.'

He said, 'You are.'

I do not suppose that he meant it literally. On the other hand, I must admit that I was beginning to look forward to my next Codein with something approaching pleasure, and it is a great relief to know that I shall now have no further need of them and can kick the habit forthwith.

Got back to office and went straight to gents where I gave myself a long, hard look in the mirror. Suddenly noticed that the area below my eyes has gone quite dark, and it was then that the horrible truth dawned on me: I was staring at the face of a potential drug addict. It just goes to show how easily the most respectable of us can unwittingly find ourselves caught up in the sordid net of depravity.

Am so relieved to have escaped that I am seriously thinking of joining one of these drug prevention organizations and using my experience to help others like me. Meanwhile I must prepare myself for the long period of cold turkey that inevitably lies ahead.

With my tooth still extremely painful, the going is going to be tough, but I think I can take it.

Saturday, September 9th

Woken early by Enid ringing to say that some friends had just arrived unexpectedly from America and would I mind terribly if we called off our theatre visit this evening?

Didn't say so, but in fact quite relieved.

Remembering our last evening à deux, back in May, and the emotional landslide that resulted, I feel that any attempt on either of our parts to stir up old embers would be bound to end in tears. I know there are young men who think it clever and amusing to carry on with a mother and her daughter at the same time, but, attracted as I am to both of them, I do not hold with it, and that's all there is to it.

Popped round to the Aldwych to return my tickets, only to

find a long queue in the foyer. From what I could make out they all seemed to be trying for *Once in a Lifetime*, and apparently without success.

Young man behind the grille most unhelpful and told me that under no circumstances could they refund money on tickets. I said that I would be perfectly prepared to change them for another evening, but that was out of the question too.

Decided to take my revenge by selling my tickets to one of the people in the long queue behind, only to find that for some mysterious reason not one of them wanted to see *Once in a Lifetime*.

I can't say I blame them.

It's at moments like these one really misses *The Times* letters column.

Sunday, September 10th

Gum very sore but am resisting Codein bravely.

Car still stammering in top gear, so decided to ginger up the system by driving down to Kent for lunch with Mother. Rang Amanda at eleven to ask if she'd like to come, but informed by Enid she was still fast asleep. Exhausted from a hard week's typing and shorthand, I suppose. When I told Enid of my plan for the day she said, 'We were expecting you for lunch to meet our American friends.' I thought she sounded rather disappointed, but reminded her that I am not the only one given to changing his mind at the last moment.

Enjoyed my drive to Kent, despite heavy traffic in Bexleyheath, which for some reason I always muddle with Bexhill. Perfect September weather so that we were able to sit in the garden with our sherry.

Mother unable to resist a series of side swipes at Tony Benn who has evidently ousted Mr Callaghan as her personal Enemy Number One.

'You know all these people at the BBC,' she said. 'Can't you get yourself onto "Any Questions" and really give him a piece of your mind?'

I said, 'Actually, I really do believe he's one of the most sincere men in British politics.'

'So was Hitler,' she replied.

'Hitler wasn't in British politics,' I said.

'Why must you always split hairs?' she said.

I don't know why I allow myself to get drawn into these absurd arguments. I blame Nigel and Priscilla myself. If they had not taken it into their heads to give her that dreadful Burmese cat for Christmas, she might have retained some vestige of sanity. I suppose I should be grateful that *she* hasn't yet taken to creeping up behind one's deck chair and sinking her teeth into one's calf for absolutely no reason.

I never thought the day would come when the sight of Denys Ramsden bumbling through the French windows would actually prove a welcome relief.

Am more convinced than ever that those two are having an affair. At one point actually caught him holding Mother's hand under the table. It's only a matter of time before I surprise the pair of them rolling round on the sofa.

After coffee Denys said he had to be getting home. He kissed Mother goodbye, stepped into his Triumph Mayflower and reversed smartly into my Maxi, completely destroying the rear offside door. In the circumstances he seemed extraordinarily unabashed. It's more than I can say for my car.

As I was leaving, Mother remarked, completely out of the blue, that she thought dentists had given up gas years ago. I felt like saying it's a pity someone doesn't give Denys Ramsden a few sniffs to settle him down.

Monday, September 11th

My third day off the drugs. A remarkable achievement considering pain in calf caused by cat's teeth. Still, it helps draw attention away from my tooth. Should I be considering an anti-tetanus shot, I ask myself.

Rang my doctor re use of gas by dentists and he confirms Mother's assertion. Am beginning to wonder if I have not unwittingly become involved in some seedy racket or other. I dread to think what happened while I was under the anaesthetic. Any day now I'll receive a lewd photograph of myself and the receptionist plus a demand for a large sum of money, I shouldn't wonder. The extraction of the tooth was probably only a cover. If so, it was in pretty poor taste.

Ruth Macmichael rang just before lunch to suggest a meeting about Product X. She sounded unusually respectful, as well she might be from now on. It's a pity I cannot say the same for the Personnel Department at Barfords. Despite constant requests, I still have no secretary of my own. Must also insist on someone coming and re-doing the sign on my door; I can't really believe they *still* haven't heard of me in Office Services.

In the meantime, have penned a stiff note to Miss Hippo concerning the continuing non-appearance of the tea trolley at my end of the corridor.

New York presentation plans coming along very well. My idea for incorporating clips from Woody Allen films in the audio-visual section makes all the difference.

After work, took car to garage. Mr Aylott still away with his knee, but Balditch says they have a spare door in the workshop and I should be able to collect it on Friday. They will also look into stammering.

Tuesday, September 12th

I think I may have succeeded in kicking the drugs once and for all. Pain in mouth and ankle barely noticeable. I can only hope now that my neck doesn't go. That would throw me on to the horns of a dilemma.

To Harley Preston in the afternoon for a meeting with Ruth about Product X.

It was a curious feeling to walk through the familiar front doors knowing that if it weren't for people like me they wouldn't be in business at all.

Announced myself to Lorraine, the pretty but bad-tempered-looking receptionist. She put down her emery board with a sigh and said, 'Was it business or pleasure?'

I wasn't going to take that sort of talk from anyone and said severely, 'I'd be glad if you'd tell Miss Macmichael I'm here.'

'What was your name again?' she said.

I pointed out that she might not be aware of the fact but I had worked there for three years until very recently.

'No,' she said, 'I'm not.'

I said with cold deliberation, 'The name is Crisp. Barfords.'

'Suits you,' she said.

I replied, 'And you'll be finding out how much in due course,' and left the building and returned to the office.

A drastic step, some may say, but I'm an old enough hand

at this game to know that it never pays to fool about with the client, and it won't do Harley Preston any harm to sweat on the top line for a bit.

Waited in my office all afternoon for a panic-stricken call from Ruth, but not a peep out of anyone. Phone finally went at six-fifteen. It was Bryant-Fenn to say he had been ringing me at home for the last half hour to invite me to a party he is giving on Friday week at some hotel near Guildford.

He said, 'I'm surprised a man in your position can get by without a telephone answering machine. I certainly wouldn't be where I am today without mine.' Wherever that might be!

He's right though. From now on, more and more people *will* be wanting to get in touch with me at odd hours of the day and night. I might seriously consider looking into the possibilities.

Wednesday, September 13th

A glorious, sunny morning, yet tinged with a sense of sadness. Arrived in the office in a strange mood. Even stranger when I found there was still no message from Ruth. Spent morning ringing round answering services. Have plumped for one in Wimbledon.

After lunch, rang Ruth and said casually that I was sorry not to have made our meeting yesterday.

She said, 'It wasn't yesterday, it's today. In half an hour.' Flew round in a taxi. Receptionist, who obviously still had no idea who I was, told me to go straight up to Ruth's office.

I said, 'Are you sure she didn't mean the board room?'

'Quite sure,' she said.

Ruth perfectly friendly, although I think she might have been a little more apologetic about Roundtree's absence. I should have thought in the circumstances he could have arranged to see his chiropodist another day.

I said, 'What? No tea then?' in a half-joking way.

She said, 'This is a business meeting', and proceeded to discuss the New York sales presentation. I do not believe I have ever been spoken to so insultingly in all my adult life. She was particularly scathing about the inclusion of the Woody Allen clips in the audio-visual section. I tried to explain that *of course* they were old hat, that was the whole point, and that they made a perfect satirical counterpoint to the projected sales figures.

She said, 'Crap. That's the trouble with this country. Jokes, jokes, jokes. That's the only thing anyone can make any more. And not very good ones at that. Well, in New York, we're pretty goddam serious about business and we leave the funnies to TV, and the sooner you understand that, the better.'

I said stiffly, 'You seem to forget, Miss Macmichael, that Product X is *our* product and the way we choose to present it to the public is our affair. You are simply here to advise us, not to teach us our job. I call the shots round here now.'

She folded the papers up into a file, handed them to me across the desk and said, 'You may be the client now, but you're still as big an ass-hole as ever. If you don't take my advice, we're none of us going to be calling any shots from now on.'

I have not as yet decided what steps to take in this sorry matter, but steps there must be.

A more immediate worry, however, is Amanda's party on Saturday. If it is to be a punk affair, as she says, I really do not think I can invite any of my friends. Except perhaps Bryant-Fenn. He'd go to a chimpanzee's tea party if it were free.

This evening a polite young Indian wearing a large ring came and demonstrated the answering machine. Japanese, of course. However, it seems to fit the bill very well. £175 a year, to be precise. It should be delivered in about a month. I can't wait.

Thursday, September 14th

At a meeting in Hardacre's office to discuss New York, Pratt said, 'Ruth is right. The Woody Allen stuff must go. The charts need clarifying, too.'

When you can't rely on your own people to back you, who can you rely on? He's obviously terrified of Ruth. On the way out, Miss Hippo handed me my passport with my American visa. It is for four years, so obviously someone is thinking long term.

Worked on charts and audio-visual till lunch, then rang Bryant-Fenn about Saturday. He accepted, needless to say. Walked up to Oxford Street in the sunshine and bought myself a box of safety pins, a lavatory chain and some pink washable hair dye.

Friday, September 15th

Spent morning putting final touches to audio-visual. Just before lunch called in at Miss Hippo's office to collect my air ticket. Rather disappointed to note that I am booked on a 747, despite request to 'UPGRADE TO 1ST CLASS IF AVAILABLE.' I chaffed her and said, 'I thought all top executives these days flew by Concorde.'

She replied, '*Top* executives, yes.'

I said, 'Just as long as I don't suffer too much from jet-lag.'

She replied, 'It shows how often you've flown the Atlantic. That only happens on the way back.'

I said, 'Not necessarily,' and left it at that.

As I was going to lunch, I suddenly realized there had been no mention of a money advance from Accounts. Have rung my bank and ordered dollars and travellers cheques for first thing Monday morning.

To garage on way home to collect car, but apparently they didn't have a new door in stock after all. I told Balditch to keep the car and have it ready by the time I get back from New York. He was obviously impressed.

Saturday, September 16th

Rang Amanda first thing to ask if there was anything I could do to help with the festivities. A man's voice replied, 'I doubt it. This is the robing room of the West London Magistrate's Court.'

Thank heaven I didn't announce my name. I have no wish to prejudice my case when it comes up. *If* it comes up. The worst part of being a criminal is the waiting.

Took the phone off the hook so as not to be disturbed and spent the morning running over my commentary to accompany the projected sales figures.

After lunch, dyed hair. Had hoped to achieve a slightly patchy effect, but while lowering right side of head into mixture, my foot slipped and I plunged my whole head in, eyebrows and all. The effect was so sensational could not resist looking at it each time I passed a mirror. By tea-time had become quite used to the colour – though not, I must say, to the curious smell.

Later, had a couple of large whisky and sodas and attempted to insert a safety pin in right cheek. According to Amanda there is a way of doing it whereby you suck in your cheek thus making the skin very thin. Can only assume she left out some vital instruction since I was quite unable to insert the point without great pain and a certain amount of blood. No amount of love is worth a nasty dose of gangrene. In the end, settled for a neat compromise by sticking a pin to each cheek with strong glue and attaching a lavatory chain to right ear lobe by ditto means.

Dressed in oldest jeans, ski-ing anorak and a pair of pointed boots I have been meaning to throw out for years. At 8.30 rang for a minicab only to realize my phone had been off the hook all day.

Arrived at Boltons in fine fettle. Door already wide open and sounds of revelry issuing into warm night air. Marched through hall and sitting room and issued into marquee in garden with a gay shout of 'Ta ra!' Everyone stopped talking and turned to stare at me. I could not believe my eyes. They were all dressed in conventional evening frocks and dinner jackets. There was a moment of complete silence and then the place erupted into laughter.

Amanda came up to me, looking enchanting in a long white billowing number. 'Oh dear,' she said, 'I've been trying to ring you all day, but your phone's been out of order. We decided at the last moment to change the theme of the party from punk to Deb's Delight. I assumed you'd come in a d.j. anyway.' Took the only course open to me and left the room with calm dignity. Rushed upstairs to guest bathroom, filled the wash basin with warm water and lowered head into it. Shampooed hair five times, but to no avail. Finally slipped down back stairs, out through side door and into street. Glimpsed two figures in intimate conversation by lighted sitting-room window. They looked very like Amanda and Bryant-Fenn to me. They're welcome to each other. I have more pressing things to worry about – chiefly how to get this wretched dye out of my hair before leaving for New York.

Before going to bed, penned a formal note to Bryant-Fenn saying I should not be able to make his party on Friday since I should be in America. Thank goodness.

Sunday, September 17th

Up at seven thirty after a wretched night's sleep to start hair washing. At noon was on my thirteenth wash when the phone rang. Rushed to answer it, hair still dripping wet. It was Amanda to ask where I had got to last night; she had been worried.

'Obviously not worried enough to tear yourself away from Bryant-Fenn's side,' I said briskly. At this she burst into tears, moaning that what should have been the happiest night of her life had turned into the most miserable. She should talk!

Put the phone down only to find that, all the time I had been talking, my hair had been dripping on to the carpet, leaving a large pink stain. It never rains but it pours these days. (A grimly apposite metaphor in the circumstances.)

Afternoon divided equally between washing hair and carpet, though without obvious success on either score. I may have to resort to some sort of hat, though quite what style I cannot think. In fact I don't seem to be able to think constructively about anything any more. I hope I haven't got water on the brain. That's all I need.

Monday, September 18th

Up early and out to the shops to buy a hat. Finally settled for a shapeless tweed affair that folds up into a little bag specially for travelling. It makes me look a bit like Rex Harrison. I cannot think why I have not treated myself to one before, pink hair or no pink hair.

Hurried home to breakfast and pack. Suddenly remembered I had still to collect my foreign currency and travellers' cheques. Flew to bank in taxi. Not only was the stuff not ready, but I was forced to waste further valuable time signing every single cheque in the presence of the cashier. He said, 'If I were you, I'd apply for an American Express card.'

Arrived at check-in desk for the New York flight to discover that the flight had been delayed for an hour.

Asked girl about possibility of being up-graded to first class. She punched several keys on her computer, and said, 'We are expecting one other first-class passenger. If he doesn't show, you're in.'

Asked if in the meantime I could wait in VIP lounge.

'Don't push your luck,' she said.

As we were boarding I was accosted by name by one of the hostesses and shown to a seat in the first-class section. Wasted no time taking off my shoes, slipping into lightweight airline slippers and stretching out luxuriously. The film, I noticed, was *Capricorn One*. I always enjoy a good thriller and have been cursing myself for missing this particular one in London. Was trying on sleeping mask when the hostess arrived to say she was very sorry but the extra passenger had turned up after all and would I mind moving back into the tourist-class section.

Nearly all seats by now taken, so forced to squash in amongst a group of chattering Chinese slap underneath the cinema screen. Not that it mattered since the tourist-class film was *Players*.

After lunch, settled down to make some last-minute changes to audio-visual script, but almost at once the entire Chinese contingent decided to fall asleep and snored so loudly I was quite unable to hear myself think.

In the end compelled to stick in earphones and watch film. I liked it no better the second time.

Despite hat wedged firmly on head, Customs man at Kennedy immensely rude about my hair and made me turn out entire contents of my suitcase. As I was doing it up, one of the buckles came away in my hand.

'That's the trouble with imitation leather,' he said.

Car ride into city so terrifying that the famous Manhattan skyline almost entirely lost on me.

The hotel seems reasonably comfortable and well appointed, if a little far from the centre of things. 8th Avenue and 22nd Street is not exactly Cole Porter country. I quite agree with the bellboy that it is convenient for Greenwich Village – not that that is a great advantage to me since the Kellerman Corporation is in East 59th Street. Still, I gather taxis are easy enough to come by, even in this part of town.

Have been here less than an hour as I write these words, and yet already I can sense the excitement of this great city coursing through my veins like young wine. Am feeling decidedly light-headed. But then, of course, I am on the 28th floor.

Tuesday, September 19th

Harry Colouris rang first thing to say some important people had just flown in from Philadelphia and did I mind very much if we put off the rehearsal till this afternoon. Couldn't have been more delighted.

8th and 22nd not in fact the easiest place to find cabs, but finally struck lucky and took material to Kellerman's offices on East 59th. Thought I'd spend rest of morning sight-seeing. Called at nearest bank to change some travellers' cheques. The clerk peered at the cheques for a long time, then said he was very sorry but he had never heard of the Bank of Scotland and had I any means of proving their bona fides. Asked to speak to his superior who said he'd heard of the Bank of England, but the Bank of Scotland was a new one on him. He said if I'd had American Express travellers' cheques, why, he'd have been happy to oblige, and his colleague said, 'Don't you have American Express cards in England?'

I said, 'It depends who recommends you,' and left it at that.

Tried several more banks with similar results. Finally tracked down a bureau de change in the Rockefeller Centre and changed £10. In my view anyone who walks round New York with large sums of cash in his pocket is asking for trouble.

Made first for Empire State Building. Am a firm believer in the E. M. Forster philosophy that the best way to get to know a new place is just to walk about aimlessly, and would certainly have gone there on foot, but one hears all too many stories of visitors being mugged in broad daylight.

Cab driver most friendly and talkative. Was sorry I couldn't place the exact street in Wembley where his brother-in-law has his take-away Chinese, but assured him I knew the general area pretty well.

As I was paying him, he said, 'Normally I won't have a faggot in my cab, but I made an exception, seeing as you're British.'

Made a mental note to speak sharply to the girl who sold me the hair dye.

View from Empire State Building all it's cracked up to be, if a little hazy. Unfortunately, effect rather spoilt by the fact that I was suddenly seized by an overwhelming desire to throw myself off the top. In spite of high fencing all round had to hold myself against back wall and will myself not to rush forward and start clambering over the wire. It is moments like this that lead one to ponder how many other strange, irrational urges lie deep within our subconscious.

To lunch at Ma Belle's on 45th Street, as recommended by Keith. They have old-fashioned telephones on the tables and you can make free calls all over New York. If you know anyone to ring, that is.

Was in the middle of my hamburger when suddenly the phone on my table rang. Picked it up and received an obscene message. It was obviously a wrong number, so replaced the receiver and asked waitress for a portion of apple pie and cream. Two minutes later, phone rang again. Message of even more pornographic nature. Decided enough was enough. Told the waitress to hold the apple pie and cream, and went to pay my bill. As I was leaving, I noticed a couple of young men, obviously pansies, looking at me, and giggling like a couple of school girls. I ignored them. I've no idea what it was all about, but am quickly coming to the conclusion that New York is a city even more obsessed with sex than London.

Discovered I now did not have enough money for a cab, so ran to Rockefeller Center where I changed £20. As a result arrived slightly late at Kellerman's. Even so, rehearsal could not have gone better, and I think we are all set for tomorrow. Afterwards Harry said, 'You know what would have really made that audio-visual? A little touch of humour. A couple of clips from a Woody Allen movie – something like that. They love to laugh, those guys from Cincinnati.'

A very embarrassing thing happened after dinner. Felt I should repay my host's hospitality by taking them all for a drink to the Rainbow Room. When the bill came, found I had not got enough money. Luckily they couldn't have been nicer about it. Decided to come clean and explained my theory about muggers.

Harry said, 'You're kidding. Give a mugger a hundred bucks, he'll take it and run. But a mugger finds you got no bread, he'll be so mad he'll beat hell out of you.'

As we were leaving, one of the guys said, 'Simon, one word of advice. Next time you come to New York, get yourself an American Express card.'

Wednesday, September 20th

I think someone was trying to break into my room last night.
I called out, 'I've got a gun in here,' and whoever it was went
away. Breakfast took an age to arrive. When it finally did, I
said to the waiter by way of a joke, 'Oh, that surely can't be
for me. I only ordered mine an hour ago.'

'You're right,' he said, and wheeled it away again.

Had meant to do some shopping in Fifth Avenue on way to
presentation, but by the time I had been to the Rockefeller
Center to change some more travellers' cheques, there was no
time.

Do not wish to tempt providence by commenting on
success or otherwise of presentation at this stage, but I don't
believe an important man like Arthur Kellerman would have
bothered to come up to me afterwards and congratulate me
if he didn't mean it. Cincinnati team also most complimentary
and expressed particular interest in the technical side of the
presentation.

One said, 'I only have one criticism. There weren't too
many laughs.'

It is most gratifying to know that my first instincts about
American business methods have been proved correct after
all. Perhaps I should seriously consider emigrating to
America. Work-wise, New York seems to be shouting 'Yes'
to me at every turn.

On the way out, Harry suggested that by way of celebration I might like to check out the famous New York night
spot, Studio 54. Returned to hotel and was slipping room
key into door when a couple of men came up behind me and
seized me by the arms. One never really knows how one is
going to behave in an emergency until it occurs, and I was
interested to notice how calm I was.

I said, 'Now look here, I'm English.'

One of the men said, 'So?'

Could see I was unlikely to make headway on moral or
touristic grounds, so immediately changed tack.

'I've got quite a lot of money on me, if that's what you're
thinking,' I said.

'That some kind of bribe?' the other man asked.

I said, 'It's an odd way of putting it, but I suppose you
could say so.'

The first man said, 'All righty. Let's see what we have here. Attempted bribery of a police officer, threatening behaviour, possible possession of a firearm without a licence. You know where that puts you? Down the tubes, baby.'

Of course, it was only a matter of time before everyone realized it was all a complete misunderstanding. Unfortunately, it meant I had to cancel my sight-seeing trip on the Circle Line boat. Still, it's not everyone who gets to experience the inner workings of Manhattan South police headquarters at first hand.

Dined with Harry at Sardi's which was a great thrill. Looked around in the hope of catching sight of some of the big Broadway stars waiting for the first editions, but as Harry pointed out, nine o'clock is a little on the early side. Took a cab to 54th Street and joined the crowds milling about outside Studio 54, all dressed in the most outlandish clothes and trying to catch the doorman's eye. Was on the point of suggesting to Harry that we called it a day when the doorman shouted out, 'The weirdo over there with the pink hair and the Ivy League boyfriend.'

Harry said, 'That's us. Let's go,' and before I could stop him he had hustled me through the envious hopefuls and in through the doors. While Studio 54 has done nothing to change my attitude towards discotheques in general, I am not so narrowminded that I am incapable of recognizing a life enhancing experience when I have one.

I'm afraid I had to draw the line at accepting invitations to dance with men, but I had a most interesting talk with a very odd-looking fellow with glasses and white hair, and danced quite a lot with a very tall girl who said she was some sort of actress. It was difficult to hear above the din but I thought she said her name was Ernest Hemingway. Could that be possible? Altogether a most stimulating and instructive evening.

The song writer got it right: New York, New York *is* a wonderful town.

My only worry is that I seem to have gone slightly deaf in one ear.

Thursday, September 21st

Had originally planned to stay till Friday, but Harry has had to fly to Chicago and, much as I'd have liked to stay on, I really cannot afford the time.

Arrived at Kennedy in good time for flight. Delighted to discover that the film in tourist class was *Capricorn One*. Found myself a seat with a good view of the screen and no one on either side of me. Was congratulating myself on my good luck when one of the hostesses leaned across and informed me that, since the flight was fairly empty, they would be very happy to upgrade me to first-class. No second invitation was needed. What I did not know until I had taken my seat was that the film in first-class was *Players*. However, thanks to airline's abundant hospitality with wine bottle, I slept soundly most of the way to London and missed it completely.

Woke, bleary-eyed and with a slight headache to learn that the film of *Players* had broken down after fifteen minutes and they had shown *Capricorn One* instead.

Arrived home to find that my American Express card had been delivered during my absence, plus a newsletter and the offer of six King Arthur plates, commissioned specially for Card Members by the International Arthurian Society. Funnily enough the Camelot legend has always interested me.

Unpacked, washed, made tea and rang Amanda.

My heart leapt with joy to hear her voice again.

'Oh,' she said, 'I wasn't expecting you.'

'I came home unexpectedly,' I said.

I suppose in the circumstances I should not be surprised or disappointed that she has arranged to attend a pop concert at Wembley with Timmy and Joanna, but I am.

On second thoughts, though, it's probably just as well, since I am feeling decidedly disorientated. Ah well, that's jet-lag for you.

Early bed with an apple and *People* magazine.

Friday, September 22nd

As soon as I got into the office, rang Bryant-Fenn to say that, since I had come home earlier than anticipated, I should now be able to accept his invitation for this evening.

'Oh,' he said, 'that's very awkward. The fact is, I've just agreed the final numbers with the hotel and frankly I'm not sure I can change them again.'

Not surprisingly, I was pretty shocked at being spoken to like that by an old friend; however, I was certainly not about to let him think I cared two hoots whether I went or not.

'I quite understand, Hugh,' I said quietly, 'There's no need to explain further.'

'I would say come along anyway and take pot luck,' he went on, 'but the thing is, the hotel is laying on individual dishes.

'Tell you what, I'll give them a quick bell and see if they can squeeze you in. No promises, mind. I'll call you straight back.' And he rang off.

Waited for an hour by the phone but no reply. Decided I had wasted enough time over this trivial matter and strolled along to Pratt's office to give him a preliminary briefing on the New York presentation. He said he was very pleased at the way it had gone. Damned civil of him, I must say. Bumped into Miss Hippo in corridor on way back to my office.

She said, 'I heard your phone ringing and took the liberty of answering it. Someone called Hugh.'

'Did he leave a message?' I asked.

'Yes,' she said. 'He said to tell you it was no go.'

'I see,' I said. 'He didn't by any chance say anything about popping in for a drink after dinner or anything?'

'No,' she said.

Looking through *Evening Standard*, discovered *Capricorn One* was showing at my local Odeon. Could not believe my luck. Rang Amanda to suggest going, but the maid told me she had gone to the country and would be back tomorrow. Rang Miss Hippo re my office door. She says a man is coming next week.

Took myself off to the cinema after supper only to learn that *Capricorn One* had come off yesterday evening.

I asked what was showing in its place.

'*Players*,' said the girl.

Saturday, September 23rd

An awful lot of nonsense is talked about jet-lag, but until one has experienced it at first hand one has no idea of how strangely it can affect one.

93

In my case, it seems to take the form of an overwhelming desire to retire to bed. I do not know if other jet-setters react in the same way, but I almost feel like writing to the *British Medical Journal* to suggest a full-scale survey into the effects of this most baffling condition.

Slept solidly till noon. Indeed I think I could have slept all day had Vanessa Pedalow not rung to ask why I was not at Hugh's 'thrash' last night. I was in no mood to pull punches.

'Because,' I told her, 'I was informed that my unexpected presence would upset catering arrangements.'

'I can't think why,' she said. 'The place was swarming with all sorts of strange people.'

I said, 'I understood from Hugh that the dishes were cooked individually. What did he give you? Half a lobster each?'

'Good Lord, no,' she said cheerfully. 'Hungarian goulash. There was plenty to go round. Tim had three helpings, Amanda had two and so did I and there was plenty left over at the end.'

This was the first I had heard of Amanda being invited, and when I asked Vanessa if she was sure Amanda was there, she replied, 'Yes, of course. So was her mother. What a nice woman and so good looking for her age.'

All very suspicious I must say.

To the garage after lunch to collect my car. The new door looks very good, and stammering completely disappeared. Is it my imagination or is the clutch much stiffer than I remember?

Sunday, September 24th

An astounding turn of events.

Denys Ramsden is dead.

Mother rang first thing with the news. It appears that while sitting on the loo, he pulled the chain and brought the whole cistern down on his head, killing himself instantaneously. Naturally I said I'd drive down to Kent straight away. The maddening thing was, I had been looking forward to a good lie-in to counteract this wretched jet-lag. Everything seems to happen to me.

Was just leaving when Amanda rang and began a long rambling explanation about Hugh's party. However, when

I told her the news she stopped short and said that she would very much like to come too. Drove straight round to Boltons and picked her up. As soon as I saw her, dressed in black, all my old feelings for her came flooding back, fresher and stronger than ever. For two pins I'd have taken her back to the flat and made passionate love to her there and then. Strange how the oddest emotions take over at the most unsuitable moments. But then, of course, in the midst of death we are in life.

It was nearly the other way round when halfway down the M2, she suddenly announced that on more than one occasion Bryant-Fenn had proposed an affair not only to her but also to Enid. Could have made a scene there and then, but decided, under the guise of family grief, to play the matter very cool indeed and made no comment.

Arrived at Mother's to find her in sparkling form, so much so, that I could not help feeling we had been brought there on a fool's errand.

'It was your idea to come,' Mother said.

I reminded her how upset she had been on the telephone.

'Oh that,' she said. 'I blame the cat myself. Staying out all night like that. I hardly slept a wink for worrying. Anyway, panic over.'

I could not believe my ears and asked her if she had any feelings for Denys whatever.

'I daresay I shall miss him,' she said. 'But really it's difficult to feel a lot of sympathy for a man who is so lazy he can't even be bothered to stand up to flush the loo.'

Amanda very subdued all day, I noticed. She couldn't do enough to help Mother. I think the message has got through.

On the way back to London I said to Amanda: 'That wig is really excellent.'

'What wig?' she said.

I said, 'That blonde wig you're wearing to cover up your green hair.'

She said, 'The green one was a wig, this is my own.'

Clutch so stiff by the time I got back to London, I could hardly move it.

Monday, September 25th

For the first time since I arrived at Barfords, the tea lady deigned to make the detour to my office with her trolley. Her name is Agnes, she wears a knitted woollen hat and shapeless slippers several sizes too large, and exudes all the charmlessness and glowering resentment that we have come to expect from our cousins from the West Indies.

'Aha,' I cried as she loomed large and menacing in the doorway, 'so you have found your way at last to the condemned cell.'

'Coffee?' she said, 'or tea?'

I asked her jokingly if there was any difference.

'I haven't got all day, dearie,' she said.

Really what is the point in trying to make these people feel at home? I honestly believe it would be easier to get a laugh out of a Martian. And yet whenever I come across a crowd of black people together, they are invariably dancing about, shrieking their heads off and slapping their thighs. What on earth do they find to laugh at? Us, I suppose.

To Parson's Green after work to view Amanda's little house. It seems pleasant enough, as late Victorian villas go, though hardly what I'd call a desirable residence, or a particularly up and coming area. Still, she seems very tickled with it, and I hadn't the heart to say what I really thought.

There is a fair amount of building work to be done and the inevitable skip is already parked outside the front door.

Amanda rushed up and down showing me which walls would be coming down, where the RSJs would be going and how the gas-fired central heating boiler will fit in the space under the stairs. To my surprise, she has already furnished one bedroom in a haphazard sort of way, and there is a sofa and a coffee table in the sitting-room.

Her enthusiasm is so infectious and she was obviously trying so hard to make me feel at home that when she suggested I stayed to supper, I fell in with the plan as eagerly as I later fell into her rather small bed. Despite cramped conditions, was immensely cheered to realize once again, despite our intellectual and mental differences, we are physically completely in accord. So much for Bryant-Fenn's little challenge.

Have taken car back to garage and Balditch has promised to have it ready by tomorrow evening.

Tuesday, September 26th

To the office in heady mood. All my worries of the last few days seem to have fallen from my shoulders like an old overcoat. The truth of the matter is that far too much of my time is devoted to taking on other people's moral and emotional burdens when I should be putting my own house in order. Why should I give a hoot because a pip-squeak like Bryant-Fenn fancies my fiancée? If our love is not strong enough to withstand the fumbling advances of a frustrated outsider then last night was nothing more than an empty charade.

Rang Ruth at Harley Preston to report on presentation. She responded with grudging praise. Could not resist putting her in her place by mentioning the Americans' comments about lack of humour.

'That figures,' she said. 'Those guys in Cincinnati always were a bunch of ass-holes.'

Amanda rang later to suggest a cinema followed by supper in Parson's Green, but I told her I had far too much work to clear up following my New York trip. Although she didn't say so, I think she was hoping to persuade me to move in with her. All in good time!

Collected car. Clutch fine and vehicle now going perfectly. I see symbolism here.

Wednesday September 27th

A ghastly thing has happened. A pop group has moved in upstairs.

Woken shortly before one by a loud twanging of guitars being tuned. Had just nodded off again when the group struck up in earnest, practically blasting me from my bed, so great was the volume of sound they made.

I stuffed some cotton wool in my ears and lay there in a fury while my bedroom reverberated with their harsh chords and heavy percussion.

Finally made up my mind to go up and say something when the sound stopped as abruptly as it had begun. I can only hope that last night was a flash in the pan, otherwise I can see I'm going to have to take steps.

Thursday, September 28th

One of the worst night's sleep I have ever had to endure in my life thanks to the extravagant musical cavortings of my new neighbours.

When, by three o'clock, the noise still showed no signs of abating, I seriously considered going up there and giving them a piece of my mind. On the other hand, one has to watch one's step with those sort of people. They're almost certainly on drugs and there's no knowing how they might react. Also, one always feels at such a disadvantage in pyjamas.

Compromised eventually by banging on ceiling with the handle of the squeegee, but merely succeeded in dislodging a large piece of plaster which came down on my bedside table, upsetting a glass of water over my pillow.

I'll give them one more chance and that's it.

Friday, September 29th

That's it. Noise last night worse than ever. Walked into the kitchen this morning to discover that a rather charming art deco meat plate that I keep propped on a shelf above the draining board had fallen on to the floor, bringing a salt and pepper mill with it. Miraculously nothing was broken. What amazes me is that no one else in the block has said anything. Still, the sort of people I have as neighbours are so feeble that if someone was being murdered in the corridor they'd claim it was nothing to do with them. Well, I'm very sorry but I'm afraid I have more sense of social responsibility than that, and if young people do not understand how to behave properly in society, then it's up to others like me to put them in their place.

Rang the Managing Agents as soon as I got in this morning and they have promised to look into the matter. In the meantime, I must do something about these bags under my eyes.

The more I think about it, the more ridiculous it is of me to strike moral attitudes where my sleeping arrangements are concerned.

Popped home after work to collect a few bits and pieces. Just to be on the safe side, took down the meat plate. Unfortunately the stupid thing took it into its head to slip out of my hand, bringing down several pieces of china, every one of which smashed to pieces on the floor. Something tells me it is high time I moved out of here.

Saturday, September 30th

My current run of bad luck continues apace. Woke early after a surprisingly good night's sleep in Parson's Green and thought I'd surprise Amanda with breakfast in bed. Slipped into my trousers and zipped up my weasel in my flies. I do not know how this happened. It is certainly not something I have ever come across before. All I know is that it proved to be one of the most painful experiences I have ever known. To add to my humiliation, the zip became inextricably jammed. Luckily, Amanda remembered that the workmen had left a pair of pliers in the kitchen but not before I had undergone several minutes of the most excruciating agony. I'm sorry I couldn't join Amanda in seeing the funny side of it, but there it is.

It may not be a serious enough case for out-patients, but we can certainly say goodbye to 'Sportsnight with Coleman' (Amanda's term for our love-making, not mine) for quite some time to come.

Stayed up after Amanda had gone to bed to watch the first in this new series of chat shows. Everyone seemed to enjoy themselves very much – and so they should with the fees they are paid, but frankly it didn't impress me. I would not have minded so much if the show had been live, but the knowledge that I was being kept up late and having my time wasted by people who were already home and in bed made the whole affair doubly irritating.

October

Sunday, October 1st

The start of the pheasant shooting season (or it would be if it were any day other than Sunday) and for me the beginning of autumn proper. My favourite season. I realize it's fashionable nowadays to pooh-pooh Keats, but he certainly got it right as far as this time of the year is concerned: it really is the season of mists and mellow fruitfulness. And yet, despite a golden walk in Richmond Park with Amanda, felt enormously depressed for most of the day. Autumn, like sex, is strangely bitter-sweet.

Monday, October 2nd

Woken at Holland Park by the postman bringing a recorded delivery letter from the West London Magistrates Court summonsing me to appear on Thursday, November 9th at 10 a.m., to answer my speeding charge. Apparently I may simply plead guilty by letter and have the case disposed of in my absence. I can imagine that a lot of people, fearful of publicity and of further damaging their case, would gladly take that way out, but I have no intention of doing anything of the sort. I am not afraid to stand up in open court and plead my case and, if it should get into the papers, I think I can handle the consequences. Justice, I believe, should not only be done but seen to be done, and you can't *see* anything by letter.

Tuesday, October 3rd

There was a time when I used to look forward to the cheery sound of the morning post plopping on to the mat. Not any more. This morning, for instance, I receive a letter from the landlords stating that they intend to put my rent up to some preposterous amount. Shall have no hesitation in taking my case to the rent tribunal. We'll see what they have to say about it. Weasel still extremely sore. I knew I was wrong to have used that Elastoplast.

Wednesday, October 4th

The thing one misses most during this *Times* strike is the obituary column. Not that I am expecting my own death to be recorded for a while yet but, as Denys Ramsden remarked only a week or two ago, 'Who wants to die in the *Telegraph*?'

In the event, his own worst fears were unhappily realized.

Thursday, October 5th

A most extraordinary thing happened tonight in the Bordelino. While I was finishing my soup, Mollie Marsh-Gibbon lit a cigarette. We were in the middle of a most interesting discussion about *À la Recherche du Temps Perdu* when a small man with a shock of grey hair got up from the next table, came across and asked in a slight Irish accent, if Mollie would put out her cigarette since it was offensive to other diners.

She said that as a matter of fact she did mind, whereupon the man said, 'What do you think about this then?' and spat in my soup. Luckily I had very nearly finished, so it didn't really matter, and we were able to laugh the matter off. Even so . . . are there no lengths these Irish fanatics will not go to to achieve their selfish ends?

Friday, October 6th

Priscilla has rung to ask us both down to Hertfordshire for the weekend on the pretext of watching James competing in his first gymkhana and have accepted. A weekend away will do us both good. Assuming my weasel picks up, that is.

Today marks the end of my sixth week at Barfords and yet the Deputy Marketing Manager is still, as far as any casual visitor to his office is concerned, is a man called Stephen Crisp. Somebody is going to be treated to one of my famous tongue sandwiches on Monday morning.

Saturday, October 7th

A beautiful sunny morning. Just the day for getting out of London. It's a pity we didn't do so earlier and thus miss the Saturday morning traffic jams all the way out to the M11.

By the time we arrived at the farm just after one, the sky had clouded over and it had started to rain. Not only that, but there was a note on the door in my sister's handwriting suggesting that we should meet them at somewhere called Archer's Field near Chelmsford for a picnic. She had drawn a rough map showing us how to get there – a little too rough, as it turned out, since we became completely lost and it was nearly two-thirty when we finally drew up amid the horse boxes.

Parked near the main ring and tracked down the Joyces huddled under the tail-gate of their Range Rover, drinking coffee from a thermos. Nearby was James in a velvet hat and jodhpurs, perched on a short fat grey pony. At our approach, he jumped up and down with excitement, shouting 'We've got the best picnic of everyone in the whole place. Chicken legs and ham and hard-boiled eggs and sausages and Coca Cola.'

I said cheerfully, 'That sounds marvellous, we're starved.'

Priscilla said, 'That's a pity. We've just this minute given your portions away to the Finch children.'

Nigel added, 'Barbara Finch doesn't seem to have a clue about catering.' I felt like saying that his wife was not exactly brilliant in that department either.

Amanda said, 'Actually, I'm not hungry at all,' which obviously endeared her to Priscilla, and from that moment on the two of them got on like a house on fire.

Nigel leered at Amanda for a while, then turned to me and said, 'She rather reminds me of that last girl you brought down. What was her name?' Considering the way he and Victoria had behaved on that occasion I am surprised he should have the gall even to mention the subject.

'I can't remember,' I said. 'She meant nothing to me.'

Strolled across to give James's pony, Misty, a closer look. Was just admiring its withers when the animal suddenly took it into its head to deposit a large load all over my suede shoes. Everyone seemed to think it a great joke. As I was scraping the stuff off, I tried to make light of the incident by saying that it made a nice change from the dog dirt in London.

Priscilla said, 'Ugh, how disgusting – straight after lunch,' and James declared in a loud voice that he felt sick. In my opinion it wouldn't do him any harm to *feel* something useful for a change, like the business side of his father's hand across his backside.

Wandered across to the collecting ring where James's class was gathering in preparation for the Bosanquet Cup.

Came upon two small boys feeding a fat brown pony with slices of ham and hard-boiled eggs. I asked them if by any chance they were the Finch boys, 'Yes' they said.

Re-joined the family group in time for James's round. Nigel and Priscilla obviously deeply embarrassed when Misty refused every jump he came to, and when James whacked him with his stick, he deliberately walked through every one, flattening them all to the ground.

I called out, 'Come in, number eighteen, your time is up.' One or two people laughed, but Nigel went white in the face and hissed, 'You can keep your London witticisms to yourself, thank you very much.' If there's one thing worse than competitive parents, it's parents who cannot take a joke at their children's expense.

Arrived back at the farm at last at six-thirty, cold and hungry. Attempted to warm myself up with a hot bath and a whisky and soda, but stomach so empty that I merely succeeded in making myself rather tight. Matters not helped by Priscilla insisting on my sleeping in the same spare room to which I was banished when I visited last year with Victoria. It was, if anything, even colder. Consequently shivered my way through supper for which we were joined by an unsmiling young man with a mass of curly hair and a ring through one ear named Andrew.

I gathered he is an agricultural student, not that that entitles him in my book to sit down at table with filthy finger nails. His manner predictably dour and charmless. Attempted to draw him into the conversation by raising various subjects of rural interest including the Common Agricultural Policy, farm subsidies, the rights and wrongs of blood sports, foot and mouth disease and so on, but I might as well have been talking to a turnip.

To bed at ten with a hot water bottle and a slightly sore throat. Harbinger, no doubt, of a nasty cold. That's what you get for leaving London. For all their jeering at urban civilization, country people are forever going down with some minor ailment or other, and is it any wonder?

Sunday, October 8th

This is positively the last time I bring a young woman to stay under this roof. A year ago almost to the day, Nigel seduced Victoria, and last night I am convinced that some sort of hanky-panky went on between Amanda and Andrew. I admit my evidence is purely circumstantial, but I'm not a fool. Girls do not develop small bruises on the sides of their necks overnight for no reason, nor do they suddenly start exuding the odour of the farmyard unless they have recently come into very close contact with it indeed. Amanda's explanation that Andrew had suddenly offered to show her the new pig unit simply will not wash. At twelve thirty at night?

Would have raised it with her had there not been more urgent matters to attend to, namely helping Priscilla to canvass on behalf of their Conservative candidate, Ivor Hitchens, who is standing in the local by-election. Had supposed there would be more to it than walking down the street banging on people's doors, announcing that Mr Hitchens was in the neighbourhood and asking if they'd like to meet him. On the other hand, it is given to few of us in these days of TV electioneering to experience an election at grass roots level, to test the nation's pulse for oneself and dip one's toe in the water of public opinion. Most encouraged to discover that not one of the householders in Church Lane, Back Street and Stortford Road who answered our knock expressed anything other than pleasure at the prospect of an exchange of views with our candidate.

Indeed, we very soon found we had left him far behind.

'He's doing far too much talking,' Priscilla muttered angrily as she strode past us. So as a result were we.

'I'm not sure if we're on the register,' one man told us.

I said, 'Well, why not talk to Mr Hitchens anyway?'

The man replied, 'I don't mind talking to him, but not to you.'

I thought it was rather uncalled for. Still, in the hurly-burly of the hustings one has to learn to take these little knocks in one's stride. All in all, a fascinating afternoon. How reassuring it is to know that in this great country of ours, each and every one of us has a small but, I believe, not insignificant role to play in the shaping of our destiny.

Throat slightly better, but car slightly worse, for no obvious reason.

Monday, October 9th

Arrived at office to find a note from Harold Hill asking me to come and see him at the earliest opportunity. Having had no dealings thus far with the chairman, I was not sure how to interpret this. Obviously it had something to do with my American trip, but what exactly? Showed note to Pippa and asked what it meant. She looked at it carefully and said, 'It means he wants you to go up and see him at the earliest opportunity.'

In the event he could not have been more friendly and invited Amanda and me to his house at Maidenhead for the day on Saturday. Of course I accepted at once. 'Good egg,' he said. As I was leaving I remarked casually, 'I rather thought this might have something to do with the New York trip.'

'What New York trip?' he said.

Rang office manager to say that if something is not done about the name on my office door by the end of the week, there's going to be trouble. 'Oh yes,' he said. 'Who are you again?' I sometimes wonder if I work here at all.

Tuesday, October 10th

I have never thought of myself as a political animal, yet I do not believe I have ever been quite so excited by anything as I was by this morning's edition of 'Yesterday in Parliament' on Radio 4.

Only those who have campaigned at grass roots level can really appreciate the cut and thrust of parliamentary argument, and I am seriously beginning to wonder if my own talent for debate is not woefully wasted in the commercial world.

If so, I realize only too well the importance of having the right woman at my side. Churchill certainly would not have got where he did without his faithful Clemmie, nor Harold Macmillan without Lady Dorothy. Whether I can depend on Amanda Trubshawe for similar support is becoming an increasing cause for doubt in my mind.

Pippa, on the other hand, would make an ideal statesman's wife.

Wednesday, October 11th

Once again my instinct has been proved correct, to wit the letter I received this morning from the chairman of the local branch of the Conservative Association in Essex thanking me for my efforts at the weekend and adding that my keen interest in the future and well-being of the Conservative Party has been noted at the highest possible level. No prizes for guessing who that refers to, and a personal message from the No. 10 direction cannot be ruled out by any means.

Thursday, October 12th

Tim Pedalow rang this morning to invite me to a wine tasting on November 8th. I have enjoyed drinking wine for many years and it has long been a source of regret to me that I am not more of a connoisseur. This may be just the opportunity I need to start educating my palate. Have told Tim that I cannot be certain of my plans so far ahead, but *en principe* would be happy to accept.

While I was out at lunch, someone changed the name on my door from Stephen Crisp to Stanley Crisp.

Friday, October 13th

One's first priority in politics is a sense of responsibility towards one's constituents, and the fact that I alone of all the tenants in the block was prepared to take the lead in putting a stop once and for all to the nocturnal cavortings of this pop group proves that I am made of the right stuff.

The fact that there turns out to be no pop group living in

the flat upstairs, only a tiny, grey-haired lady with insomnia is, as I pointed out to Amanda, neither here nor there. The fact that I was prepared to assume the responsibility is what matters. After all, I might just as easily have been confronted by a drug-crazed lunatic with a knife.

'What I can't stand about politicians,' Amanda said, 'is that they are always poking their noses into other people's business.'

I said, 'So you don't see yourself as the chatelaine of Chequers?'

'No,' she said.

Am definitely going to ask Pippa out for a drink next week.

Saturday, October 14th

To lunch with the chairman at his house at Maidenhead. It only goes to prove what a great mistake it is to have pre-conceived ideas. I am not saying I do not like Scandinavian, open-style architecture, or housing estates, or home-made wine, or fish fingers, or children under the age of five, or even devoting most of Saturday afternoon to washing Ford Cortina 1.5 Ghias; it's just that I had expected something different.

Harold (as I now call him) could not have been more welcoming. It was a pity, as he said, that they should have been out of gin *and* whisky, but I am really quite fond of straight Noilly Prat, and one drink before lunch is really quite enough for anyone.

Betty Hill is really not as bad a cook as she likes to make out. Anyone can forget to put the lamb chops in the casserole until ten minutes before one is due to eat, and I do see, when you have three small children, it can so easily slip one's mind to take them out of the deep freeze first. (The chops, that is, not the children!) On the other hand, the rice pudding was excellent, if a little hard, and perfectly complemented the stewed plums.

We had a most interesting talk over lunch, mainly about Greece where I gather Harold and Betty take a villa every summer – or did until the children came along – and I was most fascinated to learn that the large marble in the bottom of my rather small wine glass is an old Corfiot custom, used originally to ward off evil spirits.

Harold obviously much taken by Amanda. Wish I could say the same for his wife.

As we were leaving, impulsively seized fifteen-month-old Daniel, swung him with a cheerful cry high into the air, and cracked his skull smartly on the main beam. Why the Scandinavians have to build their ceilings so low I cannot imagine. Perhaps they never lift children above shoulder height indoors.

However, the doctor assured us there is no question of a fracture. Did not like to ask about chances of permanent brain damage, preferring to keep that little worry to myself for the next few years. Finally got away at about six.

One of the windscreen wipers fell off on the M4.

Sunday, October 15th

One can scarcely pick up a newspaper these days without coming across a reference to this self-improvement course that everyone is talking about.

I am the first to admit that I am far from perfect and I would certainly be interested in the possibility of tuning myself up morally and mentally. £195 seems little enough to pay for the secret of a happy life, but not if it involves spending a whole weekend at some draughty country house with a lot of people I don't know, feeling their faces, making public confessions about my sex life, and rolling round on the floor screaming my head off. The truth of the matter is that we all spend far too much time worrying about ourselves and not enough worrying about other people.

The more I think about it, the more convinced I am that I am naturally cut out for politics.

Perhaps I should make a start by taking up social work in my spare time?

Monday, October 16th

On an impulse, rang poor old Miss Weedon's bell last night on my way in from the office and asked her if there were any little chores that I could help out with.

Knowing how sensitive the elderly and impoverished can be to the merest hint of charity, I approached the matter with immense tact.

'If ever you need any little jobs done,' I told her, 'like shopping, for instance, please don't hesitate to ask.'

'Thank you,' she replied, 'but that won't be necessary. Harrods' delivery service has always proved more than satisfactory.'

Tuesday, October 17th

My weasel now completely recovered from being zipped up, though the way things have been going with Amanda since the unfortunate affair with the baby on Sunday, this is of small consolation.

To add to my problems, I find I have now contracted athlete's foot – a cruel irony, since I rarely indulge in any physical activity of any kind, on the athletics track or off. Perhaps I should. The phrase *mens sana*, etc. did not acquire popular coinage in ancient Rome for nothing.

Wednesday, October 18th

By an odd coincidence, amongst my mail this morning what should I find but a leaflet advertising a local Yoga group. Read the whole thing with the keenest interest. While the essence of Yoga is the discovery of oneself through meditation, there are many other benefits to be derived from the 12-week course, including better breathing, relaxation, weight loss, mind control and goodness knows what else. Am particularly interested in the Yoga philosophy. The first class takes place next Thursday and I have rung up already to enrol Who knows, they may be able to do something for my athlete's foot!

Thursday, October 19th

Was returning to the office in a taxi, following a working lunch at Thomas de Quincey with Gubbins, the head of our Manchester operation, when Pratt suddenly announced that if I didn't do something about Pippa very soon, he'd go round the bend. When I asked him what he meant, he replied that for the whole of this week she had been saying she must see me.

'Obviously,' said Pratt, 'she's got the hots for you, old

chap. If I were you, I'd get in there while the going's good. There's a formidable list of contenders waiting to take your place.'

If this is true, and I see no reason why Pratt should be trying to deceive me, then it is without doubt the most astonishing stroke of luck ever to come my way.

Tempted to ring her at once and fix a drink or dinner, but a) it never pays to look eager, and b) I have committed myself to a number of projects with Amanda over the next few days which I cannot possibly get out of. Nor do I wish to.

Athlete's foot showing no signs of improvement. Have been using the cream in conjunction with the powder, as per the instructions, but am beginning to wonder if these are not meant to be applied separately. If the manufacturers mean that, why on earth don't they say so? One does not need to be a professional to recognize bad marketing when one sees it.

Friday, October 20th

To the Phoenix to see the Stoppard at last with Amanda and the Pedalows.

An extraordinary thing happened during the second act when the man sitting in the row in front of us suddenly threw back his head and started uttering curious gargling noises from the back of his throat.

Tim who was sitting in an aisle seat said, 'I don't like the sound of this. I'm going to ring for an ambulance.' And leaping to his feet he hurried towards the back of the auditorium. Although the man continued to utter these horrible sounds, no one apart from us seemed the slightest bit concerned, least of all the woman seated next to him who was presumably his wife.

I turned to Vanessa to ask what she thought we should do but at that moment a man in the row behind us leaned forward and hissed in my ear, 'Quick, grab his tongue before he swallows it.'

I said, 'Are you sure?'

'Of course I'm sure,' the man replied. 'I am a dentist.'

Pushing past Vanessa, I bent over the poor fellow and shoving my hand into his open mouth, seized his tongue with my two front fingers. Suddenly the man opened his eyes and sat upright. Naturally I at once let go of his tongue.

'Who are you?' he asked in a loud voice. 'And what do you think you're playing at?'

Attempted to explain how this curious state of affairs had arisen, but he was not to be appeased.

He said, 'Things have come to a pretty pass when a man can't doze off in a West End theatre any more without inviting bodily abuse from fellow members of the audience.'

A classic case of much ado about nothing, some might say. On the other hand, if he really had been suffering a heart attack and one had pretended not to notice, one would almost certainly have been accused of gross callousness. One simply cannot win these days.

Saturday, October 21st

To the Horses of San Marco Exhibition at the Royal Academy, and not before time, since it comes off in a week. Whether the horse they had brought over from Venice was the one that Carlo Mendotti so signally failed to show me when I was in La Serenissima in May with Hugh, I have no means of telling. If so, I am sadder than ever not to have seen this magnificent work of art *sur place* in St Mark's instead of on a carpeted platform being gawped at by swarms of culture vultures who have probably never been within a thousand miles of Venice in their lives.

Afterwards, in Piccadilly, bumped into Harold and Betty Hill, up for an afternoon's shopping with the children. They seemed friendly, if detached. I was sorry that little Daniel had to scream quite so loudly when I bent down to tickle his chin. He looked sweet under his white bandage. Jason and Emma, however, could not have been more friendly and jumped up and down, pulling on my coat sleeves and generally getting over-excited. Quite why Jason had to hit me in the groin like that I can't think. I suppose he was trying to attract my attention. If so, he certainly succeeded. I admit I must have cut a rather curious figure, doubled up and groaning all over the pavement, but if Harold had only had the sense not to laugh out loud, his beastly little brat would not have assumed he was being given the go-ahead to hit me again in exactly the same place.

Is it any surprise I have decided to give Parsons Green a miss this weekend?

Sunday, October 22nd

Lunch *chez* Trubshawe. The first time in many weeks. No matter how much I protest otherwise, they are convinced I am living with – and by implication, off – their daughter.

It's a pity she does not share my eagerness to disillusion them, but I suppose that's her way of showing her independence. However, Enid has invited me on to the committee of the local branch of the Conservative Association. Have said that my new job leaves me little time for extra-curricular activities, but that I'll certainly think it over very seriously.

Mother rang this evening to tell me to watch 'Face the Music' as Lord Norwich was on. The way I'm feeling I could not have cared less if the entire House of Lords was appearing. Which reminds me, I never heard another word from Hardacre about the National Trust.

Monday, October 23rd

Rang Pippa as soon as I got in this morning and invited her to the National on Wednesday night to see the Maugham.

She sounded most surprised and said, 'Oh, really, it's not necessary to go to such lengths.'

Not wishing to take too much for granted, I said, 'What sort of lengths did you have in mind then?'

She said, 'A quick drink after work. That's all it'll take.'

Pratt was obviously right after all. I don't know whether I am more excited or alarmed. I know we are only going to the theatre, but I feel I am committing adultery already.

Tuesday, October 24th

Delayed ringing Enid while I sorted out my thoughts. The way things are going with Pippa, there seems every possibility my relationship with Amanda may soon be at an end and I would not wish to embarrass her mother by having to face her across the committee table. On the other hand, sentimentality has no place in politics, and any work on behalf of the Conservatives can do me nothing but good.

Rang her after lunch to deliver my verdict.

'Oh,' she said, 'it never occurred to me for a moment that you would refuse.'

From what I can gather, she is expecting me to get up a committee of my own to devise some sort of fund-raising event to take place early in January. When I asked her what she had in mind, she said, 'I've no idea. That's up to you.'

While I welcome the responsibility, I shudder at the deadline. But then, of course, some people are good organizers and some aren't.

Wednesday, October 25th

So nervous at the prospect of this evening I could think of nothing else all day.

Need not have worried, as it turned out, since Pippa is the easiest of companions and most amenable to every suggestion – unlike some I could mention.

What a pleasure it is to spend an evening with someone who share's one's own tastes so exactly. Noticed in the second act that one of the actors was wearing an OF tie. Must remember to look him up in the OF register – if and when the secretary decides to send me the new one.

Supper at the Bordelino devoted entirely to the subject of Harold Hill. Pippa seemed to know all about my visit to Maidenhead and wanted to hear everything about it down to the last detail. Tempted to redirect conversation into more fruitful areas, but left the restaurant sadly unprepared for any possible advance in our friendship. Supposed she would suggest my stopping off at her flat for coffee, and was naturally disappointed when she got out of the car, thanked me for a most pleasant evening, and without so much as a backward glance, disappeared inside her front door.

Now what have I done wrong?

Thursday, October 26th

Pippa polite and cheerful as ever in the office but no mention of last night. Have always prided myself on not acting the Beddoes or the Armitage as far as women are concerned. However, feel I could certainly take a leaf out of both their books over this one.

Arrived in good time for my first Yoga class. Why is it

these sort of activities always appeal to the most unattractive people? The slight hint of self-improvement and out they come, the beards, the sandals and the dirndl skirts. But then, I suppose, those sort of people are more in need of self-improvement than most.

We all trooped into the school gymnasium (unheated, of course) where our teacher, a thin woman with a monotonous voice named Mrs Hodges, taught us how to sit in the lotus position – that is to say, cross-legged on the floor, with our backs straight, our wrists resting lightly on our knees and our thumbs and middle fingers forming a figure O. She then told us about the need for proper breathing, through the nose and the mouth. As one who has been using this method for many years with considerable success, I found no difficulty with this. One or two of my fellow students, however, seemed to be making unneccessarily heavy weather of this simple device – so much so that one was tempted to ask them how they'd been breathing hitherto: through their ears?

If nothing else, evening classes are great levellers. Had hoped in the first lesson to touch on Meditation; however, when I went up to Mrs Hodges afterwards and asked her to give me a mantra she seemed positively baffled and said, 'Do you mean a lift home?' I think she must have taken me for a foreigner.

Arrived back at the flat, bathed and cleaned my teeth, and went into the sitting room to practice my lotus position in front of 'News at Ten'. Chimes of Big Ben scarcely died away when the most excruciating pain shot through my knee. Lept to my feet and hobbled on to the sofa where I lay staring alternately at Sandy Gall and my knee. I do not know which gave me less pleasure.

To bed finally in great pain, where I chose a suitably obscene mantra which I repeated over and over again until falling into an uneasy sleep.

Friday, October 27th

Knee still stiff – not that my fellow tube travellers apparently cared two hoots. Not one of them offered to give up his seat, despite my obvious limp. Humanity seems to be as much a thing of the past as manners.

So that joint should not stiffen up unduly, strolled to

nearest bookshop for a bit of a browse. Came upon a fascinating book about finger massage, which is like acupuncture but without the needles. Apparently all you have to do is locate the pressure point that corresponds to the area of the body where the pain is, then press down on it with the point of your finger, jiggle it about a bit and the pain disappears.

Looked up 'Pain in the Knee' and found that relevant point is three fingers width above top of patella on the outer side of the thigh. Turned my back on the other customers, quickly rolled up trouser leg and followed instructions as per book. Was beginning to experience definite relief when there was a tap on my shoulder. Straightened up to be confronted by shop manager who said, 'I don't know what you are doing and I don't much care, but whatever it is I'd be glad if you would not do it in my shop.' Needless to say, one or two customers started sniggering and whispering together. I looked the fellow straight in the eye and said, 'There was a time when it was considered normal practice to test the quality of goods before purchase, but perhaps I'm very old-fashioned.'

'Yes,' said the manager, 'you are.'

I replied that in that case it was a pity there weren't a few more old-fashioned people about, adding that it was most unethical of him to be offering manuals of this sort for sale on the open shelves without allowing customers the opportunity to test their efficiency.

He said, 'I suppose the next thing you'll be wanting is to bring your girlfriend in to try out *The Joy of Sex*.'

The trouble with the shopkeeper mentality is that it never knows where to draw the line. Had no intention of buying book after that and told him so. Took bus to Foyles only to find they were out of stock, so compelled to return to original shop after all.

Got home to find that the GPO had been to install the jack for my answering machine. It's only taken nine weeks.

Saturday, October 28th

Hooray, hooray. At last I've got my answering machine. The man came to install it this morning and spent a good twenty minutes showing me how to get the best from the service.

I do see that a cheerful, friendly, perhaps even slightly apologetic message is preferable to the brusquer, more formal type of greeting. Have decided to aim for an approach somewhere between the two. Charm without sycophancy should be the keynote, I think.

Spent the afternoon thinking up a suitable message which, after several bosh shots, I have finally recorded. Set machine and popped out to buy a few groceries. Returned to find no one had left any messages, but decided to leave it on anyway. I had a feeling Pippa might ring and I certainly did not wish to give the impression that I have nothing better to do on Saturdays than sit at home. Later, on an impulse, drove round to Parson's Green to find a note pinned to the door from Amanda saying she had been trying to ring me all afternoon to suggest going to the Woody Allen film, but had given up and gone out instead with Christopher.

Realized something must be wrong with the machine and rushed home to find I had left dial on wrong position. Re-set it and nipped out for some eggs before the shops shut. Got back to discover someone had called. Re-wound tape only to hear a long silence followed by the receiver being replaced. I suspect it was Pippa, but there's no way I can be sure, short of ringing up, and that would ruin the whole effect. A wretched evening. And who is this Christopher when he's at home?

Sunday, October 29th

A sleepless night, filled with doubts and anxieties. Have listed them in order of concern. I always think problems are easier to consider once they are down on paper. I suppose that's the writer in me coming out again.

Many people, faced with so many unsolved dilemmas tend to let matters sort themselves out of their own accord. I prefer a more positive attitude myself. Like Lord Mountbatten, I am a man of action and, as such, believe in taking life by the scruff of its neck and shaking it, as a dog shakes a rat. Of course it is bound to be unpleasant, and people are liable to get hurt in the process, but better that than a slow decline into a morass of indifference and inertia.

I shall begin straight away by sorting out this wretched headache that has been plaguing me since breakfast. The pressure point, I see from my finger massage book, is on the inside of one's wrist.

Monday, October 30th

Headache completely cured, but I now have an extremely sore wrist.

Morning post brings a copy of the most recent register of OFs, plus an invoice for £3.75, not including VAT. I was outraged, though not half as much as I was to find that my name is not included. Not that I could care less whether I am in there or not. It's just that the whole thing's so hopelessly incomplete. National Theatre actor also not included. But then I might have expected that.

Have written off to the secretary of the OF society, registering my complaint in the strongest possible terms and returning his insulting invoice. Father did not pay all that money in 1960 to make me a life member for nothing. No messages on the answering machine this evening.

Tuesday, October 31st

Rang Hugh early. Before I could utter a word he said, 'Whatever were you thinking of when you recorded that message for your machine? You sound like some terrible old poof.'

I said coldly, 'I can only think there is something wrong with your telephone,' and hung up on him.

November

Wednesday, November 1st

Have been reading the famous cases of Sir Patrick Hastings.
I realize that great advocacy is a thing of the past, but a well-
argued, well-delivered speech, concentrating on my hitherto
impeccable record, can certainly do me no harm. As soon as
they see the sort of person they are dealing with I feel sure
they will simply let me off with a warning.

On the way home had my hair cut extra short.

Later hunted my old school black jacket and pin-striped
trousers out of mothballs and tried them on. Stood in front
of mirror and in Churchillian style, seized my lapels, one of
which came clean away in my hand.

I think the grey double-breasted with the chalk stripe will
do just as well.

Thursday, November 2nd

Was skimming through OF news on loo this morning when
my eye alighted on the name of Dishforth. He was a House
Runt in School House at the same time as me, and for a
couple of semesters we shared a cubby together. I never
realized until now that his name was David. He was always
known throughout the school as Dirty – for all the obvious
reasons.

Typical of him to think that anyone would wish to know

what he has been up to for the last eighteen years. He always was pushy. Slightly Jewish if I remember rightly.

He is now a successful solicitor in Theobalds Road. On an impulse, rang him from the office to sound him out on my chances with the West London Magistrates. He listened politely while I outlined the facts of the case, then said, 'Are you asking for my professional advice?' I said that I certainly was.

He said, 'I'd try the human weakness ploy myself – ' he said. 'Say that you were driving along quite normally at about 20 m.p.h. when suddenly you were gripped by the most appalling attack of the trots. Naturally you needed to get home as quickly as possible for fear of soiling the upholstery.'

I said that if I'd known he was going to be so flippant, I'd never have rung him.'

He said, 'I'm being perfectly serious.'

'In that case,' I said, 'I'd *seriously* advise you to consider another profession. Like writing BBC comedy scripts.'

'Oh, I do that already,' he said. 'in my spare time of course.'

Could not resist remarking that there was no mention of this in the OF news.

'Maybe not,' he said, 'but at least I pay my debts.'

When I asked him what that was supposed to mean, he replied that I owed the society £3.75 plus VAT for a copy of the OF register.

I replied that, if it was any of his business, I was a life member and, as such, was not obliged to pay for registers.

He said, 'It *is* my business. I happen to be the new honorary secretary. And what's more, you're not a member, life or anything else. You resigned from the society six months ago.'

Friday, November 3rd

Woke with a shock to realize that I had forgotten to cancel my yoga classes. It's always a great mistake to pay for things in advance these days: there's always some good reason why you shouldn't get your money back.

Rang Mrs Hodges who said, 'I am not surprised that you didn't come back.'

When I asked her why, she said, 'Some people are serious about this sort of thing, some aren't.'

I said that, if she really wanted to know, I'd given my knee a very nasty wrench, thanks to her.

'Your excuses,' she said, 'are your own affair.'

I'd had enough of beating about the bush.

'I suppose there's no chance of my getting a refund?' I said.

'The more I think about it,' Mrs Hodges said, 'the more I think you were right to give up yoga. You're far too aggressive.'

The trouble with these left-wing, pacifist, self-improvement merchants is that one can never get a straight answer out of them.

Bumped into Pippa in lift after lunch.

She said 'Have you seen the Hills lately?'

I said that I hadn't and, more to the point, when was I going to see her again?

'You see me every day,' she said.

Why is it that everything I say nowadays is automatically misinterpreted?

Saturday, November 4th

Woken early by the phone. A voice said 'Is that Mr Crisp?' I said that it was. 'Simon Crisp?' asked the voice. I repeated that that was so. 'Oh, I'm so sorry,' said the voice, 'I wanted to speak to his answering machine,' and put the phone down.

Is it my imagination, or did it sound remarkably like Beddoes?

To the Pedalows in the evening for dinner with Amanda. Theresa and Philippe de Grande-Hauteville there. They can talk about nothing but their wretched baby. I suppose it's understandable, their being so much older than the average first-time parent. He now seems convinced that I work in Fleet Street. I could not be bothered to disillusion him.

She looking greyer than I remember.

Good conversation at dinner, mainly about the adaptation of this famous spy novel on television. I seem to be the only one who thinks it has the slightest merit. As I told Tim, the whole point about spying is that in real life it is a very slow, methodical business.

'I don't want reality', he said, 'I want entertainment.'

As an epitaph on the Pedalow gravestone it could hardly be bettered.

During coffee, Tim left the room and came back with a bag of golf clubs. He extracted a seven iron, unscrewed the head and slid out a long, thin packet which he carefully unwrapped and, amid much oohing and aaahing from the others, proceeded to make up a cigarette. With one rap hanging over my head already, I was not going to risk getting busted and, when it came to my turn to have a puff, I said, 'I happen to know a thing or two about addiction,' and passed it on.

Felt quite dizzy on the way home. I put it down to all those fumes amidst which I was forced to spend the last hour of an otherwise quite enjoyable evening.

Sunday, November 5th

The great mystery has at last been uncovered. Christopher is a dog – to be precise, a large white Pyrenean Mountain dog.

It belongs to A's antique-dealer friend Brian and his boy friend, and A looks after it when they go off for their weekends in Amsterdam.

Am not a great lover of dogs, least of all the type that rush at you the moment you open the front door, hurl their paws against your chest, then slide down, pulling great lengths of wool out of your pullover.

Had been hoping, in the light of Pippa's lack of enthusiasm, to take the dying embers of our fading love affair and coax them into flame.

Suggested to Amanda that we might spend tomorrow lunchtime looking for an engagement ring. Anyone would have thought I'd suggested a hiking holiday in the Andes from the astonished look on her face.

'An engagement ring?' she exclaimed. 'Who for?'

'For you, of course,' I told her. 'Who else?'

'You and me?' she said. 'Engaged? You're not serious.'

I replied that I had never been more serious in my life, and that I was sorry it had taken me so long to make up my mind, but that I have never believed in rushing into things. To my amazement, she burst into shrieks of laughter.

'What ever makes you think I'd want to *marry* you?' she said. I replied stiffly that I was aware that for us the path of true love had certainly not run as smooth as it might have done, but that, as far as I was aware, there had always been an understanding between us.

She said, 'The only thing I understood was that we were friends – you have obviously been expecting something more.'

I said, 'Are you trying to tell me it's all off?'

'Poor old Simon,' she said. 'It was never really on, was it?' Not for her perhaps; it certainly was for me. Still, there seemed no purpose in labouring the point, and we've left it that I'll call her in a few days. We both need time to think things over.

She said, 'It won't do any good.'

'We'll see, we'll see.' I suppose that, if I were really honest with myself, I'd have to admit I've seen this coming for some time, but now that it has, it is no easier to bear. All in all, the worst Guy Fawkes Night I can remember in a very long time.

Monday, November 6th

The most wretched start to a week I've ever known. However, the morning post brought a letter from Beddoes proposing a trip to Brussels next weekend.

Surprised to realize how much I have missed him in recent weeks. For all his bad behaviour, he is a lively companion and although we do not see eye-to-eye on moral matters, a completely fresh approach to the vexed question of my emotional and sexual life could be just what's needed. On a more serious note, I am deeply concerned over our contribution to the Common Market budget; one's knowledge of the workings of the EEC is all too sketchy and I welcome this opportunity to acquaint myself with this organization into whose hands we have so blithely committed ourselves.

Rang the European Commission HQ from the office, but no one on the switchboard seemed to have heard of Monsieur Ralph Beddoes.

Unfortunately, I was unable to give them the slightest clue as to his function, and my assurance that he is something of a big cheese led predictably to much confusion.

Finally ran him to earth this evening at his flat. He was obviously delighted to hear that I was coming and doubly so that I would be alone. Knowing him, I daresay he's laid on a couple of loose women. *Tant mieux.*

Tuesday, November 7th

Feel.I cannot let personal feelings interfere with my responsibilities towards the Conservative party, and think I may have come up with a perfect fund-raising idea. A real 1950s dance, just like the ones we always used to go to as teenagers during the school holidays. Dancing 8.30 to 1.00. Cold buffet with wine cup. A real old-fashioned eight-piece band. Quicksteps and slow quicksteps, waltzes and valetas, Gay Gordons and Dashing White Sergeants and Strip the Willow, and, of course, the Last Waltz with the lights dimmed. A Teenage Dance. It will be a sell-out. All I need now is a committee to help me organize it. Got on the phone as soon as I arrived in the office and have already co-opted Tim and Vanessa Pedalow and Theresa de Grande Hauteville. Philippe, being foreign, obviously wouldn't understand.

Terribly tempted to ask Jane Baker to help. It's very much her thing. And so, the more I think about it, am I.

Wednesday, November 8th

Rang Jane and she has said yes. We have fixed our first committee meeting for a week today.

To my nearest travel agent at lunchtime to book an economy return flight to Brussels. Unfortunately, have left it far too late and must pay full fare of £99. At those prices, is it any wonder we can't afford to stay in the EEC? On the other hand, if one cannot splash out at my age, when can one?

To the wine tasting in the evening with Tim, in a cellar somewhere off Lombard Street.

Wines in question all Burgundies from the Chambolle-Musigny region, wherever that might be. Asked Tim who said, 'What does it matter *where* it is? It's *what* it is that matters.'

Whether he actually knows anything about wine is hard to tell. At all events, he made a great fuss, sticking his nose into the glass, sloshing the stuff from cheek to cheek and smacking his lips after each swallow.

As far as I was concerned, they all tasted exactly the same. Tim said that, in his view, wine was meant to be drunk, not to be spat out into barrels of sawdust. I replied that if I had swallowed every glass I had tasted, I'd be under the table by now.

'It depends what you're used to,' he said, throwing back his head for the umpteenth time.

Oddly enough although not a single drop passed my throat, by the time we left at half-past-nine, the room was reeling and Tim had to help me into a taxi.

Had intended to spend the evening preparing my speech for the trial tomorrow, but collapsed on to the bed where I fell fast asleep and dreamt that I was Sir Patrick Hastings defending Tim Pedalow on a drunken driving charge, and losing.

Thursday, November 9th

Woke at six-thirty feeling dreadful. Bathed and dressed in dark grey with chalk stripe.

Arrived at court shortly before ten. How ironic life can be: the last time I set foot in such a place it was very much on the other side of the legal fence, as a juror.

Surprised to note how few of my fellow defendants had bothered to dress for the occasion.

Gave my name to the clerk and went to sit on a bench with my fellow criminals. Normally would not have bothered to pass the time of day with such types, but crime is a great leveller and it would have been a narrow-minded man indeed who did not welcome this opportunity of an insight into the mentality of the criminal classes.

One, a coloured man, said he reckoned he'd get eighteen months and another said he'd rather get a short stretch than a fine any day as he always forgot to pay them and finished up in the nick anyway.

Fascinated to find how quickly and easily one falls in with the criminal argot and way of thinking. I said, 'On balance, I prefer a fine.'

'What you up for then?' the coloured man asked me. I said casually, 'Oh, a little bit of this and that. You know,' and tapped the side of my nose and winked.

Soon began to wish I really were up on a more serious charge. For some reason all the others were summoned before me and it was midday when my name was finally called.

Found myself face to face with two pleasant-looking elderly men in dark suits and a grey-haired woman. The charge was read out and I was asked if I had anything to say.

Made, I think, a very good speech: succinct, witty and not too flowery.

The chairman said, 'Very interesting,' and began to confer with his colleagues in a low voice.

Finally, he looked up and said, 'If you had a real excuse to offer – you suddenly felt ill or something – I might have understood. As it is, fined forty pounds and licence endorsed.'

On way down to accounts office, asked the usher how forty rated as fines went.

'About average,' he said.

Said nothing but could not help thinking that if I hadn't shown up in person, it might have been a good deal stiffer.

Was crossing the road when I bumped into my coloured friend.

He asked me what I'd got and when I told him, he said, 'Bad luck. Next time try damage to property. I got six months suspended. See you,' and walked jauntily up the street. To rob a bank, no doubt.

Is there no justice?

Am seriously considering taking the matter up with my MP. Whoever he may be.

Friday, November 10th

Arrived home last night to find a most curious message on my machine.

'Mr Crisp,' said the voice. 'I hope you have a very enjoyable weekend.'

Laughed it off as a jape by one of my friends and went to bed.

Woke at four in a muck sweat, convinced that some lunatic had planted a bomb on the 9.30 plane to Brussels and was ringing up every one of the passengers to gloat.

Lay there sleepless till eight when I rang the airline to ask if it was possible for anyone to get hold of a copy of the passenger list.

The girl said it was out of the question, but I was taking no risks. Told them to cancel my reservation and rang British Rail to find that the boat train was leaving at ten.

Rang Beddoes to tell him of change of plan. Debated whether to leave his number on answering machine in case of emergency but finally decided against it. One doesn't want to make it any easier for burglars than it already is.

Rushed to Victoria and caught the train by seconds. Felt oddly like the Duke of Windsor going into exile.

Crossing delayed by an hour owing to bomb scare, but once under way the journey passed quickly enough. A pity it was rough. People are so stupid. If only they'd get out on deck, they'd feel 100 per cent better straight away. I certainly did. Of course, there are always exceptions – viz. the Indian next to me by the lifeboat. I suppose it was my fault for standing down-wind of him, but that did not make a faceful of regurgitated curry any more palatable.

Finally arrived at Brussels station at 9 p.m.

No sign of Beddoes. Ring his flat. Girl answers. Ralph will be there soon. Half an hour later, no Ralph. Phone again. Same girl: he's been delayed. Twenty minutes later, he rolls up in a large grey Mercedes, 'Hope I haven't kept you waiting, laddie.' Snigger, snigger 'Spot of unfinished business.' Snigger, snigger. 'We thought we'd all go out to eat somewhere, then perhaps go on to a club and meet some friends then back to my place for a night cap. . . .'

I'm sorry to be a wet blanket, but there it is. As Beddoes' Dutch live-in girlfriend, Lola, points out, we have the whole weekend ahead of us, but he won't have it. European life seems to have made him, if anything, worse.

Saturday, November 11th

A late start.

To Waterloo after lunch to view famous battlefield. A fitting outing on Remembrance weekend. Lola extremely knowledgeable about the battle. She took us first to La Belle Alliance, the inn on the far hill that Napoleon used as his HQ, thence down the valley to Hougoumont, the famous farm, so valiantly and decisively defended by the Scots Guards. Not for the first time, I found myself wondering if there is a single country in the world whose tourist industry does not owe its success to British courage, skill and initiative. Travel certainly broadens the chest.

Drove to the Lion Monument for final panoramic view of

field of battle. The huge mound, surmounted by a large lion, stands on the very spot from which the Iron Duke directed the proceedings. Arrived just as attendant with moth-eaten moustache was locking the gateway to this magnificent memorial to courage and patriotism. Reminded him in no uncertain terms who won this battle, but he shrugged his shoulders and plodded off into the gathering gloom. 'If it hadn't been for people like us,' I called out after him, 'there wouldn't be a monument for you to guard.'

'Actually,' said Lola, 'the monument was erected in memory of the Prince of Orange, son of the King of Holland.'

Even if she was right, there was no reason to be quite so smug.

Dined at the most lively fish restaurant behind the Grande Place.

Halfway through my second plate of mussels when Beddoes said, 'Hallo, you're in luck. Here's one of our Commissioners. You may not realize it in England but he is probably one of the most important men in the world right now.'

Noticed a slight hush descend over the proceedings.

As the Commissioner and his party passed our table he paused briefly and said a few words to Beddoes who in turn introduced me.

I stood up, opened my mouth to speak and belched loudly.

The Commissioner said, 'Enjoying your mussels, I see,' and passed on his way.

Beddoes said, 'Bang go our chances of being asked to dinner there.'

I said I was very sorry, but if one's career in Europe hung on a belch, then that was about all it was worth anyway.

Beddoes said 'Then that just shows how little you people in England understand about the EEC.'

I suggested that the Commissioner had probably never even noticed.

Beddoes said, 'People like that do not get where they are by not noticing things.'

To bed on a slightly frosty note. *Plus ça change*.

Sunday, November 12th

To Bruges for the day. A most fascinating medieval city. According to Lola, it is known as the Venice of the North.

Could not resist remarking that I had yet to hear of Venice being described as the Bruges of the South.

Dinner in the flat, cooked by Lola, and very nice too. Over coffee, I suggested to Beddoes that he might care to give me the low-down on this Common Agricultural Policy row.

He thought for a moment and said, 'I'd like to show you something.'

Leaving Lola with the washing-up, we got into the car and drove down a sidestreet where a number of girls sat in lighted windows, knitting scarves and flipping through magazines.

Beddoes told me, as if I hadn't guessed already, that this was the red-light district.

For an awful moment I was afraid he was going to suggest sampling the wares, but he seemed content to drive up one street and down the next, making lewd and suggestive comments as we went. It was all most embarrassing, especially as we got caught up in a one-way system and found ourselves driving up and down the same two streets half a dozen times looking for the way out. By the end, some of the girls had actually started waving at us and making provocative signs in our direction. We finally extricated ourselves and as we drove home I said to Beddoes, 'Most interesting, but I'm afraid the metaphor escapes me. What has all that to do with the Common Agricultural Policy?'

'Nothing whatever,' he said. 'I just thought you'd be interested, that's all.'

Is it any wonder the Prime Minister is having such problems achieving credibility with Schmidt and Giscard when this is the sort of back-up she has to rely on.

Monday, November 13th

Entire day spent travelling. Remarked to one of the old stewards on the boat that I felt sure in the old days, when the rich travelled to the Continent by boat, it was all much more comfortable.

'It still is,' he said, 'if you travel on the night sleeper.'

Typical of my travel agent not to have thought of suggesting it.

Arrived back at the flat to find several messages on the machine: from Pratt asking why I wasn't at the reps meeting, from Enid saying when could I give her the names of the committee, from Tim saying would I call him and from Mother wondering whether I'd made my mind up yet about Christmas. Nothing from Amanda.

Also a bill from Dirty Dishforth – 'To professional services' – £25, of all the cheek.

I definitely remember now that he had a Jewish mother.

Tuesday, November 14th

Tackled Pratt first thing. I have always believed that the best form of defence is attack, and said that, if he thought a reps meeting was more important to Barfords than an exchange of views with a European Commissioner then he might just as well start looking for a new deputy.

He said, 'I think you might have let me in on your plans.'

'There are occasions,' I said, 'in this fast-moving world of modern business, where one simply has to seize ones chances as and when they occur.'

It's this sort of petty-fogging, small-mindedness that is responsible for Britain's poor performance in world markets today.

He grudgingly conceded I might have a point. I somehow don't think we shall be hearing from that quarter for quite some time.

Had not considered it before, but I see no reason now why I should not claim at least part of my trip on expenses.

Tim rang after lunch to say that he and Vanessa had been planning a weekend trip to Moscow on Saturday week, but that she had walked out on him in Annabel's on Friday night and would I care to go in her place. I have long held the view that in this day and age no one can speak with authority about modern political life without first having visited America and Russia. To be offered the opportunity of experiencing the two extremes of the political spectrum in as many months is one that no thinking man would dream of refusing. Have told Tim I'll think about it and call him back tomorrow.

New York, Brussels, Moscow: where will it all end?

There's no doubt this is my year for seeing the world and the more my life expands, the more convinced I am that even to consider tying myself down to a married life at this exciting stage of my career would be sheer madness. I am now convinced that the break with Amanda is a blessing in disguise.

On to Moscow. I wonder if there's a potential market for Barfords there? What a feather in my cap that would be! Have made a note to write a memo to Hardacre on the subject.

Wednesday, November 15th

Rang Tim first thing to say I am definitely on for Russia. I thought he seemed most relieved. Am a firm believer in doing my homework before visiting a country for the first time, so walked to the library at lunchtime to borrow a copy of *Das Kapital*. It is a good deal larger than I had imagined, and heavier. Was glad I had the sense to take a plastic carrier bag with me, even though the handle did break on the way back. I already have the reputation at the office for being a bit of an intellectual and with all this talk of traitors at the palace I wouldn't put it past any of my colleagues to leap to the conclusion that they have a mole in their midst. Put book away in drawer and forgot all about it until I arrived home. Rang office, but no reply. Drove round, but place locked and in darkness. I don't know why I am worrying. No one ever comes to my office in daytime, so it's hardly likely they'd suddenly start doing so in the middle of the night.

Thursday, November 16th

Arrived at office at seven-thirty. Book apparently untouched – ditto waste paper basket and dirty coffee cup.

Posted off passport to travel company. I hope there's not going to be any trouble *vis-à-vis* my American visa. (Rather a good joke that.)

To Pedalows after work for inaugural committee meeting. Tim clearly relishing his new bachelor status as much as I am. Jane completely transformed, I hardly recognized her. Her skin has quite cleared up and she has given up those dreadful glasses in favour of soft contact lenses. She has even taken to wearing a little make-up. I could not take my eyes off her. Delighted to hear that she had at last given Armitage the boot. I said, 'We must get together again soon.'

'I don't think that will be possible,' she said, 'now that I'm engaged to Hugo.'

Life is all a matter of timing.

Everyone very keen on my Teenage Dance idea, although we wasted far too much time persuading Theresa that a Beautiful Baby Contest just isn't on. While I am delighted that she and Philippe have found happiness together in middle age and I do appreciate that their baby is very special to them, it isn't to everyone.

I also think that if one must bring a child to a committee meeting, one really ought to be able to think up better ways of stopping it grizzling than opening one's blouse and breast-feeding it. Natural rearing may be all the rage now but do we have to have it shoved down our throats?

It simply isn't the sort of thing one expects of Young Conservatives.

All in all, though, a most successful meeting. Tim has agreed to organize the band and the hall; Jane will do the food; Theresa is in charge of decorations; I will handle public relations and advertising.

It was unfortunate that Theresa had to come across my copy of Marx just as we were leaving. She claimed she was looking for the disposable nappies.

'What's this?' she cried, 'A traitor in our midst?'

I said coolly 'He is a foolish man indeed who rides into battle without first knowing the mind of the enemy.' Everyone laughed and the tension dissolved.

Tim said laughingly, 'That was very good. Just like Philby at his press conference in '55. You'd make a jolly good mole.'

Friday, November 17th

Is it my imagination or was the same man who got on the tube with me at Holland Park this morning still behind me as I walked down Chancery Lane? I also have the impression that there are many more clicks and buzzes than usual on my telephone, and have therefore taken to speaking through a handkerchief. As for Tim's joke last night about Philby and my making a good mole, I am not a fanciful man, but I have a definite feeling he was trying to tell me something. In fact the more I think about it, the more convinced I am that there is more to this Russian trip than meets the eye. It would not surprise me one little bit to learn that Tim is a talent spotter for the Russians. He has the perfect background: public school, Cambridge, etc., and perfect cover: respectable job in the City, entailing a certain amount of travel. What more could the KGB ask? Quite why he should consider me as a possible agent, I cannot imagine. I neither drink nor am I homosexual. Nor, on the other hand, am I in the habit of expressing dissatisfaction with the *status quo* or sympathy with Mr Brezhnev and his cronies.

I am wondering if the fact that I enjoyed that spy series on TV so much has anything to do with it. It's tiny dropped hints of this sort that spymasters seize on without one realizing it.

Could call Tim's bluff, of course, and make it quite clear from the word go that it's just not on, but on reflection think I'll bide my time and see how the land lies.

Softly, softly, catchee molee.

Saturday, November 18th

Tried to read *Das Kapital* in bed last night, but somehow just couldn't get into it. In the end fell asleep with the tome resting on my chest. Woke up in the small hours with the light still on and quite a pain in my chest.

Mollie rang after breakfast to say that she had received some details from an estate agent for a house which boasted, among other things, a 'vehicle hard-standing.' She seemed to think that highly amusing.

Tried to avoid telling her about Russia but it slipped out anyway.

She said, 'Well, all I can say is, they don't wear those fur hats for nothing.'

When I asked her to elaborate, she explained that since 80 per cent of one's body temperature escapes through the top of one's head, a fur hat in those sub-zero temperatures was very much a *sine qua non*.

The trouble with people who have hot air coming through the tops of their heads, whatever the temperature, is that one can never be entirely sure when they are telling the truth. However, I have always rather fancied myself in fur ever since Mr Macmillan went to see Mr Khrushchev. Hurried off to the shops to see what they had in stock. Was trying one on in Harrods when Tim appeared from nowhere and said, 'Don't buy a fur hat here. They have the real thing in Moscow at half the price.'

Now how did he know that if he's never been before?

And was it really plain coincidence that he should be in Harrods at exactly the same time as me?

The plot thickens.

Sunday, November 19th

To Mother's for lunch – possibly the last we shall have together. On the way down, heard a fascinating talk on the wireless on how to barbecue an entire pig.

Mother quite unconcerned about my escapade behind the Iron Curtain. All she said was, 'I hope this doesn't mean you'll be away for Christmas.'

I may be away for a great many Christmases if I don't play my cards very carefully indeed, but said nothing to her.

As I was leaving she said, 'Just make sure you wrap up warm. I don't want you going down with a cold just before Christmas.' Talk about a one-track mind.

Monday, November 20th

Took *Das Kapital* back to library on way in to work. With the best will in the world I am quite unable to get beyond page two. Goodness knows how Marx thought the uneducated masses were going to lap it up. Anyway, to my way of thinking, if one cannot get the flavour of a society by living amongst the people for a few days, one's certainly not going to get it from books.

Memo from Keith Hardacre concerning my memo to him, to the effect that likelihood of trading agreement with Russians extremely remote. On no account am I to repeat my foolish behaviour in Brussels by trying to take things into my own hands. Nothing, repeat, nothing should be undertaken on behalf of the company by any junior executive without the prior consent of a board member, and then only under the strictest supervision. Not even Christina Onassis can do as she likes and she owns her company, etc. etc.

I have never been so insulted. Am I Deputy Marketing Manager or am I some pipsqueak of no more importance than an office boy?

Rang Keith and put the question to him straight from the shoulder. He said, 'As far as this sort of thing is concerned, you are a pipsqueak of no more importance than an office boy.'

Is there no place left in Britain these days for flair and initiative? Has the lesson of my Brussels trip still not got through? For two pins I'd emigrate somewhere where my talents are really appreciated and nurtured. Possibly Russia.

Tuesday, November 21st

A disastrous start to the day.

Had dressed, shaved, breakfasted, etc. and was just on way out when I discovered hands still slightly sticky with marmalade.

Went to wash them under bath tap, owing to underpants soaking in basin. Unfortunately, had forgotten to switch knob from shower to bath and turned on tap to receive powerful jet of water on top of head. Hair completely soaked, also shirt, tie and jacket.

As a result, stepped out of front door considerably later than planned. Looked down to see small brown package leaning against door frame. Closer examination revealed that it was postmarked SW11 – a favourite haunt of anarchists and parcel-post bombers if I'm not mistaken. Also noticed my name spelt wrong. I suppose it could have been perfectly innocent, but one cannot afford to take any risks these days. It is quite possible that my name is down on someone's death list. Hurried indoors at once and rang the police.

I imagine they must be the victims of many hoaxes in the course of their work but obviously they believed this to be the real thing since they were round in less than an hour.

Have told them I am available to answer questions until Friday evening, but did not mention Russia. Also suggested making a list of possible enemies.

They said it's not necessary, but I think I'll do it anyway.

Wednesday, November 22nd

No news yet from the police. My own list of suspects shorter than I had imagined. Am curiously disappointed.

Thinking of *bêtes noires*, I see from today's *Times* that Sir Peter Hall is 49. I suppose it's the beard that makes him look older.

Also noticed that Professor K. B. S. Smellie is 82.

I wonder if he is any relation to Andrew Smellie who was so anxious we should be kept *au courant* with his career in the last but one OF news? I'm quite sorry now I chucked in my membership. I'd really have something to set my contemporaries by their ears in the next edition.

Thursday, November 23rd

Tim rang with the stunning news that he will not now be coming to Russia after all, since Vanessa has come back and they have decided to have a week's holiday in Istanbul to celebrate, but that he hoped I'd received the packet of guide books and leaflets he'd sent on Monday.

He said, 'Sorry to let you down at the last minute, but I think you'll find you'll be very well looked after.'

By his controller at the Centre, no doubt.

Friday, November 24th

Passport returned in morning post, plus visa. No query about my trip to America I notice. Parcel of leaflets returned by police.

A sudden ghastly thought occurred to me on the way to work. If Tim does do something silly, I shall have to find someone else to arrange the band and hall for the Teenage Dance.

Despite earlier rudeness on the subject, rang Bryant-Fenn to sound him out as a possible substitute.

Before I could get a word out, he said, 'I hear you're off to Moscow.'

Hedged slightly at first, but finally he wheedled the truth out of me.

'One word of advice, old man,' he said. 'Take plenty of gifts for the natives. It's the only way you'll get anything done. But, of course, I don't need to tell that to a well-travelled chap like you.'

Frankly, it was all gobbledygook to me. I said, 'No, of course not. What sort of gifts do *you* take?'

He said, 'Oh, the usual things you know: soap, chewing gum, fags, lipstick, chocolate, of course. I gather Pentel pens go down very well these days, and tights – the larger the better, knowing Russian women.'

While I have no intention of being arrested for smuggling before I've even got into the country, I have heard that it is hard to get certain goods in Russia, so perhaps the authorities turn a blind eye to this system of tipping. The problem is, how much of everything to take? Is one bar of Imperial Leather enough to ensure early morning tea and how many pairs of tights does one need for a seat at the Bolshoi?

Have decided to err on the side of generosity and take more than one really needs.

I only hope I've got the right shade of lipstick. The girl assured me that Morning Rose is very popular.

Before leaving this evening, fired off memo to the office manager asking for the name on my door to be altered a.s.a.p. I only hope it will be worth the effort.

Saturday, November 25th

Arrived at London Airport in good time for noon flight. Rest of the party the usual unlikely mixture of age and class one invariably meets on package tours. Not that I have been on that many, of course.

One quite glamorous blonde girl with a fur coat and suede boots. She is alone, but why? Tried to wangle seat next to her on flight, but edged out by tough looking, grey-haired man in sheepskin coat and corduroy suit.

They're obviously all set for a bit of a thing. I think I may have missed the boat there.

Landed up next to elderly woman named Mrs Antrobus whose son, she claimed, had been a contemporary of mine at Oxford. The name means nothing. I gather he was very keen on madrigal singing.

She said, 'Do I gather this is your first visit?' I said it was. 'It's always exciting the first time,' she said. 'This is my fifth.'

Opened my brief-case to take out my *Guide Bleu*. Mrs Antrobus took one look at the array of lipsticks, soap, etc. and exclaimed, 'Aha, a commercial traveller!' Tried to explain about tipping but nothing I said could persuade her otherwise. I can see that I am going to be stuck with the nickname 'The Traveller' for the rest of the weekend.

Long, unexplained delay at Moscow Airport while our

Intourist guide, Irena, scurried about in an aimless sort of way. Finally shepherded on to ancient bus for long, cold drive across flat empty countryside to city.

Tim's not going to like this after a lifetimes' weekending in the Cotswolds. Finally drew up at Metropole, a large, once plush Edwardian hotel, just off Red Square.

Key-lady on my landing excessively grim despite my cheery greeting. Shall obviously have to slip her something straight away, but what? And how awful if she were to refuse – or worse, send for the police. Hung about in corridor to see if anyone else slipped her anything, but decided it doesn't do to draw attention to oneself in Communist countries.

Bedroom spartan in the extreme – torn curtains and no bath plug. Hugh was right about bringing a squash ball. I assumed he was joking. Who wouldn't?

Room far too hot for my taste, so threw open window while unpacking. Temperature soon dropped owing to sub-zero conditions outside. Unfortunately, unable to close window again, and had to wedge it with *Times*. Hunted for a while for bug, but without success. Suddenly overwhelmed by conviction that mirror on wall two-way. Covered it with towel and dismantled telephone. Not knowing what inside of Russian telephone looks like normally, impossible to tell if bug inserted or not. Struggled to put it together but failed. Reassembled it as best as I could and went down to dinner.

Marinated fish, meat, potatoes and dry cake, washed down with sweet fizzy drink like Lucozade, in an echoing barn of a room, watched over by glowering waitresses.

Sat next to large girl with blonde hair who said, 'You look the sort of man who knows what's what.' I did not disagree. Her name is Belinda Bott. Rather apt. She has managed to work out that she and her ex-husband were also at Oxford at the same time as me. Am beginning to wonder if there is anyone in Moscow who wasn't.

When I asked her which college she was at, she said, 'Balliol.' Naturally I expressed surprise. 'Strictly night-time only,' she said and guffawed loudly. If I had a name like Belinda Bott, I think I'd keep very quiet indeed.

After dinner went up to third floor to look at Berioska Tourist shop which was closed. Arrived back in my room to discover that someone had closed the window, also put telephone together. Interesting. To bed humming 'Midnight in Moscow'.

Sunday, November 26th

Spotted curious protuberance high up on wall I had not noticed before. Will investigate later.

After breakfast hurried up to Berioska shop to find several shelves of fur hats. Toyed with silver fox and astrakhan, but finally plumped for more typical rabbit fur. A bargain, to my mind, at 9 roubles 20 kopeks, and a perfect fit. Astonished to find that one can pay with American Express. I'm only sorry I didn't bring my card. However, pound notes equally welcome.

Morning spent on general sight-seeing tour of city. Blonde girl and grey-haired man together again, I was sorry to see. She is rather my type. Her name is Angela and his is Ken. Did my best to avoid Belinda Bott, but without success.

'That's a nice hat,' she boomed as she slumped beside me on the coach, crushing my thigh. 'Pity about the white patch.'

I had not noticed it before, but now she mentioned it, it stood out in a most irritating fashion so that I could scarcely think of anything else all morning. Caught Irena staring at me several times during lunch.

Returned to Berioska and explained my problem re hat. Assistant in grey suit shook his head, indicating that, since he had already snipped the label from the hat, any exchange was now out of the question. I suggested he could always thread it back through, but he was not to be persuaded.

Suddenly had a brilliant thought. Snatched my Pentel pen from my pocket and thrust it into his hand. He nodded his thanks and put the gift in his pocket. Assuming that I now had the go-ahead to take the new hat, I picked it up and made to leave, but he rushed forward and seized it from me, and an undignified tussle ensued. Out of the corner of my eye I noticed his colleague picking up the telephone and dialling.

Decided to cut my losses and make a run for it. Mentioned my problem to Irena as we were getting on to bus for after-noon outing to Kolomenskoye Palace and she said if I left it with her she would see what she could do.

At dinner she arrived carrying paper bag containing new

hat. Thanked her profusely, then added quietly, 'You don't happen to have any messages for me do you?'

She said, 'Yes.'

My heart was pounding and I felt slightly sick. 'What?' I said.

She said, 'The manager of the Berioska says will you please not go to his shop again?'

Having been promised an evening at the Bolshoi, it came as a great disappointment to learn that we were booked instead at an evening of folklore dancing at the Palace of Congress in the Kremlin. No one seemed to know why. I was all for kicking up a stink, but Mrs Antrobus said, 'In Russia you must let things take their course.'

Had the definite feeling she was trying to tell me something, but what? Could there be more to her than meets the eye? She looks very much the type who might have mixed with the Cambridge crowd in the Thirties.

Suggested walking back with her to hotel after ballet, but she did not rise to any of my baits.

Had barely got back to my room when there was a knock on my door. Opened it to find Belinda Bott who said, after a long pause, 'Well don't you have something to say to me?'

I said, 'I don't think so.'

'Oh,' she said, 'Are you quite sure?' And she pushed her way into the room. Suddenly the whole picture fell into place.

Seizing her by the arm I pushed her into bathroom and turned on all the taps.

'I'm sorry,' she said, 'but I'm not that sort of girl.'

I said, 'Not what sort of girl?'

'Well,' she said, 'you know. . . .'

I said, 'But they did send you, didn't they?'

'Yes, she said.

'And?' I said.

She said, 'And nothing, I just thought, here we are, two people in a strange city without any strings. . . .'

The fact is that, if it weren't for that mirror being where it is, facing the bed, I might easily have been tempted to take her up on her blatant offer. However, one simply cannot afford to risk compromising oneself in a place like Russia. Which reminds me; I still haven't looked at that appliance on the wall.

Monday, November 27th

Up early for a last look at Red Square – on my own. Stood for a while in front of St Basil's looking, in my fur hat, like that famous photograph of Kim Philby, or is it Burgess?

I still couldn't quite believe that I was really there, right under walls of the Kremlin, facing Lenin's marble mausoleum, bang on the very spot where the might of Russia's hardware parades every year before those grim-faced Politburo members.

Was on my way back to the hotel when I realized I was being followed by a young man in a black leather overcoat. The more I quickened my pace the more he hurried after me. Had reached the metro station when I felt a hand on my shoulder. Spun round to be confronted by a grim Slav face beneath a grey fur hat.

'American?' he said in a thick Russian accent. I shook my head.

'British?' I agreed.

He said, 'Would you like to buy a belt? Very nice. Many designs on buckle. Kremlin, Red Star, Head of Lenin. . . .'

'How much?' I said.

'How much you got?' he said.

I got out a Pentel and a couple of sticks of chewing gum.

'Is that all?' he said.

I said, 'How about a couple of bars of Cadbury's Fruit and Nut?'

'Chocolate pah!' he said. 'Don't you have dollars?' I shook my head.

'Forget it,' he said. 'You British all the same. Always trying to get everything on the cheap.'

Hurried back to hotel, looking anxiously about me all the while. Suddenly realized that my new hat was really quite loose. Each time I swivelled my head, the hat stayed where it was. Decided I'd rather have a white patch than a bad fit. Ran up to Berioska to find completely new staff. Also my original hat. Explained problem to new assistant who could not have been nicer and changed it straight away.

Packed suitcase and, out of interest, climbed on chair to examine strange appliance on wall. Managed to unscrew it and was lifting it gently away when leg of chair gave way and I fell back, taking appliance and several wires with me. Left pieces where they were, grabbed suitcase and hurried down to lunch. There seemed to be considerably more activity than usual in the hall – men rushing about with bags of tools, reception clerks busy on the telephone, etc. Mentioned the fact to Irena who said, 'I think there is a problem with the central heating. One of the guests has been interfering with the thermostat in his room.'

To the Tretyakov Gallery for a quick look at the icons before leaving for the airport. Went to collect hat and coat from compulsory cloakroom and was halfway to airport before I realized I had been given someone else's hat by mistake. Not only was it far too large, but it also had an even larger white patch than my own. Oh well. Perhaps it will do as a Christmas present for someone.

Carefully avoided Belinda on plane, but that did not stop her giving me her telephone number. I did not give her mine. Ken and Angela still very much in cahoots right up to the last moment. Surprised however to find her alone on the coach going back to Cromwell Road.

I said, 'Your friend abandoned you then?'

'Yes, thank goodness,' she said. 'At last.'

I was astounded and said that we had all imagined they had really hit it off in a big way.

She said, 'You must be joking. If there's one thing I can't stand it's middle-aged married swingers. I spent most of my free time hiding in my room.'

I said, 'What a shame. I've been wanting to talk to you all weekend.'

'Now he tells me,' she said.

We have exchanged phone numbers. One never knows when one might not find oneself at a loose end in Finchley. Her surname is Tuckerman.

Tuesday, November 28th

Felt curiously detached at the office today. Mentioned to one or two people that I had just spent the weekend in Moscow, but it might just as well have been Margate for all the interest it aroused. Is it any wonder we get on so badly with our Common Market colleagues when we are all so abysmally parochial in our outlook?

Noticed on the way out this evening that someone has at

last been and changed the name on my door. To Stanley Cripps. I give up.

Wednesday, November 29th

To the Rent Tribunal to argue my case against the proposed rise.

The representative of the landlords, a pale runty-looking type with a large moustache that was obviously sapping his strength had little to offer in defence, I thought, and merely re-stated his company's wish to put the rent up. The Rent Officer then announced that, taking everything into consideration, he agreed that the new figure was very much in accord with the rents in that area and that he would be re-commending the new rent, to take effect from last September. The two shook hands and it was all over. I left without shaking anyone's hand. A more blatant case of collusion I have yet to encounter. Is it any wonder that intelligent people turn to socialism when this is the way they are treated? Not that some of us have very far to turn.

Thursday, November 30th

The more I think about it, the more I am beginning to harbour grave moral doubts concerning this Teenage Dance I'm supposed to be organizing. In a truly caring society, it's not the haves that need their pockets filled but the have-nots, and I've no doubt Mrs Thatcher is quite capable of keeping her head above water without my help. I am not and never have been anyone's catspaw. It is not too late to withdraw my support for this scheme and I shall write to The Boltons this evening to inform Enid of my decision. I also intend to abandon any ideas I might have had for standing as a Con-servative at the next election.

The fact that my change of political heart has occurred shortly after my return from Russia is purely coincidental and anyone who accuses me of starry-eyed opportunism could not be further from the mark. After all, Churchill crossed horses in mid-stream and it certainly did his career no harm in the long run.

December

Friday, December 1st

Rang Bryant-Fenn to say that I should not now be requiring his services on the Teenage Dance Committee. He said, 'That's just as well. I wasn't planning on giving them.'

For all his blatantly capitalist ways, I have always suspected that at heart Hugh is a fellow socialist, and I felt I was quite safe recounting to him my savaging at the hands of the Rent Officer. He was most sympathetic.

He said, 'If I know your landlords, they're selling off every flat that falls vacant, and for a small consideration, they'd be glad to see the back of you.'

I said, 'You've lost me there, comrade.'

'It's quite simple,' he said. 'Write to them – better still ring them up – and say you're thinking of moving, but as things are you can't afford the cost of a van, agent's fees, etc. On the other hand, if they could see their way to covering your expenses to the tune of, say, five thousand smackeroos, you could be on your way tomorrow. They'll jump at it.'

The Labour Party could do with people like Hugh.

Saturday, December 2nd

Hugh rang and said, 'I gather it's all off with Amanda Trubshawe.' No prizes for guessing who he got that bit of tittle-tattle from. I told him that, if he really wanted to know, we'd come to a mutual understanding. 'Yes', he said, 'I thought it was all over. Well you're well out of that one. I speak from experience.' What experience?

Am more than ever convinced that Hugh and she got up to something while I was in America.

Not that it matters a hoot now.

Sunday, December 3rd

Woke feeling lower than a snake's hips.

Mother rang after breakfast today to say that Priscilla had told her she needed a new pair of slippers for Christmas, but if I wanted, she'd get her the slippers and I could think of something else. No news of Tim and Vanessa. I thought they were supposed to be coming back on Thursday?

Ho ho ho.

Nothing worth reading in the papers so spent afternoon picking my eight favourite gramophone records in case I should ever be invited on to 'Desert Island Discs'. It's quite a bit harder than one might imagine.

Monday, December 4th

In the tube this morning an unusually large intake of passengers at Lancaster Gate caught me completely unawares. Put my hand up to prevent myself cannoning into the woman in front of me and suddenly found myself grasping one of her breasts. Unfortunately, there was such a squash I was unable to extricate myself and had to travel all the way to Oxford Circus jammed in this embarrassing position.

The odd thing is that the woman went on reading her *Woman's Realm* apparently without noticing a thing. Perhaps it's something that happens to her every day.

Rang the landlords as soon as I got in and laid my cards on the table more or less along the lines Bryant-Fenn had suggested.

Mr Haynes listened politely, then said, 'We shall certainly be offering your flat for sale when and if you decide to leave. It's no skin off our nose either way, but I would advise you not to try pulling any more tricks of this nature, or you could find yourself in very hot water indeed.'

Obviously the sooner I am out of that place the better. I have rung half a dozen reputable estate agents and they have promised to send me details of houses and flats at the lower end of the price scale.

Tuesday, December 5th

According to the stuff that has arrived from three of the agents, there is nothing for sale below £35,000, and for that one is lucky to get a two-bedroom flat in Tooting.

I see now what the opposition spokesman on the environment meant when he said that those hardest hit by the credit squeeze are the first-time buyers. How on earth does one climb on the property merry-go-round unless one has something to sell? Have I completely missed the boat, I ask myself? Obviously I should have bought something years ago – or better still, I should have abandoned my scruples about living with Amanda.

I've always thought of Parsons Green as being the back of beyond, but I see now that it is every bit as desirable as Belgravia and Mayfair, if not more so.

Wednesday, December 6th

Tim rang after lunch. I was amazed.

'Where are you?' I asked him. 'Russia?'

'Don't be daft,' he said 'I'm in the office. We loved Turkey so much we stayed on a few extra days.'

I felt like asking if they had any cheap houses for sale out there.

'How was Moscow?' he asked.

'It was all right,' I said 'Your friend never got in touch.'

'Who?' he said. 'Belinda?'

I asked him what Belinda had to do with it.

'Nothing, as it turned out,' he said. 'It's just that I suggested she meet up with you. Pity; she's lots of fun. Very much your type I'd have thought.'

I was astonished and said 'Since when have I gone for the Miss Piggy type?'

Tim said, 'Not only is she a lecturer in Russian and an expert on the art treasures of Moscow, but she also happens to be my sister.'

Thursday, December 7th

An astonishing thing happened in the office today.

Returned from an area planning meeting with Pratt to find a message on my desk from Keith Hardacre to say that at long last the New York presentation has borne fruit in the shape of a £250,000 contract. He was with the chairman and would I come up as soon as I got in?

Pratt shook me by the hand and said 'You're made in Barfords now.'

Was in a complete daze as we travelled up in the lift. Arrived in Harold's office to more congratulations and handshakes all round. Harold said, 'I always knew you had it in you,' and opened a bottle of champagne. He then proposed a toast: 'To the young knight who has at last won his spurs.'

As we all trooped out half an hour later, Harold said 'If there's anything I can do to help, don't hesitate to let me know.'

Felt like saying that an interest free loan on a house would not go amiss, but there'll be time for that anon.

In my euphoria, rang Pippa and suggested a celebration dinner at the Bordelino tomorrow night, but maddeningly she's tied up.

Give it time, give it time.

Friday, December 8th

A sensational turn of events. Harold Hill has resigned as Chairman of Barfords and, in the small hours, run away with Pippa to France.

Their precise whereabouts are still a mystery. So far as I am concerned, so is their behaviour. I did not realize that Harold was even aware of Pippa's existence – although the more I think about it, the more everything falls into place.

What can she possibly see in him? Like Mrs Simpson, she cannot seriously believe she is to be the consort of a king in exile.

While I am certainly no killjoy and would deny no one the chance of happiness in this life, I feel personally extremely let down.

After yesterday evening's triumph, I shall obviously be

seen from now on as a Harold Hill man and, with him out of the picture, the knives will soon be out and into my back.

Bang goes my house, if not my career.

Saturday, December 9th

On a whim, rang Angela in Finchley. Hung on for a good two or three minutes but there was no reply which is very odd since she told me she was always at home on Saturdays.

In the evening there was a man on 'Desert Island Discs' I have never heard of in my life. He claimed to be a well-known writer.

Sunday, December 10th

Rang Mollie apropos nothing in particular. She has a theory that all these trades union people are basically failed actors and the only reason they keep going on strike is because it's the only way they can get on TV.

Happened to mention the difficulty I had getting through to Finchley yesterday.

She said, 'What's this girl's name?'

I said Angela Tuckerman.

She screamed with laughter and said, 'Of course nobody answered the phone. On the Sabbath?'

I said sharply that there was no reason to suppose Angela was Jewish.

'With a name like Tuckerman?' she screeched. 'Living in Finchley?'

Monday, December 11th

Instead of going straight home after work, took the bus down to Trafalgar Square for the traditional ceremony of the lighting of the Christmas tree.

It was a most moving occasion and as the Band of the RAF struck up 'The First Nowell', a lump rose in my throat and tears welled up unashamedly in my eyes.

But then isn't that what Christmas is all about?

Tuesday, December 12th

Mother rang with the news I have been dreading all year: Nigel and Priscilla are coming for Christmas, with James. The season of goodwill is obviously destined never to get off the ground this year as far as I am concerned.

Can I honestly be blamed for not being able to raise a lot of enthusiasm about the January sales conference? Hardacre is already showing signs of carping. I'm wondering if I shouldn't have joined the Masons after all. The writing is on the wall.

Angela rang after lunch, much to my delight. Had meant to say nothing about my ringing on Saturday, but it came out anyway.

She said, 'What a shame. The phone was on the blink all day.' Perhaps she is not Jewish after all. Not that it matters a row of beans to me one way or the other. Indeed, I have always understood the Jews to be an unusually warm and generous people. She has suggested an outing tomorrow.

Why I should be so inordinately excited at the prospect of spending an evening with a girl, I don't know, but I am.

Am only sorry that she has seen the Woody Allen film twice.

I said, 'You couldn't face it a third time, I suppose?'

'No' she said.

There's nothing I admire more than a woman who knows her own mind.

Woody Allen's Jewish, of course.

Wednesday, December 13th

I have been out with several women in my life but I do not believe I have felt at once so relaxed and at ease with any of them as I was this evening with Angela. I even quite enjoyed seeing *Players* again.

Dined afterwards at the Bordelino.

It's much farther to Finchley than I thought. I hope this is not going to become a stumbling block.

Thursday, December 14th

To Harley Preston for a meeting about the New York contract.

148

Ruth Macmichael unnecessarily sharp with me, I thought, Remarked on the fact afterwards to Keith, but all he said was. 'She had a point.'

The knives are very definitely being sharpened. Still, that's big business for you. If you can't stand the heat, get out of the kitchen. That's the way I look at it.

Met Angela for a drink at the Piccadilly Hotel, then back to Holland Park for one of my specials: boeuf bourguignon. She was obviously impressed.

Had a most fascinating talk after dinner about California which she has apparently visited on numerous occasions. She was most interested to hear about my recent visit to New York, although, as she pointed out, there is very little comparison with the West Coast. San Francisco certainly sounds very much my cup of tea, and the news that she is planning to go there next week to live filled me with envy and regret.

I am really going to miss her, and told her so.

She said, 'In that case why not come with me for Christmas and see it for yourself? Who knows, you may like it and decide to stay.'

A tempting offer. However, people in my position do not alter their domestic arrangements at the drop of a hat – not ten days before Christmas, anyway.

Have said I'll think about it.

Friday, December 15th

Today could turn out to be the most momentous of my life.

Was bracing myself for the long haul back to Finchley just before midnight last night when Angela said, 'Do you really want to drive all that way?'

I asked her if she had a better idea.

'Yes,' she said.

I do not propose to go into details about what ensued. I would not wish to embarrass my children and grandchildren when they come to browse through my diary in years to come, and like so many sensitive people, I have always found 'Sportsnight with Coleman' curiously difficult to describe.

Suffice it to say that, if last night was anything to go by, Angela Tuckerman and I were made for each other. Perhaps not on a permanent basis but who knows. . . ?

Whether or not I shall take her up on her offer over America is still something of a moot point. The way things are at Barfords, I shall almost certainly have to start looking for another job soon and America for all its current problems is very much the sort of go-ahead country where I would be able to give free rein to my imagination and talents, as has already been amply proved by my recent success in New York. A £250,000 contract is a £250,000 contract in anyone's language. It is well known that news travels fast in the United States, and I should not be at all surprised to learn that my name is already not entirely unknown in California. Andrew Carnegie, Cary Grant, Dudley Moore – they all seized their chance for fame and fortune in the New World when it came their way, and for me to allow mine to slip through my-fingers, for the sake of Christmas with the cat, would be sheer lunacy.

Decisions, decisions. Still, every man must face a watershed at some stage in his life, and only he can decide which is the right path to follow.

Saturday, December 16th

After a largely sleepless night, have finally made up my mind. The crisis is past. America for Christmas it is. I have told Hardacre that I shall be taking a few extra days off over the holiday.

And with these words I lay down my pen and close my diary. Another important chapter of my life draws to a close. Now all I have to do is speak to Mother. She is going to be very cross indeed.

The Crisp Report

To Bridge and Al, with love

Memo

From: The Chairman
To: All Departments   2 January

This is to confirm that, pursuant upon the unexpected departure of Mr Harold Hill, the following appointments have been made:

Keith Hardacre, from Marketing Director to Deputy Managing Director, effective immediately.

Simon Crisp, from Department Market Manager to Special Projects Manager, this to take effect on his return from the USA.

My dear Angela,

Just a brief note to apologize once again for the unfortunate scene at the Dongs' Howdee Neighbours' party on
New Year's Day, and to say how very sorry I am that
things between us did not turn out quite as well as we had
both hoped and expected. Please apologize to Harry and
Deedee on my behalf. I shall be writing in due course, but
in the meantime, if Harry would like to forward me the bill
for the new water jug, I'll settle up with him forthwith.

As you know, I enjoy Sportsnight with Coleman as
much as the next man. However, in my book, there is
more to a relationship than that.

The point is, Angela, one's got to have something to do
between the hanky-panky, and I'm sorry to say that I
think that your suggestion that one should sit about planning the next session does not altogether fit the bill as far as
I am concerned.

As you know, my idea of travel is getting out and about
among the highways and byways, observing the natives in
their natural habitats and generally acquainting myself
with their customs and way of life. Plonk me down at a
busy pavement café with a notebook and pencil and a glass
of dry white wine and I'm as happy as a sandman. In that
way I suppose I'm a bit of a Freya Stark or Jan Morris.

Pope was right. The proper study of mankind *is* man.
But not the way you mean.

Home is where the heart is and much as I would have
liked to tell you to the contrary, I did not leave mine in San
Francisco. London very much belongs to me, I realize that
now. Which brings me on to my latest bit of news, and
pretty sensational it is too.

As you know, I was convinced that, once the chairman,
Harold Hill, had eloped to France with Pippa Robinson, it
was only a matter of time before the knives were not only

out but deeply embedded in my back. I had pinned my colours to Harold's mast pretty firmly and heads were bound to roll. It was like the abdication crisis all over again with myself in the Fruity Metcalfe role.

However, arrived in my office to find a memo from Keith Hardacre announcing that not only had he been promoted to Deputy Managing Director but that I, too, had been promoted – to the post of Special Projects Manager. This means not just a 15% rise in salary, but also a decent office at the front of the building overlooking the square, possibly a secretary of my own, and a key to the Seven Above Club – the bar on the top floor of No. 7 that only the top executives in the firm are permitted to use. Quite a feather in my cap, I think you'll agree.

My first project, if you can believe the irony of it, is to compile a special report on sex in Britain today. I am to get cracking on it straight away and the whole thing is to be delivered by the end of February. As you can imagine, I immediately rang Hardacre for an explanation.

He said, 'It is twenty-one years since the *Lady Chatterley's Lover* trial heralded the permissive society. We at Barfords think it is high time someone in this country came up with a progress report on the current state of British mores. We believe that Barfords are exactly the right sort of people to carry out a study of this sort.'

I reminded him that the Williams Committee had recently spent several years producing an excellent report along very much the same lines.

Hardacre said, 'Good point, but the fact is that we want the Crisp Report to go a good deal further than Williams and cover the entire field of sexual behaviour. Obscenity is only the tip of the iceberg, to our way of thinking.'

I could hardly believe my ears. The Crisp Report! Naturally I have every intention of accepting – once I've got my committee together, that is.

I am hardly what you might call a Masters or a Johnson. I must pass through Soho half a dozen times a week and yet never once have I felt the slightest urge to enter a porno cinema or witness a live sex show or call upon the services of a 'young model'.

Tant pis for me, some may say, and they are probably right. It is, after all, the duty of every intelligent respon-

8

sible citizen with the slightest claim to a social conscience to acquaint himself with every aspect of modern life, including the soft underbelly of the consumer society. Having been afforded this unique opportunity I cannot wait to get started.

My only real concern is that my friends – and, more importantly, Mother – should not get hold of the wrong end of the stick and jump to the conclusion that I have taken this thing on in order to satisfy some personal need or gratification.

Frankly I have better things to do with my time than waste it on the massage parlours and peep shows of London's so-called Golden Mile. However, I have always held that, if a job's worth doing, it's worth doing well, and I believe that to rub shoulders with the twilight world of bottoms and breasts can only serve to increase one's understanding of this funny old world in which we live.

Must close now and get ahead with my committee shortlist. Am wondering if John Mortimer would consider helping out in an ex officio capacity. He is very much in the public eye these days and I have always been a great fan of his.

My best to the Dongs, and don't forget about the jug, will you?

Affectionately,
Simon

PS I didn't happen to leave a pair of underpants lying around, did I? I seem to be short and can't think where they could be otherwise. If you do come across them, perhaps you would be kind enough to pop them in a strong manilla envelope? I will, of course, reimburse the postage costs.

Confidential Memo

From: Simon Crisp, Special Projects Manager
To: Keith Hardacre, Deputy Managing Director

10 January

Re: *Crisp Report Committee*

I have given this matter a lot of thought and my proposals are as follows: I should, of course, wish you and Neville to be as closely involved in the project as possible. I have been most impressed, as I know you have, by Roger Fremantle's work on the in-house magazine. We need a good editorial mind on this. I do not know what the form is re involving Harley Preston. However, my feeling is that we do not make full enough use of our marketing consultants, and Colin Armitage is one of the few people I know who is genuinely *au fait* with the sexual world. Shall I progress this or will you? I feel a female mind might have something useful to contribute, and who better than the chairman's secretary, Erica? She and her husband live near Bromley. Enough said?

Am considering the possibility of approaching John Mortimer in an advisory capacity. Ditto Clement Freud. To have a sympathetic foot in the Palace of Westminster might be very useful.

May I have your reactions to this at the earliest possible opportunity?

S.c.

Memo

To: Simon Crisp
From: Keith Hardacre   15 January

Someone's lines seem to have been crossed somewhere. All this talk of a committee is news to me. My idea was simply that you should pop into a few sex films, skim through some magazines, and collate some rough statistics on wife swapping, adultery, etc. It may have escaped your notice, but we are in the middle of a recession and we shall have to keep a close watch on every penny if we are to come through it in one piece. To give you some idea of the gravity of the situation, we are scrapping the Seven Above Club. In the circumstances, therefore, while we are 100% behind you over this one, the idea of a redistribution of manpower along the lines you suggest would be quite out of the question.

If you feel you are not up to it, please say so immediately and we will start looking round for someone else. I should value your reply within the week.

KH

Memo

From: Simon
To: Keith   16 January

May I call upon the services of a full-time secretary?

S.c.

Memo

From: Mr Hardacre
To: Mr Crisp   17 January

I have arranged for Sue Frizzell to be seconded to your department on a temporary basis.

KH

Memo

From: Simon Crisp, Special Projects Manager
To: Keith Hardacre, Deputy Managing Director
cc: Neville Pratt, Personnel, Accounts, File

18 January

Re: *The Crisp Report*

This is to confirm that, as from today, 18 January, I shall be working full-time on the above-mentioned study into the contemporary state of British mores, with direct responsibility to you.

S.c.

Private and Confidential Memo

From: Simon
To: Keith   18 January

Just a small point, between ourselves.

When you said in your memo that you wanted me to 'pop into a few sex films, skim through some magazines, and collate some rough statistics on wife swapping, adultery, etc.', what exactly did you have in mind and how far precisely do you want me to go?

11

Re massage parlours, for instance. Do you think it absolutely crucial to the authenticity of the report that I actually have a 'massage' and all that that entails? Does one really need to sit through hours of hard-core films, or would an interview with a leading pornographer fit the bill just as well? Naturally, not having a wife, it would be impossible for me to swap one with someone else's, but my not being married certainly does not preclude me technically from committing adultery. But how far is one expected to go in the interests of truth? I feel one should draw the line somewhere, but where exactly?

I look forward to your comments at the earliest opportunity.

S.C.

Memo

To: Simon Crisp
From: Keith Hardacre   19 January

Re your memo, I leave it entirely to your discretion.

Please note that I shall be away on a skiing holiday from noon today until Monday, 29 January. I look forward to your progress report then.

R. Hippo
pp. Keith Hardacre
Dictated by Mr Hardacre and signed in his absence.

Progress Report to Myself

Saturday

I know now how Winston Churchill must have felt in 1940 when he was summoned to the Palace and asked by the King if he would be prepared to form a government. He wrote at the time that he felt as if he were walking with destiny and as if his whole life had been but a prelude to that moment – and so do I. A short stint in the wilderness never did anyone any harm.

Where though to begin? Once again I find myself regretting Beddoes' disappearance to Brussels. For all his endless succession of inconsiderate and humourless inamoratae, and his fondness for jokes based upon the lavatory, my ex-flatmate was extremely knowledgeable concerning the grubbier areas of life about which most of us are, thank goodness, ignorant.

Still, I have a feeling he was planning to come to London some time in the next few weeks. I might very well drop him a line and suggest picking his brains over a rather good lunch (or, knowing his strange tastes in food, picking a rather good lunch over his brains). Ditto Tim Pedalow and possibly the awful Colin Armitage. I cannot really believe that Hugh Bryant-Fenn will have any first-hand experiences to offer, since his most personal relationship to date appears to have been with his late pet budgerigar, Percy. However, in this life there are those who do and those who know people who do, and Hugh certainly knows a few people one way and another. I've no idea who, but it can't do any harm to drop him a line.

In the meantime, I shall get on with some basic field research. Am still slightly in the dark as to the form my report should take. I daresay the nature of the material itself will determine this. Have decided to jot down all my researches in a notebook willy-nilly. Although have told Hardacre am beginning with sex shops, think I shall seize the sexual bull by the horns and plunge straight into the world of sex films.

Monday, 22 January

Never having been to a sex film, am not quite sure where to begin. Should one break oneself in with something fairly innocuous like *Flesh Gordon* or *Emmanuelle Meets the Wife Swappers* and gradually work one's way up towards the meatier stuff? Or should one go straight for the hard-core and get the worst over as soon as possible?

Sue absolutely no help whatever. Posed my dilemma to her over a cup of coffee soon after getting in this morning.

She said, 'I have never felt the slightest desire to see any films of that sort, hard, soft or otherwise, and neither, I'm glad to say, have any of my friends, so I'm afraid I can't help you.'

Reminded her in no uncertain terms that this was neither the time nor the place for a display of her Home County scruples and that, as my full-time assistant, I expected her co-operation at all times.

I said, 'You don't suppose I'm in this for fun, do you?'

'I don't see why not,' she said. 'Anyone else I know would be.'

I can see that someone's going to have to read the riot act to someone before very long.

Lunched modestly off a toasted sardine sandwich, then set off to Soho for a preliminary recce.

Had not realized before how many porno cinemas there are in this part of London. Interested to see that the word 'Swedish' features a good deal in neon. Quite why this should be, I do not know. If the de Grande-Hautevilles' au pair is anything to go by, the average Swedish girl is sulky, unalluring, and about as sexy as a cup of cold Horlicks.

Outside La Continentale in Wardour Street was a sign saying: 'This cinema is showing uncensored films of a sexual and explicit nature. Any person who may be offended or shocked by this type of material should not enter this cinema.'

How the initiate is to know if he is going to be offended or shocked without having a look first, I cannot imagine. Was jotting down exact wording in a notebook when a dark-skinned fellow with a heavy moustache, a gold chain nestling among a jungle of chest hair, and accent of vaguely

14

eastern Mediterranean extraction, strolled out of entrance and came up to me and asked if there was anything I wanted. I replied that I was merely taking down a few particulars.

'Look,' he said, 'no children in this cinema.'

'I should hope not,' I said.

'No animals,' he said.

I said with a laugh, 'You can't take your dog anywhere these days.'

He frowned and said, 'You from West End Central?'

'No,' I said. 'From Barfords actually. You may have heard of us.' I explained about the report.

He said, 'You sure you're not from the police? Mrs Whitesides? GLC?'

I shook my head.

He said, 'I don't know who you are or what you want, but I run a respectable cinema here. All completely above the line, you know?'

I said, 'This is most interesting. When you say respectable, what do you mean exactly?'

He seized me by the arm. 'Look,' he said. 'If you want to see the show, see the show, be my guest. But please, don't stand here writing in your little book. It's bad for business.'

I explained that unfortunately I had an important meeting to attend, but that I certainly hoped to sample his wares at a later date along with the rest of the paying public.

He said, 'Please yourself,' and disappeared inside.

Doubt if I shall in fact take him up on his offer. Am convinced that in any form of research anonymity is very much a *sine qua non*. One cannot imagine Egon Ronay turning up out of the blue at Le Gavroche and demanding a free meal, and while I am not for a moment suggesting that the manager of La Continentale would have attempted to get into my good books by laying on a few 'special' items, I do not believe one can get a properly balanced view without experiencing it from the public's point of view. Also, one has to be careful dealing with the underworld. Lay yourself open to bribery and corruption and suddenly you'll find you're being asked to repay the favour at a most inconvenient moment. We at Barfords cannot afford to be caught up in a squalid blackmail situation.

Decided I was not yet up to material of this strength and that I really would do better to kick off with something a bit milder.

Sat down in snack bar with cup of tea, Kit-Kat and the *New Standard* and began browsing through entertainments pages. Unfortunately, titles gave very little hint as to the content of the films on offer. One film, *Phantasm*, carried with it the promise (or possibly threat) 'Sex will never be the same again.' Is one to understand from this that those who see the film will find their personal lives altered in some dramatic fashion? Or does the phrase have a wider significance? Have all our lives been in some mysterious way transformed by one film? Have made a mental note to have a look in the next time I am passing.

Further down the page, my eye was caught by the news that the Cinecenta at Piccadilly Circus was showing the first ever Triple-X programme, comprising *The True Blue Confessions of Mary Millington*, plus *Boys and Girls Together*, and *Scandinavian Erotica* – an 'X-certificate shocker – includes scenes from hard-core movies previously banned for general viewing'.

This sounded very much the sort of thing I ought to be cutting my sexual teeth on.

Was paying my £2.90 at Cinecenta box office when suddenly remembered this was the same cinema I had once visited many years ago, which had a little balcony to one side of the auditorium where they served light teas during the performance. The combination of *Nudes in the Snow* and a toasted tea cake is an experience I shall always treasure.

Sadly, the old place has undergone the indignity suffered by all cinemas these days of being sliced up into a series of long, thin rooms, so that one has the sense of watching a film in a hotel corridor.

Not that either *Blue Confessions* or *Scandinavian Erotica* would have looked or sounded any the better by being shown in the Odeon, Leicester Square.

The highlight of the proceedings came when Mary Millington, once a popular sex star, declared, 'It's not the sleep of the just that counts; it's the sleep of the just after.'

No one laughed though. They were probably all asleep. I know I nearly was.

Was interested to note that, in the interval, despite the fact that I am a lifelong choc-ice man, found myself going instinctively for a cone – something I have not done since childhood. Man in next seat ate two! It just goes to show the sort of effect a short exposure to pornography can have on even the strongest-minded amongst us without our realizing it. Goodness knows how I shall react when I start getting down to the real hard-core stuff, though have a feeling they may not sell ice creams in this kind of cinema.

Decided to put the interval to good use by making a spot survey of the sort of people who make up the audiences in the Jaceys, the Cinecentas and the Moulins of Britain.

Of the thirty or so present, half appeared to be Chinese waiters – on their afternoon off, I daresay. Of the remainder 40% were in the 45–65 age bracket, and, in socio-economic terms, C1/C2/D, at a rough guess. The rest were quite young couples. The pair in front of me were very lovey-dovey and I made a mental note to keep my eye on them to see if the nature of the entertainment had any interesting effects on them.

Was halfway through a rough head-count of rainwear when the lights dimmed and *Boys and Girls Together* started.

The story was set in London. It began, like *Scandinavian Erotica*, with an aeroplane landing. Am wondering if these sex film producers have some sort of tie-in with the airlines. If we're not careful, they'll soon be giving us in-flight blue movies.

The hero, a young American, was soon through customs and on his way to Hampstead, where he appeared to have fixed himself up in advance with accommodation in a large Victorian house.

The house had six rooms. Number 1 was occupied by a black man doing press-ups; 2, by a nude blonde having a shower; 3, by a long-haired Japanese youth thumbing through a pansy magazine; 4, by a black girl eating a banana; and 5, by a dopey-looking white girl sitting on the loo.

No sooner had the American set foot in his room than he was thumbing through a girlie magazine.

After a while, we saw the loo lady ironing a pair of

panties. The Japanese, who had a kitten, was washing his. (Panties, that is, not kitten.) The blonde, whose name was Ilsa, was listening to the wireless.

The black man stared gloomily for a long time at a photograph of a rather frumpy black girl (his girlfriend back home in Trinidad presumably, but possibly his mother) before suddenly snatching it off the wall and tearing it into shreds.

The black girl in No. 4, meanwhile, was sticking up a poster of the pop singer Roger Daltrey, and in No. 3 the Japanese was enjoying an extremely satisfying dream about a young fellow-countryman playing tennis.

No one, it seemed, had pressing engagements, or regular employment. Perhaps it was the weekend.

There then followed a sensational chain of events.

First, the white girl slipped on a bar of soap in the bathroom and gave herself a cheap and unexpected thrill with the loo brush. Next, the black man found the kitten wandering around the corridor and took it back to its Japanese owner who, by way of saying thank you, invited the somewhat bemused fellow on to the bed to join him in some hanky-panky.

Meanwhile in No. 4, the coloured girl had fallen in love with a huge carrot while preparing herself a salad lunch.

The American, miraculously transported to Soho, was enjoying a good deal less luck. But then anyone who hands over twenty pounds to a tart in the street is asking for trouble and even I, who know nothing of these things, could have told him she was going to make a run for it.

Back in Hampstead, Ilsa and the other white girl were contriving to brush against each other a good deal in the bathroom doorway and showing distinctly lesbian tendencies, and the two tinted gentlemen were getting extremely overexcited by a very noisy singer on the TV. In fact, one way and another, the entire cast seemed to be making pretty heavy weather of it.

Now the black girl found herself being pursued in the street by a white-haired tramp in a dirty mac. Evidently he wasn't her type, although for my money it was a toss-up between him and the carrot. He was surprisingly nifty on his feet for one apparently so decrepit, but luckily the girl could shift a bit too, and in no time at all she was outside

18

the house being comforted by the American who arrived at that moment, penniless, from the opposite direction.

In relief and gratitude, she took him up to her room and, while our two nancy boyfriends sat happily in a nearby pub watching a drag act, she made him a cup of coffee which she promptly poured into his crutch.

'Let me look,' she said. 'I'm a part-time nurse. A little massage is all that's needed.'

Would have thought that was the last thing that would have helped. And yet it certainly seemed to be doing wonders for both of them, and, as the American pointed out, 'It's not as scalded as all that.'

Could not resist glancing at the couple in front who appeared to have gone to sleep. Unless they, too, were up to no good. The man next door was tackling his third King Cone.

Meanwhile the lesbians were still fondling each other, the men had taken to biting each other's bottoms, and the massage had produced predictable results.

Decided the young couple in front definitely asleep.

Came the dawn and the milkman arrived, but no one was up earlier than this household (no joke intended), and by eight o'clock they were all hard at it again.

Later, they all went walking in the sunshine in Regent's Park.

Suddenly everything turned blue and they started to dream of who they would really like to be with. The black man fancied the carrot lady, Ilsa fancied the American, and the loo lady fancied the Japanese pansy.

Next, they were all in Hampton Court maze, bumping into each other and laughing and generally getting into a frightful muddle. In the end, though, they all ended up with the right partner and, because it was a nice day, they rushed off into the long grass and got busy.

Later, black and carrot got busy at home; ditto loo and Japanese on the roof.

Suddenly, for no apparent reason, they were all to be found sitting cross-legged in a circle on the grass without a stitch on, holding hands and kissing each other, while a choir sang 'All Together Now'.

And then the lights came up.

Rather regret now that I had not plumped for bill in

adjoining cinema: *Flesh Gordon* ('more laughs than lechery', – the *Guardian*) and *Deadly Weapons* starring the Incredible Chesty Morgan (72-32-36 – 'Seeing is believing. The outstanding attraction everyone is talking about.') Shall definitely have to make time for a return visit.

Home then by underground, convinced that everyone in the carriage knew where I had spent the afternoon.

Straight into a good hot bath followed by an individual steak and kidney pie and *Panorama*. I feel like a man who has just been let out of prison after a long stretch.

To bed early where I slept badly and dreamt constantly that Mrs Gurney from the flat downstairs was making a salad and chasing me round the kitchen with a huge carrot, and Miss Weedon from next door had unexpectedly developed the largest breasts in the world.

Tuesday

Had not in fact planned to resume my diary. However, can think of no better way of maintaining a day-to-day account of my researches. Not so much a diary perhaps as a writer's notebook along the lines of Maugham's.

Had barely got in this morning when the phone rang. It was Hugh Bryant-Fenn to say that my letter had arrived by the first post and that he would be delighted to give me all the assistance he could and what aspects of the subject particularly interested me.

I said, 'I realize you're not exactly a sexual athlete, Hugh, but . . .'

'I don't know who you think you are that you should make assumptions about other people's private lives with so much confidence and so little knowledge,' he said.

Was quite taken aback by this unexpected outburst. However, have not spent the last few months handling the firm's corporate image without developing an instinct for defusing awkward misunderstandings.

I said with a laugh, 'Come of it, Hugh. Knowing the sort of bloke you are. . .'

He said, 'How do you know what sort of bloke I am? Just because you once tagged on to me in Venice, that hardly entitles you to make value judgements on my sexual behaviour. I'll tell you one thing: the sort of man who allows his friend's budgerigar to die and then tries to cover up the fact by palming him off with a cheap double is not guaranteed to meet with great success with women.'

I said, 'I'm very sorry about the budgerigar, Hugh, but that's hardly the point.'

'On the contrary,' he said, 'it is very much the point. You doubtless see yourself as one of the world's great philanthropists, but the truth is you're as mean as all get out, and if there's one thing that women can't abide it's meanness.'

Pretty rich stuff coming from a man who's never once picked up a restaurant, hotel or airline bill in the last ten years.

I said, 'Hugh, for all I know you may be the world's greatest gift to women. Frankly, I could not give a row of beans one way or the other. It's quite obvious to me you have nothing useful to contribute towards this project, so let's just leave it at that, shall we?'

'Fine,' he replied. 'Your loss, not mine. Don't say I didn't offer.'

'I won't,' I said, and put the phone down on him. Looked up to find Sue standing in the doorway.

She said, 'I always think you can tell a lot about a man from the way he sounds on the phone.'

I said, 'Don't worry; I'm not always as bad tempered as this.'

'I don't mean you,' she said. 'I mean him.' She nodded towards the telephone.

'Who?' I said. 'Hugh?'

'Is that his name?' she asked. 'I only caught the Bryant-Fenn bit. I like the name Hugh. It's reassuring and manly. It reminds me of good tweed suits and lawns and labradors in front of a blazing log fire.'

'So you reckon Hugh's pretty hot stuff, do you?' I said.

She frowned. 'What a very vulgar expression,' she said. 'I merely said that, to judge from his voice, he sounded an attractive man.'

I laughed and said, 'You wouldn't say so if you saw him.'

'How do you know?' she said, and left the room, slamming the door behind her.

I enjoy the company of spirited women. The only drawback is that you never know from one minute to the next where you are with them.

On an impulse, rang Tim Pedalow. He's the sort of chap who knows the way the world wags, sexually speaking. He's always travelling here, there and everywhere on business, and no one's going to try to tell me he retires to his hotel room every evening after a quiet dinner and reads his Gideon Bible.

Despite the curiously open marriage they affect, Tim and Vanessa have always struck me as being a very physical couple, held together by a strong mutual interest in Sportsnight with C.

Tim said he was most interested to hear about my project. I said that I had always understood that he and Vanessa were confirmed hedonists.

'We were,' he said, 'until our last trip to California. Now we're confirmed disciples, and apostles, of the New Celibacy.'

I said that sounded a typical trans-Atlantic fad, if ever I'd heard one.

He said 'You may well laugh, but I can tell you, it's sweeping America and it's only a matter of time before it catches on over here.'

I said that I was very sorry but I wasn't quite sure what he was talking about.

He said, 'Don't be daft. You know very well what celibacy is. You've practised it enough yourself over the years. The retreat from sex was bound to happen on a huge scale sooner or later. It's the natural response to years of sexual overkill by people like Heffner and Guccione. It promotes an altogether higher and more everlasting sense of fulfilment.'

I replied that, following my own experiences in San Francisco, he could definitely count on my support in his new movement once I'd got my report out of the way.

He said, 'Yes, well, it's a greater sacrifice for some than for others.'

'You mean like Hugh Bryant-Fenn?' I said.

'Hugh?' he exclaimed. 'Don't be silly. He's the biggest ram this side of the Thames.'

I said, 'Hugh? A ram? Are you sure?'

'Ask any girl in London,' he exclaimed. 'You must have

heard of Hugh's famous big red book.'

Apparently Hugh is in the habit of recording in a large red notebook a blow by blow account of every encounter he enjoys with a member of the opposite sex.

'It must be a very slim volume,' I said,

'Don't you believe it,' said Tim. 'Poor old Theresa de Grande-Hauteville – Milne that was – once made the mistake of accepting an invitation from Hugh for dinner. He took her to some El Cheapo in Fulham, then back to his place for coffee. She popped into the loo to powder her nose and came back into the sitting room to find Hugh, stark naked, reclining on the chaise longue, smoking a large cigar and looking decidedly pleased with himself. As soon as she appeared, he sprang to his feet, sat her down with the red book with the words, "Why don't you have a look through this? I'll just see about the coffee," and tripped off into the kitchen. She waited till he was out of the room, nipped out into the hall, grabbed her coat and disappeared into the night.'

I said, 'But I saw them not so very long ago at your drinks party, chatting away as though nothing had happened.'

Tim said, 'As far as they're concerned, nothing did. That's why they're still friends.'

I said, 'Do you think Hugh might know anything about tarts, massage parlours, that sort of thing?'

'Probably,' he said. 'Why not ask him yourself?'

Tim Pedalow may be a lousy stockbroker, but I could almost forgive him the £420 he lost me a year ago for what he told me today.

Rang Hugh after lunch. Apologized for my irritable behaviour earlier and assured him that I had never for a moment doubted his expertise in the field of how's-your-father. I added that he had always been high on my list of experts to be interviewed, and suggested a good, long lunch (at my expense, of course) to chat things over.

He said, 'I knew you'd come round to it in the end. Unfortunately, I can't make lunch this week. I'm already committed to a couple for my column in *Bedroom* magazine.'

Made a mental note to quiz him about the men's magazine market.

He went on, 'And then, of course, on Friday I'm lunching with Sue.'

'Who's Sue?' I asked him.

He said, 'Your secretary, of course. Who else?'

'I never realized you knew my secretary,' I said.

'I don't,' he replied cheerfully. 'But we got on so well on the telephone and she has such a sexy voice that I suggested a meeting.'

I don't know why I should be so angry; she means nothing to me. But I am.

I said, 'Next week then?'

'You're on,' he said.

For some reason, am strongly reminded of those stories one used to read in the *News of the World* when one was at school – about dentists in the suburbs who gave their female patients gas and then took advantage of them. The really sexy ones were nearly always extremely unattractive. Things do not appear to have changed.

Thought about taking in a couple of hard-core porn shows on way home, but there was a rather good wildlife programme I wanted to see on BBC1 at 8.05. Besides, the vision of a naked Bryant-Fenn reclining on a chaise longue brandishing his confessions while my secretary busied herself in the kitchen was more than enough naked flesh to contemplate for one day.

Wildlife programme well up to BBC standards. Had not realized before that mute swans mated in that way, or that sex is so much a part of our lives without our realizing it. It's probably simply because I'm more sexually attuned than usual.

Wednesday

Walked into office this morning just as phone started ringing. Picked it up at once.

A man's voice said, 'Good morning, Miss Lovely Voice. Guess who?'

I said, 'Who exactly did you wish to speak to?'

'Is that you, Crisp?' the voice asked.

I said that it was.

'Oh, it's Hugh here. I thought you were somebody else.'

'Evidently,' I said.

He said, 'Actually it was you I wanted to speak to.'

He went on to explain that a friend of his was laying on a film show in Ashford, of all places, on Saturday night and would I like him to get me in on it?

I said, 'By an odd coincidence, I happen to be staying near Ashford for the weekend with my mother. What sort of film show?'

Hugh said, 'All I can tell you is that a friend of his has just made a film about W.B. Yeats which she hopes to sell to a television company. This is by way of being a sneak preview for a few close friends. It sounds just up your street.'

Why he should think this, I cannot imagine. However, have taken down particulars and said I'll look in if family commitments allow.

Hugh said, 'I think you'll find it'll be worth your while.' And he rang off.

Must confess to being rather intrigued. There has to be more to this than meets the eye, but what? May make the effort or may not. I'll see how I feel.

Must remember to ask Hugh if he knows Fiona Richmond. Shall have to think about buying a ticket for her latest show at the Whitehall, although it doesn't require a particularly fertile imagination to picture the sort of thing one is in for.

In many ways, am quite glad to be without a girlfriend for a while. I can imagine only too well what Jane would have had to say about my various outings. Strange how much I still miss having her around, though. It is some weeks now since we worked together on our abortive Young Conservative Dance and she announced she was engaged.

Which reminds me, I still haven't had a reply to my letter to Armitage. I am convinced there are several folds in the soft underbelly of the London entertainment scene in which he has dipped more than the occasional toe. Will try to ring him tomorrow.

Also nothing from Beddoes in Brussels.

To Soho again after lunch to make a serious start on the hard-core scene. Began my researches in Brewer Street. Wherever I looked my eye was dazzled by the neon lights of yet another sex-related premise, as I believe these places are known in official circles. Can hardly believe that I pass along these streets so often, yet apparently notice so little. But then, of course, one has better things to look out for from the back of a motorbike than thrusting breasts and provocative bottoms. So much for this so-called all-out porn war declared by the Conservatives on the Greater London Council.

Where is one to begin? The blurbs all promise so much. 'You'll never see anything sexier'; 'The latest in hard-core porno films'; 'All 100% hard-core porn. £3.50 for two-hour show'; 'All the best in hard-core from America, Denmark, Sweden, Great Britain, Germany'.

Hot Between the Legs, Country Bumkins, Up She Comes, Swedish Teenage Doll . . . What can they all be about? One hardly feels inclined to approach the oily-skinned scruffs who call out at one as one passes, and ask for a synopsis. To judge from my previous expedition into these foreign parts, 'Show now on, gents' is probably the only English phrase they know.

Am also slightly concerned about this business of club membership. Have not had a chance yet to check up on the legal ins and outs, but a voice somewhere at the back of my brain tells me that one has to wait twenty-four hours from the time of paying one's initial membership fee before one is officially a member. Or am I thinking of gambling clubs? At all events, would not care to be the innocent victim of some random police raid. Being the special case I am, I daresay one could persuade the authorities to keep one's name out of the papers, but there's always *Private Eye*. Not that Mother has ever subscribed to this excellent magazine, but I have a feeling Denys Ramsden's nephew takes it, and I wouldn't put it past him to go shooting his mouth off at a cocktail party. News travels fast in English villages.

Legal considerations apart, £3.50 seems a lot to shell out when, for only 50p, one can enjoy an equally rude experience in one's own private booth in the nearby Love Shop.

Changed a pound note at the desk and made my way into the gloomy interior, peering as I went at the titles pinned up on the doors. Very much torn between *Lay-By Lovers, Erotic Lesbians* and *Open for Anything*. Settled in

26

the end, though, for *Gripped by Lust*. Not that this feeble tale of a burly judo instructor and his two attractive young female pupils gripped me – with lust or anything else.

Closed door, inserted coin and projector began to whirr. It soon became obvious from the grainy image flickering on the back of the door that, unfortunately, I had happened upon a very early instalment of the story.

After the burly instructor had watched the two girls throwing each other onto the floor, he sent one of them away for a shower and called the other back for some private tuition. To his surprise, she quickly had him flying through the air. He was obviously annoyed, if not aroused. Not that one could tell in those loose judo clothes.

Meanwhile, back in the dressing room, the less favoured girl was sitting in front of a mirror giving her neck and shoulders a bit of a rub. Before long, her hand had wandered unconsciously onto her bosoms and she was giving them a bit of a rub too. Then, before one knew what, she was giving every part of her body a good going over.

Meanwhile, back in the gym . . .

The money had run out.

Sat there for a while in the dark, wondering whether to change another pound. Things were obviously about to hot up, and very probably within the next 50p's worth. Decided to chance my arm and nipped out to desk. Slight delay owing to sudden arrival of a team of rowdy football supporters, rather the worse for wear. By the time I had transacted my business my booth was occupied.

I do not know which made me angrier: the fact that I would now never know who gripped who, or that someone else was even now enjoying the fruits of my extremely unsatisfying spadework.

Marched straight out without a second glance, across the road and into the Erotic 1 & 2 cinema complex. This was an altogether superior establishment, well-lit and welcoming. There was even a man washing the floor. Headed straight for booths. It's extraordinary to think that, only a couple of days ago, I would have been nervous and ill at ease entering a place like this, yet now I can walk in as easily and shamelessly as if I were about to see *Snow White and the Seven Dwarfs* at the Chelsea Odeon.

Choice of films considerably more attractive here. Finally chose one called *Rodox*. A suggestive if somewhat enigmatic title. I hoped I wasn't in for any corporal punishment.

Took my seat, inserted coin, but nothing happened. Pressed equivalent of Button A several times. Still nothing.

Made my way outside to glass booth to seek guidance. Inside, two men were watching a tennis tournament. Stan Smith was in action; I couldn't see who his opponent was. Would have given a lot to be at home watching the same thing with my feet up and a cup of tea and a couple of ginger biscuits at my side.

Explained my predicament re non-working of projector. One man looked round behind him where a stack of video cassette players were hard at work. Was reminded of a self-service garage. 'That's funny,' said the man. 'Should be okay.'

His colleague looked up briefly. The score, I could see, was deuce. 'Press the tit and stick your finger up the hole,' he said.

Returned to booth and sat there for several minutes, pondering advisability of following his bizarre instructions. Presumably he was referring to the small hole beneath the box where the money goes in. However, it has always been my policy in life never to stick my finger into anything unfamiliar and I was not about to start now. Anything could happen. Even electrocution. Worse still if I got my finger stuck and they had to send for the fire brigade to haul me out.

'Stick your finger up the wossit,' I heard the man calling outside the door.

The possibility then occurred to me that, by doing so, I might in some mysterious way enjoy a sexual thrill – electronically perhaps. Very gingerly I did as I had been told. There appeared to be nothing inside that would furnish me either with a sensation or my money back.

I returned to the booth. I hoped there wasn't going to be any trouble. These sort of people have a habit of turning ugly, I'm told, if they think a customer is trying to make monkeys out of them. However, they couldn't have been nicer and gave me another coin without a murmur. It's that sort of behaviour that makes one feel inclined to go back to

28

a place. In the circumstances, felt quite happy to ask them what the word MITTON meant on the bottom of every door sign.

'It's German,' one of them told me. '*Mit ton*. With sound.'

No whacking with sticks, I'm glad to report, but plenty of good old Rodox, provided by a man with a large moustache and a silly grin on his face, another with long hair and a permanently pained expression, and a blonde girl with an American accent.

Ton excellent. It certainly added to the whole thing no end, although there is a limit to the expressions of muttered ecstasy even the most articulate lover can dream up, and these three had definitely come to the end of theirs long before my 50p ran out.

Decided I owed it to the management to treat myself to another 50p's worth. Scouted round for a suitable sequel only to discover that all the booths were showing *Rodox*. Plucked up my courage to point out this fact to the man in the booth.

'Don't be a prat,' he said. 'That's the name of the effing distributor.'

Stan Smith seemed to be losing.

Place by now positively bustling with customers going about their business with all the dignity of men about to telephone their wives from Victoria Station to say there was a delay on the Oxted line and they'd be home a few minutes late.

Was feeling rather like a spot of lesbianism for a change, but unfortunately a small negro with a beard beat me to it, so settled on *Thai Tease* instead.

I don't know about Thai but a tease it certainly was. Not only was it a cartoon, but it appeared to have nothing whatever to do with the subject for which we were all gathered together under this unlikely roof. I do not believe I have ever been more disappointed over anything in my life. Thought I had probably pushed my luck quite far enough with the men in the booth, so left silently just as Stan Smith saved game point.

One way and another, as fascinating and educational an afternoon as I have spent in a long time.

Two points arise:

1. Is one to understand that there are many more women eager for a spot of straightforward, no-nonsense Sports-night than one might think? If so, how is it that all the ones I ever meet seem to make such heavy weather of it?

2. 50p for a two-minute thrill is a good deal more expensive than may at first appear – especially for those of us old enough to remember the days of ten-shilling notes.

Interesting footnote: is it my imagination or am I suddenly quite keen at the prospect of a return visit? And, if so, should I be happy that I am throwing off my inhibitions, or alarmed at being so rapidly depraved?

To bed in thoughtful mood.

Thursday

Surprised and disappointed to have heard nothing still from Armitage. Obviously do not wish to give him the impression that I am running round after him, but must get on. Rang him immediately following a time-wasting Progress Report meeting on the Kellerman contract.

Apparently he had received my letter but just hadn't had time (or manners) to reply.

'I knew you'd call sooner or later,' he said.

I came straight to the point. 'You remember you once sent me to a massage parlour . . . ?'

'Vaguely,' he said. 'Why? Got a stiff neck again, have you? Or a stiff something else?' And he gave a vulgar guffaw.

I was in no mood for his style of crude innuendo and decided to knock the stuffing out of him straight away. 'Noel Annan,' I said, 'did not agree to be chairman of his distinguished commission because he had secret longings to be a radio interviewer, nor was Bernard Williams planning a career in obscenity.'

There was a pause and then Armitage said, 'So?'

I said, 'So . . . if I had wanted an excuse to patronize low haunts, I could have thought up an easier one than this.'

He said, 'So you're asking me to take you to some low haunts, is that it?'

'In a word,' I said, 'yes.'

'Massage parlours.'

'That depends,' I said.

'On what?' he said.

'Look, Armitage,' I said, 'I think I should tell you that I am perfectly capable of carrying out all the research necessary for this survey without anyone's help. I'm not some naive nincompoop, you know. I have been around.'

Armitage said, 'You don't have to justify yourself to me, old cock.'

I suppose I should not blame Armitage for trying to score off me. He has never properly recovered from losing his job to me as Assistant Group Head at Harley Preston last year, of course. However, cannot allow finer feelings to cloud one's judgement where business is concerned.

I said, 'Since we're on the subject, you wouldn't happen to know anything about contact magazines, would you?'

He said, 'Personally I have never felt the need to advertise for my pleasures. Why not try *Time Out*? Their lonely-hearts columns are full of that sort of thing.'

Having never subscribed to trendy way-out journalism, had always assumed *Time Out* to consist of nothing but long, serious reviews of lunchtime performances of incomprehensible left-wing plays in disused warehouses in Shoreditch, profiles of underground pop groups with silly names, and listings of demos by the Socialist Workers' Party. Was astonished upon buying my first copy, therefore, to discover that it is a perfectly straightforward guide to what's on in London. I cannot think how I can have survived all these years without it. It is obviously essential reading for anyone with the slightest interest in metropolitan life.

Turned to classified pages at back of magazine. I had no idea that so many young people experienced such difficulty in finding friends.

TALL, ATTRACTIVE, INTELLIGENT, FUN-LOVING CHAP, 24, enjoys T.S. Eliot, Astaire, Ayckbourn, drinking and eating – in or out. You are female, any age, quite tall, interesting. Photo.

AMUSING, INTELLIGENT BACHELOR, 37, wide tastes, own flat, car. Knows what's what. Seeks lively, attractive girl with eye to adventure. Photo/phone desirable.

HANDSOME STALLION seeks thoroughbred older mare with own cosy paddock.

Why men with so much to offer are not already fighting off women every minute of their lives I cannot think.

The women sound even less in need of an agony column.

BLONDE, TALL, SENSUOUS GIRL, 25 seeks well-educated, handsome, tall guy for fun evenings. No serious involvement.

ATTRACTIVE, INTELLIGENT BLONDE, 30, seeks loving, humorous, free-thinking male counterpart.

SENSUOUS CONTINENTAL LADY, 32, slim, intelligent, wide interests, seeks kind, good looking romantic male for wining and dining. Possibly more.

Cannot decide what is implied by phrases like 'fun-loving', 'possibly more', 'free-thinking' and so on. Are they a code for what I think they are? Or am I rapidly acquiring an over-developed sense of *double entendre*?

Feel my report requires a section on sex by advertisement, but how am I to present a true picture without personal experience? Am seriously considering putting in an ad myself and seeing what sort of replies I get. But would it be within my brief to follow up the most promising? Doubtless Hardacre thinks that, by leaving it to my own discretion, he has made things easier. In fact I am in even more of a muddle than ever. A restaurant critic can hardly describe the latest trattoria without first eating the food and drinking the wine and, as the late Kenneth Tynan once said (or was it Sheridan Morley?), the theatre critic's job is to tell his readers what it was like to be in a certain theatre on a certain night.

First things first though: I've devised a short advertisement along the lines quoted. I have rung the magazine in question and gather that, if I'm slippy about it, I will be just in time for next week's issue.

It reads:

ATTRACTIVE, SENSITIVE STALLION, 37. Fun-loving, adventurous, wide range of unusual tastes. Has been around a bit and knows the score. Seeks sophisticated, free-thinking, sensuous partner(s) for entertaining get-together, possibly more. Photo/phone please.

32

I do not think that leaves much room for doubt as to what I have in mind. If it brings in as large a response as I think it will, £14.90 will be little enough to add to my expenses chit.

Despite box number, am slightly concerned about putting my real name and address on the booking form. Just to be on the safe side, have given office address and an assumed name. Have a feeling this may be illegal, but no time to check now. Must make a note to inform post room that, if a package should arrive addressed to Mr John Ashford, it is for me.

Bryant-Fenn rang just before lunch and said he was calling to make sure I had Desmond's address for Saturday night and to check that I was still definitely coming.

I repeated that I would certainly try to make it, but that I could not guarantee that Mother had not committed me to some soirée or other in the village, in which case I was sure he would understand.

At this he became obviously agitated and said that he would not understand. The film show was to begin at nine sharp and if I could not make it I was to say so now.

I cannot imagine what all the fuss is about. However, rang Mother who said that, if I couldn't be bothered to come down for Christmas, it was perfectly obvious that I had no time for her or her circle and that I could keep my clever London friends as far as she was concerned. If I thought she had nothing better to do than waste time trying to integrate me into Kent society, then I had another think coming and would I be down in time on Saturday to pop into Ashford and pick up the cat's antibiotics from the vet, his surgery closed at noon, had I remembered?

Rang Hugh straight back and told him I was definitely on.

'Good,' he said. 'As long as I know who's coming. Will you be bringing anyone with you?'

I said that I didn't think Mother was that much of a Yeats fan but, if he wanted me to give someone a lift, I'd be happy to oblige.

'No, no,' he said. 'That's fine. Just as long as I know.'

Am beginning to wonder if all this eating out isn't beginning to turn his head.

To Soho again after lunch to complete my survey on

hard-core films. After much deliberation, decided to plump for hard-core club in Brewer Street which was showing a six-film programme consisting of *The Teenager, Surprise Orgy, Kinky Lips, Sex Fantasy, Date with Vanessa* and *Analitis*, which I always thought was the name of a haemorrhoid cream.

'Two fifty, squire,' said the man at the box office. The fact that he was English I found strangely reassuring. Thought I ought to come clean straight away and confess that I was not actually a member.

'Don't you worry about that, my son,' said the man. 'Straight through the doors and down the stairs.'

Picked my way down steep, narrow staircase and into tiny, smoke-filled room. The film clattered scratchily through a glass panel at the back and on to a pocket handkerchief-sized screen.

Nearly all three rows of seats occupied by silent staring customers but managed to squeeze on to end of back row, took out my notebook and prepared for the worst. I cannot say that I was disappointed.

Goodness knows which of the films was which. Only one, which was faintly Germanic, actually had a story and dialogue. It concerned a virginal young blonde and her wicked auntie who ran a brothel – with the inevitable results.

The other five claimed no such pretensions to dramatic art. They consisted merely of men Sportsnighting with women in a number of different positions to the accompaniment of moans, groans and muttered imprecations.

I'm surprised the man next to me managed to sleep so soundly throughout with all that noise going on.

Was quite unable to doze off myself and was forced to sit there in the dark staring expressionlessly up at the screen like my fellow voyeurs while yet another moustachioed ex-lorry driver struggled undecorously out of his underpants and socks on the Dralon in somebody's front room in Ealing and braced himself to meet the onslaught of yet another uninviting crutch.

The female anatomy has never had my vote as Aesthetic Object of the Year at the best of times, and nothing that I saw this afternoon has persuaded me to change my mind. I had no idea cameras could zoom in as close on anything as they did on those gaping wounds. Had the man next to me woken up suddenly and looked up at the screen he might have been forgiven for thinking that he had arrived in the middle of an episode of *Your Life in their Hands*.

From the titillation point of view, they rated somewhere between a half and one out of ten on my personal scoreboard. On the other hand, as sex education films, showing what goes where and how, they could hardly be bettered.

As far as the performers went (generally too far), I do not believe I have seen so many unattractive people captured for posterity on celluloid in one afternoon. I am told on quite good authority that many of the people who take part in rude films are out-of-work actors. If so, I can perfectly see why.

Friday

Devoted morning to penning a memo to Hardacre in anticipation of his return on Monday morning. Unable to dictate, however, as Sue did not deign to roll in until nearly eleven, airily announcing by way of excuse that she had been to the hairdresser. Hoped it was not for Bryant-Fenn's benefit, but did not like to ask. Is it my imagination or am I slightly jealous?

Left rough draft of memo on her desk and took an early lunch myself.

On way back to office, popped into local newsagent to buy evening paper. Noticed one of the popular dailies was carrying a story on the proliferation of strip clubs in the Midlands – graphically illustrated, to judge from the extremely well-endowed performer on the front page. Could not resist commenting on this to sour-faced woman behind counter.

The woman being served in front of me said, 'They'll do anything to sell papers these days.'

'Bloody disgusting, if you ask me,' said the shopkeeper. 'Printing that sort of stuff with kiddies around.'

'Too right,' said the other woman. 'And they wonder why the youth of Britain is depraved.'

'You see articles about it in the papers,' said the shopkeeper.

'Yer,' said the other. 'In papers like these, more than likely.'

'Bloody disgraceful,' agreed the shopkeeper.

Bought my paper, turned and found myself face to face with a revolving rack jammed solid with glossy men's magazines – *Penthouse, Men Only, Mayfair, Knave, Whitehouse, Romp, International Model Directory, Escort,* and many more. Funnily enough, have been thinking that sooner or later I must get in a supply of these for research purposes. Picked up special Caligula issue of *Penthouse* for idle flick through.

The woman behind the counter said, 'No use trying to do that. I've stuck them all up with sellotape.'

I said with an ironic laugh, 'Yes, well, you wouldn't want kiddies seeing this sort of thing, would you?'

She lit a cigarette and coughed horribly. 'It's not that,' she croaked. 'It's to stop dirty sods like you coming in here, picking them out, having a quick flip through and putting them back again.'

I said cheerfully, 'Well, you certainly succeeded in my case,' and made to put the magazine back. Unfortunately, the rack was so full that I had to force the thing in and, in doing so, slightly tore the front cover.

'You'll have to buy it now, won't you?' said the woman, coughing. Had no alternative but to pay up.

I said pointedly, nodding towards the offending newspaper, 'A slight case of double standards, wouldn't you say?'

She stubbed out her cigarette and put her hands on her hips. 'I've nothing against sex,' she said. 'In its proper place.'

Suddenly noticed a small cardboard box on the counter containing a number of copies of something called *The Sex Maniac's Diary*. It looked rather fun and only £2.75.

I said, 'I'll have one of those.'

'I thought you would,' she said.

Have made a note to include a section on sex among the middle-aged.

Saturday

To Kent soon after breakfast. Mother still going on about

36

Christmas, despite my making special detour to collect cat's medicine – and paying for it.

A cold, damp day, so spent most of afternoon in front of TV watching the rugger international followed by wrestling. Am wondering if I should include a section on sex in sport? Had always understood women not generally excited by the sight of the male nude body and, if Sue's experience is anything to go by, they never buy male pinup magazines. Yet I have never seen women work up such a head of steam over anything as that front row did in the Fairfields Hall, Croydon, at the sight of 'Flash' Gordon sorting out 'Pretty Boy' Cartwright over three rounds. I'm surprised the Soho pornographers have not thought of adding an extra booth specializing in male wrestling for female customers. There'd be a fortune in it. Fortunately, Mother so engrossed in cat's gippy tummy that I was not called upon to explain my present occupation.

After supper I announced that I had to go into Ashford for a bit.

She said, 'But aren't you going to watch *Dallas*? I thought you liked *Dallas*. That's why I got supper ready early, so that you could watch *Dallas*.'

Told her not to wait up for me, but I knew she would anyway.

Had rather more difficulty finding Hugh's friend's house than had anticipated. For some reason, had not imagined that anyone he knew would live in quite such a suburban street. Met at the door by Desmond's wife, Anthea, a pale, skinny girl with lank fair hair and slightly protruding teeth. Surprised to hear I was the first arrival, even though it was already nearly 8.45.

Anthea took my anorak and led me through to the sitting room. Floral patterned carpet and striped Regency wallpaper. At one end a small screen had been erected. Ashtrays and bowls of crisps and peanuts had been placed at strategic intervals. A projector was propped up on a small table, beside which a burly, balding man with a heavy moustache was mending a plug.

'Desmond,' I cried, striding forward with arm outstretched. 'Thank you so much for asking me. My name's Crisp.'

'Actually,' said Anthea, 'this is Ray, from the local

garage. He's very kindly lent us his projector and agreed to show the films.'

Ray nodded at me in an offhand manner. He didn't look the Yeats type to me.

After a couple of minutes, Desmond himself arrived. He was about my age, on the short side, with a mass of shaggy black hair. His T-shirt had OXFORD UNIVERSITY written across it.

'Aha,' I said, 'another Oxford man, I see. Which college were you?'

'I wasn't,' he said. 'I bought it in a secondhand shop in Canterbury.'

We then went through to the next room where French bread and cheese and pâté and two-litre bottles of Valpolicella and large cans of Ruddles had been laid out on the dining room table.

Desmond poured us all a glass of wine and said, 'Are you new to this sort of thing?'

'Oh no,' I said. 'We quite often have parties like this in London.'

'Oh, that's all right then,' he said. 'Only Hugh did mention something about you needing a bit of persuasion, shall we say?'

At that moment the doorbell went and suddenly the room was full of people, laughing and kissing and shrieking at the tops of their voices.

Desmond tried to introduce me to them all, but the only names I caught were those of Lady Somebody-or-other and her daughter who, I gathered, was the director of the film. They had brought with them a silent young man with very close-cropped hair and a ring through one ear, and someone I took to be his girlfriend. Also a scruffy blonde woman and her husband who was tall and thin with glasses and a beard. They hailed apparently from New Zealand. I said that I had always wanted to go to New Zealand, to which the woman replied that she couldn't think why anyone should want to go there. She had spent her entire life trying to get away. In my experience, it never pays to try to make conversation with disgruntled colonials.

A minute or two later, there was another ring and Hugh appeared, looking foolish in jeans and leather jacket, with a flimsy silk scarf round his neck held by a little gold ring. If there's one thing I can't bear it's people who aim low, sartorially speaking, and miss. I felt quite embarrassed – though not half as much as I was when I saw that the girl clutching his arm was none other than my secretary, Sue.

Naturally I kept my surprise to myself and behaved as I would with any old friend. I even kissed Sue on both cheeks. Bang go my chances of getting another letter decently typed, I daresay.

Made mistake, as I always do, of asking Hugh what he was up to, whereupon he launched into a long and detailed account of his latest curriculum vitae. Not only has he been asked, in his capacity as Wig and Hairpiece Editor of *Barbershop Quarterly*, to undertake a six-week lecture tour next autumn in the Far East on the subject of The Toupée and its Place in the Developing World, but he is to be the chairman, if you please, of a new TV quiz show about food and wine called *Pass the Port*. He tried to explain the rules to me but I simply couldn't make head or tail of it – nor did I wish to. Sue, I'm sorry to say, seemed to be taken in by the whole thing. I'm beginning to have second thoughts about her. Soon everyone was tucking into the French bread and Valpolicella, and by the time we all adjourned to the sitting room, one or two were in a very merry mood indeed.

As Anthea was turning out the lights, Bryant-Fenn whispered to me, 'Never mind, it'll make good copy for you.'

The first thing to appear on the screen was a dealer film for Skoda cars. While I was mildly interested to learn of the vehicle's good roadholding and low fuel consumption, the connection between the Czechoslovakian motorcar industry and William Butler Yeats completely eluded me. Could only assume this was the price Mr and Mrs Desmond had to pay in return for Ray's services for the evening. There was a short break while the garage man laced up the next film and we settled back to twenty minutes of unrelieved boredom while someone with an Irish accent intoned line after line of lugubrious verse over endless shots of rain-swept countryside.

The sigh of relief that went up simultaneously with the lights was only too audible. Frankly, I have always suspected Yeats of being an overrated poet and am now more convinced of it than ever.

And then the most astonishing thing happened. The lights went down, the projector whirred once more into life, and on the screen appeared the vision of two people deeply embroiled in as steamy a session of Sportsnight with C as you could wish to see.

I could not believe my eyes. Obviously, by an astounding stroke of luck, I had fallen upon one of those groups of blue movie enthusiasts one reads about in certain Sunday newspapers. The story was as insubstantial, the inquisitiveness of the camera as intrusive and the physical appearance of the two protagonists every bit as unattractive as I'd remembered from my afternoon at the ciné club. The only difference was that, while those films had been flecked throughout with the scratches of a thousand showings, this one was blurred and contorted by strange colours, wispy gauzes and sudden flashes of bright lights.

On and on it ground. Once someone coughed gently, but apart from that and the whirring of the projector the whole spectacle took place in total silence. But all bad things must come to an end, and with one final leap and judder, the couple concluded their bizarre performance.

Had assumed that everyone would get to their feet, make muttered excuses and leave as quickly as possible. Far from it. There they all sat, chatting politely with one another and discussing the finer points of the film as calmly as if they had just sat through *The Seventh Seal*. Suddenly the scruffy New Zealand woman stood up and made her way to the front.

'If any of you have any questions, I'd be glad to answer them,' she said.

Suddenly realized to my astonishment that this was the woman in the film. Not only that, but she had also directed it. Or rather, as she put it so graphically, 'set the camera and us in motion'. To add to the confusion, the bearded man she had come with and who I had understood to be her husband, was not the man in the film.

She blithely explained that all the funny marks on the film were specially made by herself during processing, with paint, with silver strips, and with tiny feathers. 'I wanted this to be the first ever truly *art* blue movie,' she explained.

Everyone, it seemed, was bursting to ask her something – even Lady Thing, who piped up, 'Wasn't it rather difficult ensuring the camera was pointing at the right place?'

'It was all right,' answered the New Zealander, 'as long as we didn't kick it over.'

Everybody roared. As I was leaving, could not resist buttonholing Desmond. 'Is there much of this sort of thing going on round here?' I asked him.

'Much of what sort of thing?' he asked.

'Well,' I said, 'you know, blue movie clubs and so on.'

'I don't know what you mean,' he said. 'We happen to be the Ashford Branch of the W.B. Yeats Appreciation Society, and if you came for any other reason, then I am only sorry Hugh asked you.'

And he closed the door on me.

I give up. Am I going sex mad or what?

Home for an early night with a hot-water bottle and a glass of warm milk, only to find Mother still glued to *Parkinson*.

'Why aren't you on this sort of programme?' she asked.

'Because I'm not famous enough,' I answered.

'That's no excuse,' she said. 'Neither was Michael Parkinson till he got on and now look at him.'

Could not bring myself to reply.

Sunday

Woken at nine by Mother with a cup of tea and the news that the weather was, if anything, worse than yesterday but that bright periods were expected, moving slowly into the east by late afternoon.

'By which time,' I said, 'it will be dark and I will be gone.'

'There's no pleasing you sometimes,' she said. 'I blame it on the sort of life you live in London.'

'What sort of life?' I said.

She said, 'Well, since you've brought up the subject, I might as well tell you that when I rang your office last Thursday to find out what time you'd be down, whoever it was who answered the phone said you'd gone to Soho and were not expected back.'

'Well?' I said. 'I expect I'd gone there to lunch.'

'At four o'clock in the afternoon?' she said, and left the room.

Thank heavens she did not find my *Sex Maniac's Diary*. I wouldn't put it past her to go through my things while I'm out. Even my sock drawer.

Had not had a chance to look through it myself until today. Waited till she had gone to Sung Eucharist and settled down to it over coffee and biscuits.

The first thirty or so pages are packed with fascinating information for those who make a hobby of hanky-panky in all its shapes and forms. There's a Good Orgy Guide containing addresses in France, Germany, the United States and Australia, though not, I'm sorry to say, in Great Britain. A pity, since this is an area that will obviously need looking into.

Am quite amused by the Catalogue of Sex Games ('some traditional, some standard, some rarely attempted'), although I suspect that, if someone suggested Guess the Length of My Husband to me by way of an icebreaker at a party, I might easily be tempted to make an excuse and leave. That way I could be sure of avoiding such later delights as Ready, Steady, Gonads, Pantie Pickin' and the Eurovision Prong Contest.

I cannot think of an occasion off-hand when the phrase *Je suis masochiste; j'ai besoin d'un(e) sadique* would spring readily to the lips, but a list of foreign phrases of a sexual nature could certainly prove useful to one or two people I know.

The most interesting section of all for me is the one entitled Source Guide to the Best Sex in the World. Here, listed alphabetically, is all the information the most enthusiastic connoisseur of how's-your-father could possibly need.

Am fascinated to learn that the Messila Beach Hotel in Kuwait is highly recommended for women on the lookout for frustrated men, and that the Los Gatos Lodge in California is so full of loose women that there is a permanent queue ten yards long of men waiting to get in. I do not imagine that I will be in the area again myself in the very near future, but if ever I am and I'm at a loose end, I shall certainly try to get along.

Cannot make up my mind whether I am amused by the diary or shocked. My instinct is to put it away in a drawer and forget about it. On the other hand, I do need a pocket diary, thanks to the tight-fistedness of my so-called business friends, and if anyone were to comment on my curious choice, I could always laugh it off as a joke.

Except with Mother, of course.

Monday, 29 January

Memo

To: Keith Hardacre
From: Simon Crisp   29 January

Re: *The Crisp Report*

Welcome back! Just to let you know how things are going on the above front.

Have already completed sex film section and am due to tackle sex shops very shortly. Also have various irons in the fire re massage parlours, orgies, wife swapping, etc.

A couple of quick ones: am still a little vague about this tricky problem of *first-hand* research. It's one thing to sit through a pornographic film, but massage parlours and brothels raise quite different moral points. Also expenses. Shall obviously have to interview one or two people over lunch. Would not wish Barfords to be shown up in a mean light.

Do you by any chance know, or know anyone who knows, Fiona Richmond?

S.c.

Beddoes rang in the afternoon to say that he will be coming over on February 14th. Am not sure whether to read anything into choice of date or not. At all events, he says he will be delighted to provide me with a crash course on London after dark.

Could not resist saying that I hoped it would involve rather more than cruising up and down the red-light district waving at girls through the car window, which had been the high spot of my recent visit to Brussels.

He said, 'That depends who's picking up the tab,' and emitted one of those suggestive laughs that helped make sharing a flat with him such a misery.

Am already beginning to wonder if I was wise to bring him into this. Frankly, the sooner Hardacre comes back with a firm answer about expenses, the happier I shall be. Why is it that some people cost you money as soon as look at you?

No sign of Sue all day. I can see I'm definitely going to have to read the riot act to that young lady.

Tuesday

Rang Hugh first thing to thank him for Saturday evening.

He said, 'Pity you had to rush away like that. It developed into a very interesting evening.'

I said, 'Unfortunately, I do not share your friends' passion for Yeats.'

'What's Yeats got to do with it?' he said, and chuckled knowingly.

The trouble with people whose lives are continually directed by PROs is that they get into such a habit of talking in riddles that in the end one can't even ask them the time of day without the help of an interpreter.

Felt sure he was trying to tell me that, as a result of the blue movie, someone overstepped the mark. I came straight to the point. 'You don't mean an o-r-g-y, by any chance, do you?' I asked him.

'I don't know what you're talking about,' he replied. 'Ray showed us the films he'd shot on holiday in Peru, that's all. No o-r-g-i-e-s in that, as far as I can remember. A lot of Inca ruins though. And llamas. Jolly enterprising for a local garage man, I'd say. Wouldn't mind having a look at South America myself one day. Another string to my bow. Take a few snaps, work up a few stories, it'd be a sure-fire hit on the luncheon club circuit. Seventy-five quid a time, first class rail fare, free nosh, no trouble. I'll have to see someone at an airline about fixing up a freebie.'

I said, 'I should be glad if you would explain how it is that, if everyone at Ashford is as innocent as you claim, we sat through fifteen minutes of the most blatant pornography I have ever witnessed.'

Hugh said, 'Oh that. We always have to put up with one of those when we meet at Desmond's. Ray has a penchant for that sort of thing and, unless we allow him to run one or two, he sulks and won't lend us the projector.'

I said, 'But I thought the film had been made by that blonde New Zealand girl.'

'So it was,' said Hugh.

I said, 'But I understood her to be a friend of Lady Thing's daughter.'

Hugh said, 'There are some people in this life who are perpetually adding two and two together and making five.' And he rang off.

Heavens knows what it's all about. No one else seems to.

Sue deigned to roll in shortly after ten.

'Good afternoon,' I said. 'And where were you all yesterday?'

'Round and about,' she said. 'Doing things for Mr Pratt mainly.'

'Like what, for example?' I said.

'Oh,' she said, waving an airy arm, 'you know – the usual sort of things one does: taking dictation, typing up minutes of meetings, booking restaurants, having lunch.'

I said, 'But what are you doing working for Pratt? You're meant to be *my* secretary.'

She said, 'Oh I met him on the way in and he asked me if I was very busy, and I said no, you were out most of the time anyway, and he said could I spare a moment to help him out as his secretary is away ill. Personnel hadn't been able to rustle him up a temp at short notice.'

I said, 'But this is disgraceful. Why didn't someone have the common courtesy to come and say something to me?'

Sue said, 'I assumed Neville had.'

Rang Neville at once and made my feelings known in no uncertain terms.

He said, 'Sorry, old man. I thought it had all been fixed up between you and Keith.'

Immediately rang Keith who was in Stockholm again, according to Miss Hippo. Apparently he sent me a memo yesterday afternoon. I said that I had certainly received no communication of any sort along those lines. She said she was sure she had sent it and that was that.

Shortly before lunch, one of the spottier messenger boys stuck his head round the door and said, 'Mr Mann?'

I told him he must have got the wrong office.

'Funny,' he said. 'Says here Room 302, Mr D.O. Mann.'

I said, 'You'd better let me look at that,' whereupon the boy rushed across the room, threw the envelope on the desk and rushed out again, wearing the stupidest grin I've ever seen.

Opened envelope to find Keith's memo. On looking more closely at envelope, realized that someone had not only pasted a thin strip of paper over my name and written the false name on top, but that 'Man' did not have two n's as I had at first assumed.

I detect the hand of the post room in this somewhere. Could kick up a stink, but have decided it's probably better to do nothing. Those who undertake work of this nature must expect a certain amount of scorn and abuse. If Lord Longford could put up with it and retain his dignity, so can I.

Memo

To: Simon Crisp
From: Keith Hardacre   29 January

Thank you for your note. Unfortunately, am just off to Sweden for a four-day conference so am unable to deal with your queries for the moment. Can you wait until next week? In the meantime, feel you should be hurrying things along a bit. You haven't gone quite as far into the subject as I'd hoped.

R. Hippo
Dictated by Mr Hardacre and signed in his absence.

Considering the effect a report of this kind is bound to have on the corporate image of Barfords both here and abroad, feel I am not commanding the respect I should.

Wednesday

On reflection, am quite relieved Sue has been taken off my hands for a bit. I really don't have enough work for her here. More importantly, despite her unfortunate liaison with Bryant-Fenn, feel we could definitely make music together, given the right circumstances, and those do not include working closely together in an atmosphere of blatant sexuality.

In my experience, sex should be kept under wraps, like a Christmas present, if it is to work at a personal level, and to be discussing the subject all day long is enough to put anyone off the whole thing for good.

A more pressing problem, however, is how I should proceed re adultery. Am certainly not prepared to break a Commandment for the sake of mere sociology, nor can I think of anyone with whom I could possibly arrange to do so in the short time at my disposal.

May have to resort to a marriage guidance counsellor.

Friday

Great excitement. Today's the day my ad came out in *Time Out*. Hurried early to newsagent to be sure of getting a copy.

Turned to back pages and for a moment could not spot it at all. Realize now I should have gone for semi-display, as the girl had suggested. The wording certainly has the right feeling of sophisticated know-how, but will anyone ever find it?

Suddenly realized to my horror that, in my effort to keep the cost down, had completely failed to specify gender of sensuous partner(s) being sought. Does this mean I can expect a mailbag filled with strange requests from gay guys? Or, an even more alarming prospect, bi-guys?

I hope this is not going to end in tears.

Saturday

To Whitehall Theatre in the evening to see Fiona Richmond in her latest sex comedy. Decided to take pot luck and arrived a few minutes before curtain-up.

Interested to note that, while rest of West End theatre is struggling to attract audiences, Miss Richmond appears to be pulling them in in their hundreds. In fact, had quite a job getting a decent seat at all. Seriously toyed with idea of telling them who I was, but would not have wanted the news that a writer was out front to filter backstage. I know how these things can affect performances.

Audience in lively mood. Had distinct impression most of them had come straight on from the pub. At all events they were in good voice – especially a couple in my row.

Had certainly expected an evening of skimpy swimwear and possibly the occasional fleeting glimpse of a bosom or two, but was not prepared for the half dozen naked girls who strolled on to the stage in the first few minutes. The two men in my row, however, were evidently very much at home.

'Get 'em off,' came the shout the moment the girls appeared.

Scarcely a scene took place from then on in which they did not participate verbally from the dress circle.

'Someone's coming,' cried one of the girls at one point, looking anxiously into the wings. 'It's a man.'

'Not me, darling,' shouted one of the jokers.

Jokes of course depend very much on the sort of mood one is in, and I'm afraid that, when one is wearing one's reporter's hat, one cannot expect to join in the roars of laughter with quite the gay abandon displayed by the rest of the audience.

In the circumstances, was relieved not to be in the front row of the stalls and thus a butt for the comedian's saucy repartee. 'Enjoying it, sir? Yes, I can see you are. Sticks out a mile,' etc.

Fiona Richmond certainly lived up to her reputation as Britain's Number One Sex Symbol in every sense of the word. She has a wonderfully warm personality and a magnificent figure, which she shows off to advantage at every possible opportunity. It's hard to believe she's a vicar's daughter. Yet a friend of Tim Pedalow's cousin knew someone who was married by her father. Either that or prepared for confirmation.

In the interval, strolled round the foyer and bars, making mental sociological thumbnail sketches of members of the audience. While one was a million miles from Alan Bennett country in purely audience terms, in terms of the characters he portrays, there was a rich vein of comic raw material here which Alan could certainly tap to his advantage. In fact, might seriously consider dropping him a note along those lines. I think he'd appreciate it. As a writer, I know I would.

On way from loo, noticed a door marked PRIVATE. CHARGING ROOM. Is this where particularly rowdy customers are taken when things get out of hand, one wonders?

Curious how in second half of show one scarcely noticed nudity and rude language. In fact, characters with clothes on seemed positively out of place. I imagine one gains the same impression after one has been in a nudist colony for a few days. Perhaps I should see for myself. Am always being accused of being too inhibited. A bit of good, honest, down-to-earth sun worshipping might help me to be more carefree with my body.

After the show, on an impulse, went to the stage door and asked to see Miss Richmond.

I am not one of these trendy theatre goers who will insist on 'going round', as they say in theatrical circles, on the thinnest pretext and hobnobbing with the actors. And although the connection through Tim's cousin's friend might seem to many rather too vague for comfort, felt myself duty-bound, as a fellow student of the sexual scene, to introduce myself.

Explained who I was to the doorkeeper who passed the information on to the star by telephone. Finally he told me that she would see me briefly, but that she had a dinner engagement and would I mind waiting a moment or two while she had a shower. Someone would be down to fetch me.

Could hardly believe my good fortune. At the same time, I was as nervous as a schoolboy on his first date.

After a while, a young man appeared and escorted me upstairs in the lift. I said, 'Does Miss Richmond have many journalists coming to see her?'

'Search me, mate,' he said. 'I'm only a stagehand round here, not a bleeding press agent.'

Fiona's dressing room occupied by a young man

49

lounging on a settee drinking a glass of red wine.

'Help yourself,' he said, indicating the bottle.

Wondered if he was her dinner date.

Having read one of her pieces in an old copy of Armitage's *Men Only*, in which she 'road-tested' different men, reckoned he was in for a pretty lively evening. Frankly he looked a bit frail for the task to my way of thinking.

Fiona arrived, fresh from her shower. She is smaller than I imagined but none-the-less attractive for that. Unable to comment on her figure owing to towelling dressing gown pulled tightly around her. However, the bone structure of face quite superb.

Unfortunately, she made no attempt to introduce me to her friend. However, flattered and surprised to discover she knew my name. Could not resist commenting on the fact and said that I had not realized my reputation had spread quite so far.

'Actually,' she said, 'the stage doorkeeper just rang and told me.'

We chatted idly for a minute or two about the show. Not wishing to appear too sycophantic, I said that I had been a keen theatre goer for many years and had even at one time contemplated treading the boards myself, following critical acclaim for my performance as the Earl of Surrey in a college production of *The Shoemaker's Holiday* at Oxford, but I was something of a novice when it came to live sex shows. Was going on to explain my views on censorship when she cut me short by pointing out that she considered the expression 'sex show' to be damning with faint praise. It had in fact been adapted from a comedy written by a well-known French dramatist and, as such, was no different from many other West End successes.

This was fascinating stuff. I've often heard it said that there is a great deal more to Fiona than just a beautiful body and there was no doubt in my mind that on the evidence of her conversation so far I was dealing with a keen and original mind.

Surprised to discover as I walked back to the car that I was actually quite jealous of her dinner date. Also that the car had been towed away for being parked on a double yellow line.

This meant my having to take a taxi down to the Kennington Car Pound, wait around for an age while the man on duty finished his cup of tea and filled out various forms etc., and then take another taxi home because I had stupidly forgotten to come out with any money and was thus unable to pay the £29 fine.

An irritating, depressing and expensive end to an otherwise fascinating day.

On the credit side, have agreed with Fiona that I will call her in the week to arrange a proper interview, and can probably swing the fine on expenses. Assuming I have a proper expense account, that is.

Monday, 5 February

The start of the Sex Shop Week and the day on which I expect to receive a definite answer from Hardacre re expenses, etc.

Decided to begin at shop I once visited last year to buy sex manual for Jane. Am still slightly baffled as to why a place like that should carry books on car maintenance as an aid to relieving tension. On the other hand, anyone could be forgiven for believing that Auto-Therapy was about something quite different.

Doubtless Jane passed it on to Armitage when she went to live with him in his converted workman's dwelling in Camberwell. I can think of no better outlet for his over-developed sexuality than the Natchford Special he was always on about.

Shop every bit as crowded with shifty-looking browsers as I remember it. As a comparatively old hand, found myself entering with a jauntiness that was certainly lacking the last time I crossed this particular threshold.

Began on ground floor. Would not have believed it was possible to think up so many ways of increasing one's enjoyment of Sportsnight with Coleman. Naturally, as a man, am extremely sympathetic towards anyone who experiences difficulty in getting himself geared up for a session. However, the day I have to rely upon a tube of Erector Prompt for a spot of hanky-panky I'll seriously consider going into a monastery.

Assuming one has set things in motion, as it were, the next thing one has to worry about is keeping it all going.

51

Hence the huge stocks of sprays specially designed to stop you getting overexcited too early and thus mucking up the whole thing for all concerned.

One in particular, called Stud, seems to be more successful than most – so much so that they even offer free brochures telling you all about the product. It comes in a tiny gold and white aerosol can, about the size of those things people use to conceal their bad breath, and is apparently 'unchallenged throughout the world for quality, effectiveness and satisfaction in reducing oversensitivity'.

All you do is, about five minutes before you think Sportsnighting is about to reach a serious stage, whip out your tiny tube and give your weasel three or four quick squirts. Quite what the effect of this is I can only guess. Presume it makes everything numb, in which case I'd imagine the whole object of the exercise is largely negated anyway. There is, of course, the added danger that the well-equipped ladies' man might forget which tube is which and, following a garlicky meal, give his mouth a quick one-two and be unable to taste a thing for the next fortnight.

For those who suffer from the opposite problem there are Erotic Explosion Creams and Orgasm Boosters.

Weasel enlargers are evidently another popular line these days. The treatment, as far as one can gather, involves a transparent plastic tube and a small hand pump. Quite how this has the desired effect is difficult to see without actually spending £9.95 and finding out for oneself. Frankly I think Barfords have better things to do with their money in these hard times than waste it on increasing the size of their executives' weasels.

On the other hand, for a mere £7.75 it is possible – if the blurb on the box is to be believed – to create the illusion of magnitude with the use of a simple device known as The Butch Harness. By all accounts it will maintain 'the fullness and allure of the slight erection, particularly when worn with jeans or tight trousers'.

Was most intrigued. Is it really possible to go round for hours on end with a slight you-know-what and, if so, is such a physical condition really guaranteed to have women going weak at the knees?

Decided I had pussyfooted around for long enough. The

time had come to put the whole issue to the test. Luckily, the box fits neatly into one's overcoat pocket.

Decided against a talking blow-up rubber lady ('Designed by a man who wants her as much as you do, she is ever eager, every ready and never says no. Comes complete with underwear set and vibratory control'); ditto a pair of Dancing Bullets, said to be 'an exquisite pleasure source known to the ancients'. (Am not sure whether this refers to the Greeks and Romans etc. or OAPs.)

Interested to note how few women one sees in sex shops. *Tant mieux* for all our sakes.

Re rubberwear, leather underpants, plastic macs etc., I'm afraid it all leaves me rather cold. However, may well return to this subject at a later date.

To the magazine section next for a browse. These fall roughly into three categories:

a) The good old standbys – *Penthouse, Mayfair, Men Only, Rustler*, etc.
b) The ones that give the impression of being saucier because they are wrapped in cellophane and cost five times as much.
c) The ones that cater for those with an eye to curious physical deformities – e.g. *Bounce: Real Life Experiences of Big-Breasted Women*, *Superdong*, and *Bra Busters* – all featuring men and women beside whom the Elephant Man would have appeared positively normal.

Had in fact been planning to do my survey of the men's magazine market at a later date, but decided to hurry things along a bit by buying a small selection of the more popular range straight away – *Whitehouse, Knave* and *Men Only* to add to my Caligula edition of *Penthouse*.

Luckily there was a newspaper stand right outside the shop so that I was able to carry my purchases home concealed in a copy of the *Radio Times*.

Paused for a last look at lighted window. Was slightly puzzled by a couple of large gold balls hanging by a string which I hadn't noticed before. Stared at them for a long time but quite unable to guess their possible function.

Felt it was only my duty to pop back and get to the

bottom of the mystery. 'Excuse me,' I said *sotto voce*, to assistant, 'but can you possibly tell me what those gold balls in the window are for?'

'They're Christmas decorations,' he said. 'I've been meaning to take them down for weeks.'

Would have to pick on someone with a particularly penetrating voice.

On way out again, who should I bump into but Philippe de Grande-Hauteville, of all people.

When I explained that I was doing some very interesting research, he said, 'For the BBC, I suppose?'

If I've told him once, I've told him a dozen times that I do not work for the Corporation, but it's like talking to a brick wall. Either he's very much stupider than everyone takes him for, or else he could do with a refresher course in conversational English.

A far greater worry, though, is that he is bound to mention our meeting to Theresa and, knowing what a gossip she is, it will be round all my friends, including Jane, in no time. I see no alternative but to ring them all up and explain the situation before she has had a chance to get on the phone. But I'm going to have to move fast.

Looked in quickly at the office on the way home, but no reply to my memo from Hardacre so decided to call it a day.

Tried Butch Harness during *Nine O'clock News* despite severe looks from Angela Rippon.

Everything seemed to attach where it was meant to, and the all-important ring was a nice snug fit.

Instructions do not specify whether or not underpants to be worn. I understand there are men in responsible positions who are in the habit of going to the office pantless. I have often suspected Neville Pratt of being such a type, although I have no actual proof one way or another. Slipped into pants and trousers, therefore, and went into bathroom to check on effect, which as far as I could see was negligible. Have written myself a note in capital letters to BUY PAIR TIGHT JEANS a.s.a.p. tomorrow.

During weather forecast, noticed slight tingling sensation. Presume this to be 'physical pleasure' referred to on packaging. Must definitely wear it to work tomorrow and test it under field conditions.

A busy and interesting day all round. Am only sorry not to have heard yet about expenses. All this is costing me a lot of money.

Tuesday

Woke at 5.30 with a shock to realize I had completely forgotten to ring the Pedalows, Jane, etc., to explain about my presence in sex shop yesterday. Could not get back to sleep for worrying about it. Finally could stand suspense no longer and rang Tim shortly after 7.30. Vanessa answered. She did not sound pleased. Explained the situation as best I could and said I was sure she'd understand.

She said, 'Do you mean to tell me you woke us up at this ungodly hour to tell us you went to a sex shop yesterday?'

'It's not the *fact* that I went that matters,' I said, 'but the *reason* I'm anxious to get across.'

She said, 'You're a grown man now, Simon.' And she put the phone down.

There are some people with whom one can never say a thing without it being taken the wrong way.

Never mind. Better safe than sorry.

Had no sooner put the phone down than remembered I should have asked her for Jane's number.

To work wearing Harness. No one on underground appeared to notice or care. Am not sure whether I'm disappointed or relieved. Paused to examine trousers in shop windows and, to my eye, effect quite striking. It may have rated a niggardly five out of ten for 'visual pleasure', but for 'physical pleasure' it earned itself a considerably higher score. Alarmed to note, however, that by the time I reached office, weasel had gone curiously numb.

To loo at once to check on form. Horrified to discover it was quite blue and swollen.

Tried to remove Harness but ring completely stuck. Drastic steps clearly called for. Opened loo door and darted out into washroom to find soap. In my anxious state, forgot to pull up trousers and fell heavily on tiled floor knocking breath from my body just as Hardacre walked in.

'Hallo,' he said. 'On to deviationism already are we?' and walked out again before I could utter a word.

Crawled back into loo and closed door just as someone else came in. Realized I had forgotten to dampen soap, so had to do so with flushing loo water which sprayed up my arm, soaking my cuffs and half my sleeve.

Soaped weasel as best I could and by dint of much physical effort, not to say pain, succeeded after several minutes in easing ring off. Pain redoubled as circulation returned. So much so that compelled to sit there for fully fifteen minutes, despite furious bangings on door by desperate customer.

Thought about taking myself up to third floor to see Sister but decided too much explanation required. Finally plucked up strength to totter back to office to find Sue back at her desk doing her nails.

Her first words were, 'Why are you walking like Groucho Marx?'

'I've got a slight backache,' I replied.

Later, rang Fiona and fixed to have lunch with her at the Coconut Grove, wherever that may be.

Thought of ringing Theresa to get Jane's number, but obviously she has drawn her own conclusions about my meeting with Philippe anyway and did not wish to seem to be protesting too much. Gritted my teeth, therefore, and against my better judgement called Armitage instead.

He said, 'I thought you'd be sniffing around now Jane's no longer engaged.'

This was news to me but I was certainly not going to let him know that. I came back like a whiplash. 'Why must you assume that everyone's motives are base?' I said.

'Because,' he said, 'they usually are.'

I said wearily, 'If you don't know where Jane is, you only have to say so. There's no need to make a Margaret Drabble novel out of it.'

He said, 'Careful. Remember who you're speaking to. I'm that chap who holds the key to all those naughty places you dare not go to alone.' And he rang off.

I had a feeling that once one started to delve into this subject, all sorts of creepy-crawlies would come out of the woodwork.

Later, dictated memo to Hardacre.

Memo

To: Keith Hardacre
From: Simon Crisp   6 February

Surprised not have heard anything from you yet re my expenses. Have already spent nearly £65 of my own money on this project and the figure could easily rise to £100 or more before I've finished. Can we therefore agree an expenses budget a.s.a.p.?

Re personal involvement in research: have decided to play this by ear, as suggested.

S.c.

Home early after a long and action-packed day.

After supper, watched a fascinating TV programme about life at Radley College, the famous boys' public school. I seem to remember there was talk at one time of my going there. Or was it Repton? As it turned out, either would have been acceptable.

By a curious coincidence, programme focused on sex life of three rather precocious senior boys. We saw them campaigning for the Gay Liberation Front in school's mock elections, being interviewed in one of the studies, and taking part in a house dance to which girls had been invited.

This was fascinating stuff for any public school boy of my generation because, of course, in my day the nearest one ever came to meeting a girl in term-time was in a house play when one or two of the younger boys were dressed up to play the female parts. Anyone caught with an actual girl was for the high jump.

The rules were relaxed marginally in my last two years when a Sixth Form dance was arranged with a nearby girls' boarding school – or against, as my friend Rex Dunwoody so wittily put it.

It just goes to show how things have changed in public schools that the three boys featured were able to claim that they could cycle out and see their girlfriends from a neighbouring school every day if they felt like it, and that they were allowed to bring their own girls to the house dance.

On the strength of this excellent programme, am

seriously considering including a section on sex in the public schools.

Shall resist natural temptation to carry out my research in one of the so-called top schools – Eton, Winchester and so on – and go instead for the old *alma mater*. Terms of reference are so important in this kind of work, and to be in a position to compare schoolboy mores over a twenty-year period could be very interesting indeed. It's the sort of thing the *Sunday Times* might easily fall upon with whoops of joy, and possibly large sums of money.

Will ring the school secretary first thing in the morning. Or should I go straight to Dickie Dunmow? As a housemaster, I seem to remember his being more open-minded than most. Except, that is, when it came to Latin verse.

Wednesday

Still far from comfortable. As an experiment, the Harness has been a bit of a flop all round. A quantitative survey at grass roots level of weasel envy/admiration could have made a fascinating footnote to the sex shop section – but not at the expense of impotence or possibly even gangrene.

To the office in sombre mood to find a memo from Hardacre awaiting me on my desk.

Memo

To: Simon Crisp, Special Projects Manager
From: Keith Hardacre, Deputy Managing Director

6 February

Thank you for your memo. Of course you will be reimbursed for any small out-of-pocket expenses that may arise in the course of your enquiries, such as taxi fares etc. But surely it should be possible to interview informants at a time and place where refreshments are not an automatic feature of the proceedings? Apart from the unnecessary expense incurred, I have personally found it almost impossible to concentrate and make useful notes at the same time as tackling half a lobster or pondering a wine list.

As far as the purchase of magazines etc. goes, most erotic literature is available on the open shelves these days and I should have thought it perfectly feasible for you to acquire all the information you need from such publications without in fact having to go so far as to purchase them.

I hope this answers your questions.

KH

Not so much answered as avoided, I'd say. Am beginning to wonder if the powers that be are taking the Crisp Report as seriously as they should.

After lunch, wrote to Dickie Dunmow explaining what I am up to and asking if it might be possible to come down to the old place and interview one or two boys of different ages regarding their attitudes to girls, sex etc. I shall be most interested to see what he has to say.

Odd that I have so far received no response to my advertisement in *Time Out*. Still, I daresay these things take time to filter through.

Thursday

Was looking through my girlie magazines last night when I chanced upon an advertisement featuring a man in a tight and extremely revealing pair of trousers. The copy read: 'BUST 'ER WITH THE THRUSTER. We'll guarantee that your smooth talk and witty repartee will not be the only thing to hold her attention when you're dressed up in your eye-catching new thrusting undergarment. Thanks to its unique and easy-to-wear design, THE THRUSTER will raise your confidence, her high hopes, and much else besides! Your quietly arrogant, obviously raring-to-go appearance will ensure that she is already looking forward to the end of the evening before it has even begun. And only you will know why!'

This could be just the thing I am looking for as a safe, effective replacement for my Butch Harness.

Do not quite understand why one needs to be over eighteen to order it but have decided to plump anyway. £6.95 plus 50p for postage and handling is surely not going to break the bank as far as Barfords is concerned, and the evidence it will inevitably throw up will be invaluable.

One often hears it said that women are not interested primarily in a man's appearance. We shall see.

Friday

Cannot believe I have had no replies to my advertisement, even though I did try to cut corners by not going for the semi-display.

Shortly before lunch, went down to post room to check if there were any letters for John Ashford. Who should I find there but the spotty messenger who tried to make a monkey out of me the other day. As I came in, he grinned at his friends in a knowing way and one or two of them tried unsuccessfully to conceal a snigger behind their hands.

Treated them to one of my famous icy stares and asked if they happened to have any letters for Mr Ashford.

The spotty one said, 'No one of that name working here, chief.' Unfortunately, he said it in such a serious tone of voice that it was impossible to tick him off for his obvious cheek.

I said, 'I hope you're telling me the truth. I happen to be using the name pseudonymously for a very important reason.'

'Enough said, squire,' he said, winking and tapping the side of his nose.

For two pins would have boxed his ears. As it was, left the room without a word. Caught my hip painfully against the edge of the counter as I did so, but I don't think anyone noticed.

A miracle occurred this afternoon when, for only the second time since joining the company, Agnes, the West Indian tea lady, actually brought me a cup without my having to ask her.

I said jokingly, 'Well, this is a turn-up for the books, Agnes.'

To my amazement she actually smiled at me, a thing I have only ever seen her do to her fellow Trinidadians. 'Big sexy man like you, Mr Samson,' she said, 'get everything he want from big sexy ladies.' And rolling her eyes and waggling her enormous hips, she traipsed out noisily on her large, slippered feet.

It would be nice to think that at least one member of the staff here accords me the degree of respect to which I am entitled, even if it is only the tea lady.

Was slipping on overcoat prior to leaving for home when Neville Pratt's new assistant, Matthew Chinnery, stuck his head round the door and tossed a large manilla envelope onto my desk. 'These found their way to me by mistake,' he said. 'Someone suggested they might be something to do with you. I can't imagine why.' And with a nod he disappeared.

Opened the envelope and out slipped half a dozen letters, pinned together, all addressed to Box 248 and all beginning 'Dear Attractive, Sensitive Stallion. . .' Was so embarrased, I shoved the whole lot into my briefcase and hurried out to the lift.

On way out of front door, spotted Chinnery and a couple of his cronies chatting with Dawn, the receptionist. As I passed, they straightened up, all innocence, needless to say. Glanced back quickly to find them giggling together and holding their noses like a lot of school-children.

Someone round here is to feel the rough side of my tongue before very long.

Weasel slightly better. I *would* say functioning normally, but unfortunately am not in a position to make such a claim.

Saturday

Less than three weeks to go before the report is due to be delivered, yet I feel I have barely scratched the surface of the subject so far.

Am all right on sex films, sex shops and the like, but what about live sex shows? Prostitution? Massage parlours? Adultery? Orgies? Homosexuality? The more I think about it, the more I wonder where it will all end.

George Washington really hit the nail on the head when he said 'So much to do, so little time'. Or was it Mahatma Gandhi?

Frankly, cannot wait for Beddoes to arrive on

Wednesday. Never have I been in as much need of good, practical advice as I am at this moment.

In the meantime, must press on with work in hand. After breakfast settled down to my *Time Out* letters. Had hoped that my intriguing wording might have attracted rather more replies, but six is a start, I suppose. There are probably more to come.

Am not quite sure what I'd been expecting. Perhaps nothing quite as crude as COME TO OUR ORGY invitations, but certainly one or two suggestions of a pretty blatant nature. Was surprised, therefore, by the first one I picked out:

Dear Attractive, Sensitive Stallion,

You sound very much my type and I should like to meet you. I am thirty years old but look younger, so my friends assure me! I am slightly on the tall side for some people's tastes. I am five foot eight inches, but slim, with a fairly good figure and lightish hair. I do not smoke and am not what you might call a drinker, except for the occasional glass of wine with my dinner! Like you I have a wide range of quite unusual tastes. I very much enjoy eating out in nice but not too expensive restaurants, theatre, films, walking in the country, animals, music (pop but not too heavy!), conversation, meeting people etc.

I see you are adventurous. I enjoy adventure too. Last year I took my moped to Normandy and had a fascinating camping holiday.

I don't know quite what you mean by free-thinking. I do not have any romantic attachments, but then, of course, if I did I wouldn't be writing to you!

Unfortunately, I do not happen to have a spare photograph of myself and anyway I'm not very photogenic. Perhaps it would be best if we were to meet for a drink and a chat and see how we get on before we start exchanging personal mementoes.

I look forward to receiving a call from you soon.

Yours sincerely,
Julie Brown

Her address was a street I have never heard of, somewhere in SE24.

Of the rest, one was matter of fact to the point of rudeness:

'You can have my phone number but not my photograph. If you want to send me a snap of yourself, that's up to you. You could be my type, but obviously I can't tell without meeting you. The next move is yours. You are the tenth ad I've replied to, so you'd better remember your box number when you ring.

Yours
Fran Holland

She'll need to write to more than ten if she's going to stand the slightest chance of success. Could she be one of these dominant types one gathers are all the rage these days? Am tempted to get in touch with her out of sheer curiosity. Ditto with 'Alan' who has seen fit to send me his business card without explanation.

Am also intrigued by short, sharp note from foreign girl called Marie-Lise. She doesn't say what nationality but I suspect French:

Hallo, stallion,
Not sure what you want but have written anyway. I am only twenty but am sophisticated and have been around. I enjoy good restaurants, travel by air, staying in first-class hotels, clothes, dancing etc. You say you know the score, so you will understand what I mean. Ring mornings only. If I am not in, you can leave your name on the answering machine. I look forward to hearing from you, big boy.

Thought it might be useful to have the foreigner's angle on sex in Britain, so took a bow at a venture and rang her number.

Surprised that she seemed to have such difficulty remembering our recent correspondence. Put this down at first to her lack of familiarity with the language, particularly when she started talking about services. Convinced that I had become unwittingly caught up with religion in some shape or form, I said that unfortunately I was not as regular about that sort of thing as I would like, but that I'd be prepared to fit in with her plans up to a certain point.

She said that depended on what I had in mind and started quoting large sums of money at me. By now I was in a complete muddle and told her that there had obviously been some sort of mistake.

She said, 'Those are my rates, take it or leave it.'

I said, 'In the circumstances, I think I'll leave it.'

'That's fine by me,' she said, 'you're the customer.'

I can only think that she thought I had something to do with a shop.

Decided that, all in all, Miss Brown sounded my best bet. She is probably very typical of the sort of people who look for love through the columns of magazines.

She sounded rather charming on the phone and seemed quite surprised that I had called. When I asked her why, she said, 'It's just that I wasn't sure whether I'd made myself sound attractive enough.'

We have arranged to meet for a drink in the bar at the Piccadilly Hotel on Monday evening at six. Am quite looking forward to my little adventure.

Had seriously thought of trying out one of these Paul Raymond sex shows that I am always passing in Soho and always meaning to investigate – *Rip Off* at the Windmill Theatre 'The Erotic Experience of the Modern Era, now in its 5th Great Year'; or *The Festival of Erotica* at Raymond's Revuebar 'New Acts, New Girls, New Thrills, now in its 23rd Sensational Year'.

They both sound pretty hot stuff.

In the end, though, decided to shelve both of them and take myself off to an altogether more congenial and familiar stamping ground, the National Theatre, to see if I couldn't squeeze into *The Romans in Britain*. There's been such a hooha about it recently.

Frankly, it takes more than a bit of full frontal male nudity to keep me awake at night, and besides, as Harold Hobson rightly said in his letter to *The Times*, one cannot begin to discuss a play as controversial as this without having seen it first.

Rumour had it that, what with the Leader of the Greater London Council, Sir Horace Cutler, walking out during a performance, and Mrs Whitehouse threatening to take everyone to court without even seeing it, it was impossible to get a ticket for love or money.

In the event, arrived a few minutes before curtain-up, bought myself a stand-by ticket for £3.50 without the slightest difficulty and took my seat in the eighth row.

An altogether fascinating evening. Strong meat it certainly is. I had no idea such language was bandied about or such things shown on the London stage. But then, strong subjects call for strong language and the famous homosexual rape occupied only a few moments out of nearly three hours. The only thing that upset me was that the nude young Celts made me feel so dreadfully overweight.

During the interval was standing in the bar when I overheard a bearded man saying to a woman, 'I mean, all right, if we have to have homosexual rape we have to have it. But quite honestly, as far as I'm concerned, there's just too much of everything.'

Suddenly something about the woman caught my eye. Looked at her more closely and realized with a shock that it was Enid Trubshawe, the mother of my ex-fiancée, Amanda, and the wife of my ex-chairman, Derrick. Whoever the bearded man was, it certainly wasn't her husband. What was more, he was holding her by the hand, and the looks she was giving him expressed considerably more than passing interest in his critical views.

Would happily have slipped away unobserved, but was so intrigued to find out what was going on that I could not resist calling out her name. Noticed she quickly unhitched her arm, and although she carried the whole thing off with her usual charm and elegance, the word guilt was written all over both their faces.

'Do you know Gerald Campsey-Ash?' she said in a vague, slightly wobbly voice.

I said that I'd never heard of him but that it was certainly a name with a nice old-fashioned English ring to it.

The man said, 'I'm Campsey-Ash and I happen to be Welsh.'

Enid explained that I had been, until recently, one of Derrick's bright young hopefuls.

'Bright at work perhaps,' he said.

'Gerald and I are great theatre goers,' Enid said.

'Oh yes?' I said, pretending innocence.

'You know what Derrick's like about the theatre. Luckily Gerald's got his finger in a lot of showbiz pies, so he's always getting tickets and rushing me off to all the best things. Derrick couldn't approve more.'

A more blatant case of the lady protesting too much I've yet to encounter.

I said casually, 'What do you think of the play? Pretty strong stuff, eh?'

'Personally I think it's rather fun,' she said.

Naturally, asked about Amanda. Enid had just about time to tell me that she was engaged to someone in the army when the bell went and we had to resume our seats.

Second half rather less sensational – although have a feeling its effect lessened slightly by (a) the shocking news of A.'s engagement and (b) my catching E. in obvious flagrante.

Have a distinct feeling I may have got my adultery chapter!

Sunday

Woke in the small hours in a cold sweat with the realization that I have made no headway whatever with homosexuality.

Apart from the man who ran the Workers' Workshop in Covent Garden I once attended with Victoria, I do not believe I have met any gays, as we must now learn to refer to them. At least, not knowingly.

Feel I should start making inroads into this strange world about which one hears so much but has such little personal experience. A gay nightclub would be an obvious starting point, but that could lead to all sorts of complications and misunderstandings.

Though hardly a young Lord Alfred Douglas, I am not without my good points and there's no knowing what these sort of people go for. I understand that some of them can be quite rough. The fate suffered by the young Druid at the hands of the brutish Roman soldiers is still too fresh in my mind for comfort.

So far completely stumped as to how this most delicate of areas should be tackled, but tackled it must be.

Got down to the Sunday papers soon after Alistair Cooke's *Letter from America*. What a first-class broadcaster he is. I somehow cannot imagine him sitting in his Fifth Avenue apartment riffling through dirty magazines or slipping furtively in and out of blue movie houses, even under the pretence of a journalistic assignment. His familiar voice only serves to remind me of how far I still have to go in order to achieve the big breakthrough that everyone needs to achieve public recognition.

Settled down in more sombre mood than usual with the Sunday papers. By an extraordinary coincidence, came upon a fascinating article about an apiarist called Howard Johnson who has just started up a thing called the National Campaign for the Knowledge, Encouragement and Rights of Sexual Freedom, or NACKERS for short.

Although Mr Johnson is not prepared at this stage to 'name names', he claims to have already enlisted the support of 'several distinguished public figures in the arts and public life' and believes that the tide of opinion is turning against the nation's most famous watchdog to such a degree that, before long, thousands will be flocking to his cause.

His campaign war cry is Stamp Out Do-Gooders, and he calls upon every man and woman in the country who believes in individual freedom to SOD along with him.

Must get in touch with Mr Johnson at the earliest opportunity.

Had been planning to spend afternoon working on critical appreciation of girlie magazines. However, in my book, Sunday is a day that should be devoted to the spirit rather than the flesh. I realize that everything God made is beautiful in its own particular way, but given a choice between grass, blue skies and fluffy white clouds, and thrusting bosoms and splayed crutches, I know which inspire me to nobler thoughts.

Set off for Hyde Park after lunch.

Every time I stroll there under the chestnuts, among the dogs and nannies and kite fliers, I find my thoughts turning to poor, sad, misunderstood little J.M. Barrie who trod these same wooded paths eighty years ago, plotting adventures for Peter Pan. I feel sure that, if only I had a nice dog to keep me company, my imagination would also be aroused to comparable heights.

Was sitting on one of the benches watching some middle-aged men sailing their model yachts when I overheard two small children deep in conversation.

He: 'You're a lesbian.'

She: 'So what? You're a homosexual.'

He (after suitable pause for thought): 'Well, what about intercourse then?'

She: 'What about it?'

He: 'I don't know, but I don't think it's very nice.'

Home for tea and crumpets and the children's Sunday serial on BBC TV.

A charming and welcome interlude in this strange period of my life. They say that sex keeps you young, but I'm beginning to think quite the opposite is true.

Monday, 12 February

A dismal Monday morning, made more so by cold, damp drizzle and the phone call I received from Ruth Mac-michael ringing from Harley Preston to ask what all this was she had heard about my spending my time among the strip clubs and peep shows of Soho.

Had forgotten how aggressive she can be on the phone when she wants and how quickly she can get one's hackles up with her abrasive trans-Atlantic manner.

I said politely, 'If you are referring to the report I am compiling on the state of British morals in the 1980s, I'm sure we can arrange to have a copy sent to you as soon as it is published.'

'Jesus,' she said, 'you're even more full of shit than I remember. You English guys are all the same. Your idea of the sexual revolution is buying *Penthouse* and not wrapping it inside the evening paper. You don't deserve to be allowed near women, you know that? Treat them rough and they'll respect you for it, right? The idea that a woman might have a mind of her own never even comes into it.'

Tried to put my point of view, but once these American women get the bit between their teeth there's no stopping them.

'Your whole approach is an insult to women,' she went on, 'and if your report comes out the way I think it will, then watch out, baby, because the shit's really going to start flying, and I mean flying. I'm only trying to help you because I kind of feel responsible for you – even though you are an ass-hole.'

I said, 'Thank you for your advice, although frankly I cannot see it is any of your business.'

'On the contrary,' she replied. 'As a woman who is sick to death of being exploited as a sex object, I think it is very much my business.'

The mistake all these women libbers make is in assuming that any man is the slightest bit interested in them from any point of view whatever. Indeed, if I was as unattractive to look at and listen to as the majority of them, I'd keep very quiet indeed.

I said politely, 'In that case, perhaps you would care to suggest in which areas one *should* be looking?'

'Try TV commercials, popular song lyrics and jokes for a start,' she said. 'They'll tell you far more about the way people are thinking about sex than any amount of blue movies.'

I said, 'Oh, I'm sorry; I thought you were going to tell me something I didn't know.' And before she could utter another word, I put the phone down on her. She may have a point or she may not. For the time being, I'd prefer to keep an open mind on the subject.

In the meantime, have many more urgent matters on my plate – adultery being not the least among them. Have shilly-shallied for long enough over this one, and the time has now come for action.

Rang The Boltons shortly before noon. Interested to find that Enid's voice still affects me as strongly as ever. I merely said that I wished to see her on a matter of some delicacy.

She said, 'You always were a mysterious young man.' I did not deny it.

I am to lunch with her at The Boltons on Thursday.

To the Piccadilly Hotel after work for my blind date with Miss Brown. Chose a corner table with a good view of the entrance, ordered a large whisky and soda, sat back and took in the scene.

Few things appeal more to the imaginative temperament than the transient life of a big city hotel. Oscar Wilde, Arnold Bennett, Kipling, Hemingway – these are just a few of the artists who have produced some of their best work in hotels and one can see why. After only a few minutes in the Piccadilly bar, my fingers began to itch for the typewriter keys and ideas for no less than three short stories sprang unbidden to my mind.

After a few minutes, a stunning blonde with a magnificent figure dressed in black walked into the bar, looked around briefly and sat at the next table but one to me. She was obviously waiting for somebody. At one point, caught her eye and smiled knowingly but I don't think she can have seen me.

Finished my drink to discover it was already twenty past six. Strolled out to lobby on off-chance there had been a misunderstanding re exact location of rendezvous. No one obviously looking for anyone, so returned to bar and ordered another drink.

Blonde girl also showing signs of having been stood up. At 6.30 nipped to loo and came back to find her talking animatedly to a swarthy, rather Arabic-looking chap with a moustache. There are those who find middle-eastern looks attractive but I can't see it myself and I must admit to feeling rather disappointed by the girl's taste. She was probably one of those loose creatures one hears about who hang around in hotel lobbies in the West End, touting for business with oil sheiks.

Finally decided enough was enough. Paid my bill and was about to leave when my date appeared from the direction of the lobby and stood in the entrance to the bar, looking about her in an obvious way.

As I'd suspected, Miss Brown had overstated her charms. I suppose I couldn't blame her, but still, I hadn't imagined she would turn out to be *quite* so plump, nor that she would be the type to wear quite so much make-up. Put it down to nervousness. That or an unfortunate complexion.

On the other hand, it was only work as far as I was concerned. I wasn't being asked to marry the girl. Took a deep breath and strolled across to her. 'Hallo,' I said. 'I'm Simon Crisp.'

'I wouldn't give a monkey's if you was the Aga Khan, darling,' she said. 'I'm booked this evening.' And she walked back into the lobby, followed shortly afterwards by the blonde and her Arabic boyfriend.

Hung around for a few more minutes, but at seven o'clock decided to call it a day. Ate a disgusting hamburger at one of these plastic American-style places and felt slightly sick.

Arrived home to find that my suit stank to high heaven of fried food. Also that I had stepped in a dog dirt somewhere and walked it all over the flat.

Would have changed and gone out to the local Odeon for the last performance of *The Blue Lagoon*, but assumed Miss Brown would be ringing with an explanation. Wrongly, as it turned out.

To bed at midnight with a mug of Milo and the new Ed McBain. Milk slightly sour and lumpy.

Like Ruth Macmichael.

Tuesday

A beautiful sunny day. Along with the clouds have disappeared all my worries and irritations of yesterday, and a clear blue sky heralded one of the great events of my life and one which will certainly set Beddoes by the ears and no mistake: lunch with Fiona Richmond.

Bathed and shaved with special care – rather too special unfortunately since the new blade nicked my neck in no fewer than four places. Also washed hair. Breakfasted lightly and cleaned teeth well afterwards. Am not a great believer in the philosophy of the after-shave lotion; however, more by way of a controlled experiment than for reasons of personal advancement, I decided to try some out on Fiona.

Chose one that I was given for Christmas two years ago and which I understand to be particularly favoured by women. Slapped it on enthusiastically only to remember too late about the nicks on my neck. Quickly tried to wash it off with a soaking flannel but even so the pain was excruciating. Also got water down my shirt front.

Was halfway to work when I realized I had chosen a shirt with a particularly tight collar, so that every time I turned my head it gave my nicks a nasty little tug. By the time I arrived at the office, my neck a mass of small red spots and my collar flecked with blood.

Could not decide whether to buy something that would conceal ravaged neck or splurge out two or three quid on a new shirt.

Arrived in office just as phone was ringing. It was Miss Brown. In the circumstances, adopted a considerably sharper tone than is my wont.

I said, 'I rather thought you might have phoned last night.'

'*Me?*' she exclaimed. 'Phone *you*?'

'Well,' I said, 'you did stand me up.'

She said, 'I like that! I sat there for half an hour and there was no sign of you.'

I said, 'Sat where? Euston Station?'

'What's Euston Station got to do with it?' she said. 'We agreed to meet in the bar of the Piccadilly Hotel and that's where I was. Why? Were you at Euston?'

'No, of course not,' I said. 'I was at the Piccadilly too.'

She said, 'Well, why didn't you come and talk to me? I gave you a perfectly good description.'

I said, 'All right. Let me tell you. I sat there for an *hour* and the only single girl I saw in all that time was a very glamorous blonde who told the waiter she was waiting for someone.'

'Of course, you idiot,' she said. 'You.'

I said, 'Do you mean to tell me that that was you?'

'How many other single women did you count?' she said.

I said, 'But you went off with some ghastly middle-eastern type.'

She said, 'If you must know, he's my cousin and he's neither ghastly nor is he from the middle east. He happens to live in Romford and our meeting was entirely fortu-itous. Since you obviously decided to rat on our arrange-ment, he took me out to dinner.'

I said, 'But this is a ghastly misunderstanding. I mean, what's a girl like you doing answering advertisements in Lonely Hearts columns?'

She said, 'I've no idea. But if you're the sort of person one ends up with, I don't think I'll bother again.'

Consoled myself with thought of lunch with Fiona.

Slipped out after coffee and bought myself a small tin of make-up. Chose as neutral a colour as I could find.

The young girl who served me said, 'I think you'll find it'll suit your colouring very well. My boyfriend swears by it, and he's slightly dark too.' No comment.

Just time to dash off a quick memo to Hardacre.

Memo

To: Keith Hardacre
From: Simon Crisp   13 February

Re: *Your memo of the 6th*

As you know, I'm the last to mix pleasure with business. On the other hand, I feel it would be a pity to spoil the ship for ha'p'orth of tar. Wouldn't you agree?

S.C.

Unfortunately, with Sue being off with a cold and my typing being rather on the rusty side, plus an unusual shortage of taxis, had to apply make-up to neck en route and arrived at Coconut Grove rather later than I'd hoped and in a muck sweat.

Luckily, Fiona delayed too, so was able to be at table to greet her when she arrived. Was mildly disappointed that when the waiter showed her across, more heads did not turn and stare. But perhaps the sort of people who frequent places like this are used to celebrities.

Happily, one of the waiters must have recognized her because, before we had time to order one of their exotic cocktails, someone came across and offered us each a glass of champagne on the house.

Am often reading interviews with TV and film stars in which the writer sets the scene by telling us that he met his subject in this restaurant or that bar, and embellishes the questions and answers with descriptions of who ordered what, and how they sipped at their white wine and Perrier water as they talked.

Hardacre is right for once. One obviously has to be very experienced at journalism of this type to be able to order, eat, drink and take in the atmosphere of the place at the same time as asking all the right questions and writing down the answers. For while I came away with a definite impression of having enjoyed an excellent couple of hours in the company of a friendly and amusing girl, I can recall very little of our conversation.

I suppose I *was* rather nervous and perhaps four glasses of wine *is* excessive for someone who never normally drinks at lunchtime, but surely not so excessive as all that?

Nor are my notes very much help. Have read them through several times and am no nearer deciphering the illiterate scrawl than before. They read: 'Big with school-boys – more humour – Mayfair definitive old men – pussy sculpted – larger than life – blue and silver – looks like a shoe – Penthouse frilly aprons? – 16-year-old virgin up to 70-year-old something – like to move it while doing it – estate agent – ring up Arabian embassy – heavy with orgies – pillow sniffing – very geometrical.'

What can it all mean?

I do remember one curious incident. As we were getting up to leave, she said, 'Are you in any way connected with the theatre?'

I told her that I had always been a keen theatregoer and, where possible, first-nighter, and that I had been very much involved in amateur theatricals at Oxford.

She said, 'Yes, I know. You told me all that the other night. What I meant was, are you by any chance performing now? I mean today?'

Remembering her famous 'road-testing' series, was suddenly struck by the thought that by 'performing' she might be referring to something quite different. However, did not wish to appear to be taking too much for granted, so waited until we got out into the street, slipped a hand under her elbow and said quietly, 'Of course, there are performances and performances.'

'You're telling me,' she said.

I gave a light knowing laugh and hailed a cab. 'Where to?' I asked her as she climbed in.

'Bayswater,' she said, closed the door and drove away, leaving me standing on the pavement.

Gave my chin a puzzled rub and found my hand covered in some strange sticky brown substance.

As soon as I got back to office, went straight to gents to discover that the make-up I had applied to my neck had run down into my collar and mingled with the bloodstains to create as unattractive an effect as I have seen since that day at school when Kippax's boil burst.

Only hope this had nothing to do with Fiona's abrupt

decision to break off our cordial dialogue. If so, it was a cruel stroke of fate. I suppose I can't blame her. You certainly wouldn't catch me testing a man who appeared to be in the latter stages of bubonic plague.

Still, the more I think about it, the more I am sure I am well out of it. Fiona has a wicked sense of humour and I should hate to find myself portrayed as one of her rare failures. Was thinking of ringing her to explain about neck, but frankly, if ever there was a case of quitting while one is ahead, it is this.

Shouldn't wonder if I don't see a sudden change of attitude from the messenger boys. F. is very popular among teenagers and it's only a matter of time before news of my relationship with her filters through to the post room. If I have anything to do with it, that is.

Wednesday

The most bizarre start to a day that I can remember for many a year. Was in bath when front door bell went. I called out, 'Leave it on the mat and I'll collect it in a minute.'

A girl's voice replied, 'I can't. This has to be delivered in person.'

Scrambled out of bath, threw a towel round my waist and flung open door to be confronted by a couple of extremely buxom girls dressed in skimpy gym tunics and school boaters, with their hair done up in pigtails. Before I could open my mouth, they began to sing at me at the tops of their voices.

The next thing I knew, Miss Weedon from the flat opposite had opened her door and was standing there in her dressing gown and curlers, with Poppy her nasty little pug barking under her arm. At that moment, realized that the girls were in fact delivering a sung message of an extremely suggestive nature, finishing up with words to the effect that they hoped today would be a memorable Valentine's Day that I would remember for years to come.

I do not think I have ever been more embarrassed in my life.

Had I been fully dressed, I daresay I could have carried off the situation with a witty riposte that would have sent all of us, including Miss Weedon, off to work with a smile on our faces and, who knows, perhaps even a song in our hearts.

Unfortunately, am never at my wittiest when half naked and soaking wet, especially at eight o'clock in the morning. Looking the girls firmly in the eye I said, 'I'm sorry, there must be some mistake,' and closed the door firmly and politely in their faces.

As I walked back to the bathroom, one of them called through the letter box, 'There's more to come. Don't you want the rest of it?'

I called back over my shoulder, 'One verse is more than enough for me,' and got back into my bath.

A certain amount of whispering and giggling ensued, followed by high-pitched barking, some screams and Miss Weedon's voice calling out, 'And don't come back. This is a respectable block of flats. Not a music hall.'

My reputation amongst members of the residents' association is shaky enough as it is without my having it further damaged by accusations of gross moral turpitude.

An even greater worry is the realization that, for the first time in fifteen years, I have forgotten to send Mother a Valentine card. I don't seem to be able to get anything right these days.

To Roland Gardens en route for the office to interview the founder of NACKERS. A short tubby man in a tight-fitting black and yellow striped jersey opened the door to me and introduced himself as Howard Johnson. He took me through to a sitting room filled with cases of stuffed bees, offered me a cup of tea and disappeared into the next room. He appeared a few minutes later bearing two small wooden bowls filled with some steaming and curiously smelling liquid. Whatever it was, it certainly wasn't PG Tips.

'It's a little honey and herbal mixture of my own devising,' he explained. 'A real pick-me-up at this time of the morning, I always find.'

For him perhaps, but not for me. Pretended to sip at it before placing it on floor beside me.

We had a most fascinating talk about the rights and wrongs of censorship. I can quite see how some people might find Howard and his ideas rather extreme, and I am not entirely persuaded that anything should go on stage, screen and on TV. Like Mother, I am not exactly looking forward to the day when we shall be treated to the sight of people doing big potties in our sitting rooms.

On the other hand, Howard is quite right. People should be shocked from time to time. I was shocked by parts of *The Romans in Britain* and I certainly feel a better man for it.

Nor apparently am I alone in my radical thinking. John Mortimer, Clement Freud, Melvyn Bragg, Moira Lister, Janet Suzman, Ted Willis, Derek Nimmo – these are just a few of the public figures Howard is thinking of approaching with a view to their becoming NACKERS committee members. Not only that, but he has asked me if I would also be prepared to serve. Have not committed myself entirely yet, but have said I will give the matter serious thought. I have long been aware that, when it comes to standing up and being counted, I have been sadly backward in coming forward. This could be just the opportunity I have been looking for to break into public life in no uncertain terms.

Have in the meantime agreed to act as steward at a NACKERS public meeting to be held in the Smith-Beresford Rooms in Bloomsbury on Sunday week. Hope there won't be any trouble. One court appearance a year is more than enough for a man in my position.

Left for Heathrow in good time to meet Beddoes' plane. Even so, became caught up in traffic jam at Talgarth Road roundabout and another at airport underpass, and only just arrived in time.

Rushed inside to find plane delayed by twenty minutes. Unable to park, so drove round for a while listening to radio. Needle of petrol gauge obviously faulty because suddenly ran out and had to push car to petrol pumps. As a results, arrived back at terminal several minutes later than expected.

Passengers pouring out of customs but no sign of Beddoes.

After a while, stream became a thin trickle and finally dried up altogether. Asked member of airline staff if Brussels passengers through yet.

He said, 'Good Lord yes. They've all been and gone half an hour ago.'

I said, 'But the notice board said the plane was twenty minutes late.'

'Obviously it changed its mind,' he said.

Waited another half an hour, but still no sign of him. Drove back to Holland Park in a rage. Sat about in the flat twiddling my thumbs and doing desultory dusting until half past eight.

By now feeling decidedly hungry. Remembered I had not bought any food because expecting to eat out with Beddoes. Rushed round corner to delicatessen to find the manager locking the door and walking off up the street.

Arrived back in flat as phone was ringing. Picked it up to hear Beddoes' cheery voice saying that he was at Victoria Station and why hadn't I been at the airport to meet him?

I told him that I certainly had been there and, more to the point, where had he been?

He said, 'I hung about in the central concourse, then went to have a drink in the Panorama Bar.'

I said, 'There's no Panorama Bar at Heathrow.'

He said, 'Who said anything about Heathrow? I was at Gatwick.'

Sat through an indifferent western followed by Barry Norman making facetious comments about films which I had neither seen nor, in most cases, wished to.

Beddoes finally turned up at 11.30, rather the worse for drink, I thought. 'Cheers,' he kept saying as he wandered round the room, sitting on each of the chairs in turn and messing up the carefully plumped cushions.

I said, 'All I can say is thank heavens you arrived before I put my pyjamas on. I'm starved. Where are we eating?'

'I've no idea where you're going,' he said. 'I've eaten already and frankly I'm ready for my bed. Nightcap first though.' And he reached into a plastic bag and produced a half-empty quart bottle of Famous Grouse whisky. 'Nothing like it for staving off the old pangs,' he said. 'Puts hairs on your chest too. You could do with a few.'

I remember being told once by a nutritionist that one should never make the mistake of substituting alcohol for good nourishing food. She obviously does not suffer from thoughtless and unreliable friends. By one o'clock we'd finished the Grouse and heard all about Beddoes' latest amorous exploits in Amsterdam, when he gave a loud belch and said, 'Well, it's the steaming pit for me, laddie. Got to get myself in shape for the next few days.'

Reminded him of our night life arrangement.

'I am,' he said yawning loudly, 'entirely at your disposal. You tell me what you want and I'll lay it on – within reason of course. Oh, by the way, I'd almost forgotten. What happened to those two lovely schoolgirls? I thought you might have asked them back this evening.'

I might have guessed Beddoes had a hand in it somewhere.

I said, 'Oh them. Was that your idea? Rather amusing, I thought. Where did you find them?'

He tapped the side of his nose. 'Oh, you know, laddie,' he said. 'Friends of friends, if you get my meaning. I trust they provided the full service. At those prices they should have given you a haircut and redecorated the sitting room.'

'Actually', I said, 'I thought one verse made the point more than adequately.'

Beddoes frowned. 'But they did come in and . . . er . . . everything, didn't they?'

'Certainly not,' I said. 'I was in the bath at the time and very late for work. I merely thanked them and sent them packing.'

Beddoes seemed appalled. He said, 'But they had strict instructions to give you a Valentine's Day greeting that you would remember till the day you die.'

Beddoes has an irritating tendency to talk in riddles when he's had a few drinks, and frankly I was in no mood to pursue the matter further.

I said, 'Well, whatever it was they were meant to do, the point was well made and much appreciated. Thank you for going to all that expense on my behalf.'

'You must be joking if you think I can afford that sort of thing on the salaries they pay us in Brussels,' he said. 'No, I told them to charge it to you at Barfords. I knew you'd have a decent expense account.'

Thursday

Finally collapsed into bed shortly before two, only to be woken a few minutes later by an insistent ringing on the front door bell. Answered it to find myself face to face with

79

a scraggy blonde with a marked Scottish accent, dressed from head to toe in red tartan, asking if Ralph was at home.

I replied, not very graciously I'm afraid, that it was true that he was a guest in my home and who should I say was asking for him?

She said that her name was Norma, that she was an air hostess, that she had met Beddoes on the flight over that evening, and that, on learning that she had problems over accommodation, he had given her my address and said that I'd be only too happy to offer her a bed.

At that moment, Beddoes appeared in the doorway of his room, dressed, as usual, in nothing but his towelling dressing gown. 'Oh good,' he said to Norma, putting an arm round her waist. 'I thought you might have lost the address.'

'No such luck,' she said, and smiled in a knowing sort of way.

Beddoes called out to me, 'Don't bother to stay up, laddie. I can manage on my own now.'

Turned into my own room, but could not resist a final crack. 'Don't mind me,' I said. 'Help yourself. I only live here.'

'Thanks,' said Beddoes, 'I already have.' And he held up a bottle of whisky I'd carefully concealed in the larder in case of emergency. With that the two of them disappeared into the bedroom.

I had forgotten how noisy Beddoes and his women can be when Sportsnighting is under way. Evidently Brussels has done nothing to dampen his ardour. *Au contraire.* I simply cannot imagine what he can possibly get up to that induces such a bedlam.

Am beginning to suspect he's the sort of man who uses a weasel enlarger. Also seriously considering introducing him to Ruth Macmichael. She'd take him down a peg or two and no mistake.

Morning post uninspiring except for a letter from Dickie Dunmow saying he couldn't quite understand what I was after but suggesting I come down to the school on Monday week and we can talk it over. Is it worth my while mugging up some Catullus between now and then, I ask myself? It might make all the difference.

On the way out to work called out to Beddoes and

reminded him we had some important business to complete.

'Haven't we all, laddie?' he called out.

Beddoes is like the flu. When you haven't got it, you can't for the life of you remember what all the fuss was about, and the moment you do, all you can think about is how soon it will go away again.

Arrived at office shortly after 9.30 to find Sue already at her desk, telephone at her ear and pencil poised over pad. Could not believe my eyes. When she'd finished I said, 'Well, this is a turn-up for the books. What are you up to? A little research of your own?'

'Actually,' she said, 'I was making an appointment at the hairdresser. Must fly.'

Once again compelled to open my own mail.

She arrived back just as I was leaving for lunch with Enid. I hardly recognized her. All the straggly rat-tails had completely disappeared, to be replaced by a neat gamin cut which makes her look about fifteen. I had never realized before what a pretty girl she can be when she tries. She has the most enormous eyes, a perfect complexion and excellent bone structure. Must admit was completely bowled over.

In matters of sex I have always maintained that one must let the heart rule the head. Women invariably respond to a man who catches them unawares and bowls them over, and when, on a mad impulse, I asked her to join me for a drink after work, I can't say I was all that surprised that she accepted.

Set off for The Boltons feeling more confident than I can remember for years. Enid as charming and poised as ever in navy blue. My exuberant high spirits obviously infectious. I have never seen her on better form.

We had a delicious hot prawn dish to start with, followed by saddle of lamb and syllabub, with a Niersteiner, a Château Talbot and brandy.

Although far from tight, I was certainly merry and told some excellent jokes of a slightly risqué nature which she was obviously too ladylike to laugh at out loud, but clearly relished in her own quiet way.

Though not normally a great tittle-tattler, could not resist giving her the lowdown on the famous Harold Hill affair. After all, it's not every day that chairmen of large companies like Barfords elope with one's secretary.

'Are you quite sure you should be telling me all this?' she asked.

'Oh why not?' I said. 'We're people of the world, and you're not going to tell me your husband hasn't been tempted to stray from the straight and narrow before now.'

Was congratulating myself on my deftness at drawing the conversation round to the question of adultery in general and hers in particular, and was surprised that she should appear so puzzled by my comment.

She said, 'I'm afraid I'm not quite with you.'

I winked and said, 'Well, you know . . . power being the most potent aphrodisiac and so on.'

Enid put down her glass. 'Are you saying that Derrick is unfaithful to me?' she asked.

It has always been a golden rule with me that once one has got into a thing one must have the courage of one's convictions and carry it through to the end with style and panache.

'All I'm saying,' I said, 'is that in an open marriage like yours – and I'm not saying anything against open marriages . . .'

She said, 'This is all gibberish to me. What's an open marriage in normal, everyday speech?'

I said, 'Sorry about the sociological jargon. What I mean is, you go your way, so I am presuming he goes his.'

'I don't know where you got this idea from,' she said. 'As far as I am aware, we are both going in approximately the same direction.'

Sorely tempted to get out notebook and jot down *aide memoire* re behaviour of people when caught out in adulterous situations, but did not wish to inhibit her in any way.

'Approximately,' I prompted. 'Except of course for theatre-going.'

'What is all this about?' she asked, suddenly rather cross.

Decided it was time to bring things to a head. 'Enid,' I said. 'I'm talking about adultery and you know it. I'm talking about the National Theatre and *The Romans in*

Britain and you and Gerald whatever-his-name-is.'

She burst into shrieks of laughter. 'Me?' she said. 'And Gerald? Are you mad? He's my brother.'

This may or may not have been a clever cover-up. At all events, decided not to pursue the matter further at this stage. Nor to ask after Amanda.

Back to the office in pensive mood to find a message from Beddoes asking me to ring him as soon as possible.

Rang the flat and got engaged signal. Knowing Beddoes of old, assumed he was still occupied with Norma and had taken phone off hook in order not to be disturbed, so thought no more about it. Repeated the process at approximately ten-minute intervals for the next hour with similar results. By now beginning to experience familiar signs of irritation with which Beddoes is so closely identified in my mind.

Finally, in a rage, rang exchange to explain that I was the Middlesex Hospital trying to contact a brain surgeon who had absent-mindedly left his phone off the hook and would they mind putting the screamer on, since this was something of an emergency.

The girl said she would just try the number herself and came back in a moment or two later with the news that 'the subscriber was in conversation'.

I said, 'In point of fact, *I* happen to be the subscriber. He is merely a guest in my house. Executives at the European Commission may not be familiar with telephone bills but we are.'

The girl said, 'I thought you said your friend's a brain surgeon.'

'He helps out part-time,' I said. 'Still, if you're not prepared to put yourself out to save lives, that's your decision.'

Finally got through. Beddoes as cool as a cucumber in the face of my fury. He said, 'What do you think I've been doing on the phone for the last couple of hours?'

I said, 'Ringing friends apparently.'

'Quite,' he said. 'Not perhaps friends in the sense that you'd understand the word, but they're certainly always very friendly to me whenever I ring up.'

'You don't mean prostitutes, do you?' I said.

'If you must put it so crudely,' he said, 'yes.'

I said, 'You did point out, I hope, that I only want to interview them? I think we can take the hanky-panky for granted.'

'*You* may be able to,' he said.

I decided the time had come to get a few things straight. I said, 'Now look here, Beddoes. I'm very grateful to you for your help in this matter, but I'm afraid I have a limited budget, and if you think I am going to be a party to your having a good time at Barfords' expense, I'm afraid you've got another think coming.'

Beddoes chuckled. 'We'll see, laddie,' he said. 'We'll see.'

We certainly shall.

Got into the lift at one point in the afternoon to find myself face to face with the spotty messenger and a couple of his cronies. Tried to pretend they weren't there, but their ill-disguised sniggers and obscene gestures final provoked me to speech.

I said, 'Were you a better behaved bunch, I'd have brought my friend, Fiona Richmond, down to the post room to meet you all.'

'Oh what a shame,' said Spotty, 'because I was going to introduce you to Raquel Welch.'

To the Horse's Neck Wine Bar for a drink with Sue at 5.30. For someone of only nineteen she really does have an excellent sense of humour. Could not resist a little gentle probing re her friendship with Bryant-Fenn.

'Who?' she said.

'Hugh,' I said. 'Hugh Bryant-Fenn. You know. Old Sex Pistol. Blue films in Ashford and all that.'

'Oh,' she said vaguely, 'I'd forgotten all about him. Isn't he a friend of yours or something?'

'Sort of,' I said. 'And yours, too, I thought.'

'Hardly,' she said. 'Poor old chap. He needs a psychiatrist, not a girlfriend. They're all the same, these middle-aged swingers. All talk and no action.'

I said, still feigning innocence, 'But I'd always understood him to be something of a ladies' man. He has a considerable reputation.'

'If he has,' she said, 'it's entirely in his own mind.' And to my delight she went on to describe how she, too, had fallen prey to his famous red book ploy.

She said, 'I can't see the point of all that slow build-up stuff myself. It nearly always means there's nothing at the end of it. I mean, if a bloke takes you back to his place for the obvious reason, either he wants to get on with it or he doesn't.'

It is not often a girl sets my heart racing these days, but talking to Sue, I could feel the years dropping away from me. It was as if I were twenty-one again.

I said, 'I couldn't agree more. I'm a man of action and few words myself, as you've probably realized. I think girls can pretty well reckon to know where they stand with me.'

Asked her if she was doing anything for dinner tomorrow night. She said that, by an odd coincidence, she and her flatmates were throwing a small party and why didn't I come? Evidently she doesn't think of *me* as being middleaged, and who can blame her?

I said that unfortunately I had a friend staying.

She said, 'Bring him too. We could do with some more men.'

Is it my imagination or did she place a little extra emphasis on the word 'men'?

Beddoes out again when I got home. He arrived back with Norma at about 10.30, made coffee, poured out the last remaining drops of my whisky and settled in front of the TV set.

I said, 'Actually I was rather hoping to have a look at the theatre awards. I've seen them every year now for seven years.'

Later, as he was on his way to bed with Norma, I asked him if by any chance he knew how one went about finding an orgy.

I might have been asking him to introduce me to the head of the Mafia from the look of pained disbelief that crossed his face. 'What do you take me for?' he said. 'A sex maniac?'

I don't know why I bother.

Friday

Time is running out and I am still no nearer finding an orgy. Am still convinced the chairman's secretary, Erica, knows more than she cares to admit, and decided the moment had come to put my theory to the test. To my surprise, got straight through to chairman who informed me rather sharply that Miss Thompson was out shopping. For what? one wondered. Kinky gear perhaps?

In order not to waste time, slipped out to see if I could track down any of these contact magazines in which, if Pratt is to be believed, people advertise their peculiar interests.

Had understood that publications of this nature freely available on newsagents' stands etc. Consequently had embarrassing conversation with newspaper seller near Piccadilly Circus underground station who got it into his head that I was a keen amateur electrician and kept trying to palm me off with magazines dealing with computers and electronics. In the end I'm afraid one or two heated words were exchanged. It was all quite unnecessary.

Eventually tried 'adult' magazine shop. Place strangely deserted except for one young man with Scottish accent standing at cash desk discussing the gay scene in London with shop manager.

Shelves well-stocked with the sort of publications I had in mind. Tried to look inside to make sure but all stuck together with sellotape. Picked out two anyway – *In Touch* and *Hallo*. £3.50 each.

Had just settled down with *Hallo* and sardine and tomato sandwich in office when Beddoes rang to say that his lunch date in the City had fallen through and would I care to stand in for his guest?

You don't live with somebody as long as I have lived with Beddoes to know something about their tastes in food, and his are lower than average. Have never myself subscribed to this craze for so-called fast-food, which the Americans will insist on forcing down our throats, and sitting about in some garishly lit plastic and formica establishment chewing soggy chips and tasteless rissoles out of a cardboard box is not my idea of a gastronomic treat. Thanked him therefore for the kind thought and told him that, with so much on hand, was having a working lunch.

'What a pity,' he said. 'You're always saying how much you'd like to eat at the Connaught. Never mind. Another time. See you later anyway. Shall we say six o'clock in the bar of the Mayfair?'

To coffee machine, only to discover something had gone wrong again with the selector mechanism, so that I ended up with a cup of hot water.

Have always been told that many more people advertise their charms and special interests than one might think, but had never realized it was done quite as blatantly as it is in this sort of publication. If the black and white snaps which accompany many of the ads are anything to go by, I can hardly believe that many of them produce a single reply. My age-old theory about sexiness being nearest to ugliness has never looked closer to holding water.

Might seriously consider following up one or two of the more colourful suggestions on offer if only one knew what one was letting oneself in for. It's the sort of world where, if you don't know what you're up to, it could all too easily end in tears.

By the same token, was not exactly over the moon at the prospect of the evening's entertainment. Whatever it was that Beddoes had laid on, I could only hope it would not involve dressing up in a PVC mac and having my bottom smacked.

A propos of which, suddenly realized to my horror that I had become so caught up in my research that I had completely forgotten to cash a cheque. Bank now closed, ditto cashiers. Would girls take American Express? The phrase 'That'll do nicely, sir' suddenly acquired a whole new meaning.

After quick wash and brush-up, set off shortly before six for the Mayfair.

Beddoes tried very hard to appear nonchalant, but any fool could see he was as excited as a schoolboy on his first outing to London.

I said, 'What were you thinking of doing about dinner?'

'Hadn't thought,' said Beddoes, swigging his vodka and tonic. 'I'm easy. A hamburger will do me fine. I couldn't face another heavy meal after the Connaught.'

'Who did you ask in the end?' I said.

'No one,' he said. 'I just ate for two.'

In the end, after more drinks and a bowl or two of peanuts, had completely lost appetite. At least Beddoes had the grace to offer to pay. Not that that did a lot towards alleviating the feeling of faint nausea that swept over me as we rumbled past Harrods. Matters not helped by Beddoes' particularly evil-smelling cheroot. I'm surprised the taxi driver didn't say something.

I remarked that we appeared to be heading away from the part of London traditionally associated in one's mind with ladies of the night. Beddoes merely laughed and said, 'Wait and see, laddie.'

Eventually we drew up outside a terraced house in a street off Redcliffe Square, of all the unlikely venues. While I paid off the taxi, Beddoes announced our arrival over the entryphone.

The taxi driver said to me under his breath, 'Ought to be ashamed of yourselves.'

When I asked him what he meant, he said, 'Don't blame me if your whatsit drops off,' and drove away up the street.

Was sorry not to be going with him.

We made our way up the broad, carpeted staircase to the third floor and paused for breath outside No. 5.

The door was opened by a comfortable-looking middle-aged woman in a blue patterned, frock. Her greying hair was done up in a rather elaborate style and a pair of spectacles hung by a cord round her neck.

'Mr Cripps?' she asked in a quiet, educated voice.

'Six out of ten,' said Beddoes. 'I'm Beddoes, he's Crisp. By name, though not always by nature.'

She did not seem to think that at all funny. 'My name's Mrs Archer,' she said. 'The girls are expecting you. At least, Debbie is. Vicky has just popped out for a minute. Come on through. May I take your coats?'

She chattered on about the weather, the traffic, the problems of getting taxis, the cost of things.

In the sitting room, a small, pale girl was curled up in one of the armchairs, embroidering. She looked like someone's secretary having a quiet evening in – so much so that I couldn't help wondering if we hadn't blundered into someone's home.

Mrs Archer said, 'Debbie, offer our guests a drink. Or perhaps you'd prefer tea or coffee?'

Wishing at all events to keep a clear head, I said that a cup of coffee would suit me very well.

'My friend leads a very sheltered life,' said Beddoes. 'Unlike me, I'm afraid.' He laughed loudly. 'A large whisky and soda for me if you please, with ice, but easy on the soda.'

Debbie said, 'It makes a change to meet someone who doesn't drink.' And she disappeared into the kitchen.

Though far from being my type, Debbie looked very much a girl who would understand the sort of thing I was after, so decided to make my position clear straight away.

Slipped out of the room, closing the door behind me. Hurried along passage and into kitchen where Debbie was laying up a tray with cups, sugar bowl, coffee pot, After Eight Mints, etc.

I said it was all very different from what I'd been expecting.

She said, 'Is this your first time?'

I replied with a laugh, 'First and last, I hope. I'm not your average client, you know.'

She said, 'Oh really?'

'Good Lord, no,' I said. 'I'm here for a very special reason. I expect Beddoes mentioned something about it on the phone.'

'No,' said Debbie. 'He didn't. What sort of special reason?'

I said, 'Oh it's really very straightforward. You're obviously an intelligent girl. I think you'll find you'll be able to give me everything I need.'

She said rather nervously, 'That depends. I don't go in for dressing up or S & M or anything like that.'

Clearly some sort of interpreter was called for. Luckily, at that moment Beddoes appeared in the doorway.

'Hallo, hallo,' he said suggestively. 'What are you two love-birds up to then? Happy families in the kitchen, is it?'

Seizing him by the arm, I manoeuvred him back into the sitting room. 'Someone's lines appear to have become crossed somewhere,' I said, and described the curious turn our apparently simple conversation had so abruptly taken.

Beddoes said, 'Leave it to me, laddie.'

A moment or two later, the two of them returned, giggling like a couple of naughty children.

'I think Debbie understands what you have in mind now,' said Beddoes, and they both giggled even harder. I couldn't see the joke myself.

Eventually Debbie pulled herself together sufficiently to pour me a cup of black coffee and offer me an After Eight.

'Would you like to watch some TV?' she said.

Naturally assumed that what she *really* meant was, did I want to watch one of the pornographic tapes which I've heard they keep handy in this sort of place to help nervous customers get more sexed up. I replied by way of an in-joke that in my view there was never very much to watch on telly on Friday nights.

Beddoes said that, in the continuing absence of Vicky, he wouldn't mind looking in for a while.

'Tape or live?' Debbie asked.

'Tape for me every time,' said Beddoes, 'I like to live dangerously.'

While she was selecting something suitable, I slipped next door for a quick wash and brush-up. Returned a couple of minutes later to find Debbie gone and Beddoes, with another large whisky and soda in one hand and a cheroot in the other, watching Sir Huw Weldon examining a large, elaborately carved piece of furniture.

I said, 'I never knew Huw Weldon went in for this sort of thing.'

'What sort of thing?' he said. 'This is *Royal Heritage*. Charles II and the later Stuarts. I missed this particular one the first time round. Look at that carving.'

By an odd coincidence, the Charles II programme had somehow eluded me too, and I had given up all hope of ever seeing it. However, had no sooner settled down with a second cup of coffee and another After Eight than Debbie stuck her head round the door and announced that she was ready if I was, and that Vicky was back.

Suggested to Beddoes that he watch something else for the time being and that we watch *Royal Heritage* together later.

He replied that there might not be a later and that he had always believed that, unless one seized the moment in this life, one invariably regretted it. 'I suggest you seize yours,' he said, 'and I'll seize mine.'

Marched purposefully towards the door and pulled it open to find myself face to face with our old flatmate Victoria. Was so astounded, all I could think of saying was, 'What in the world are you doing here?'

She replied coolly, 'I might ask you the same thing.'

I said, 'I'm researching.'

'I might have guessed it,' she said. 'Well, I work here.'

Assumed at first that this was all an elaborate plot dreamed up by Beddoes, but obviously he was as taken aback as I was.

She told us that things hadn't worked out between her and Mike Pritchard, thanks largely to the very attack of alopecia that had sent Victoria rushing from my side to his last spring.

'It was like Samson and Delilah,' she said. 'With his hair went his strength, if you see what I mean. In the end he became so depressed he went back to Babs and the children. He's a producer with local radio somewhere in the north. The kids call him Radio Savalas.'

I said that was all very unfortunate but that still did not explain how she came to be doing what she was.

'It happens,' she said. 'Actually, for the first time in my life I've found my true métier.'

I said, 'But I thought your great aim in life was putting the world to rights.'

'It still is,' she said. 'Only now I tackle the problems in a more personal way. How can man hope to be free until he throws off his sexual shackles? I see myself as the first truly left-wing sex therapist. It's extremely satisfying, I can tell you. For all concerned.'

Beddoes, who has to make a joke of everything, said, 'Funnily enough, I've been suffering from a rather embarrassing complaint myself recently.' And he put his arm suggestively round Victoria's waist. 'Your place or yours?' he said, leering horribly.

Victoria extracted herself neatly from his fumbling embrace. 'I'm sorry,' she said, suddenly serious. 'I couldn't possibly go with either of you. It would be quite out of the question.'

Beddoes said, 'You're joking. Not even for old time's sake?'

'Especially not for that,' she said.

I said, 'I suggest that in the circumstances we call it a day. It's all been most interesting and I think I've certainly got enough to be getting on with.'

Beddoes said, 'You may have. I certainly haven't.'

I said, 'The trouble with you, Beddoes, is that you never know where to draw the line. Now then, how much do we owe you girls for your time?'

Beddoes continued to complain in a facetious way, but the girls' attention was by now firmly fixed on the question of money.

Debbie said, 'That's up to you.'

I said, 'Would twenty cover it?'

'Twenty each?' said Victoria.

'Good heavens no,' I said. 'Between you. I'm not made of money.'

'You must be joking,' she said.

'How much then?' I said.

She said, 'Most punters wouldn't expect to get out under a hundred.'

Felt myself go quite weak at the knees. I said, 'But we didn't actually, you know . . .'

She said, 'That was your choice, not ours.'

I said that I would have thought that chatting was a good deal less wearing and should therefore be charged at a considerably lower rate.

Victoria said, 'It may be less wearing for you, but as far as we're concerned, it's merely another way of taking advantage of our experience and, if anything, it takes longer.'

Beddoes said, 'In that case, I'm certainly going to have my money's worth.' And before I could stop him he had grabbed the unfortunate Debbie and marched off down the passage with her.

I said to Victoria, 'I expect you're used to this sort of behaviour.'

She said, 'All punters are the same, and as far as I'm concerned, Beddoes is just another punter.'

I said, 'That hardly sounds like the tart with the heart of gold.'

'Can't afford to be,' she said. 'I've got a living to make.'

I said, 'I know what you mean. I could never really be a punter.'

She said, 'Either you are or you aren't. Some people are doers; you just like talking about it. You were always like that in the flat and you haven't changed.'

I wasn't about to have her taking a high moral tone with me. I said, 'I happen to be doing my job. I suppose that next you'll be trying to tell me the Deputy Managing Director of Barfords is a secret voyeur.'

'Keith Hardacre?' she said. 'I know bloody well he is. He's one of my oldest clients.'

For only the second time in my life, rendered utterly speechless. Unfortunately, before I could recover sufficiently to press Victoria for further information, Beddoes came marching along the passage, very red in the face, pulling on his jacket, and pursued by an anxious-looking Debbie.

'This is the last time I do you a favour,' he shouted.

When I asked him what on earth he was talking about, all he would say was, 'Ask her.' And he pointed at Debbie.

'It's no good,' she said, her eyes brimming with tears. 'I can't manage with people I fancy.'

'Excuses, excuses,' muttered Beddoes.

I said, 'But you ought to be flattered.'

'Flattered?' he shouted. 'Who needs flattery? I can get that any day of the week for nothing.' And still shouting, he marched out of the front door.

Decided the only way to defuse the situation was to pay up as quickly as possible and leave. Unfortunately, American Express card not received quite as graciously as in the TV ads. I had a good mind to tell Hardacre to settle up the next time he was round, but in the end the girls settled for a personal cheque.

I said to Victoria, 'See you again one of these days perhaps.'

'I doubt it,' she said.

So do I somehow. Business and pleasure make uneasy bedfellows.

Beddoes silent and bad-tempered all the way home in the taxi. I should have thought if anyone had a grudge to bear, it was me against him.

Still, it shouldn't be too difficult to get my £200 refunded, knowing what I now do about Keith Hardacre's extra-curricular activities. But the trousers, though old, are irreplaceable.

Saturday

An anxious afternoon of indecision while Beddoes tried to make up his mind whether or not to visit parents in Gravesend.

Unfortunately, made cardinal error of letting slip about Sue's party, and from then on there was no getting rid of him. Nor of making any useful progress re putting my notes in coherent shape.

In the end, felt duty bound to ring Sue and explain dilemma. Painted Beddoes in worst light possible.

'He sounds fun,' she said. 'Bring him along.'

I pointed out that he would almost certainly behave badly.

'That's what parties are for, isn't it?' she said.

For some, perhaps. The moment we arrived I knew I had made a terrible mistake. Music too loud, people too young, food too unpalatable, drink too undrinkable, Sue too taken up with her chums even to look at me.

Decided the only solution was to use the event as the basis for my Sex Among Flatsharers section, and wandered about, notebook and pencil in hand, observing.

Beddoes clearly in his element, since every time I saw him he was on his way into or out of one of the bedrooms and each time with a different girl.

For some reason was reminded of an incident that occurred in a flat I once shared in the sixties. Was smiling fondly at the memory of those far-off golden days when I was aware of a girl standing looking at me and saying something. 'What?' I said.

She said, 'I said a penny for them.'

I smiled and shook my head. 'You wouldn't understand.'

'Try me,' she said.

She had such a pretty smile that I did as she asked. She listened most attentively and when I got to the bit about the sheets, she said, 'Is that it?'

I said, 'I told you you wouldn't understand. I don't suppose you've heard of Profumo either, or Christine Keeler, or the Cuban missile crisis, or Freddie and the Dreamers.'

She said, 'I remember my parents talking about someone

called Christine Keeler. Wasn't she a famous tennis player?'

It was like talking to Amanda Trubshawe all over again. Of course, I should have recognized the warning lights straight away and left at once, but was so delighted at finding a captive subject at last, my only thought was to get her into a quiet corner and pump her for information.

I said, 'Is there a quiet room where we could go?'

Unhappily, she got quite the wrong end of the stick and before I knew what, I was grappling with her amongst a pile of coats on a mattress on the spare room floor.

'I hope you don't mind,' she panted. 'I'm a very physical person.'

I said that I was pretty robust myself – under normal circumstances.

'You can't get circumstances more normal than these,' she muttered, and rolled onto her back, pulling me hard on top of her. As she did so, my notebook and pencil fell out of my hand and disappeared among the coats. Anxious to recover them at once before they became lost for ever, I leaned over and scrabbled around with my left hand.

At that moment, my neck went.

'That's it,' I said. 'My neck's gone stiff.'

'It's the only thing that has,' said the girl.

She stood up. 'My mother was right,' she said. 'You're all the same, you middle-aged guys. Tired in the evening, hungry in the daytime and randy in the morning.'

And with that she left the room, slamming the door and leaving me in the dark, searching for my precious notes.

Located them but not Beddoes. Left him to get on with it and drove home. Very slowly.

Sunday

A wretched night. Neck so bad, unable to move an inch without great pain. So terrified Beddoes might come back at any minute and ring the front door bell, that didn't get a wink all night.

Spent morning with papers. Neck slightly easier after bout of self-manipulation in bath.

Even so, did not wish to risk muscle spasm with large movements of the arms, etc., so for the first time for years bought *Mirror* and *People* instead of usual heavies. And thank heavens I did. For what should I come across but a fascinating exposé of the fast-growing British craze for striptease? It seems that while audiences have been declining in Soho, due to the high prices, elsewhere in Britain, in pubs, at cricket and rugger club dinners, stag nights, even business conferences, a striptease act is now considered very much an accepted part of the proceedings.

Feel this is definitely something that needs investigating. I have been concentrating far too heavily on London and the Home Counties, and a brief visit to the provinces can only help to add an extra dimension to my study. By a lucky coincidence, am due to go to Manchester with Pratt on Wednesday to give a talk to our northern salesmen about my New York trip and the Kellerman contract.

Must try to arrange for us to take in a Mancunian strip club or two while we are there. Pratt will probably be only too delighted and we can put it on his expenses.

Speaking of which, have at last itemized my exes to date:

	£
Adult films	9.00
Theatres	9.50
Magazines	8.00
Sex shop goods	15.00
Time Out advertisement	14.90
Lunches with various experts	80.00
Taxis/transport	30.00
Refreshments (sundry)	25.00
Sundry expenses incurred during interviews/research etc.	250.00
	441.40

I do not believe anyone could complain about that. Sex is an expensive business these days, as Hardacre should know!

Beddoes finally deigned to roll in just after lunch, looking far too pleased with himself for my liking.

'What happened to you?' he said. He indicated my surgical collar. 'Trying out a few new positions, were you?'

'Only one,' I said. 'It's called lowering oneself to other people's level.'

He said, 'You have a positive talent for leaving at just the wrong moment.'

'Some of us,' I said, 'can tell the difference between right and wrong.'

He went on, 'You go round for weeks searching in vain for an orgy, and yet you can't see one when it comes up and hits you between the eyes.'

Apparently things did get out of hand last night, as I thought they might; marks were overstepped and lines not drawn.

Beddoes elaborated, 'It wasn't until that boyfriend of Sue's appeared that things really started to warm up.'

'Boyfriend?' I said.

'Chappie she works for in your office,' Beddoes said. 'Begins with a T, I think.'

'Pratt?' I said.

'I thought so,' said Beddoes. 'But what imagination!'

I doubt if I have ever felt more wretched than I did at that moment.

Beddoes said, 'Cheer up. It may never happen.' Then he added with a laugh, 'It hasn't so far anyway.'

I said, 'I thought you were going to Gravesend.'

He looked at his watch. 'It hardly seems worth it now,' he said.

I said, 'In that case, I wonder if you'd mind awfully going back to Belgium.'

'My flight's not till ten,' he said.

I said, 'You've managed to occupy yourself perfectly well so far today; I'm sure you'll be able to think up something equally amusing for the remaining few hours of your stay. Goodbye, and I suggest that next time you fancy a weekend in London, you book into a hotel. That's obviously where you think you've been for the last few days.'

At that, I rose and left the room in dignified silence, but caught the pocket of my sports jacket on the door handle as I did so, giving it a slight tear.

Went to my room, closed the door firmly behind me and locked it.

Heard Beddoes pottering about uncertainly for a few minutes. He then went into his room, pottered about some more and then came along the passage. He paused outside my door. 'I'll be off then, laddie,' he said. 'See you anon when you're in a better mood. You probably need a few early nights. And a bottle or two of Sanatogen. Money's on the table.'

The moment the front door had closed, hurried back into the sitting room, catching my other pocket as I did so, and there on the table, propped up against the vase of dried flowers, was an envelope with my name on it. Inside were five twenty-pound notes. Have not as yet made up my mind whether to keep them.

Took a couple of Veganin and spent the rest of the afternoon in bed, trying not to think about anything or anybody.

Got up at seven, bathed, got into my pyjamas and dressing gown, and was just settling down in front of the TV with a plate of scrambled eggs and Penelope Keith when the phone went.

It was Vanessa Pedalow in floods of tears, saying that Tim had left her again, this time for good, and could she see me.

Must admit that, amused as I generally am by the Pedalows, my heart sank. Guessed it would take her at least half an hour to get to me, so that at least I wouldn't have to miss Penelope and the detective series. I said, 'See you here in about half an hour then.'

She said, 'Tim's taken the BMW and the Mini's on the blink. I'll never get a taxi round here at this time on a Sunday evening. You couldn't possibly be an angel and come and fetch me, could you?'

Wouldn't have minded turning out quite so much if I had been able to move my head while driving. Vanessa, however, so taken up with her own tale of woes, she did not appear to notice anything amiss, despite several heavy hints.

Barely had we got into the flat than she said, 'Something smells delicious.'

I said it was only scrambled eggs on toast.

'Only!' she exclaimed. 'I'd give my right arm for a plate of eggs – scrambled, poached, anything.'

I said, 'I think there's only one left.'

I was going to add that I was keeping it for breakfast, but before I could get the words out, she said, 'I don't mind.

I'm not greedy. It's just that, what with one thing and another, I haven't eaten all day.'

When she had polished off my last egg, my last two slices of bread and my last drop of milk, she launched into a long and involved account of Tim's latest sexual escapade. It appeared to involve the wife of his oldest friend and represented, according to Vanessa, the end of the line as far as she and Tim were concerned.

'Goodness knows what he sees in her,' she said.

Never having clapped eyes on the lady in question but keen to help, I made a few stabs in the dark.

'Perhaps,' I said, 'he's going through an early middle-age crisis and she seems to represent something in his life which he feels, quite wrongly I'm sure, that you cannot provide.'

'Such as?' she said, rather snappily.

'I've no idea,' I said. 'Perhaps she just feels sorry for him. Or vice versa.'

'Balls,' said Vanessa. 'She's got big boobs, that's all.'

'Aha,' I said. 'So you think sex is at the bottom of it?'

'Isn't it always?' she said.

I said, 'But I thought you had both taken up this new celibacy thing one hears is sweeping across the western world.'

Vanessa said, 'It's certainly swept through our little corner of it, I can tell you. Mainly since Tim took up with this stupid girl.'

'But I'd always thought you two enjoyed a full and active sex life,' I said.

She said, 'It depends on what you call full and active. I'm always reading articles in the newspapers that talk about couples making love two and a half times a week on average. I'm jolly grateful if we manage it once every three months.'

If what Vanessa had told me was a true representation of the sex life of the average thirty-five to forty-year-old professional married couple, then I was on to something which, if published, could set the whole world of sociology by the ears and rock the very foundations of middle-class life in Britain today.

I said to her, 'Would you be prepared to give me a long, searching interview on the subject?'

She said, 'The way I'm feeling right now, I'd be prepared to have an affair with you.'

I laughed and said, 'No, seriously, Vanessa, would you?'

'Have an affair with you?' she said. 'Why not? Why should I be the one to miss out on all the fun?'

Having never been on the receiving end of a proposition of this kind from a married woman before, was not quite sure how to react. I must admit I have always secretly had a soft spot for Vanessa. She is a little tall for my liking and her manner can be rather on the sharp side, but in many ways she is very much my type.

I told her that I was as familiar with the way the world wagged as the next man, but that I was not used to going in for this sort of thing in quite such a matter-of-fact sort of way.

'Me neither,' she said. 'But frankly I'm sick to death of all this open-mindedness and mutual understanding that goes with modern adultery. One's natural reaction is not to go rushing straight home and confess all, but to carry on sneakily behind the other one's back and hope they never find out. That's what gives the whole thing its spice. Elaborate plans, elaborate excuses, coded telephone calls, cheap hotel rooms, Mr and Mrs Smith, dark glasses, slouch hats: adultery as it always used to be and as it should be. That's what I'm in the mood for right now. If you don't fancy it, you only have to say so.'

I said, 'Well, if you think it'll be all right. Where did you have in mind? Here? Now?'

'Good Lord, no,' she said. 'It's got to be somewhere with a warm, cosy atmosphere. This place is about as sexy as a Borstal.'

She went on to explain that she had some friends with a flat in Mayfair, just off Curzon Street. They were away in California at the moment and had left her the key and asked her to look after it for them. She said that it was the perfect setting for an affair – nice and central, well-heated and furnished, and the chances of running into Tim in that area were remote.

She added, 'I always think these things go better on neutral ground, don't you?'

I've no idea. All I know is that somehow or other I have

agreed to spend the night with her there on Tuesday.

Sorry to have missed Penelope Keith.

Monday, 19 February

A restless night, filled with erotic dreams involving Jane, of all people. In one, we were in an enormous penthouse suite on top of the Dorchester Hotel, about to get busy on a centrally heated circular bed when Tim appeared in the room, disguised as a waiter, and broke my neck.

Woke up in even greater agony than last night.

Great excitement at breakfast. The Thruster has arrived at last. It is rather like a solid cricket box which you simply tie inside your underpants and 'wait for the incredible reactions which are sure to follow'.

Decided not to wear it to work. All my trousers are really too loose-fitting for the effect to be fully appreciated.

However, took it with me in briefcase and en route slipped into boutique and bought myself tightest pair of corduroy trousers I could get into. Slightly alarmed to note that right thigh soon went quite numb, but assistant said that was normal with people with 34-inch waists who try to squeeze into 32-inch trousers and that, as soon as the waist-band had begun to stretch, the circulation would quickly return. He also suggested I give up underpants in favour of briefs.

To gents immediately on arrival in office to insert Thruster. Am quite relieved I am not better equipped in biological sense.

Had not realized lump would be quite so prominent. However, there's no doubt it gives one a certain *je ne sais quoi*, and I found myself walking along corridor with a decidedly jaunty gait, even though to and fro movements of legs rather more constricted than usual.

Passed several secretaries on the way and made a point of stopping and chatting to them about this and that. I think they must have been so nervous at being spoken to by an executive of my level that they never even noticed.

Strode into office feeling like Clint Eastwood. Sue already at desk and on phone – to Pratt no doubt, mulling over happy memories of Saturday night. Gave her a cold stare and marched through to inner sanctum.

Unfortunately, unable to sit down without extreme discomfort, so perched nonchalantly on edge of desk and waited. By the time Sue eventually appeared, bottom as sore as everything else.

Dictated a few letters etc., but made no reference to Saturday night's activities, nor to Thruster. Nor, I'm sorry to say, did she. She is going on the principle, presumably, that silence implies innocence.

I wasn't having any of that, and announced in a loud voice that I was just going to the third floor to see Pratt. I pronounced his name with special emphasis.

'Right,' she said, and didn't even look up.

Strolled up and down various corridors for several minutes but unable to provoke the slightest reaction from anyone. Perhaps people take it for granted that this is the natural result of wearing very tight-fitting trousers. Like ballet dancers in their tights.

Arrived back at office to be told by Sue that I had a visitor. Went through to find the chairman's secretary, Erica, sitting in my swivel chair, thumbing through one of my contact magazines.

She said gaily, 'I hope you don't mind. I was looking for a piece of paper to write you a note, opened the first drawer to hand and found these. I would never have guessed this was your sort of thing.'

I said, 'It isn't actually,' and went on to explain what I was up to.

She said, 'Why didn't you come and ask me? I could have told you all you need to know.'

Was so relieved I burst out laughing. 'That's wonderful,' I said. 'When can I come and talk to you?'

She said, 'Any time you like. I'm just off skiing in America for three weeks. They say people really swing in those Rockies resorts. Shall we say about mid-March?'

As she was leaving, she turned and said, 'There's something different about you. Don't tell me.' She stared at me for a moment, then said, 'I know what it is. You've got fatter.'

I suppose she is the expert on swapping etc. she claims to be – though a girl who can seriously put a large weasel down to overeating cannot altogether be trusted to know what's what.

Passed several more people on way to coffee machine and back but still no reaction. Decided the time had come to bring things to a head. Marched up to Sue's desk and asked her straight out if there was anything about me she'd noticed.

She said, 'Your trousers are two sizes too small. A man in your position ought to be able to afford properly cut clothes.'

'Anything else?' I said.

She looked me up and down. 'Not really,' she said. 'Apart from whatever it is you've pushed inside your flies.'

To Harley Preston after lunch, in Thruster, for meeting about Manchester Regional Sales Conference.

Ruth looking softer and more feminine than I have ever seen her. She must be in love. Decided this was as good a moment as any to bury the hatchet, and began by giving her one of my beaming smiles.

'May I say,' I said, 'how very pretty you're looking today, Miss Macmichael?'

'Never mind all that,' she said. 'I met a friend of yours on Friday. Name of Ralph Beddoes. He doesn't hang about, does he?'

I said, 'Don't tell me you actually fell for that brutish English male-chauvinist charm?'

'There are,' she said, 'male chauvinists and male chauvinists. Naturally, I could never consider any serious long-term relationship with a man like that, but for a one off I've got no complaints. Sex in the afternoon has a charm all of its own.'

I don't think I've ever seen her looking quite so excited about anything.

I said, rather pointedly, 'Well, as long as you enjoyed yourselves, that's the main thing, isn't it?'

'We certainly did,' she said. 'My God, your apartment's uncomfortable though.'

The meeting went extraordinarily smoothly considering, and everyone seemed to think my speech fitted the bill very nicely. Even Ruth had only two criticisms to make – both levelled, as usual, against my use of humour.

As I sat down afterwards, felt something give in my waistband, but assumed this to be part of stretching process and thought no more about it.

103

Later, we came to the section dealing with the presentation of sales charts.

A very odd thing happened. Was on the point of running through them for third time, when suddenly Roundtree came across carrying a chair and asked if I'd prefer to sit down. I said that I was perfectly happy standing.

'Are you sure?' he said.

'Perfectly thank you, Roundtree,' I said.

Afterwards, he came up to me, I thought to congratulate me. Instead, he took me to one side and asked if I was sure I was up to the presentation.

I said, 'Why? Are the figures still confusing?'

'No, no,' he said. 'Physically I mean. That leg of yours. It looks so painful. Water on the knee, is it?'

I looked down to discover that my knee had indeed swelled horribly. In panic, seized it in both hands and suddenly realized that what I was holding was the Thruster. Thank heaven for tight trousers, otherwise it might have slipped right down to the floor.

I straightened up, looked Roundtree firmly in the eye and said in a loud voice, 'It's kind of you to ask, Roundtree, but it's nothing. An old skiing accident. Lauberhorn actually. Years ago now, but it can blow up in the cold weather. I've got used to it, I hardly ever notice it.'

And limping slightly, I left the room.

Tuesday

Woke early with sinking feeling in pit of stomach. For a moment or two could not think why, then suddenly remembered today was the day I was due to start my affair with Vanessa Pedalow.

At all events, it's bound to be interesting, and I'm still very short of stuff for my adultery section.

After breakfast, packed a small overnight bag. Toothbrush, shaving tackle, flannel, brush and comb etc. a must, of course, but would one be able to use these people's towels? And how about dressing gown and slippers in case one wanted to sit about and chat over a drink during a refreshment break? And pyjamas? Have tried on occasions sleeping in the nude, but it has never been a great success, owing to the fact that I spend all night dreaming I am wandering around the streets without any clothes on and wake up feeling exhausted. Also, one never knows how well off people are for blankets. In the end, settled for a neat compromise by slipping in a T-shirt, just in case. I read somewhere that they're rather a turn-on for certain types of girls.

My biggest headache, though, (or should I say neck-ache?) is my soft collar. My neck, though definitely improving, is by no means 100 per cent and, if I don't wear my collar at night, I could undo all the good work to date. A difficult decision, but on balance would prefer to lose Vanessa than another cervical disc.

My attention so taken up with tonight's adventure that was scarcely able to concentrate on anything else all day.

I'm afraid that, when Bryant-Fenn rang this morning to say when were we having our lunch, I gave him very short change indeed. Have agreed to meet him at 1.15 tomorrow at this new French place in Covent Garden everyone keeps banging on about.

Pratt called in on the pretence of wanting to check some last-minute figures for Friday, but I'm too old a campaigner to be taken in by that sort of ploy. As he was leaving, I said, in a loud voice, 'How's your love life these days, Neville?' Of course he pretended innocence. He must take me for a bloody fool.

Could not resist a little dig at Sue as I was leaving. 'Enjoyed the do the other night,' I said casually. 'Sorry I had to leave early. Had to be up early in the morning. Pressure of work, you know.'

She said, 'Yes, I'm sorry we didn't have a chance to chat. You know what it's like at one's own party. Pity you couldn't have stayed a few more minutes. Things really livened up.'

'So I heard,' I said, raised my eyebrows suggestively, and left.

Met Vanessa in small Italian restaurant near Grosvenor Square, as arranged. Amused to note she was wearing sunglasses, even though lighting in restaurant very subdued.

I said, 'I like your disguise.'

She said, 'Actually, I've got pinkeye and it's extremely painful.'

Somehow struggled through a plate of saltimbocca, half a carafe of red wine and some desultory conversation, but my eye more on door than on table. I've known Vanessa to be better company, too.

Finally, paid our bill, sneaked out into street, and began to walk down South Audley Street. I do not think I have felt less like having an affair in my life.

'Isn't this fun?' I said.

'No,' she said.

Blocks of flats newer and smarter than I had imagined – just behind Hilton. I don't think anyone saw us going in. Anyway, it's always difficult to recognize someone when he has an overcoat over his head.

Hurried into lift. Vanessa pressed one of the buttons and soon we were standing in thick pile carpet outside solid-looking pine door. I do not believe I have ever seen quite so many locks and anti-burglar devices in my life.

Flat small, neat and furnished in a mixture of modern and traditional styles. Procter prints, drink bottles in antique baby's cradle, etc. It was like walking into a *Sunday Times Colour Magazine*.

Went to kiss Vanessa who said, 'I'm convinced that at any moment the front door is going to open and Bill and Lucy are going to walk in.'

I said, 'But I thought you said they were in California.'

'They are,' she said, 'but what guarantee's that?'

I said, 'Why don't we lock all the doors and set the burglar alarm, and then if Bill and Lucy do come back unexpectedly, we'll have time to get up and get dressed while they're unravelling it all.'

Quickly undressed and put on T-shirt, dressing gown and slippers, and cleaned teeth. Came back into sitting room just as Vanessa was putting last touches to burglar alarm.

We were halfway through *News at Ten* and our whisky and sodas when she remembered she'd left all her night creams in a vanity case in the boot of the car.

I said I'd go and went to unlock front door, but without success. Vanessa became rather irritable at this and launched into a long attack on men's inability to do anything when it was really needed. Delighted, therefore, when she, too, unable to crack locks.

Slightly less delighted when, after half an hour's combined struggling, it became clear that we were going to have to ring for the porter.

In our anxiety to escape, it had slipped our minds that we were both moderately déshabillés, with the result that the porter arrived to find us still struggling into our day clothes and we had to buy his silence with a tenner. Since I was now out of pocket completely, Vanessa compelled to drive me home in the Mini. I asked if she'd like to carry on where we'd left off in my flat, but she said that enough was quite enough for one day – perhaps another time.

To judge from this evening's events, adultery not quite all it's cracked up to be. On the other hand, we had probably got to know each other better through adversity than we would have done through straightforward Coleman, and actually my neck is really not yet up to coping with unknown pillows.

To bed in cheerful mood.

Wednesday

As I travelled in to work this morning, could not help looking about me at my fellow passengers and wondering how many of them had ever tried adultery and, if so, whether they had had better luck with it than I had. Cannot say that many of them looked the type. But then, who does?

Just as one cannot imagine one's parents getting down to a spot of uninhibited hanky-panky, so one cannot really believe that most people one sees have ever entertained a rude thought or indulged in saucy behaviour in their lives.

Of course, there are always exceptions, one of them being Sue. Am still haunted by a mental image of her, Pratt and Beddoes rolling around among the coats in the spare room in her flat. Cannot make up my mind whether I am more or less keen on her as a result. All I do know is that her presence in the outer office is extremely disturbing. For two pins would suggest having her removed to another part of the building were it not for the fact that, with less than a week to go, she still hasn't begun typing up the report.

As soon as I arrived this morning, therefore, suggested

she make a start on the sex film section. Have told her there's plenty more where that came from.

Is it my imagination, or has a new note of respect crept into her voice? Perhaps I should have brought her to heel a long time ago.

Sent off my expenses to Hardacre with a covering memo.

Memo: Private and Confidential

From: Simon Crisp
To: Keith Hardacre   21 February

Herewith my expenses, as discussed. I think you'll agree they're modest enough.

When one is asked to deal with a subject as wide-ranging as this, one is bound to run up against the odd snag. If I am to do full justice to this survey, and thus to Barfords' public image, I shall need to extend the deadline by a few days, especially since I have had to take time off for this Manchester presentation.

I feel sure you will agree.

Vicky sends her love. Need I say more?

S.C.

Met Bryant-Fenn at 1.15 as agreed. Restaurant done up in style of old-fashioned French brasserie. Hugh just polishing off large *pastis* as I arrived.

He said, 'This couldn't suit me better. I've been meaning to write the place up for my column for weeks. Trouble is, I've been rather overspending on my budget recently, so your invitation came like a lifeboat to a drowning man.'

About to point out that he had invited himself, but when you're in the position of having to get a lot of information out of someone in a very short space of time, you take care not to rock the boat.

Cannot imagine that the readers of *Bedroom* magazine rate high among the world's gastronomes, but that did not deter Bryant-Fenn from ordering the most expensive things on the menu. My onion soup, though at £1.80 it undoubtedly helped to counterbalance his smoked salmon stuffed with lobster at £4.50, tasted every bit as uninspiring as it looked.

108

Hugh said, 'This smoked salmon is out of this world. Your soup looks dull.'

I said, 'It is rather. Perhaps I could have a taste of yours?'

'If there's one thing I can't bear in restaurants,' he said, 'it's people who choose badly and then try to compensate by picking at others' food.'

Was not about to make the same mistake twice, so announced that I wished to change my tournedos for something rather more exotic.

Hugh said, 'Why not try the calves' brains? It would help me if you had something typically French. I think you'll find it rather amusing and it'll go very well with this excellent Bordeaux.'

I do not believe I have ever had a more unappetizing plate of food placed before me in my life. Calves' brains are certainly no joke to my way of thinking.

'Anything the matter?' said Hugh, tucking into his *filet de boeuf*.

I said, 'Actually, I've rather lost my appetite.'

'You know why, don't you?' he said. 'You shouldn't have had that onion soup. It's far too filling.' And he launched into a long boring monologue about proteins and carbohydrates and polyunsaturates.

Tried on several occasions to bend the conversation to figures and thence to girlie magazines, but without success.

Finally, over the cognac and coffee, I said that, to judge from the letters I have been reading in *Bedroom* and similar publications, his readers had appetites of a quite different kind.

'Really?' said Hugh. 'I wouldn't know about that. I only ever read my own columns.'

I said, 'But what about your competitors? *Penthouse, Men Only, Whitehouse* and so on.'

Hugh said, 'I've no idea. I never look at them.'

I said, 'But I thought you told me you were an expert on this sort of thing?'

'Did I?' he said. 'I can't think why. Perhaps it was a joke.'

I replied that our lunch certainly hadn't been a joke.

He said, 'I quite agree. They run a pretty serious kitchen here. I'm so glad you brought me. It saved my life. Must dash. May I leave you to deal with *l'addition*?' And without so much as an apology he stood up and walked out of the door.

L'addition came to just under £50!

Rang Vanessa as soon as I got back to the office to explain that I had had second thoughts re our affair, but somehow or other I seem to have agreed to try again, same time, same place tomorrow night.

Does too much sex soften the brain, I ask myself?

Thursday

Bryant-Fenn rang this morning. Assumed it was to apologize for not keeping his side of the bargain in the matter of the lunch, but, as usual, I overestimated his finer feelings.

He said, 'The thing is, as you may know, I've recently started handling the public relations for Dorothy.'

'Who's she?' I said. 'A pop singer?'

Hugh tutted irritably. 'Dorothy,' he said. 'You know, the new niterie in Kensington High Street. Bianca Jagger and all that. I was wondering if you'd be interested in coming along one evening and having a look – on the house. Come Saturday; there should be some big names about. Bianca mentioned something about looking in. You could talk to her. I'll be there. Shall we say about ten, in the bar? Bring someone if you want.' And he rang off.

I may take him up on his offer or I may not. Have always been rather curious to see what goes on in these places and, knowing the sort of prices they charge for membership, it's unlikely that the opportunity will occur again in the near future. Oddly enough, have always been rather keen on Bianca. If I do go, shall almost certainly not take a companion.

A memo arrived from Hardacre this afternoon.

Memo

From: Keith Hardacre
To: Simon Crisp   22 February

Subject: *Sex Report*

I disagree. Your expenses are far higher than I'd hoped or

110

expected. It is really necessary to go *everywhere* by taxi? As for the £200, said to cover 'sundry expenses', I couldn't possibly sanction this without some sort of breakdown.

Re completion date. I'm afraid I cannot allow any extension on this.

Good luck with the Manchester presentation, and please return my love to Vicky next time you see her.

KH

The older I become, the more convinced I am that I am not made for the cut and thrust of big business. Or for blackmail apparently.

Vanessa rang to say that her Mini had conked out again and could I pick her up from the San Frediano at 10.30.

Washed a few smalls, hoovered right through, packed a small holdall with shaving tackle, notes for speech, etc, and arrived at San Fred to find her standing just inside doorway, looking decidedly cross.

She said, 'You took your time.'

Pointed out that, according to my watch, it was exactly 10.30.

She said, 'You do take life literally.'

That may or may not be so, but I do object to being treated like a husband before I have even become a lover.

As we drove up the Brompton Road, she snuggled up against my arm and said in a lovey-dovey voice, 'Don't you want to know who I've been having dinner with?'

'Not specially,' I said.

'Of course you do,' she said. 'Well, if you must know, it was Tim.'

I nearly drove off the road.

'It's all right,' she said. 'I told him I was having an affair, but didn't mention your name.'

Am not sure whether to take this as a compliment or not.

Since I would be away the whole of the next day, decided to put the car in a garage and be done with it.

Vanessa said she would go on up to the flat with the luggage and pour drinks, etc. Suddenly realized I did not actually know flat number.

Neither, for some reason, did she. However, agreed that

111

she should take things up and then come down again and meet me in the lobby.

Car park slightly further away than I'd imagined. Got back to find her peering out through plate glass front doors.

She said, 'I was beginning to think you'd got cold feet.'

I laughed reassuringly and, in the lift going up, kissed her properly for the first time.

'This is more like it,' she said, and we kissed again. Confidence certainly breeds confidence.

Arrived at fourth floor to find flat door closed. 'Hallo,' I quipped. 'Is this symbolic?'

'No,' she said. 'It's bloody disastrous. I've left the keys inside.'

Pointed out that it was hardly the end of the world, since the porter obviously had a spare set.

We tried several doorbells without success and finally struck lucky on the ground floor in the shape of a man with close-cropped white hair, beard and slightly petulant voice, who told us that the porter lived in the basement in No. 2.

Hurried downstairs to find note pinned to door of porter's flat, announcing that he'd gone to stay with his sister overnight and would be back at eight the next morning.

This was a cruel blow, since my train to Manchester left just before seven and all my notes, not to say shaving tackle, clean shirt, etc., were inside the flat.

Had no alternative but to call it a day.

Got back to garage to find it locked for the night.

I said, 'Never mind. It isn't the end of the world. We'll get a taxi back to my place.'

'It may not be the end of the world,' said Vanessa, 'but it certainly is of our so-called affair. I've never had this trouble with anyone before.' And with that she hailed a passing taxi and drove off up South Audley Street.

Unfortunately, although I walked up and down for nearly half an hour, not a single free taxi came my way. Finally hailed one in Berkeley Square. Arrived home at midnight.

Was paying off the taxi when suddenly remembered I had left flat keys in car. Porter most unsympathetic. He hasn't heard the end of this by a long chalk.

Arrived at last in flat only to find I had inadvertently left electric heater full on all day. I dread to think how this could affect my quarterly bill. On the other hand, I suppose I should thank my lucky stars I caught it when I did. At least the evening was not a complete disaster.

Friday

How I do hate alarm clocks. I very rarely use them but when I do, I find I am awake every two minutes waiting for them to go off.

Woke exhausted and with splitting headache at six. Ascot heater on blink, so forced to bath in tepid water. Got out old electric shaver, plugged in and gave chin an appalling shock.

Rang all the taxi rank numbers I could find but without success. Once again forced to take to pavements.

Eventually turned up at Euston at 8.45. Absolutely no sign of Pratt. Assumed he must have gone on ahead without me, so, with sinking heart, rushed to ticket counter in hope of catching 8.55. Huge queues, needless to say.

By 8.52 had almost reached front when felt tap on shoulder. Spun round to find Pratt who said, 'Hallo, what happened to you?'

'Unexpected personal tragedy,' I said. 'I assumed you must have gone on.'

He said, 'Actually, I've only just arrived. The presentation's been put off till this afternoon. I thought we could have breakfast here and catch the 9.55. I tried to ring you at home last last night but there was no reply.'

As we were pulling out of the station, Pratt said, 'I do think you might at least have shaved.'

'I happen,' I said, 'to be growing a beard.'

'If I may say,' said Pratt, 'this kind of fringe activity would best be confined to holiday periods.'

'So, if *I* may say so,' said I, 'should inter-staff liaisons.'

As was only to be expected, Pratt pretended he had no idea what I was on about and, when I spelt it out in words of four letters, he actually claimed that he had no interest in my secretary beyond a professional one. He had never been near her flat in his life and, if ever he heard that I had been spreading rumours to the contrary, I could expect to be receiving a sharp note from his solicitor. And talking about notes, where were mine?

I replied that, like him, I found I always got away with things more easily if I played it off the cuff.

Arrived at ballroom of hotel just as salesmen were breaking off for a buffet lunch. A gloomier, more bored-looking bunch of individuals it would be hard to imagine.

Fortunately, Dave Stammers, who has just been appointed Northern Regional Manager, grabbed us and whistled us off to his private suite for champagne and smoked salmon sandwiches.

He said to me, 'You're on second from last. They'll be pretty jaded by then, so I'm relying on you to send them off in a cheerful and optimistic frame of mind. After all, if someone like you can pull off the Kellerman deal, there's hope for all of us.' He roared with laughter, slapped me on the back and poured out another glass of champagne.

Took the opportunity to question him re investigating local strip clubs for the Crisp Report. Stammers slapped me on the back yet again and poured out more champagne. 'Don't you worry about that, lad,' he said. 'It's taken care of already.'

The trouble with drinking at lunchtime is that, at the time, it slips down easily enough and it is only later that the effects begin to be felt. While I wouldn't say I was drunk exactly, by the time the proceedings were under way again at 2.15, was feeling decidedly merry.

By half past three, however, showing every sign of sobering up. Feeling in need of Dutch courage, slipped out and made my way up to Stammers' suite, where topped up liberally with Moët et Chandon Non-Vintage and arrived back much refreshed in time to hear my name being announced.

Salesmen looking even more sorry for themselves than before lunch, though not half as much as I was when I realized I couldn't remember a single word of what I had been planning to say.

Luckily, can be pretty nifty on my feet when pushed and, before I knew what, heard myself announcing that everybody took marketing far too seriously nowadays and that the sooner we put the jokes back into selling, the sooner we would have Britain back on an even keel.

I then described, rather wittily I thought, the struggle I had had with our marketing consultants over including some clips from Woody Allen films in the audio-visual part of the Kellerman presentation. The entire audience stared at me with a look of such blank incomprehension that, on an impulse, decided to give them a small taste of my famous Allen impersonation with which I used to bring the house down at Oxford parties.

It was a pity I couldn't remember it word for word, and one or two of the jokes didn't come off quite as well as they used to. However, I think the flavour came through, which is the main thing. Could have gone on for longer than I did had Stammers not jumped up on the platform and drawn things to a premature conclusion. A pity, because it brought a huge cheer.

After that, the most extraordinary thing happened. Dave gestured to me to stay where I was and, seizing the microphone, announced, 'And now, gentlemen, by special request of Mr Crisp, an extra item for your pleasure and inspiration. A young lady to show you the real meaning of figures. She's just back from Leningrad, where she was a great hit in Conservative Clubs, and last month she graced the centrefold of *Exchange and Mart*. May I present Barbara!'

The lights went out, a single spotlight was aimed at the side of the stage and, to the music of 'The Stripper', into it slinked a very pretty and curvaceous girl wearing a long dress on which were written the words: BARFORDS SALES UP 5%?

At this the entire audience burst into raucous cheers and laughter.

Barbara then proceeded to do a most seductive striptease. Each time she removed a garment she draped it over me and there was another underneath suggesting an even higher percentage, until she had no clothes on at all, whereupon she turned round and stuck out her bottom on which was printed: 30% YES!

The audience roared its approval.

She then came prancing over to me, seized her garments, tossed them to one side and, to my horror, started to undo my tie. To a man, the audience shouted, 'Get 'em off'. For an awful moment I was afraid she might take them at their word. But, of course, nothing more came of it. Barbara put a finger against my lips, seized me by the hand and dragged me off to the accompaniment of loud cheers and catcalls.

Luckily, I am the sort of man who can take a joke but, even so, the very fact that they should even contemplate such gimmicks makes me wonder if Barfords is the sort of company to which I should be making a lifetime's commitment.

Pratt came up to me afterwards and said, 'Still fancy a strip club?'

I laughed it off, but could barely bring myself to speak to him the whole way back to London. I also had one of the worst headaches of my life. My neck's much better though.

Saturday

Pretty much of a washout, thanks to continuing headache and hangover.

Vanessa rang after lunch to say she had collected the things from the flat and did I want to come round and pick them up.

I said, 'I suppose you didn't remember to pick up my car while you were about it?'

'No,' she said.

I told her I'd be round at about three.

Unfortunately, got caught up in demo round Hyde Park Corner and did not get there until nearly four.

Was waiting in hall while she went into sitting room to fetch my holdall, when a voice that I can only describe as artisan called out from upstairs, 'Are you going to be all afternoon, darling?'

Looked up to see a muscly young man in jeans and T-shirt, with curly hair and tattoos on his arms, leaning over the banisters. We stared at each other for a moment, then he withdrew as suddenly as he had appeared.

When Vanessa returned, I asked her who he was.

She said vaguely, 'Oh, he's my jobbing builder. He's come to give me an estimate for a labouring job.'

Said nothing but, if I'm not very much mistaken, there's rather more to this than meets the eye. One often hears it said that women are not averse to a spot of rough trade from time to time. It will make a very telling footnote to the adultery section.

Watched *Dallas* in the evening. Am wondering if I should consider a brief comparative study of sex in the country versus sex in the city.

To Dorothy later. Bad-tempered-looking girl on door claimed never to have heard of me. Explained that I was there as a guest of Mr Bryant-Fenn.

'Who?' she said.

I repeated the name very slowly and loudly.

'Is he a member?' she said.

'He's your public relations officer,' I said. 'And, if I may say so, you are badly in need of one.'

After that, she became very rude indeed and I was forced to see the manager. A smooth-faced young man – all velvet and lace ruffles – eventually arrived and said that Hugh was not in the club and that, as far as he knew, they were not expecting him that evening.

I pointed out that I was not just anyone, but had come specially to write about them for a very important publication.

The manager shrugged. 'We've got a waiting list as long as a gorilla's arm,' he said. 'Who needs publicity? Still, if you'd like to come and have a drink and see what it's all about, you're very welcome.'

I said, 'Please don't feel you have to invite me,' in an ironic sort of way.

'Who needs *bad* publicity?' he said.

He dumped me in a large, squashy armchair in a corner of the bar and ordered me a large whisky and soda.

I declined his invitation to sample the dining room, but said that I might certainly tread a measure or two on the dance floor a little later.

He said, 'Things don't normally get going till after midnight.'

I replied that I would be quite happy to sit there soaking up the atmosphere.

'Just so long as you don't soak up the whisky,' he said, and we both laughed.

I remarked casually, 'Oh, by the way, I gather Bianca might be in this evening.'

'Who?' he said.

Spent the next couple of hours watching the so-called beautiful people at play. Some of the girls quite pretty but most of the men appeared to have been born in rather sunnier climes.

At one point, went through to next room to check action on dance floor. Only one couple caught my attention. He was tall, blond and good-looking; she was slim and graceful with straight, fairish hair. They were obviously in love.

As they came towards me, suddenly realized with a terrible shock that the girl was Amanda. Would have given anything to avoid meeting them, but she recognized me before I had a chance to move. She introduced the young man as her fiancé, name of Giles de Something.

She said to me, 'I didn't know you were a member. I've never seen you here before.'

'Nor I you,' I said blithely. 'The fact is, I don't get out much these days. I'm very busy.'

Amanda said to Giles, 'Simon is a big cheese in marketing.'

'Congratulations,' said Giles.

'Giles is a poor Army officer,' she told me.

At that moment, the barman arrived and asked us what we'd like to drink. They both looked at me. Had no option but to order. A fresh orange juice for Amanda, a large gin and tonic for Giles, and a small whisky and soda for me.

Reached in my pocket for money only to realize that I had stupidly come out without my wallet. I said in a low voice to the barman, 'I'll sign for these.'

When he handed me the bill, I wrote with a flourish across the bottom: *Hugh Bryant-Fenn*.

'Excuse me, sir,' said the barman. 'You've forgotten to add your membership number.'

At that precise moment, the manager appeared from nowhere and said, 'Don't worry, Robert. These people are with me.' And, crossing out Hugh's name, he signed his own.

'I hope you've had everything you need,' he said, putting particular emphasis on the word 'everything'.

I said I hadn't enjoyed an evening so much for a long time.

'Good,' he said. 'I'm only sorry to hear you won't be in again for a while.'

118

'Oh what a pity,' said Amanda. 'I was hoping to catch up on the news. Why?'

'Pressure of work,' I said. 'Please remember me to your mother.'

She said, 'I don't see her as much as I used to now that she and Daddy have split up.'

So I was right after all.

She went on, 'I wouldn't have minded if she'd found herself someone amusing. Even you would have been better than the poofy old quasi-theatrical pseud she lives with now.'

I said, 'He wouldn't happen to be called Gerald Campsey-Ash, would he?'

'Good Lord, no,' she said. 'Gerald's my uncle.'

The manager couldn't have been nicer as he accompanied me to the door.

A large car drew up as I was walking away up the road, and a young woman stepped out and walked quickly towards the door of the club.

Could have sworn I heard the manager saying, 'Bianca, darling . . .'

Sunday

Set off for Bloomsbury in good time for NACKERS meeting.

Am not quite sure what one's duties as a committee member will amount to in the months to come, but my appointment as a steward for tonight's gathering, whatever else it involved, obviously meant being there well in advance of time. Crowd handling is a tricky business, especially if one is not fully in command from the word go.

Unfortunately, experienced rather more difficulty locating hall than I had anticipated. As a result, arrived with only five minutes to spare. Place unexpectedly quiet, although fully lit. Thinking meeting must already be under way, tiptoed across lobby and in through large panelled door, only to find room completely deserted. Made my way down aisle between neatly arranged rows of wooden chairs and up on to platform.

Five minutes had passed when the door at the end of the room opened and a man in blue overalls and a peaked cap shuffled in. 'You Mr Johnson?' he called out.

I said no, but that I was expecting him any moment.

'The hall was booked for seven-thirty,' the man grumbled.

I pointed out that I happened to be a committee member and that it was only twenty to eight.

'I wouldn't care if you was Shirley Williams,' he said, 'as long as someone pays for the room and you're out of here by nine at the latest.'

By eight o'clock it was perfectly obvious that something had gone badly wrong. Unfortunately, had come out without Johnson's phone number, and no joy from Directory Enquiries.

Hung on till the bitter end, just in case, but eventually forced to admit defeat, and wrote out cheque for £25.

I'd like to know how I'm going to explain *that* on my expenses sheet.

The moment I got home, rang Howard Johnson's number but got unobtainable tone. I can't say I'm surprised. I daresay the same will hold true for my £25.

Next, rang Sue to enquire re progress of typing, only to learn that she has gone down with flu and will not be in for at least a week.

I said, 'You don't think you could do it in bed if I were to bring the material round to the flat?'

'No,' she said.

'Fair enough,' I said. 'I daresay we'll manage somehow. By the way, while I've got you on the phone, perhaps you could clear up a mystery that's been puzzling me. Are you, or are you not, having a thing with Neville Pratt?'

'Pratt?' she croaked. 'You must be joking. How could anyone have a thing with anyone with a name like that?'

I said, 'But you are having a thing with someone in Barfords?'

'No,' she said, 'I'm not.'

I said, 'Beddoes distinctly told me that somebody from the office came to your party the other night and played a leading role in your orgy.'

Sue said, 'Is everyone going round the twist? What orgy? We played Scrabble and danced a bit, that's all.'

'Never mind what you did or didn't do,' I said. 'Do you absolutely promise me that no one from the office came to your party?'

'Yes,' she said.

'And you're definitely not having a thing with anyone in the office?'

'No,' she said. And put the phone down on me.

Am seriously beginning to wonder if I might not be having a nervous breakdown without realizing it. They do say overwork can affect one in all sorts of strange ways.

Still, sufficiently *compos mentis*, I'm glad to say, to remember to ring Armitage re our proposed visit to a massage parlour. To judge from the enthusiasm with which he agreed to meet me on Tuesday afternoon, he must have been having a pretty lean time of it in the last few weeks, in every sense of the word. I reminded him that he had promised in return to give me Jane's telephone number, which he duly did.

'A bargain's a bargain,' he said.

'Not for some I know it isn't,' I said, and rang off.

Rang Jane on her 673 number, which I have a feeling is somewhere the other side of Clapham Common, but no reply. I can't quite remember now what it is I'm so keen to get in touch with her about.

Thought about ringing Beddoes in Brussels to challenge him over the Sue and Pratt business, but decided I had put up with enough flannel for one day and watched Melvyn Bragg's excellent arts programme instead.

What a clever young man he is. I bet he didn't get where he is today by wasting his time with second-rate has-beens. And neither in the future shall I.

Monday, 26 February

To Alma Mater for the day. Had every intention of setting off early. As Dickie Dunmow had said when I telephoned to confirm the arrangements, 'The sooner you get here, the sooner you can tell us what you want to know and the sooner we can decide whether we will tell you.'

Unfortunately, thanks to Sue's unexpected absence, was forced to spend two hours battling with Personnel over a temporary typist.

Miss Bintree finally agreed to release a dim but pretty creature called Una who, within five minutes of arriving in my office, had received visits from practically every messenger in the building, each one of whom actually had the sauce to claim to be her fiancé.

Finally became so incensed by sounds of giggling as I was trying to get through to Dickie re my slight change of plan that I was compelled to read the riot act. As luck would have it, the messenger in question turned out to be the spotty youth who had tried to make a monkey out of me over the matter of my mail.

I said in my iciest voice, 'I'm afraid my secretary has a great deal of work to do. If you must meet her, you're welcome to do so during the lunch hour. But, in the meantime, I must ask you to be about your business.'

I turned and walked back into my office. As I did so, the spotty messenger made a lavatorial noise. When I challenged him, he said, 'Oh didn't you know, Mr Mann? Una suffers from a rare stomach complaint. She's under the doctor. I don't think it's very nice of you to talk like that in front of her.'

The maddening thing is that he could have been telling the truth. However, I suspect from the smothered giggles that this youth is, for reasons that I cannot fathom, merely bent on confrontation at all costs. However, if he thinks he is going to get a rise out of me, he's got another think coming.

I said very quietly, 'If I catch you in here again for no good reason, you'll be suffering from a rare complaint of the backside.'

Meant of course that he would be feeling the end of my boot, but should have known that he would deliberately choose to misunderstand me.

'Fancy a bit of rough trade from time to time, do you squire?' he said, rolling his eyes suggestively.

I said, 'Any more lip out of you and I'll be speaking to the head of the post room about you.'

He said, 'Not before I've told him a thing or two about you and your nasty suggestions. And I've got a witness.'

Responded to this feeble attempt at blackmail with a brief look of withering scorn, and left for the fresh wholesome air of the Weald of Kent which I breathed so happily

122

for four and a half happy years.

Parked in Pegram's Piece only to be informed by officious Under Magister that it was reserved for staff only. Luckily, he was not only unknown to me but several years younger and, when I pointed out that I was (a) an OF, (b) on school business *and* (c) had an appointment with Mr Dunmow, he quickly caved in. I thought he would.

Skirted Apthorpe's Bottom and bounded up front steps of School House like the young lion I once was. Entered Back Passage and was almost knocked down by gang of small boys running full tilt towards Toggers' Room. From sheer force of habit called out, 'No running in Back Passage!'

All the boys ran on heedlessly, except one, obviously a New Squit, who said, 'Who are you?'

I said, 'I'll show you who I am, you nasty little Squit,' and seizing him by the ear I marched him along to Toggers', threw open the door and pointed at the wall above the Old Fireplace where the house honours board hung, only to realize too late that I was pointing at a huge collage of nude pinups cut from girlie magazines.

I suppose in the circumstances I cannot blame the boy for crying out 'Help! Assault!' nor his chums for coming to his rescue. However, I still maintain it was not necessary for *all* twenty of them to use quite so much force to bring me to the floor, and I really do think they could have frogmarched me along to Dickie's study quite satisfactorily without going to the lengths of tying my thumbs behind my back.

It was a pity, too, that Dickie chose not to take a rather more severe line with them. The words, 'Hallo, Crisp. Started your researches already, I see,' could hardly fail to carry with them the implication of approval, however faint.

I might have expected him to assume that my sole purpose for being there was to dig up more dirt on the old homosexuality chestnut.

He said, 'I know you left-wing journalist types; always the first to pick on some trivial aspect of public school life and blow it up out of all proportion. Anything for a bit of sensationalism. Still, that's what sells papers, eh?'

123

Opened my mouth to put the record straight, but once Dickie gets a bee in his bonnet about something, it takes more than reasoned argument to shift it.

'The fact is,' he went on, 'the boys have got many better things to think about than sex.'

'Such as?' I said.

'The usual things,' he said, 'O and A levels, carpentry, the school play, rugger . . .'

I said that surely rugger was merely one of many substitutes for releasing sexual aggression.

Dickie said, 'I had hoped we might have been able to clear up this matter in a few minutes between ourselves, but you newshounds will never take anyone's word for anything will you? If you don't believe me, you might try talking to some of the boys. Beaumont and Fletcher have got free periods. They should be in their cubby now.'

He led the way up to Top Swine Level and knocked on the door of Big Cubby. From inside came the sound of scuffling and whispering, and finally one of them gave us permission to come in. They were both at their desks, apparently hard at work, but, to my way of thinking, looking rather flushed and guilty. Dickie said, 'This is Mr Crisp OF. He's doing an article about homosexuality in the public schools and he'd like to ask you a few questions.'

Could not help commenting on the eye-catching display of nude pinups with which every wall was covered.

Dickie said, 'A few comely females scantily clad can hardly be said to amount to wholesale depravity – especially as the display of . . . er . . . toilet areas is strictly forbidden.'

After he had gone, Beaumont said, 'The real stuff's behind you, if you're interested.'

I turned to find, sellotaped to the back of the door, half a dozen of the fullest frontal shots of women I have ever seen.

Fletcher said, 'Dickie never sees them because he always stands with the door open against the wall.'

Could not resist roaring with laughter and slapping my thighs, which obviously endeared me to the boys because they were soon revealing all sorts of fascinating things about what they really get up to in schools these days. For instance, most of the senior boys seem to have girlfriends in the girls' boarding school about three miles away.

Beaumont said, 'We can see them five times a week if we really feel like it.'

'Trouble is, we're usually too shagged,' said Fletcher.

'From rugger?' I said.

'No', said Beaumont. 'Wanking.'

They then told me that they have house and school dances once or even twice a term for Swine and upwards.

'Trouble is,' Fletcher said, 'they only give you a quarter of an hour after the dance for any unfinished business, so to speak.'

'The shed behind Upper Bummers is very popular,' said Beaumont.

'If you don't mind upper splinters in your upper bummer,' said Fletcher.

I said, 'According to Dickie, all this homosexual stuff is a thing of the past?'

'Oh, we still eye the New Squits and mark them out of ten,' said Fletcher.

'But it's nothing serious,' said Beaumont.

I said, 'You mean you don't get up to anything?'

'If we did,' said Beaumont, 'you don't think we'd tell you, do you?'

We all roared. Despite our age differences, I think we understood each other.

'Got a ciggy on you?' Beaumont said suddenly.

Was naturally hesitant about encouraging smoking in Cubbies but, as they pointed out, if only one smoked and someone came in, I could always say it was me.

As they were puffing away merrily, Fletcher said, 'How much will we get for all this?'

I said, 'Six of the best, I shouldn't wonder.'

Beaumont said, 'What Fletchy means was how much will your paper pay us for these sensational revelations?'

'Bearing in mind we might be among the ranks of the unemployed school leavers by this time next week,' added Fletcher.

I pointed out that I did not actually work for a paper and that there was no question of payment for information supplied for a survey of this kind.

Beaumont said, 'Mr Dunmow's going to be very upset

when we tell him how Mr Crisp OF offered us cigarettes in return for information, isn't he, Fletch?'

'Very,' said Fletcher.

Unfortunately, I could see their point.

The two of them whispered together for a while, then Fletcher said, 'Tell you what. Beau's been gated for the last week and he's rather anxious to see his girlfriend. Supposing we were to get a message to her, then you could drive across to Bedenham this afternoon during games, pick her up and bring her back here. If anyone challenges you, you can say she's your wife or your secretary. She'll stay for half an hour or so and then you can drive her back again.'

I said, 'I don't know if you are both planning to go into the blackmailing business when you leave here, but I suggest you try cutting your teeth on someone a good deal less gullible.' And with that I stood up and left the room.

Was crossing Apthorpe's Bottom just as the Refec Bell was ringing out from Tommy Tiddle, when I felt a pull on my sleeve and turned round to find it was the New Squit whose ear I had pinched earlier.

He pressed a pound note into my hand and said, 'Be a good chap and slip across to the newsagent's and get me the new *Men Only*, will you?'

Am not by nature a violent man, but there are occasions when even my patience is exhausted and a good sharp shock is more salutary than a thousand words of admonition.

As luck would have it, no sooner had the flat of my hand made contact with the back of the boy's head than round the corner appeared the very same boys who had come to his rescue in Toggers' earlier on. Decided discretion the better part of valour, and with cries of 'Help! Assault! Child-beater! Stop thief!' ringing in my ears, I legged it for Arthur's Opening.

Hurtled into Pegram's Piece only to find my car had disappeared. Not daring to stop, headed for Black Hole and ran straight into officious Under Magister who informed me coolly that, since I had chosen to break the rules about parking, he had asked the police to come and tow the vehicle away.

By now the boys had almost caught up with me. The Under Magister grabbed my coat; but I shook him off and ran like the devil towards Main Gate. Luckily, I managed to lose them all in the back streets of the town, but my luck was short-lived, since it cost me twenty quid to retrieve my car from the police pound.

How I can ever have spent the last twenty years singing the praises of the place I cannot imagine. Had I not already cancelled my subscription to the OF Society a year ago, I would have no hesitation in doing so here and now. I shall certainly make it quite clear that it is the last place for which I shall be entering my sons. If ever I have any, that is.

Halfway to London, it suddenly occurred to me, apropos of Beaumont and Fletcher's little ruse, that the only girls' school in the vicinity was at least twenty miles away, and it was not called Bedenham but High Heath. What their purpose can possibly have been in trying to persuade me otherwise is anybody's guess. Thank goodness my natural instinct to call their bluff did not let me down.

Tuesday

Arrived in the office this morning expecting to find the entire film section typed out and ready for Xeroxing, only to be told by Una that, because I hadn't told her whether I wanted it double or single spaced, she had decided to do nothing and wait until I got back.

I pointed out in terms that left her in little doubt as to my disappointment that the whole thing was due to be delivered tomorrow and that I had no alternative but to ask her to work through the lunch hour and, if necessary, right through the night. At which point she burst into floods of tears, said it was not her fault and that she had never worked for anyone so cruel in her life. And with that she gathered up her personal effects and left the room.

Realizing there was almost certainly no chance of getting anyone else in time, sat down there and then and started typing away as fast as is humanly possible with only two fingers. By lunchtime, had managed to produce eight reasonably clean pages. Rang Armitage to suggest postponing our massage parlour visit until another day.

He said, 'I haven't got another day.'

I said, in that case, would he mind if we didn't meet for lunch first.

'Not if you don't mind missing out on a certain amount of background material,' he said.

Had no alternative but to say I'd meet him in San Giuliano as agreed.

Typed out one more page, made a botch, tried to erase it, made a hole in the paper, threw it in the waste-paper basket and set off for Soho. Armitage already at the table nursing a Campari and soda and nibbling on *grissini*.

Had I the slightest inkling of what he was about to describe, I certainly would not have ordered a starter of the cured meat covered with olive oil and black pepper.

Had never realized before that he had travelled quite so extensively in the Far East, nor that he was in the habit of taking at least one holiday every year in Manila or Bangkok. In his estimation these are the sex capitals of the world.

'Never has a city been more aptly named,' he said.

'What?' I said. 'Manila?'

'No,' he said. 'Kuala Lumpur.' He then proceeded to describe in vivid detail a typical afternoon's visit to a typical oriental massage parlour.

Apparently the great trick is to pick out a couple of girls and get them to give you a Chinese Sandwich. This involves one of them lying down, the customer lying on top of her and then the second girl lying on top of the customer.

Could not quite make out what happens then, but gather everyone wriggles about a good deal and a jolly time is had by all.

I said, 'This is all very interesting, Armitage, but my report specifically covers the sexual life of the British.'

'Oh,' said Armitage blithely, 'I've never been to a place like that in London.'

'Why not?' I asked him.

'Well,' he said. 'It's always so cold isn't it?'

As I was paying the bill, remarked that I hoped that whatever he had laid on by way of a practical demonstration would represent considerably better value.

'I don't know what you mean,' he said. 'As a way of getting one into the right frame of mind, a good spicy Italian lunch with plenty of rough red wine takes a lot of beating.'

128

Did not like to say so, but have never felt less in a mood for anything in my life.

Was tempted on more than one occasion to dodge down a side alley, grab the first taxi that came my way and head back to the office and the IBM golf-ball. Yet something drew me on. Was it curiosity? Conscientiousness? An absurd wish not to let Armitage down? Even an unconscious message from my libido? Who knows? Perhaps a liberal helping of all four.

After a while I asked Armitage where he was taking me – Bangkok?

He said, 'I told you, I don't know the London scene. I thought we'd have a look around and pick one out at random.'

It was hardly the moment to remind him that the whole purpose of my asking him along was that one's path should be made smoother and easier through his knowledge and expertise, not rutted and potholed with doubt and uncertainty. If I had wanted the blind to lead the blind, I could have brought Mother.

Suddenly Armitage stopped dead in his tracks. 'This looks the sort of thing,' he said, peering in through a corner window hung with multicoloured strips of plastic.

'How do you know?' I asked him.

'They're all much of a muchness,' he said.

The sign above the main window proclaimed it to be the Scando-Thai Saunarama and Massage Centre.

It all sounded extremely respectable – so much so that I could not help but ask Armitage if he was sure this was quite the sort of place I had in mind.

Armitage said, 'Not losing your nerve by any chance, are you?'

I said that nothing could be further from my mind.

'Good,' he said. '*A nos moutons* then.' And before I knew what, we were through the door and standing in front of the reception desk where a sensible-looking girl in a white blouse and tweed skirt said, 'What did you two gentlemen have in mind?'

Armitage leered at her and said, 'What are you offering?'

She said, 'Royal Sauna, Massage and Shower is £15; VIP Assisted Sauna, Massage and Shower, with body shampoo and cologne, comes to £25.'

'What's the difference?' Armitage asked.

'The VIP's assisted, the Royal isn't,' she said.

Armitage said, 'Oh I think the assisted for us, don't you, Crisp?'

I said whatever was easiest.

'Makes no difference to us one way or the other,' said the receptionist.

I said that perhaps she could be a little more specific.

'Assisted includes hand relief,' she said. 'Extras have to be discussed and arranged with the girl in question.'

Felt like asking if I could forgo the hand relief in favour of an interview at the same price, but decided to play cards close to the chest at this stage of proceedings.

The girl said, 'So that'll be two assisted then?'

We both nodded.

'That'll be fifty pounds,' she said, 'including VAT.'

'And relief,' said Armitage.

I said that I was rather short of cash, as it happened, but she said I could pay by cheque with a cheque card or credit card, whichever I preferred. This is not the first time I have found myself reflecting what a strange world it is where one can get pleasure on credit.

She then showed us through to a small room with some rather cheap armchairs in one of which a dark-haired, plump young man was smoking a scented cigarette and watching a middle-aged woman on TV interviewing another woman with a large snake round her neck.

After a while, two girls came into the room. Both were dark-haired and both wore T-shirts and very short shorts. They introduced themselves as Carol and Liz. I thought I had rather the better of the bargain with Carol, but there wasn't a lot in it.

I remarked that I hoped we would be in separate rooms.

Liz said, 'What do you take us for?'

'We don't go in for kinks here,' Carol said.

I said, 'No chance of a Chinese Sandwich then?'

'Coffee, tea and soft drinks,' said Liz, 'but no food.'

Carol led me into a small room containing a wooden chair, a wash basin, a wooden trolley on wheels containing various powders and unguents, a small pile of towels and a box of Kleenex, and a couch of the sort you see in doctors' waiting rooms, covered with a white sheet. The decor

130

consisted largely of nude girls swimming up a silver wall-paper.

Carol said, 'If you'd like to get undressed and lie on the table.'

'Completely?' I said.

She said, 'Well I can hardly be expected to give you a VIP Assisted in a double-breasted suit, now can I?'

Was standing there, feeling rather cold and foolish, when she suddenly said, 'Will you be requiring any extras?'

'Such as?' I said.

'That's up to you,' she said. 'French?'

'No, no,' I said. 'English and proud of it. Born just outside Chatham as a matter of fact. I can never remember whether that makes me a Kentish Man or a Man of Kent. Do you know that part of the world by any chance?'

She said that she was happy to say she had never been within fifty miles of Chatham and that she hadn't got all day and would I mind getting on the table, face down.

I said, as I settled myself on to the couch, 'I was wondering, do you see any moral dilemma in the job you do?'

'I see a lot of frustrated old sods,' she said, 'and a lot of overweight bodies. Not a lot else.'

I said, 'Wouldn't you say frustrated is a relative term?'

'All right then,' she said. 'Frustrated is a relative term. Talcum or Baby Oil?'

'What's the difference?' I said.

'Do you suffer from dry skin?' she said.

I said that I did rather.

'I'll give you the oil then,' she said, and took her T-shirt off.

Have often wondered how one would behave if one knew with absolute certainty that in the next few moments one was going to die. I imagine one's feelings are not dissimilar to those I experienced as Carol poured oil on to my back and started to rub up and down my spine. One simply closes one's eyes and says to oneself, 'This is it,' and awaits the inevitable. Was interested to note how calm I was. In fact, after a while, was beginning to feel extremely relaxed, not to say sleepy. I remember feeling a slightly different sensation in the small of my back and asked her what it was. I think she said something like 'Look, no hands' and then I must have dozed off, because the next thing I knew she was manhandling me onto my back.

I heard her say, 'My, my, this won't do at all, Mr Crisp. We're going to have to try a little harder, aren't we?' when the most excruciating cramp shot through my leg.

Almost without thinking, leapt off the table and hobbled round the room, rubbing the back of my thigh and trying to straighten out my leg to relieve the pain. Unfortunately, in my agony, did not look where I was going and cannoned straight into Carol who fell backwards with a shriek onto the trolley which carried her headlong into the wall with a crash before hurling her senseless onto the floor.

I did not see there was any reason for the manager to take quite such a strong line with me. It was an accident, as I tried to explain, and I can't help thinking that Carol must experience many worse things in her line of business than a small bump on the head. I also think they might have permitted me to have a quick shower before getting dressed. Johnson's Baby Oil is all very well in its place, but not directly beneath a shirt and tie and double-breasted wool and worsted suit.

As for my demanding a proportion of my money back, I believe I was entirely justified. Apart from the lack of shower, I could hardly be said to be a satisfied customer in any sense of the word. May take the matter further or may not.

As I was being shown the door, Armitage appeared looking well pleased with himself. 'Judging from the noise,' he said, 'you got more than you bargained for.'

Couldn't be bothered to answer and, ignoring further enquiries, hobbled up the street in search of a taxi.

Was wrestling with the intricacies of golf-ball, page twelve of the report and continuing sharp pains in the thigh when Armitage rang to enquire after my health and to thank me for a most satisfactory afternoon.

I said, 'The only person whose health interests me round here is my secretary. She claims to have taken to her bed with flu.'

'Correction,' said Armitage. 'She has taken to *my* bed.'

'Since when?' I demanded.

'Since about a fortnight ago,' he said.

I said, 'You didn't happen to go to a party at her flat about ten days ago, did you?'

'Yes,' he said.

Have a feeling I may have damaged telephone in my anger.

Rang Beddoes from home on the cheap rate later that evening. I made it clear I was in no mood to beat about the bush.

'You told me that Pratt came round to Sue's party that night and misbehaved. Yet now I learn that it was, in fact, Armitage.'

Beddoes said, 'Oh I'm sorry if I misled you. I thought you asked me if he was a prat, and he was.'

Really, as if I could give a row of beans whether Sue is having a thing with Pratt, Armitage or the entire Australian cricket team. Here am I supposedly the leading expert on sex in Britain today, yet I have not had a thing with anyone for the last six weeks. Indeed, my sex drive has reached such an all-time low that I cannot even keep awake during a topless massage.

Steps will clearly have to be taken.

Wednesday

Today I am due to deliver the Crisp Report. Not only am I dead on my feet after an entire night at the golf-ball (and I'm still only on page 75), but I am suddenly convinced that a section on How to Improve Your Sex Life and Make Yourself More Attractive to the Opposite Sex is absolutely crucial to the report's success.

Home at six for a bath, shave and breakfast, then back at the keys by 7.30.

Called Miss Hippo at ten to assure her that report on its way. She said, 'Mr Hardacre is in Stockholm all this week. I'll give him your message when he comes in on Monday morning.'

I said, 'In that case, since I am without a secretary, I wonder if you would be kind enough to help me out with some typing?'

'I am a personal assistant,' Miss Hippo said, 'not a typist. There are plenty of those in the pool.' And she put the phone down on me.

133

Rang typing pool to be informed by Miss Bintree that, owing to illness, she was short-staffed as it was and that anyway she couldn't risk having any more of her girls upset.

Have worked out that, if I can keep up an average of forty-five pages a day for the next four days, that will give me just enough time to work up my remaining notes, and research and write Improvement Section. Where, though, to begin?

By an astonishing coincidence, was skimming through newspaper while tackling sardine and cucumber sandwich and coffee in O Sole Mio coffee bar, when what should my eye alight upon but an article about how a hairdresser called Ricci Burns transformed a young executive, not unlike myself, into a modern sex symbol. Cannot say that I have ever been a great fan of the boiler suit, nor is anyone likely to catch me mincing about with make-up all over my face. However, am most impressed by the tousled, devil-may-care hairstyle, and feel sure that to place oneself in Mr Burns' hands for an afternoon would prove a fascinating experiment.

Rang his PR who couldn't have been more helpful and made an appointment for me for four o'clock.

Arrived at his West End salon by taxi in pouring rain. Everything was white: walls, floor, furniture. Even the hairdressers were dressed in specially designed white creations.

Mr Burns, his white shirt contrasting magnificently with his lean, tanned face and his glossy black hair, rushed forward to greet me for all the world as if Mick Jagger had just walked in off the street.

It was all a far cry from Jack's round the corner from my flat, with his cracked basin, his Durex advertisements, his dog-eared pile of *Weekend* magazines, his nicotine-stained fingers and his perennial hacking cough.

First, I was handed over to a young man who made me sit with my head resting backwards over a basin while he gave my hair the most thorough washing of its life.

While waiting for Mr Burns to attend to me, I drank an excellent cup of coffee and tried to spot some of the famous film stars, TV personalities and beauties who have helped to make him the superstar among hairdressers that he is today. One blonde girl at the end reading *Vogue* might have been Liv Ullman, except that those sort of women tend to look the same with wet hair.

After about ten minutes, a young man came across and told me that Mr Burns was ready for me.

'Now, Mr Crisp,' he said. 'You're all mine.' And running his fingers through my locks, proceeded to insult Jack's handiwork in no uncertain terms. 'You've got a beautifully shaped head,' he told me, 'but no one's cut *into* your hair. They've just gone round the edges, as usual.'

Had not realized before that in this sort of place an assistant does all the donkey-work of actually holding your hair, while the great man himself merely wields the scissors.

I cannot pretend that, after years of Jack's heavy-handed assaults on my hair, I responded naturally to such luxury, but the experience was not an unpleasant one, and I must admit that the carefree styling did give me a certain youthful *je ne sais quoi*.

I did enquire about make-up, simply out of curiosity, but Ricci said that, apart from face-bronzing gel and eyelash dye, make-up for men was not nearly as popular as one might think.

I said that I was very glad to hear it, but supposing someone were to come to him and ask him to give them a few simple hints on how to make himself more attractive to women, what would he suggest?

He thought for a moment and said. 'A good haircut, a fortnight's diet, regular exercise, and self-confidence – though that probably comes with the other three.'

I said, 'All right. We've dealt with the hair; what about the rest?'

Ricci looked me up and down and said, 'If I were you, I'd start off with a simple diet – an orange and black coffee for breakfast, cottage cheese and an apple for lunch, and chicken, fish or meat and plenty of green vegetables for dinner. Then I'd take myself off to a good health club, like that one in Kensington, where they have a gym, sauna, massage, sunbeds and so on. Then I'd buy myself some nice clothes, a nice pair of jeans, a polo neck sweater, a nice belt, you know. I'd have lunch with Molly Parkin. Oh, and I'd start taking ginseng. It does wonders for your libido.'

I pointed out that I wasn't really asking for myself. It was all hypothetical and in the interests of research.

'You could have fooled me,' he said.

Am not used to being spoken to this way by hairdressers. However, at that moment he informed me that the whole thing was on the house. I have never been one to look a gift horse in the mouth and, at £20 a haircut and with the whole expenses issue balanced on a knife edge, this was not the moment to start doing so.

Normally, would have had no hesitation in taking a taxi home, but this evening, anxious to check women's reaction to my new looks, plumped instead for tube. Interested to notice that not a single woman gave me so much as a second glace. Of course it *was* the height of the rush hour. The only positive reaction came from a burly working type who I bumped into by mistake on the escalator in my anxiety to get to the chemist before the shops shut.

'Sorry,' I called after me.

'Get out of it, you poof,' he called back.

Thank heavens I'd had the foresight not to try the make-up.

Bought box of ginseng tablets, half a dozen large oranges and a pound of sprouts to go with the rump steak in my deep-freeze compartment. Also made slight detour and called in at health club.

It is obviously extremely well-equipped, and the people who run it appear to know what they are talking about. The atmosphere is casual and friendly and, if the signed photographs of film and TV celebrities that line the stairs to the gym are any indication of the type of clientele one can expect to rub shoulders with in the sauna bath, this could well turn out to be very much my sort of place. £190 a year seems little enough to shell out for a healthy body. It's not quite White's, but the people who sit about in leather armchairs in St James's do not do so in order to improve their sex lives.

At all events, took a brochure and said I'll ring tomorrow and talk further.

Arrived home starving and opened freezer compartment to find steak gone and note saying, 'Man cannot live by bread alone, laddie, especially with a lady to entertain. Cheers, Ralph.'

136

Am glad now I decided to keep the hundred pounds.

Potatoes obviously out of the question, so had to content myself with huge plate of sprouts. Dull but nutritious.

After *Nine O'Clock News*, took my first ginseng tablet. Have never had a lot of time for orientals. However, when it comes to sex, am perfectly prepared to bow to their superior wisdom. Ginseng is not called 'The Man Root' for nothing. Indeed, I had erotic thoughts for the rest of the evening, especially about Jane. She seems to be constantly in the forefront of my mind these days.

Rang her number on off-chance but no reply.

Also mystified by Ricci Burns' suggestion re lunch with Molly Parkin. Is one to understand that this might lead to useful information for the report or what?

To bed in puzzled mood – also with slightly gippy tummy. Am wondering if ginseng is not just another form of natural laxative. If so, what possible reason could Ricci have had for recommending it? There's nothing sexy about senna pods.

Thursday

Arrived at office at 7.30 and straight to golf-ball. By 10.15 had completed ten more pages and had obtained Molly's phone number from Ricci's PR.

For some reason got it into her head that I was an obscene book salesman. Fortunately, we were able to uncross our lines before too much damage was done, and she has agreed to meet me for lunch at Langan's Brasserie. One is always reading about this place in the newspapers. I understand it to be a haunt of the rich, famous and trendy, but have never had the opportunity to try it out for myself.

She said, 'Langan's is very sexy. You've got to be sure and make a good entrance, though. In a big hat preferably.'

Frankly, it's all gobbledygook to me, but affected to be familiar with modern café society language and, when she asked exactly what it was I wanted to know, I said cryptically, 'Everything.'

I think she's intrigued and puzzled. I can't say I'm surprised. I'm pretty much out of my depth myself. In fact, the longer I continue with the subject, the more I have the feeling that everything is getting slightly out of hand.

But then isn't sex most of the time?

Typed furiously till one when bought a Cox's Orange Pippin and a small pot of cottage cheese from nearby delicatessen. Tummy still rather wobbly but at the same time feeling altogether more lithe and on my toes. Normally never give any of the secretaries a second glance in the lift, yet this morning caught myself treating Caroline from Personnel to one of the frankest and most searching looks I have ever given anyone. Pleased to note from the puzzled expression on her face that my essential masculinity had struck home in no uncertain terms.

After a while, she said, 'What have you done to your hair?'

I said, 'Nothing much. I just thought it was time I gave it a little pzazz. Do you like it?'

'I'm not sure,' she said.

She was obviously so intrigued she completely missed her floor. I shouldn't be at all surprised if this little encounter doesn't bear fruit before very long.

As the senior instructor at the health club reminded me when I called round in the afternoon for a chat, 'A really fit man is like a thoroughbred stallion in looks and performance. Stamina on the exercise machines means stamina in bed, believe you me.'

Am not sure I'm prepared to put in a three-hour routine three times a week for five years like the muscle-bound hulk with the spotty back I watched lifting seventy kilos on the lateral pull-down machine. But then, as the instructor said, 'These tasty young birds don't want a gorilla on their hands.'

Have told them I will make a definite decision re membership first thing Monday morning. The odd thing is that I was only in the place for a few minutes yet I feel fitter already.

Am up to page 145. Only another hundred to go.

Friday

Lunch with Molly Parkin informative, encouraging and unnerving, all at the same time.

Surprised to discover my blue motorcycling outfit caused even more heads to turn than her gold sou'wester. I had the devil's own job trying to persuade her that, while eminently practical at 30 mph in driving rain, it did not make for ideal luncheon wear.

At all events, we had a fascinating chat. She was particularly sound on how to attract members of the opposite sex. She said that the more sexually active one is, the stronger the sexual scent one puts out and the more likely one is to 'pull something' as she so quaintly puts it.

Meanwhile, she has suggested a routine that she assures me is an absolute winner every time:

1. The moment you meet a girl, look her straight in the eye.
2. Let your eyes drop to her lips.
3. Go back to her eyes. All this should take a matter of seconds.
4. Drop your gaze discreetly to her bosom. By this stage she should have a reasonable inkling of what you have in mind.
5. Weigh in with a complimentary remark, such as, 'What a great haircut; where did you have it done?' She now knows you are more aware of her body than her mind.
6. Get cracking with the chat. There is no greater aphrodisiac than talking about oneself, so get her to do just that.

For some people, apparently, all this comes as second nature, but those of more reticent disposition should practise first in front of a mirror.

Could not take my eyes off her lips and bosom for the rest of the meal, but obviously it was a bit late for all that and, when I went to peck her on the cheek as we were leaving, she shook me firmly by the hand and marched off to look for a taxi. I took it as a compliment to my professionalism.

Stayed on in the office till nearly eight and managed to get to page 170. Took golf-ball, plus notes, paper, correcting fluid etc. home with me in a taxi.

Thank heavens for the ginseng. It's certainly given me the extra energy I need. Sat through TV this evening till after eleven without falling asleep once. Tummy still slightly on the move. Am wondering if sprouts three nights running is really wise. May very well switch to cauliflower tomorrow. Or possibly even carrots.

Practised eye movements briefly in front of bathroom mirror but my heart not really in it.

To bed with a glass of unsweetened lemon juice and the *TV Times*. I don't know which sets my teeth on edge more.

Saturday

Woke feeling as if someone had hit me over the head with a sandbag, only to discover to my horror that it was 2.15 in the afternoon.

Had no sooner got down to typing at three than power failure put paid to chances of catching up on nearly four hours' worth of lost time.

Was groping way to kitchen in dark when phone rang. It was Jane to say that she was just back from an extended skiing holiday and had heard from the Pedalows that I was anxious to get hold of her.

I do not believe I have ever been more relieved to hear anyone's voice than I was to hear hers at that moment. Have always believed that, deep down inside, she and I were really meant for each other all along. For two pins would have chucked golf-ball, typed pages, notes and everything else to do with this assignment clean out of the window and rushed round to her there and then, had she not already arranged to have dinner with her brother.

Remembering his talent for bumming lifts off people etc, I said, 'Just as long as he's not planning on taking you somewhere cheap and cheerful round here. We're having a power cut.'

She said, 'Actually we're going to the Connaught.'

'The Connaught?' I exclaimed. 'Your brother?'

'What's so extraordinary about that?' she said. 'His car hire business is doing very well.'

I said I was glad to know I wasn't the only one whose career had blossomed.

We have arranged to meet on Monday evening for a drink at the Piccadilly Hotel. Am so excited I can hardly think of anything else.

Even so, the moment lights came on again, applied my

mind once more to task in hand, and by two a.m. had reached page 200.

Would have had quick mirror practice before turning in, but by then eyes capable of only one movement.

Sunday

Had most erotic dream about Jane I have ever known. Am not sure what I have to thank for it. Who cares? All I do know is that, the moment when I erased the last typing error and banged down the last full stop of the Crisp Report was, for me, one of the high spots of my marketing career.

One hears it said that writing a book is rather like having a baby. I have always thought that, as similes go, this one oversteps the mark. All I can say is that, having suffered the birth pangs myself and known the joy of seeing the fruits of my labour lying in a neat pile beside the typewriter, I shall definitely take care not to get pregnant again for a very long time!

Monday, 5 March

Woke at six. Quite unable to get back to sleep again for excitement.

Up finally twenty minutes later for a long eye-movement session. One of them seems to be rather sore. Hope I haven't been overdoing it.

Am now into fifth day of diet and ginseng and, eye apart, have never felt fitter or more cheerful in my life.

Arrived at work bang on dot of nine, dropped off golf-ball and marched straight up to Hardacre's office. No sign of anyone, so dumped report firmly on middle of his desk where he can't possibly miss it.

By way of celebration, had white coffee with sugar from machine.

The moment I got into my room, wrote off to health club enclosing entrance form and cheque for £190.

Thought I might slip down there for a spot of weight training during lunch hour.

Was in fact on way out to buy track suit, gym shoes

etc. shortly after noon when Miss Hippo rang to say she had Keith Hardacre for me.

Could not conceal my glee as I said, 'Morning Keith. Any comments?'

He said, 'Not really, except to thank you for all the hard work you've put in and to tell you that, unfortunately, we have decided we won't be going ahead with the report after all.'

I said, 'I'm sorry Keith, I'm not with you. What do you mean we won't be going ahead? We *have* gone ahead. At least, *I* have. What do you think all those bits of paper on your desk are?'

Keith said, 'Yes, well, they certainly look interesting from what I've managed to skim so far. Some of it will come in useful as a starting point if ever we decide to go ahead at a later date.'

'What do you mean, starting point?' I said. 'I've been knocking myself out for six weeks over this.'

'And don't think we don't appreciate it,' said Keith. 'Of course, I realize now we should never have expected you to do any more than scratch the surface. It's obviously far too big a subject for one person to cover fully. Silly to have thought otherwise really. Still, it's all good experience after all, and I daresay there were a few fringe benefits to be enjoyed along the way. Now then, I'd like you to liaise with Pratt. I think you'll find he's got some interesting ideas for a new marketing strategy for Scandinavia. You'll be working with him again, so if you wouldn't mind moving back to your old office as soon as possible. By the way, an old colleague of yours from Harley Preston is joining us today on the sales side. Colin Armitage. First-class fellow.'

I may resign or I may not. It depends on the sort of response I get from the various publishers when I present them with the manuscript of my journal. Barfords may not recognize a best seller when they see one, but I can think of one or two people who will.

Anyway, was far too excited at the prospect of meeting Jane again to give a hoot one way or the other.

In the event, barely recognized her. I thought she had improved out of recognition when I saw her last year at the Pedalows', but that was without the deep Alpine suntan.

Was so taken aback I almost forgot the eye routine.

'What a great suntan,' I said, when I had completed it. 'Where did you get it?'

'I've already told you,' she said. 'I've been skiing. And why are you leering at me in that horrible way, Simon? It makes you look like those middle-aged men you see outside dirty cinemas. And what *have* you done to your hair?'

I said, 'I suppose you're going to tell me you don't like that either?'

'Not at all,' she said. 'It's wonderful. It makes you look ten years younger. You've lost some weight too. It suits you. Very sexy. I could quite fancy you.'

I often think life is like a huge elephant. One minute it is trampling you underfoot, scarcely aware of your existence; the next it has seized you by its trunk and lifted you gently and triumphantly onto its broad, safe, comfortable back.

Was naturally disappointed when Jane told me about the Austrian ski instructor and the baby she is expecting in a few months' time. Personally, I can think of many places I'd rather set up home in than Obergurgl.

On the other hand, find I am able to absorb the shock of her news with an insouciance of which I would have been quite incapable only a few weeks ago. The instructor at the health club was right: You're only as good as you feel, and I do not believe I have ever felt leaner, fitter and more virile in my life. Think big and think positive; that's my motto from now on.

I may decide to pop out to Obergurgl and sort the matter out with Hans, man to man, or I may not.

Jane is not the only fish in the sea by a long chalk and, with a potential best seller on my hands, I shall soon be in a position to pick and choose women at will.

Barfords' loss is certainly going to be my gain in every sense of the word.

First things first, though; I must sort out these wretched expenses.

CHRISTOPHER MATTHEW

FAMILY MATTERS

More than five years have elapsed since Simon Crisp last kept an account of his rich and varied life as an up-and-coming, often accident-prone, but always well-intentioned bachelor-about-town. Now at last his marriage to Belinda and the imminent arrival of his first-born have urged him to take up his pen once again and afford us a fascinating glimpse into his new existence as husband, father and breadwinner.

A Royal Mail service in association with the Book Marketing Council & The Booksellers Association.
Post-A-Book is a Post Office trademark.

MORE TITLES AVAILABLE FROM
HODDER AND STOUGHTON PAPERBACKS